Modern

Short Stories

A CRITICAL ANTHOLOGY

Robert B. Heilman   UNIVERSITY OF WASHINGTON

GREENWOOD PRESS, PUBLISHERS
WESTPORT, CONNECTICUT

To R. C. H., the co-editor

Contents

FANTASY

METHODS OF CHARACTER STUDY

SYMBOLISM

THE EDITOR TO THE TEACHER

In putting together a volume of short stories for students, an editor soon discovers a problem of choice in almost every step he takes. He can make a collection of old favorites and thus risk having simply another anthology, undistinguishable from the others; or he can depend primarily upon untried stories, and risk appearing to be interested only in novelty. He can select stories solely because they are excellent, or because they are representative, without thought of the relation of the stories to each other; or he can determine first the organization of his volume, and then, as well as he can, fit the stories into it.

The stories in the present volume have not been picked either as old reliables or as startling novelties. Some of the stories have not been anthologized before, and some are quite familiar. The distribution of new and old is largely accidental, for the matters of age and fame have been subordinated to two other criteria.

The first of these is the criterion of interestingness, of having a fairly immediate appeal to the student reader. We might well argue, against possible objections, that there is no necessary antithesis between immediate interestingness and excellence. However, that is not the point. Our first business is to get the student to read the story not because it is an assignment but because it engages his curiosity or imagination. Then we are in a good position to go ahead and ask him to consider *how* his attention has been held and *whether* it has been fairly held. The best we can hope is that by the end of a course he will have a more critical sense of what is interesting, or at least that the tendency to yield assent easily or to withhold it stubbornly will have been somewhat modified by his examination of what is in a story, and of what goes on there.

Interest also implies variety, and the student should constantly feel the element of differentness as he reads new stories. Indeed, this perhaps superficial device for holding attention actually leads into the basic critical study of the stories. For the essential difference between stories may best be seen if they are also held together by likeness of one kind or another. The second criterion in the selection of stories, then, has been their possession of likeness with difference. The likeness may be either in method or in theme. Thus a number of stories that are extremely different in subject matter but alike in their use of symbolism are grouped together. This is of course a fairly conventional classification. Slightly less so, perhaps, is the bringing together of a number of fantasies which at the same time may be sharply distinguished both in tone and in the kinds of non-realistic devices employed. Another series of stories all use either a child's point of view or a contrast of adult and children's points of view, but work from situations which are markedly different. A trio of stories—those by Mansfield, Huxley, and Greene—all deal with "triangles" but are so dissimilar in their total effects that their common point of origin is hardly apparent until attention is called to it. Perhaps the principle of likeness-with-difference is most vividly illustrated in the juxtaposition of Joyce's "A Little Cloud" and Thurber's "The Secret Life of Walter Mitty." Thurber's comedy of a dreamer and Joyce's sardonic contrast of a man of the world with a "little man" of Dublin are far removed in method and effect; but the fact is that though they move in opposite directions, they have the same starting point.

This statement of the identity of Walter Mitty and Little Chandler may be protested against as a tour de force, a wrenching of the context, a torturing of what the stories say. To such a protest the editor could only agree. For it is the basic assumption of the book that *what* the story is depends upon *how* the author puts the parts together, and not on the summarizable ingredients which may be described as the "contents." To identify a story in terms of the unformed raw material that one may infer from the finished story is indeed a wrenching of the context. But such a wrenching of the context does serve a pedagogical purpose: it is a clear way of making students see how contexts differ, and how a different structure makes an entirely different story. No student will think of "A Little Cloud" and "The Secret Life of Walter Mitty" as essentially similar stories; but if, by distorting the completed work, the teacher can make the student see that the stories were at some hypothetical earlier stage tangent and theoretically could have moved side by side toward the same objective, the student will be able to see not only differences but the meaning of difference—the individual choices and emphases which make one work unique instead of a loose counterpart of another. And he will also be acquiring the tools which will enable him to see why one story is better than another.

The editor has endeavored to use the general method of likeness-with-difference very flexibly. Stories may be related in terms of subject *or* theme *or* method; the treatment of the comparable elements may provide only a starting-point for the comments; the clusters of related stories are kept small, and the clusters themselves contrast with each other; and a number of stories do not fall into clusters at all. The general order of stories in the book is not inevitable (in the main, the more demanding stories come in the second half of the book), and the teacher may wish to rearrange them according to his own preferences. But if the comments, which often compare a story with one that precedes or follows, are to be used, the stories would best be done in an order which takes some account of their interrelationships.

A final word on selection: not all interesting stories or similar or contrasting stories are good stories, and the ones which have been chosen should make it possible for the student to distinguish a considerable range of stories, from those which in critical terms are fine achievements to those which are only partly successful. Probably not more than one or two stories have in them something of the meretricious. In the rest, the problem is one of seeing how effective are the means used (what works or doesn't work), and of the quality of the insight which finds expression in the means used (the completeness, richness, or maturity of what the story says). Incidentally, a prospective editor who reads some four or five hundred short stories is surprised how many good stories he comes across—and how few very good ones. Many writers have some sensitiveness, a sense of effect, a considerable mastery of technique; relatively few have the fullness of imagination which can make the reading of their tales an essentially illuminating experience.

So much for the selection and arrangement of stories; now for a word on the editor's comments, where again there has been a problem of choices. One alternative is to let the stories speak entirely for themselves, the student prompted only by a question or two; the other alternative is to analyze very fully throughout. The present editor has tried to steer between the two dangers—the extreme of giving no help at all, and the extreme of doing all the work for the instructor, who properly resents being left emptyhanded. On each story there is a brief comment—the average length is a page or two—which endeavors to raise several basic issues about what the author is doing. The intention is to stay within a readable length and within these limits to give the student a start in analyzing the story and to provide the instructor with one angle of attack if he wants to use it. The instructor may disagree, and if he does, the student has the advantage of being in on a critical debate. It is to be hoped, of course, that the comments can sustain themselves well enough to be, at least part of the time, something more than a target. Naturally, however, the more complex and imaginative the story, the greater the diversity of the readings for which some case can be made. The interpretation of a number of the stories in this volume ought to evoke considerable discussion.

The editor's comments endeavor (1) to suggest why a story is one kind of story rather than another, (2) to point out the specific methods by which an author secures his effects, and (3) to introduce the criteria which may be used in judging the quality of the story. All these points might be discussed with reference to each story. If they were, the discussions would be interminable; so each comment deals only with a critical question or two that seem especially pertinent to the story under consideration. In one story, point of view is more important than in another, in another irony, in another contrast, and so on. Thus the critique arises naturally out of the story and is related to it rather than to a preordained pattern of instruction. By the end of the book a considerable number of critical issues have been presented, and each one has been taken up several times.

It is obviously not the primary business of the student to learn a terminology for the criticism of short stories, and conceivably stories might be well read and judged without the conscious use of a set of critical terms. But certain problems do recur; they are most conveniently discussed by means of terms which are commonly used; and at least nothing is to be lost by the student's acquiring some familiarity with them. Certain basic terms are used repeatedly, so that after reading a number of comments on stories the student should have a working knowledge of several dozen rather useful terms.

The editor suspects that a body of questions systematically appended to each story becomes an onerous burden which is finally forgotten about by both students and teachers. He has therefore included questions only when they seem to grow naturally out of the discussion which he has begun. Sometimes a question points to the conclusion of a discussion which is deliberately left unfinished.

All of the methods used to make this a workable handbook for a critical reading of the short story—the selection of stories, the arrangement of them in an order which sets up illuminating relationships, the comparisons, the arguments set forth in the analyses, the leading questions asked—do not always point the way to novel conclusions. If the methods do work, they should at least sharpen the reader's insight into the stories. In the last twenty-five years we have learned a good deal about the analysis of literary form, and this book, it is hoped, applies some of the most useful of the critical methods which are now well known. We no longer believe that summarizing a plot, or locating the climax, or telling what a story is "about" is a very fruitful approach to it. Rather we try to see how the story is put together, what materials the author has chosen, what he emphasizes, what are his methods of development, how he communicates an attitude—in a word, what are the structure and tone of the work. By these means we see both what it is and what it is not, how it succeeds or fails. This is to say that we doubt the old axiom that matters of taste cannot be argued about. Tastes do differ. But this book assumes that they may be reconciled, that there are general principles of literary excellence to which many kinds of stories may be referred, and that the individual preference may be trained to find common centers of value.

ROBERT B. HEILMAN

Seattle, Washington

DIFFERENT KINDS

OF STORY

W. Somerset Maugham

William Somerset Maugham, one of the most prolific, popular, and versatile playwrights and fiction writers of the twentieth century, was born in 1874 and trained in medicine, which he never practiced. He has lived in England and France and traveled widely in the South Seas and the Orient, always taking voluminous notes to be used in subsequent writings. During World War II he made his home in the United States. His central aim in writing has always been readableness, and his better works tend to fall somewhere between those that are purely transitory and those that achieve critical acceptance as enduring work. His most serious piece of fiction is the partially autobiographical *Of Human Bondage* (1915); and *The Moon and Sixpence* (1919), based on the life of the artist Gauguin in Tahiti, is very interesting. "Rain," his best-known short story, was very successful in a stage version. A number of his plays —*Our Betters, The Circle,* and others—have been repeatedly anthologized. His experience in the British Secret Service during World War I led to the novel *Ashenden.* Two semi-autobiographical works, *The Summing Up* and *A Writer's Notebook,* have appeared in recent years.

The Facts of Life

IT WAS Henry Garnet's habit on leaving the city of an afternoon to drop in at his club and play bridge before going home to dinner. He was a pleasant man to play with. He knew the game well, and you could be sure that he would make the best of his cards. He was a good loser; and when he won was more inclined to ascribe his success to his luck than to his skill. He was indulgent, and if his partner made a mistake, could be trusted to find an excuse for him. It was surprising then on this occasion to hear him telling his partner with unnecessary sharpness that he had never seen a hand worse played; and it was more surprising still to see him not only make a grave error himself, an error of which

THE FACTS OF LIFE From *The Mixture as Before* by W. Somerset Maugham. Copyright, 1933, 1934, 1935, 1936, 1937, 1938, 1939, 1940 by W. Somerset Maugham, reprinted by permission of Doubleday & Company, Inc.

you would never have thought him capable, but when his partner, not unwilling to get a little of his own back, pointed it out, insist against all reason and with considerable heat that he was perfectly right. But they were all old friends, the men he was playing with, and none of them took his ill humour very seriously. Henry Garnet was a broker, a partner in a firm of repute, and it occurred to one of them that something had gone wrong with some stock he was interested in.

"How's the market today?" he asked.

"Booming. Even the suckers are making money."

It was evident that stocks and shares had nothing to do with Henry Garnet's vexation; but something was the matter; that was evident, too. He was a hearty fellow who enjoyed excellent health; he had plenty of money; he was fond of his wife and devoted to his children. As a rule he had high spirits, and he laughed easily at the nonsense they were apt to talk while they played; but today he sat glum and silent. His brows were crossly puckered, and there was a sulky look about his mouth. Presently, to ease the tension, one of the others mentioned a subject upon which they all knew Henry Garnet was glad to speak.

"How's your boy, Henry? I see he's done pretty well in the tournament."

Henry Garnet's frown grew darker.

"He's done no better than I expected him to."

"When does he come back from Monte?"

"He got back last night."

"Did he enjoy himself?"

"I suppose so; all I know is that he made a damned fool of himself."

"Oh. How?"

"I'd rather not talk about it if you don't mind."

The three men looked at him with curiosity. Henry Garnet scowled at the green baize.

"Sorry, old boy. Your call."

The game proceeded in a strained silence. Garnet got his bid, and when he played his cards so badly that he went three down not a word was said. Another rubber was begun, and in the second game Garnet denied a suit.

"Having none?" his partner asked him.

Garnet's irritability was such that he did not even reply, and when at the end of the hand it appeared that he had revoked, and that his revoke cost the rubber, it was not to be expected that his partner should let his carelessness go without remark.

"What the devil's the matter with you, Henry?" he said. "You're playing like a fool."

Garnet was disconcerted. He did not so much mind losing a big rubber himself, but he was sore that his inattention should have made his partner lose too. He pulled himself together.

"I'd better not play any more. I thought a few rubbers would calm me, but the fact is I can't give my mind to the game. To tell you the truth I'm in a hell of a temper."

They all burst out laughing.

"You don't have to tell us that, old boy. It's obvious."

Garnet gave them a rueful smile.

"Well, I bet you'd be in a temper if what's happened to me had happened to you. As a matter of fact I'm in a damned awkward situation, and if any of you fellows can give me any advice how to deal with it I'd be grateful."

"Let's have a drink and you tell us all about it. With a K.C., a Home Office official and an eminent surgeon—if we can't tell you how to deal with a situation, nobody can."

The K.C. got up and rang the bell for a waiter.

"It's about that damned boy of mine," said Henry Garnet.

Drinks were ordered and brought. And this is the story that Henry Garnet told them.

The boy of whom he spoke was his only son. His name was Nicholas, and of course he was called Nicky. He was eighteen. The Garnets had two daughters besides, one of sixteen and the other of twelve, but however unreasonable it seemed, for a father is generally supposed to like his daughters best, and though he did all he could not to show his preference, there was no doubt that the greater share of Henry Garnet's affection was given to his son. He was kind, in a chaffing, casual way, to his daughters, and gave them handsome presents on their birthdays and at Christmas; but he doted on Nicky. Nothing was too good for him. He thought the world of him. He could hardly take his eyes off him. You could not blame him, for Nicky was a son that any parent might have been proud of. He was six foot two, lithe but muscular, with broad shoulders and a slim waist, and he held himself gallantly erect; he had a charming head, well placed on the shoulders, with pale brown hair that waved slightly, blue eyes with long dark lashes under well-marked eyebrows, a full red mouth and a tanned, clean skin. When he smiled he showed very regular and very white teeth. He was not shy, but there was a modesty in his demeanour that was attractive. In social intercourse he was easy, polite and quietly gay. He was the offspring of nice, healthy, decent parents, he had been well brought up in a good home, he had been sent to a good school, and the general result was as engaging a specimen of young manhood as you were likely to find in a long time. You felt that he was as honest, open and virtuous as he looked. He had never given his parents a moment's uneasiness. As a child he was seldom ill and never naughty. As a boy he did everything that was expected of him. His school reports were excellent. He was wonderfully popular, and he ended his career, with a creditable number of prizes, as head of the school and captain of the football team. But this was not all. At the age of fourteen Nicky had developed an unexpected gift for lawn tennis. This was a game that his father not only was fond of, but played very well, and when he discerned in the boy the promise of a tennis player he fostered it. During the holidays he had him taught by the best professionals, and by the time he was sixteen he had won a number of tournaments for boys of his age. He could beat his father so badly that only parental affection reconciled the older player to the poor show he put up. At eighteen Nicky went to Cambridge and Henry Garnet conceived the ambition that before he was through with the university he should play for it. Nicky had all the qualifications for becoming a great tennis player. He was tall, he had a long reach, he was quick on his feet and his timing was perfect. He realized instinctively where the ball was coming and, seemingly without hurry, was there to take it. He had a powerful serve, with a nasty break that made it difficult to return, and his forehand drive, low, long and accurate, was deadly. He was not so good on the backhand and his volleying was wild, but all through the summer before he went to Cambridge Henry Garnet made him work on these points under the best teacher in England. At the back of his mind, though he did not even mention it to Nicky, he cherished a further ambition, to see his son play at Wimbledon, and who could tell, perhaps be chosen to represent his country in the Davis Cup. A great lump came into Henry Garnet's throat as he saw in fancy his son leap over the net to shake hands with the American champion whom he had just defeated, and walk off the court to the deafening plaudits of the multitude.

As an assiduous frequenter of Wimbledon, Henry Garnet had a good many friends in the tennis world, and one evening he found himself at a city dinner sitting next to one of them, a Colonel Brabazon, and in due course began talking to him of Nicky and what chance there might be of his being chosen to play for his university during the following season.

"Why don't you let him go down to Monte Carlo and play in the spring tournament there?" said the Colonel suddenly.

"Oh, I don't think he's good enough for that. He's not nineteen yet, he only went up to Cambridge last October; he wouldn't stand a chance against all those cracks."

"Of course, Austin and Von Cramm and so on would knock spots off him, but he might snatch a game or two; and if he got up against some of the smaller fry there's no reason why he shouldn't win two or three matches. He's never been up against any of the first-rate players, and it would be wonderful practice for him. He'd learn a lot more than he'll ever learn in the seaside tournaments you enter him for."

"I wouldn't dream of it. I'm not going to let him leave Cambridge in the middle of a term. I've always impressed upon him that tennis is only a game and it mustn't interfere with work."

Colonel Brabazon asked Garnet when the term ended.

"That's all right. He'd only have to cut about three days. Surely that could be arranged. You see, two of the men we were depending on have let us down, and we're in a hole. We want to send as good a team as we can. The Germans are sending their best players, and so are the Americans."

"Nothing doing, old boy. In the first place Nicky's not good enough, and secondly, I don't fancy the idea of sending a kid like that to Monte Carlo without anyone to look after him. If I could get away myself I might think of it, but that's out of the question."

"I shall be there. I'm going as the nonplaying captain of the English team. I'll keep an eye on him."

"You'll be busy, and besides, it's not a responsibility I'd like * ask you to take. He's never been abroad in his life, and to tell you the truth, I shouldn't have a moment's peace all the time he was there."

They left it at that, and presently Henry Garnet went home. He was so flattered by Colonel Brabazon's suggestion that he could not help telling his wife.

"Fancy his thinking Nicky's as good as that. He told me he'd seen him play and his style was fine. He only wants more practice to get into the first flight. We shall see the kid playing in the semi-finals at Wimbledon yet, old girl."

To his surprise Mrs. Garnet was not so much opposed to the notion as he would have expected.

"After all the boy's eighteen. Nicky's never got into mischief yet, and there's no reason to suppose he will now."

"There's his work to be considered; don't forget that. I think it would be a very bad precedent to let him cut the end of term."

"But what can three days matter? It seems a shame to rob him of a chance like that. I'm sure he'd jump at it if you asked him."

"Well, I'm not going to. I haven't sent him to Cambridge just to play tennis. I know he's steady, but it's silly to put temptation in his way. He's much too young to go to Monte Carlo by himself."

"You say he won't have a chance against these crack players, but you can't tell."

Henry Garnet sighed a little. On the way home in the car it had struck him that Austin's health was uncertain and that Von Cramm had his off days. Supposing, just for the sake of argument, that Nicky had a bit of luck like that—then there would be no doubt that he would be chosen to play for Cambridge. But of course that was all nonsense.

"Nothing doing, my dear. I've made up my mind, and I'm not going to change it."

Mrs. Garnet held her peace. But next day she wrote to Nicky, telling him what had happened, and suggested to him what she would do in his place if, wanting to go, he wished to get his father's consent. A day or two later Henry Garnet received a letter from his son. He was bubbling over with excitement. He had seen his tutor, who was a tennis player himself, and the Provost of his college, who happened to know Colonel Brabazon, and no objection would be made to his leaving before the end of term; they both thought it an opportunity that shouldn't be missed. He didn't see what harm he could come to, and if only, just this once, his father would stretch a point, well, next term, he promised faithfully, he'd work like blazes. It was a very pretty letter. Mrs. Garnet watched her husband read it at the breakfast table; she was undisturbed by the frown on his face. He threw it over to her.

"I don't know why you thought it necessary to tell Nicky something I told you in confidence. It's too bad of you. Now you've thoroughly unsettled him."

"I'm so sorry. I thought it would please him to know that Colonel Brabazon had such a high opinion of him. I don't see why one should only tell people the disagreeable things that are said about them. Of course I made it quite clear that there could be no question of his going."

"You've put me in an odious position. If there's anything I hate it's for the boy to look upon me as a spoilsport and a tyrant."

"Oh, he'll never do that. He may think you rather silly and unreasonable, but I'm sure he'll understand that it's only for his own good that you're being so unkind."

"Christ," said Henry Garnet.

His wife had a great inclination to laugh. She knew the battle was won. Dear, oh dear, how easy it was to get men to do what you wanted. For appearance' sake Henry Garnet held out for forty-eight hours, but then he yielded, and a fortnight later Nicky came to London. He was to start for Monte Carlo next morning, and after dinner, when Mrs. Garnet and her elder daughter had left them, Henry took the opportunity to give his son some good advice.

"I don't feel quite comfortable about letting you go off to a place like Monte Carlo at your age practically by yourself," he finished, "but there it is, and I can only hope you'll be sensible. I don't want to play the heavy father, but there are three things especially that I want to warn you against: one is gambling, don't gamble; the second is money, don't lend anyone money; and the third is women, don't have anything to do with women. If you don't do any of those three things you can't come to much harm, so remember them well."

"All right, Father," Nicky smiled.

"That's my last word to you. I know the world pretty well, and believe me, my advice is sound."

"I won't forget it. I promise you."

"That's a good chap. Now let's go up and join the ladies."

Nicky beat neither Austin nor Von Cramm in the Monte Carlo tournament, but he did not disgrace himself. He snatched an unexpected victory over a Spanish player and gave one of the Austrians a closer match than anyone had thought possible. In the mixed doubles he got into the semifinals. His charm conquered everyone, and he vastly enjoyed himself. It was generally allowed that he showed promise, and Colonel Brabazon told him that when he was a little older and had had more practice with first-class players he would be a credit to his father. The tournament came to an end, and the day following he was to fly back to London. Anxious to play his best, he had lived very carefully, smoking little and drinking nothing, and going to bed early; but on his last evening he thought he would like to see something of the life in Monte Carlo of which he had heard so much. An official dinner was given to the tennis players, and after dinner with the rest of them he went into the Sporting Club. It was the first time he had been there. Monte Carlo was very full, and the rooms were crowded. Nicky had never before seen roulette played except in the pictures; in a maze he stopped at the first table he came to; chips of different sizes were scattered over the green cloth in what looked like a hopeless muddle; the croupier gave the wheel a sharp turn and with a flick threw in the little white ball. After what seemed an endless time the ball stopped and another croupier with a broad, indifferent gesture raked in the chips of those who had lost.

Presently Nicky wandered over to where they were playing *trente et quarante,* but he couldn't understand what it was all about, and he thought it dull. He saw a crowd in another room and sauntered in. A big game of baccara was in progress, and he was immediately conscious of the tension. The players were protected from the thronging bystanders by a brass rail; they sat round the table, nine on each side, with the dealer in the middle and the croupier facing him. Big money was changing hands. The dealer was a member of the Greek Syndicate. Nicky looked at his impassive face. His eyes were watchful, but his expression never changed whether he won or lost. It was a terrifying, strangely impressive sight. It gave Nicky, who had been thriftily brought up, a peculiar thrill to see someone risk a thousand pounds on the turn of a card and when he lost make a little joke and laugh. It was all terribly exciting. An acquaintance came up to him.

"Been doing any good?" he asked.

"I haven't been playing."

"Wise of you. Rotten game. Come and have a drink."

"All right."

While they were having it Nicky told his friend that this was the first time he had ever been in the rooms.

"Oh, but you must have one little flutter before you go. It's idiotic to leave Monte without having tried your luck. After all it won't hurt you to lose a hundred francs or so."

"I don't suppose it will, but my father wasn't any too keen on my coming at all, and one of the three things he particularly advised me not to do was to gamble."

But when Nicky left his companion he strolled back to one of the tables where they were playing roulette. He stood for a while looking at the losers' money being raked in by the croupier and the money that was won paid out to the winners. It was impossible to deny that it was thrilling. His friend was right, it did seem silly to leave Monte without putting something on the table just once. It would be an experience, and at his age you had to have all the experience you could get. He reflected that he hadn't promised his father not to gamble, he'd promised him not to forget his advice. It wasn't quite the same, was it? He took a hundred-franc note out of his pocket and rather shyly put it on number eighteen. He chose it because that was his age. With a wildly beating heart he watched the wheel turn; the little white ball whizzed about like a small demon of mischief; the wheel went round more slowly, the little white ball hesitated, it seemed about to stop, it went on again; Nicky could hardly believe his eyes when it fell into number eighteen. A lot of chips were passed over to him, and his hands trembled as he took them. It seemed to amount to a lot of money. He was so confused that he never thought of putting anything on the following round; in fact he had no intention of playing any more, once was enough; and he was surprised when eighteen again came up. There was only one chip on it.

"By George, you've won again," said a man who was standing near to him.

"Me? I hadn't got anything on."

"Yes, you had. Your original stake. They always leave it on unless you ask for it back. Didn't you know?"

Another packet of chips was handed over to him. Nicky's head reeled. He counted his gains: seven thousand francs. A queer sense of power seized him; he felt wonderfully clever. This was the easiest way of making money that he had ever heard of. His frank, charming face was wreathed in smiles. His bright eyes met those of a woman standing by his side. She smiled.

"You're in luck," she said.

She spoke English, but with a foreign accent.

"I can hardly believe it. It's the first time I've ever played."

"That explains it. Lend me a thousand francs, will you? I've lost everything I've got. I'll give it you back in half an hour."

"All right."

She took a large red chip from his pile and with a word of thanks disappeared. The man who had spoken to him before grunted.

"You'll never see that again."

Nicky was dashed. His father had particularly advised him not to lend anyone money. What a silly thing to do! And to somebody he'd never seen in his life. But the fact was, he felt at that moment such a love for the human race that it had never occurred to him to refuse. And that big red chip, it was almost impossible to realize that it had any value. Oh, well, it didn't matter, he still had six thousand francs, he'd just try his luck once or twice more, and if he didn't win he'd go home. He put a chip on sixteen, which was his elder sister's age, but it didn't come up; then on twelve, which was his younger sister's, and that didn't come up either; he tried various numbers at random, but without success. It was funny, he seemed to have lost his knack. He thought he would try just once more and then stop; he won. He had made up all his losses and had something over. At the end of an hour, after various ups and downs, having experienced such thrills as he had never known in his life, he found himself with so many chips that they would hardly go in his pockets. He decided to go. He went to the changers' office, and he gasped when twenty thousand-franc notes were spread out before him. He had never had so much money in his life. He put it in his pocket and was turning away when the woman to whom he had lent the thousand francs came up to him.

"I've been looking for you everywhere," she said. "I was afraid you'd gone. I was in a fever, I didn't know what you'd think of me. Here's your thousand francs and thank you so much for the loan."

Nicky, blushing scarlet, stared at her with amazement. How he had misjudged her! His father had said, don't gamble; well, he had, and he'd made twenty thousand francs; and his father had said, don't lend anyone money; well, he had, he'd lent quite a lot to a total stranger, and she'd returned it. The fact was that he wasn't nearly such a fool as his father thought: he'd had an instinct that he could lend her the money with safety, and you see, his instinct was right. But he was so obviously taken aback that the little lady was forced to laugh.

"What is the matter with you?" she asked.

"To tell you the truth I never expected to see the money back."

"What did you take me for? Did you think I was a—cocotte?"

Nicky reddened to the roots of his wavy hair.

"No, of course not."

"Do I look like one?"

"Not a bit."

She was dressed very quietly, in black, with a string of gold beads round her neck; her simple frock showed off a neat, slight figure; she had a pretty little face and a trim head. She was made up, but not excessively, and Nicky supposed that she was not more than three or four years older than himself. She gave him a friendly smile.

"My husband is in the administration in Morocco, and I've come to Monte Carlo for a few weeks because he thought I wanted a change."

"I was just going," said Nicky because he couldn't think of anything else to say.

"Already!"

"Well, I've got to get up early tomorrow. I'm going back to London by air."

"Of course. The tournament ended today, didn't it? I saw you play, you know, two or three times."

"Did you? I don't know why you should have noticed me."

"You've got a beautiful style. And you looked very sweet in your shorts."

Nicky was not an immodest youth, but it did cross his mind that perhaps she had borrowed that thousand francs in order to scrape acquaintance with him.

"Do you ever go to the Knickerbocker?" she asked.

"No. I never have."

"Oh, but you mustn't leave Monte without having been there. Why don't you come and dance a little? To tell you the truth, I'm starving with hunger, and I should adore some bacon and eggs."

Nicky remembered his father's advice not to have anything to do with women, but this was different; you had only to look at the pretty little thing to know at once that she was perfectly respectable. Her husband was in what corresponded, he supposed, to the civil service. His father and mother had friends who were civil servants, and they and their wives sometimes came to dinner. It was true that the wives were neither so young nor so pretty as this one, but she was just as ladylike as they were. And after winning twenty thousand francs he thought it wouldn't be a bad idea to have a little fun.

"I'd love to go with you," he said. "But you won't mind if I don't stay very long. I've left instructions at my hotel that I'm to be called at seven."

"We'll leave as soon as ever you like."

Nicky found it very pleasant at the Knickerbocker. He ate his bacon and eggs with appetite. They shared a bottle of champagne. They danced, and the little lady told him he danced beautifully. He knew he danced pretty well, and of course she was easy to dance with. As light as a feather. She laid her cheek against his and when their eyes met there was in hers a smile that made his heart go pit-a-pat. A coloured woman sang in a throaty, sensual voice. The floor was crowded.

"Have you ever been told that you're very good-looking?" she asked.

"I don't think so," he laughed. "Gosh," he thought, "I believe she's fallen for me."

Nicky was not such a fool as to be unaware that women often liked him, and when she made that remark he pressed her to him a little more closely. She closed her eyes, and a faint sigh escaped her lips.

"I suppose it wouldn't be quite nice if I kissed you before all these people," he said.

"What do you think they would take me for?"

It began to grow late, and Nicky said that really he thought he ought to be going.

"I shall go too," she said. "Will you drop me at my hotel on your way?"

Nicky paid the bill. He was rather surprised at its amount, but with all that money he had in his pocket he could afford not to care, and they got into a taxi. She snuggled up to him, and he kissed her. She seemed to like it.

"By Jove," he thought, "I wonder if there's anything doing."

It was true that she was a married woman, but her husband was in Morocco, and it certainly did look as if she'd fallen for him. Good and proper. It was true also that his father had warned him to have nothing to do with women, but, he reflected again, he hadn't actually promised he wouldn't, he'd only promised not to forget his advice. Well, he hadn't; he was bearing it in mind that very minute. But circumstances alter cases. She was a sweet little thing; it seemed silly to miss the chance of an adventure when it was handed to you like that on a tray. When they reached the hotel he paid off the taxi.

"I'll walk home," he said. "The air will do me good after the stuffy atmosphere of that place."

"Come up a moment," she said. "I'd like to show you the photo of my little boy."

"Oh, have you got a little boy?" he exclaimed, a trifle dashed.

"Yes, a sweet little boy."

He walked upstairs after her. He didn't in the least want to see the photograph of her little boy, but he thought it only civil to pretend he did. He was afraid he'd made a fool of himself; it occurred to him that she was taking him up to look at the photograph in order to show him in a nice way that he'd made a mistake. He'd told her he was eighteen.

"I suppose she thinks I'm just a kid."

He began to wish he hadn't spent all that money on champagne at the night club.

But she didn't show him the photograph of her little boy after all. They had no sooner got into her room than she turned to him, flung her arms round his neck, and kissed him full on the lips. He had never in all his life been kissed so passionately.

"Darling," she said.

For a brief moment his father's advice once more crossed Nicky's mind, and then he forgot it.

Nicky was a light sleeper, and the least sound was apt to wake him. Two or three hours later he awoke and for a moment could not imagine where he was. The room was not quite dark, for the door of the bathroom was ajar, and the light in it had been left on. Suddenly he was conscious that someone was moving about the room. Then he remembered. He saw that it was his little friend, and he was on the point of speaking when something in the way she was behaving stopped him. She was walking very cautiously, as though she were afraid of waking him; she stopped once or twice and looked over at the bed. He wondered what she was after. He soon saw. She went over to the chair on which he had placed his clothes and once more looked in his direction. She waited for what seemed to him an interminable time. The silence was so intense that Nicky thought he could hear his own heart beating. Then, very slowly, very quietly, she took up his coat, slipped her hand into the inside pocket and drew out all those beautiful thousand-franc notes that Nicky had been so proud to win. She put the coat back and placed some other clothes on it so that it should look as though it had not been disturbed, then, with the bundle of notes in her hand, for an appreciable time stood once more stock-still. Nicky had repressed an instinctive impulse to jump up and grab her; it was partly surprise that had kept him quiet, partly the notion that he was in a strange hotel, in a foreign country, and if he made a row he didn't know what might happen. She looked at him. His eyes were partly closed, and he was sure that she thought he was asleep. In the silence she could hardly fail to hear his regular breathing. When she had reassured herself that her movements had not disturbed him, she stepped, with infinite caution, across the room. On a small table in the window a cineraria was growing in a pot. Nicky watched her now with his eyes wide open. The plant was evidently placed quite loosely in the pot, for, taking it by the stalks, she lifted it out; she put the bank notes in the bottom of the pot and replaced the plant. It was an excellent hiding place. No one could have guessed that anything was concealed under that richly flowering plant. She pressed the earth down with her fingers and then, very slowly, taking care not to make the smallest noise, crept across the room and slipped back into bed.

"Chéri," she said, in a caressing voice.

Nicky breathed steadily, like a man immersed in deep sleep. The little lady turned over on her side and disposed herself to slumber. But though Nicky lay so still, his thoughts worked busily. He was extremely indignant at the scene he had just witnessed, and to himself he spoke his thoughts with vigour.

"She's nothing but a damned tart. She and her dear little boy and her husband in Morocco. My eye! She's a rotten thief, that's what she is. Took me for a mug. If she thinks she's going to get away with anything like that, she's mistaken."

He had already made up his mind what he was going to do with the money he had so cleverly won. He had long wanted a car of his own and had thought it rather mean of his father not to have given him one. After all, a feller doesn't always want to drive about in the family bus. Well, he'd just teach the old man a lesson and buy one himself. For twenty thousand francs, two hundred pounds roughly, he could get a very decent second-hand car. He meant to get the money back, but just then he didn't quite know how. He didn't like the idea of kicking up a row, he was a stranger, in a hotel he knew nothing of; it might very well be that the beastly woman had friends there; he didn't mind facing anyone in a fair fight, but he'd look pretty foolish if someone pulled a gun on him. He reflected besides, very sensibly, that he had no proof the money was his. If it came to a showdown and she swore it was hers, he might very easily find himself hauled off to a police station. He really didn't know what to do. Presently by her regular breathing he knew that the little lady was asleep. She must have fallen asleep with an easy mind, for she had done her job without a hitch. It infuriated Nicky that she should rest so peacefully while he lay awake, worried to death. Suddenly an idea occurred to him. It was such a good one that it was only by the exercise of all his self-control that he prevented himself from jumping out of bed and carrying it out at once. Two could play at her game. She'd stolen his money; well, he'd steal it back again, and they'd be all square. He made up his mind to wait quite quietly until he was sure that deceitful woman was sound asleep. He waited for what seemed to him a very long time. She did not stir. Her breathing was as regular as a child's.

"Darling," he said at last.

No answer. No movement. She was dead to the world. Very slowly, pausing after every movement, very silently, he slipped out of bed. He stood still for a while, looking at her to see whether he had disturbed her. Her breathing was as regular as before. During the time he was waiting he had taken note carefully of the furniture in the room so that in crossing it he should not knock against a chair or a table and make a noise. He took a couple of steps and waited; he took a couple of steps more; he was very light on his feet and made no sound as he walked; he took fully five minutes to get to the window, and here he waited again. He started, for the bed slightly creaked, but it was only because the sleeper turned in her sleep. He forced himself to wait till he had counted one hundred. She was sleeping like a log. With infinite care he seized the cineraria by the stalks and gently pulled it out of the pot; he put his other hand in, his heart beat nineteen to the dozen as his fingers touched the notes, his hand closed on them and he slowly drew them out. He replaced the plant and in his turn carefully pressed down the earth. While he was doing all this he had kept one eye on the form lying in the bed. It remained still. After another pause he crept softly to the chair on which his clothes were lying. He first put the bundle of notes in his coat pocket and then proceeded to dress. It took him a good quarter of an hour, because he could afford to make no sound. He had been wearing a soft shirt with his dinner jacket, and he congratulated himself on this because it was easier to put on silently than a stiff one. He had some difficulty in tying his tie without a looking glass, but he very wisely reflected that it didn't really matter if it wasn't tied very well. His spirits were rising. The whole thing now began to seem rather a lark. At length he was completely dressed except for his shoes, which he took in his hand; he thought he would put them on when he got into the passage. Now he had to cross the room to get to the door. He reached it so quietly that he could not have disturbed the lightest sleeper. But the door had to be unlocked. He turned the key very slowly; it creaked.

"Who's that?"

The little woman suddenly sat up in bed. Nicky's heart jumped to his mouth. He made a great effort to keep his head.

"It's only me. It's six o'clock and I've got to go. I was trying not to wake you."

"Oh, I forgot."

She sank back onto the pillow.

"Now that you're awake I'll put on my shoes."

He sat down on the edge of the bed and did this.

"Don't make a noise when you go out. The hotel people don't like it. Oh, I'm so sleepy."

"You go right off to sleep again."

"Kiss me before you go." He bent down and kissed her. "You're a sweet boy and a wonderful lover. *Bon voyage.*"

Nicky did not feel quite safe till he got out of the hotel. The dawn had broken. The sky was unclouded, and in the harbour the yachts and the fishing boats lay motionless on the still water. On the quay fishermen were getting ready to start on their day's work. The streets were deserted. Nicky took a long breath of the sweet morning air. He felt alert and well. He also felt as pleased as Punch. With a swinging stride, his shoulders well thrown back, he walked up the hill and along the gardens in front of the Casino —the flowers in that clear light had a dewy brilliance that was delicious—till he came to his hotel. Here the day had already begun. In the hall porters with mufflers round their necks and berets on their heads were busy sweeping. Nicky went up to his room and had a hot bath. He lay in it and thought with satisfaction that he was not such a mug as some people might think. After his bath he did his exercises, dressed, packed and went down to breakfast. He had a grand appetite. No continental breakfast for him! He had grapefruit, porridge, bacon and eggs, rolls fresh from the oven, so crisp and delicious they melted in your mouth, marmalade and three cups of coffee. Though feeling perfectly well before, he felt better after that. He lit the pipe he had recently learnt to smoke, paid his bill and stepped into the car that was waiting to take him to the aerodrome on the other side of Cannes. The road as far as Nice ran over the hills, and below him was the blue sea and the coast line. He couldn't help thinking it damned pretty. They passed through Nice, so gay and friendly in the early morning, and presently they came to a long stretch of straight road that ran by the sea. Nicky had paid his bill, not with the money he had won the night before, but with the money his father had given him; he had changed a thousand francs to pay for supper at the Knickerbocker, but that deceitful little woman had returned him the thousand francs he had lent her, so that he still had twenty thousand-franc notes in his pocket. He thought he would like to have a look at them. He had so nearly lost them that they had a double value for him. He took them out of his hip pocket into which for safety's sake he had stuffed them when he put on the suit he was travelling in, and counted them one by one. Something very strange had happened to them. Instead of there being twenty notes, as there should have been, there were twenty-six. He couldn't understand it at all. He counted them twice more. There was no doubt about it; somehow or other he had twenty-six thousand francs instead of the twenty he should have had. He couldn't make it out. He asked himself if it was possible that he had won more at the Sporting Club than he had realized. But no, that was out of the question; he distinctly remembered the man at the desk laying the notes out in four rows of five, and he had counted them himself. Suddenly the explanation occurred to him; when he had put his hand into the flower pot, after taking out the cineraria, he had grabbed everything he felt there. The flower pot was the little hussy's money box, and he had taken out not only his own money, but her savings as well. Nicky leant back in the car and burst into a roar of laughter. It was the funniest thing he had ever heard in his life. And when he thought of her going to the flower pot sometime later in the morning when she awoke, expecting to find the money she had so cleverly got away with, and finding, not only that it wasn't there, but that her own had gone too, he laughed more than ever. And so far as he was concerned there was nothing to do about it, he knew neither her name nor the name of the hotel to which she had taken him. He couldn't return her money even if he wanted to.

"It serves her damned well right," he said.

This then was the story that Henry Garnet told his friends over the bridge table, for the night before, after dinner when his wife and daughter had left them to their port, Nicky had narrated it in full.

"And you know what infuriated me is that he's so damned pleased with himself. Talk of a cat swallowing a canary. And d'you know what he said to me when he'd finished? He looked at me with those innocent eyes of his and said: 'You know, Father, I can't help thinking there was something wrong about the advice you gave me. You said, don't gamble; well, I did, and I made a packet; you said, don't lend money; well, I did, and I got it back; and you said, don't have anything to do with women; well, I did, and I made six thousand francs on the deal.'"

It didn't make it any better for Henry Garnet that his three companions burst out laughing.

"It's all very well for you fellows to laugh, but you know, I'm in a damned awkward position. The boy looked up to me, he respected me, he took whatever I said as gospel truth, and now, I saw it in his eyes, he just looks upon me as a drivelling old fool. It's no good my saying one swallow doesn't make a summer; he doesn't see that it was just a fluke, he thinks the whole thing was due to his own cleverness. It may ruin him."

"You do look a bit of a damned fool, old man," said one of the others. "There's no denying that, is there?"

"I know I do, and I don't like it. It's so dashed unfair. Fate has no right to play one tricks like that. After all, you must admit that my advice was good."

"Very good."

"And the wretched boy ought to have burnt his fingers. Well, he hasn't. You're all men of the world, you tell me how I'm to deal with the situation now."

But they none of them could.

"Well, Henry, if I were you I wouldn't worry," said the lawyer. "My belief is that your boy's born lucky, and in the long run that's better than to be born clever or rich."

COMMENT

The central appeal of Maugham's popular story lies, of course, in the pleasant unexpectedness of Nicky's experiences at Monte Carlo—his good luck at gambling, at lending, and with the "little lady." Perhaps there is even more than that; there is a good picture of the feelings of the young man in these experiences. But in the main we are invited to enjoy the ironic opposite of the bad luck which Nicky might normally be expected to meet in his adventures. Irony—which is present when an outcome runs counter to expectations—is, of course, one of the devices by which very mature literary effects may be secured. But here the question is whether the irony suggests a profound insight into experience —an insight which is not content to take various aspects of life at their face value or in terms of popular conceptions, or whether the irony is created only by the author's arbitrary turning upside down of the expectations we would normally have in the circumstances he has described. Is this not what Maugham has done in this story? Has he not merely made an appeal to an uncritical reader's love of unexpected good luck?

Maugham has in part done just this. Yet he has not quite been content to let the story stop at this simple level; he has not merely let the reader enjoy Nicky's good fortune. That he has wanted to do more is shown by the fact that he has used a framework, in which the chief character is Henry Garnet. He has complicated his rather simple material by having the story focus partly on Henry. Henry has had an ironic experience too—for him, an ironic disappointment. Is this irony, although it springs out of the other one, as arbitrary as the other, or does it shed a kind of light on human experience generally, or at least on parental experience generally?

Note that Nicky's story is told almost without getting into Nicky's character at all. Except for a certain ingenuity which he shows in the girl's room, he is less active than passive; he does not do things, but things happen to him. The character is not individualized—any young man would do. Yet the nature of the materials is such that a real problem of character keeps constantly occurring to the reader: Nicky keeps feeling more and more proud, confident, and even morally self-satisfied. How will his experiences eventually affect him? Maugham knows that this is a real issue. This he shows in the framework story, which acts as a commentary on Nicky's experience: Henry says of his son, "It may ruin him." But then Maugham drops it; Henry is apparently primarily concerned about looking like a fool, and the story ends on a platitude. What is more, Henry's worried state has been shown only by his errors and bad temper in bridge. A final effect of triviality is caused by this casual presentation of parental concern about a real issue. We need not be unduly solemn about a story which has no serious intention, but we should see how it falls short because it does not develop the implications of the materials, which the author himself shows that he is aware of.

A. E. Coppard

Although now very well known as a writer of short stories, Alfred Edgar Coppard did not begin to create his reputation—in fact, did not even begin to write—until virtually middle-aged. He was born in England, where he has always lived, in 1878; his first volume of short stories, *Adam and Eve and Pinch Me,* appeared in 1921. This was some time after he had moved to Oxford and come under the influence of the university and of students with literary interests. Before then he had engaged in various kinds of work—as a tailor's apprentice, as a professional sprinter, and as a clerk. He was self-educated. He has published several volumes of poetry and better than a dozen volumes of short stories. Although he can write in the vein of conventional realism, his most characteristic manner involves the use of fantasy and symbol. His writing is sometimes called "lyric."

Fifty Pounds

AFTER tea Philip Repton and Eulalia Burnes discussed their gloomy circumstances. Repton was the precarious sort of London journalist, a dark deliberating man, lean and drooping, full of genteel unprosperity, who wrote articles about *Single Tax, Diet and Reason, The Futility of this, that and the other,* or *The Significance of the other, that and this;* all done with a bleak care and signed P. Stick Repton. Eulalia was brown-haired and hardy, undeliberating and intuitive; she had been milliner, clerk, domestic help and something in a canteen; and P. Stick Repton had, as one commonly says, picked her up at a time when she was drifting about London without a penny in her purse, without even a purse, and he had not yet put her down.

"I can't understand! It's sickening, monstrous!" Lally was fumbling with a match in front of the gas fire, for when it was evening, in September, it always got chilly on a floor so high up. Their flat

FIFTY POUNDS From *The Collected Tales of A. E. Coppard.* Reprinted by permission of Alfred A. Knopf, Inc. Copyright, 1927, 1948, by Alfred A. Knopf, Inc.

was a fourth-floor one and there were— Oh, fifteen thousand stairs! Out of the window and beyond the chimneys you could see the long glare from lights in High Holborn, and hear the hums and hoots of buses. And that was a comfort.

"Lower! Turn it lower!" yelled Philip. The gas had ignited with an astounding thump; the kneeling Lally had thrown up her hands and dropped the matchbox, saying "Damn" in the same tone as one might say good morning to a milkman.

"You shouldn't do it, you know," grumbled Repton. "You'll blow us to the deuce." And that was just like Lally, that was Lally all over, always: the gas, the knobs of sugar in his tea, the way she . . . and the, the . . . O dear, dear! In their early life together, begun so abruptly and illicitly six months before, her simple hidden beauties had delighted him by their surprises; they had peered and shone brighter, had waned and recurred: she was less the one star in his universe than a faint galaxy.

This room of theirs was a dingy room, very small but very high. A lanky gas tube swooped from the middle of the ceiling towards the middle of the table-cloth as if burning to discover whether that was pink or saffron or fawn—and it *was* hard to tell—but on perceiving that the cloth, whatever its tint, was disturbingly spangled with dozens of cupstains and several large envelopes, the gas tube in the violence of its disappointment contorted itself abruptly, assumed a lateral bend, and put out its tongue of flame at an oleograph of Mona Lisa which hung above the fireplace.

Those envelopes were the torment to Lally; they were the sickening, monstrous manifestations which she could not understand. There were always some of them lying there, or about the room, bulging with manuscripts that no editors—they *couldn't* have perused them—wanted; and so it had come to the desperate point when, as Lally was saying, something had to be done about things. Repton had done all *he* could; he wrote unceasingly, all day, all night, but all his projects insolvently withered, and morning, noon and evening brought his manuscripts back as unwanted as snow in summer. He was depressed and baffled and weary. And there was simply nothing else he could do, nothing in the world. Apart from his own wonderful gift he was useless, Lally knew, and he was being steadily and stupidly murdered by those editors. It was weeks since they had eaten a proper meal. Whenever they obtained any real nice food now, they sat down to it silently, intently and destructively. As far as Lally could tell there seemed to be no prospect of any such meals again in life or time, and the worst of it all was Philip's pride—he was actually too proud to ask anyone for assistance! Not that he would be too proud to accept help if it were offered to him: O no, if it came he would rejoice at it! But still, he had that nervous shrinking pride that coiled upon itself, and he would not *ask;* he was like a wounded animal that hid its woe far away from the rest of the world. Lally alone knew his need, but why could not other people see it—those villainous editors! His own wants were so modest and he had a generous mind.

"Phil," Lally said, seating herself at the table. Repton was lolling in a wicker armchair beside the gas fire. "I'm not going on waiting and waiting any longer, I must go and get a job. Yes, I must. We get poorer and poorer. We can't go on like this any longer, it's no use, and I can't bear it."

"No, no, I can't have that, my dear. . . ."

"But I will!" she cried. "Oh, why are you so proud?"

"Proud! Proud!" He stared into the gas fire, his tired arms hanging limp over the arms of the chair. "You don't understand. There are things the flesh has to endure, and things the spirit too must endure. . . ." Lally loved to hear him talk like that; and it was just as well, for Repton was much given to such discoursing. Deep in her mind was the conviction that he had simple access to profound, almost unimaginable wisdom. "It isn't pride, it is just that there is a certain order in life, in my life, that it would not do for. I could not bear it, I could never rest: I can't explain that, but just believe it, Lally." His head was empty but unbowed; he spoke quickly and finished almost angrily. "If only I had money! It's not for myself. I can stand all this, any amount of it. I've done so before, and I shall do again and again I've no doubt. But I have to think of you."

That was fiercely annoying. Lally got up and went and stood over him.

"Why are you so stupid? I can think for myself and fend for myself. I'm not married to you. You have your pride, but I can't starve for it. And I've a pride, too, I'm a burden to you. If you won't let me work now while we're together, then I must leave you and work for myself."

"Leave! Leave me now? When things are so bad?" His white face gleamed his perturbation up at her. "O well, go, go." But then, mournfully moved, he took her hands and fondled them. "Don't be a fool, Lally; it's only a passing depression, this; I've known worse before, and it never lasts long, something turns up, always does. There's good and bad in it all, but there's more goodness than anything else. You see."

"I don't want to wait for ever, even for goodness. I don't believe in it, I never see it, never feel it, it is no use to me. I could go and steal, or walk the streets, or do any dirty thing—easily. What's the good of goodness if it isn't any use?"

"But, but," Repton stammered, "what's the use of bad, if it isn't any better?"

"I mean . . ." began Lally.

"You don't mean anything, my dear girl."

"I mean, when you haven't any choice it's no use talking moral, or having pride, it's stupid. Oh, my darling," she slid down to him and lay against his breast, "it's not you, you are everything to me; that's why it angers me so, this treatment of you, all hard blows and no comfort. It will never be any different, I feel it will never be different now, and it terrifies me."

"Pooh!" Repton kissed her and comforted her: she was his beloved. "When things are wrong with us our fancies take their tone from our misfortunes, badness, evil. I sometimes have a queer stray feeling that one day I shall be hanged. Yes, I don't know what for, what *could* I be hanged for? And, do you know, at other times I've had a kind of intuition that one day I shall be—what do you think?—Prime Minister of the country! Yes, well, you can't reason against such things. I know what I should do, I've my plans, I've even made a list of the men for my cabinet. Yes, well, there you are!"

But Lally had made up her mind to leave him; she would leave him for a while and earn her own living. When things took a turn for the better she would join him again. She told him this. She had friends who were going to get her some work.

"But what are you going to do, Lally, I . . ."

"I'm going away to Glasgow," said she.

"Glasgow?" He had heard things about Glasgow! Good heavens!

"I've some friends there," the girl went on steadily. She had got up and was sitting on the arm of his chair. "I wrote to them last week. They can get me a job almost anywhere, and I can stay with them. They want me to go—they've sent the money for my fare. I think I shall have to go."

"You don't love me then!" said the man.

Lally kissed him.

"But *do* you? Tell me!"

"Yes, my dear," said Lally, "of course."

An uneasiness possessed him; he released her moodily. Where was their wild passion flown to? She was staring at him intently, then she tenderly said: "My love, don't you be melancholy, don't take it to heart so. I'd cross the world to find you a pin."

"No, no, you mustn't do that," he exclaimed idiotically. At her indulgent smile he grimly laughed too, and then sank back in his chair. The girl stood up and went about the room doing vague things, until he spoke again.

"So you are tired of me?"

Lally went to him steadily and knelt down by his chair. "If I was tired of you, Phil, I'd kill myself."

Moodily he ignored her. "I suppose it had to end like this. But I've loved you desperately." Lally was now weeping on his shoulder, and he began to twirl a lock of her rich brown hair absently with his fingers as if it were a seal on a watch chain. "I'd been thinking we might as well get married, as soon as things had turned round."

"I'll come back, Phil," she clasped him so tenderly, "as soon as you want me."

"But you are not really going?"

"Yes," said Lally.

"You're not to go!"

"I wouldn't go if . . . if anything . . . if you had any luck. But as we are now I must go away, to give you a chance. You see that, darling Phil?"

"You're not to go; I object. I just love you, Lally, that's all, and of course I want to keep you here."

"Then what are we to do?"

"I . . . don't . . . know. Things drop out of the sky. But we must be together. You're not to go."

Lally sighed: he was stupid. And Repton began to turn over in his mind the dismal knowledge that she had taken this step in secret, she had not told him while she was trying to get to Glasgow. Now here she was with the fare, and as good as gone! Yes, it was all over.

"When do you propose to go?"

"Not for a few days, nearly a fortnight."

"Good God," he moaned. Yes, it was all over then. He had never dreamed that this would be the end, that she would be the first to break away. He had always envisaged a tender scene in which he could tell her, with dignity and gentle humour, that . . . Well, he never had quite hit upon the words he would use, but that was the kind of setting. And now, here she was with her fare to Glasgow, her heart turned towards Glasgow, and she as good as gone to Glasgow! No dignity, no gentle humour—in fact he was enraged, sullen but enraged; he boiled furtively. But he said with mournful calm:

"I've so many misfortunes, I suppose I can bear this, too." Gloomy and tragic he was.

"Dear, darling Phil, it's for your own sake I'm going."

Repton sniffled derisively. "We are always mistaken in the reasons for our commonest actions; Nature derides us all. You are sick of me; I can't blame you."

Eulalia was so moved that she could only weep again. Nevertheless she wrote to her friends in Glasgow promising to be with them by a stated date.

Towards the evening of the following day, at a time when she was alone, a letter arrived addressed to herself. It was from a firm of solicitors in Cornhill inviting her to call upon them. A flame leaped up in Lally's heart: it might mean the offer of some work which would keep her in London after all! If only it were so she would accept it on the spot, and Philip would have to be made to see the reasonability of it. But at the office in Cornhill a more astonishing outcome awaited her. There she showed her letter to a little office boy with scarcely any fingernails and very little nose, and he took it to an elderly man who had a superabundance of both. Smiling affably the long-nosed man led her upstairs into the sombre den of a gentleman who had some white hair and a lumpy yellow complexion. Having put to her a number of questions relating to her family history, and appearing to be satisfied and not at all surprised by her answers, this gentleman revealed to Lally the overpowering tidings that she was entitled to a legacy of eighty pounds by the will of a forgotten and recently deceased aunt. Subject to certain formalities, proofs of identity and so forth, he promised Lally the possession of the money within about a week.

Lally's descent to the street, her emergence into the clamouring atmosphere, her walk along to Holborn, were accomplished in a state of blessedness and trance, a trance in which life became a thousand times aërially enlarged, movement was a delight, and thought a rapture. She would give all the money to Philip, and if he very much wanted it she would even marry him now. Perhaps, though, she would save ten pounds of it for herself. The other seventy would keep them for . . . it was impossible to say how long it would keep them. They could have a little holiday somewhere in the country together, he was so worn and weary. Perhaps she had better not tell Philip anything at all about it until her lovely money was really in her hand. Nothing in life, at least nothing about money, was ever certain; something horrible might happen at the crucial moment and the money be snatched from her very fingers. Oh, she would go mad then! So for some days she kept her wonderful secret.

Their imminent separation had given Repton a tender sadness that was very moving. "Eulalia," he would say; for he had suddenly adopted the formal version of her name: "Eulalia, we've had a great time together, a wonderful time, there will never be anything like it again." She often shed tears, but she kept the grand secret still locked in her heart. Indeed, it occurred to her very forcibly that even now his stupid pride might cause him to reject her money altogether. Silly, silly Philip! Of course it would have been different if they had married; he would naturally have taken it then, and really, it would have *been* his. She would have to think out some dodge to overcome his scruples. Scruples were *such* a nuisance, but then it was very noble of him: there were not many men who wouldn't take money from a girl they were living with.

Well, a week later she was summoned again to the office in Cornhill and received from the white-haired gentleman a cheque for eighty pounds drawn on the Bank of England to the order of Eulalia Burnes. Miss Burnes desired to cash the cheque straightway, so the large-nosed elderly clerk was deputed to accompany her to the Bank of England close by and assist in procuring the money.

"A very nice errand!" exclaimed that gentleman as they crossed to Threadneedle Street past the Royal Exchange. Miss Burnes smiled her acknowledgment, and he began to tell her of other windfalls that had been disbursed in his time—but vast sums, very great persons—until she began to infer that Blackbean, Carp and Ransome were universal dispensers of heavenly largesse.

"Yes, but," said the clerk, hawking a good deal from an affliction of catarrh, "I never got any myself, and never will. If I did, do you know what I would do with it?" But at that moment they entered the portals of the bank, and in the excitement of the business, Miss Burnes forgot to ask the clerk how he would use a legacy, and thus she possibly lost a most valuable slice of knowledge. With one fifty-pound note and six five-pound notes clasped in her handbag she bade good-bye to the long-nosed clerk, who shook her fervently by the hand and assured her that Blackbean, Carp and Ransome would be delighted at all times to undertake any commissions on her behalf. Then she fled along the pavement, blithe as a bird, until she was breathless with her flight. Presently she came opposite the window of a typewriting agency. Tripping airily into his office she laid a scrap of paper before a lovely Hebe who was typing there.

"I want this typed, if you please," said Lally.

The beautiful typist read the words on the scrap of paper and stared at the heiress.

"I don't want any address to appear," said Lally; "just a plain sheet, please."

A few moments later she received a neatly typed page folded in an envelope, and after paying the charge she hurried off to a District Messenger office. Here she addressed the envelope in a disguised hand to *P. Stick Repton, Esq.*, at their address in Holborn. She read the typed letter through again:

DEAR SIR,

In common with many others I entertain the greatest admiration for your literary abilities, and I therefore beg you to accept this

tangible expression of that admiration from a constant reader of
your articles who, for purely private reasons, desires to remain
anonymous.

Your very sincere

WELLWISHER.

Placing the fifty-pound note upon the letter Lally carefully folded
them together and put them both into the envelope. The attendant
then gave it to a uniformed lad, who sauntered off whistling very
casually, somewhat to Lally's alarm—he looked so small and careless to be entrusted with fifty pounds. Then Lally went out, changed
one of her five-pound notes and had a lunch—half-a-crown, but it
was worth it. Oh, how enchanting and exciting London was! In two
days more she would have been gone: now she would have to
write off at once to her Glasgow friends and tell them she had
changed her mind, that she was now settled in London. Oh, how
enchanting and delightful! And tonight he would take her out to
dine in some fine restaurant, and they would do a theatre. She did
not really want to marry Phil, they had got on so well without it,
but if he wanted that too she did not mind—much. They would go
away into the country for a whole week. What money would do!
Marvellous! And looking round the restaurant she felt sure that no
other woman there, no matter how well-dressed, had as much as
thirty pounds in her handbag.

Returning home in the afternoon she became conscious of her
own betraying radiance; very demure and subdued and usual she
would have to be, or he might guess the cause of it. Though she
danced up the long flight of stairs she entered their room quietly,
but the sight of Repton staring out of the window, forlorn as a
drowsy horse, overcame her and she rushed to embrace him crying
"Darling!"

"Hullo, hullo!" he smiled.

"I'm so fond of you, Phil dear."

"But . . . but you're deserting me!"

"O no," she cried archly; "I'm not—not deserting you."

"All right." Repton shrugged his shoulders, but he seemed happier. He did not mention the fifty pounds then: perhaps it had not
come yet—or perhaps he was thinking to surprise her.

"Let's go for a walk, it's a screaming lovely day," said Lally.

"Oh, I dunno." He yawned and stretched. "Nearly tea-time, isn't it?"

"Well, we . . ." Lally was about to suggest having tea out somewhere, but she bethought herself in time. "I suppose it is. Yes, it is."

So they stayed in for tea. No sooner was tea over than Repton remarked that he had an engagement somewhere. Off he went, leaving Lally disturbed and anxious. Why had he not mentioned the fifty pounds? Surely it had not gone to the wrong address? This suspicion once formed, Lally soon became certain, tragically sure, that she had misaddressed the envelope herself. A conviction that she had put No. 17 instead of No. 71 was almost overpowering, and she fancied that she hadn't even put London on the envelope—but Glasgow. That was impossible, though, but— Oh, the horror!—somebody else was enjoying their fifty pounds. The girl's fears were not allayed by the running visit she paid to the messenger office that evening, for the rash imp who had been entrusted with her letter had gone home and therefore could not be interrogated until the morrow. By now she was sure that he had blundered; he had been so casual with an important letter like that! Lally never did, and never would again, trust any little boys who wore their hats so much on one side, were so glossy with hair-oil, and went about whistling just to madden you. She burned to ask where the boy lived, but in spite of her desperate desire she could not do so. She dared not, it would expose her to . . . to something or other she could not feel, not name; you had to keep cool, to let nothing, not even curiosity, master you.

Hurrying home again, though hurrying was not her custom, and there was no occasion for it, she wrote the letter to her Glasgow friends. Then it crossed her mind that it would be wiser not to post the letter that night; better wait until the morning, after she had discovered what the horrible little messenger had done with her letter. Bed was a poor refuge from her thoughts, but she accepted it, and when Phil came home she was not sleeping. While he undressed he told her of the lecture he had been to, something about Agrarian Depopulation it was, but even after he had stretched himself beside her, he did not speak about the fifty pounds. Nothing, not even curiosity, should master her, and so she calmed herself, and in time fitfully slept.

At breakfast next morning he asked her what she was going to do that day.

"Oh," replied Lally offhandedly, "I've a lot of things to see to, you know; I must go out. I'm sorry the porridge is so awful this morning, Phil, but . . ."

"Awful?" he broke in. "But it's nicer than usual! Where are you going? I thought—our last day, you know—we might go out somewhere together."

"Dear Phil!" Lovingly she stretched out a hand to be caressed across the table. "But I've several things to do. I'll come back early, eh?" She got up and hurried round to embrace him.

"All right," he said. "Don't be long."

Off went Lally to the messenger office, at first as happy as a bird, but on approaching the building the old tremors assailed her. Inside the room was the cocky little boy who bade her "Good morning" with laconic assurance. Lally at once questioned him, and when he triumphantly produced a delivery book she grew limp with her suppressed fear, one fear above all others. For a moment she did not want to look at it: Truth hung by a hair, and as long as it so hung she might swear it was a lie. But there it was, written right across the page, an entry of a letter delivered, signed for in the well-known hand, *P. Stick Repton*. There was no more doubt, only a sharp indignant agony as if she had been stabbed with a dagger of ice.

"O yes, thank you," said Lally calmly. "Did you hand it to him yourself?"

"Yes'm," replied the boy, and he described Philip.

"Did he open the letter?"

"Yes'm."

"There was no answer?"

"No'm."

"All right." Fumbling in her bag, she added: "I think I've got a sixpence for you."

Out in the street again she tremblingly chuckled to herself. "So that is what he is like, after all. Cruel and mean!" He was going to let her go and keep the money in secret to himself! How despicable! Cruel and mean, cruel and mean. She hummed it to herself: "Cruel and mean, cruel and mean!" It eased her tortured bosom. "Cruel and mean!" And he was waiting at home for her, waiting with a smile for their last day together. It would *have* to be their last day. She tore up the letter to her Glasgow friends, for now she *must* go to them. So cruel and mean! Let him wait! A 'bus stopped beside her and she stepped on to it, climbing to the top and sitting there while the air chilled her burning features. The 'bus made a long journey to Plaistow. She knew nothing of Plaistow, she wanted to know nothing of Plaistow, but she did not care where the 'bus took her; she only wanted to keep moving, and moving away, as far as possible from Holborn and from him, and not once let those hovering tears down fall.

From Plaistow she turned and walked back as far as the Mile End Road. Thereabouts, wherever she went she met clergymen, dozens of them. There must be a conference, about charity or something, Lally thought. With a vague desire to confide her trouble to some one, she observed them; it would relieve the strain. But there was none she could tell her sorrow to, and failing that, when she came to a neat restaurant she entered it and consumed a fish. Just beyond her three sleek parsons were lunching, sleek and pink; bald, affable, consoling men, all very much alike.

"I saw Carter yesterday," she heard one say. Lally liked listening to the conversation of strangers, and she had often wondered what clergymen talked about among themselves.

"What, Carter! Indeed. Nice fellow Carter. How was he?"

"Carter loves preaching, you know!" cried the third.

"O yes, he loves preaching!"

"Ha ha ha, yes."

"Ha ha ha, oom."

"Awf'ly good preacher, though."

"Yes, awf'ly good."

"And he's awf'ly good at comic songs, too."

"Yes?"

"Yes!"

Three glasses of water, a crumbling of bread, a silence suggestive of prayer.

"How long has he been married?"

"Twelve years," returned the cleric who had met Carter.

"Oh, twelve years!"

"I've only been married twelve years myself," said the oldest of them.

"Indeed!"

"Yes, I tarried very long."

"Ha ha ha, yes."

"Ha ha ha, oom."

"Er . . . have you any family?"

"No."

Very delicate and dainty in handling their food they were; very delicate and dainty.

"My rectory is a magnificent old house," continued the recently married one. "Built originally in 1700. Burnt down. Rebuilt 1784."

"Indeed!"

"Humph!"

"Seventeen bedrooms and two delightful tennis courts."

"Oh, well done!" the others cried, and then they all fell with genteel gusto upon a pale blancmange.

From the restaurant the girl sauntered about for a while, and then there was a cinema wherein, seated warm and comfortable in the switching darkness, she partially stilled her misery. Some nervous fancy kept her roaming in that district for most of the evening. She knew that if she left it she would go home, and she did not want to go home. The naphtha lamps of the booths at Mile End were bright and distracting, and the hum of the evening business was good despite the smell. A man was weaving sweet stuffs from a pliant roll of warm toffee that he wrestled with as the athlete wrestles with the python. There were stalls with things of iron, with fruit or fish, pots and pans, leather, string, nails. Watches for use—or for ornament—what d'ye lack? A sailor told naughty stories while selling bunches of green grapes out of barrels of cork dust which he swore he had stolen from the Queen of Honolulu. People clamoured for them both. You could buy back numbers of the comic papers at four a penny, rolls of linoleum for very little more—and use either for the other's purpose.

"At thrippence per foot, mesdames," cried the sweating cheapjack, lashing himself into ecstatic furies, "that's a piece of fabric weft and woven with triple-strength Andalusian jute, double-hotpressed with rubber from the island of Pagama, and stenciled by an artist as poisoned his grandfather's cook. That's a piece of fabric, mesdames, as the king of heaven himself wouldn't mind to put down in his parlour—if he had the chance. Do I ask thrippence a foot for that piece of fabric? Mesdames, I was never a daring chap."

Lally watched it all, she looked and listened; then looked and did not see, listened and did not hear. Her misery was not the mere disappointment of love, not that kind of misery alone; it was the crushing of an ideal in which love had had its home, a treachery cruel and mean. The sky of night, so smooth, so bestarred, looked wrinkled through her screen of unshed tears; her sorrow was a wild cloud that troubled the moon with darkness.

In miserable desultory wandering she had spent her day, their last day, and now, returning to Holborn in the late evening, she suddenly began to hurry, for a new possibility had come to lighten her dejection. Perhaps, after all, so whimsical he was, he was keeping his "revelation" until the last day, or even the last hour, when (nothing being known to her, as he imagined) all hopes being gone and they had come to the last kiss, he would take her in his arms and laughingly kill all grief, waving the succour of a flimsy banknote like a flag of triumph. Perhaps even, in fact surely, that was why he wanted to take her out today! Oh, what a blind wicked stupid girl she was, and in a perfect frenzy of bubbling faith she panted homewards for his revealing sign.

From the pavement below she could see that their room was lit. Weakly she climbed the stairs and opened the door. Phil was standing up, staring so strangely at her. Helplessly and half-guilty she began to smile. Without a word said he came quickly to her and crushed her in his arms, her burning silent man, loving and exciting her. Lying against his breast in that constraining embrace, their passionate disaster was gone, her doubts were flown; all perception of the feud was torn from her and deeply drowned in a gulf of bliss. She was aware only of the consoling delight of their reunion, of his amorous kisses, of his tongue tingling the soft down on her upper lip that she disliked and he admired. All the soft wanton endearments that she so loved to hear him speak were singing in her ears, and then he suddenly swung and lifted her up, snapped out the gaslight, and carried her off to bed.

Life that is born of love feeds on love; if the wherewithal be hidden, how shall we stay our hunger? The galaxy may grow dim, or the stars drop in a wandering void; you can neither keep them in your hands nor crumble them in your mind.

What was it Phil had once called her? Numskull! After all it was his own fifty pounds, she had given it to him freely, it was his to do as he liked with. A gift was a gift, it was poor spirit to send money with the covetous expectation that it would return to you. She would surely go tomorrow.

The next morning he awoke her early, and kissed her.

"What time does your train go?"

"Train!" Lally scrambled from his arms and out of bed.

A fine day, a glowing day. O bright, sharp air! Quickly she dressed, and went into the other room to prepare their breakfast. Soon he followed, and they ate silently together, although whenever they were near each other he caressed her tenderly. Afterwards she went into the bedroom and packed her bag; there was nothing more to be done, he was beyond hope. No woman wants to be sacrificed, least of all those who sacrifice themselves with courage and a quiet mind. When she was ready to go she took her portmanteau into the sitting-room; he, too, made to put on his hat and coat.

"No," murmured Lally, "you're not to come with me."

"Pooh, my dear!" he protested; "nonsense."

"I won't have you come," cried Lally with an asperity that impressed him.

"But you can't carry that bag to the station by yourself!"

"I shall take a taxi." She buttoned her gloves.

"My dear!" His humorous deprecation annoyed her.

"O bosh!" Putting her gloved hands around his neck she kissed him coolly. "Good-bye. Write to me often. Let me know how you thrive, won't you, Phil? And"—a little waveringly—"love me always." She stared queerly at the two dimples in his cheeks; each dimple was a nest of hair that could never be shaved.

"Lally darling, beloved girl! I never loved you more than now, this moment. You are more precious than ever to me."

At that, she knew her moment of sardonic revelation had come—but she dared not use it, she let it go. She could not so deeply humiliate him by revealing her knowledge of his perfidy. A compassionate divinity smiles at our puny sins. She knew his perfidy, but to triumph in it would defeat her own pride. Let him keep his gracious, mournful airs to the last, false though they were. It was better to part so, better from such a figure than from an abject scarecrow, even though both were the same inside. And something capriciously reminded her, for a flying moment, of elephants she had seen swaying with the grand movement of tidal water—and groping for monkey-nuts.

Lally tripped down the stairs alone. At the end of the street she turned for a last glance. There he was, high up in the window, waving good-byes. And she waved back to him.

COMMENT

Coppard's story has some rough resemblances to Maugham's "The Facts of Life": The main action involves a young man and a young woman, there is a financial windfall, the young man in effect makes off with the young woman's money, and he is entirely self-confident and pleased with himself. But these similarities serve chiefly to show what an entirely different kind of story Coppard has written. Luck plays a negligible part in "Fifty Pounds": the coincidence of the legacy's coming at a time of need is used not to settle a difficulty the author cannot manage otherwise, but to cause new difficulties. It is a starting point, not a solution. The treatment of character is not secondary to the presentation of pleasantly surprising events, but is the chief business of the story: the author is mainly concerned with revealing the character of Phil. The plot is ingenious, but it is rooted in matters of character: Lally makes the anonymous gift because she thinks Phil's pride would not permit him to accept money from her, and through the gift she discovers the exact nature of his pride. Further, the story is full of irony, but the irony, instead of being produced by an author's arbitrary upsetting of what might be expected, is a matter of character and is a means of revelation. When Lally thinks Phil is sensitive and proud, and tries to act in accordance with his sensitivity and pride, the irony of her mistake does not exist merely for its own sake or for a shock: rather the irony points up the character of Phil, which now becomes clear both to Lally and to the reader. Finally, the very ending contrasts interestingly with Maugham's. Whereas Henry Garnet's final words are rooted in a rather trifling self-centeredness and vanity, Lally's final action involves an admirable kind of pride: she is content to rest in her painful knowledge and will not condescend to inflict humiliation on her dishonest lover. The story ends on this insight into her character.

Other points that the student will wish to consider are these: the means by which, in the first half of the story, we are prepared for Phil's eventual conduct; the usefulness, in the story, of the things Lally sees and hears during the day after she discovers that Phil did receive the money; and the author's purpose in first having her bitterly angry with Phil, and then of putting her through various changes of mind and feeling.

Caroline Gordon

Caroline Gordon is one of the numerous Southerners who have won literary distinction in the present century. She is the author of six novels, of which *Penhally* and *Aleck Maury* are especially notable. Her short stories have appeared in many periodicals and have been collected in a volume entitled *The Forest of the South* (1945). She also writes criticism of fiction. She was born in Kentucky in 1895, the descendant of two lines of tobacco planters, and was educated at Bethany College. She has been a reporter on the Chattanooga *News* and a teacher of English at the North Carolina Women's College. She is the wife of Allen Tate, the poet and critic.

The Last Day in the Field

THAT was the fall when the leaves stayed green so long. We had a drouth in August and the ponds everywhere were dry and the watercourse shrunken. Then in September heavy rains came. Things greened up. It looked like winter was never coming.

"You aren't going to hunt this year, Aleck," Molly said. "Remember how you stayed awake nights last fall with that pain in your leg."

In October light frosts came. In the afternoons when I sat on the back porch going over my fishing tackle I marked their progress on the elderberry bushes that were left standing against the stable fence. The lower, spreading branches had turned yellow and were already sinking to the ground but the leaves in the top clusters still stood up stiff and straight.

"Ah-h, it'll get you yet!" I said, thinking how frost creeps higher and higher out of the ground each night of fall.

The dogs next door felt it and would thrust their noses through the wire fence scenting the wind from the north. When I walked in the back yard they would bound twice their height and whine, for meat scraps Molly said, but it was because they smelled blood on my old hunting coat.

They were almost matched liver-and-white pointers. The big dog had a beautiful, square muzzle and was deep-chested and rangy. The bitch, Judy, had a smaller head and not so good a muzzle but she was springy loined too and had one of the merriest tails I've ever watched.

When Joe Thomas, the boy that owned them, came home from the hardware store he would change his clothes and then come down the back way into the wired enclosure and we would stand there watching the dogs and wondering how they would work. Joe said they were keen as mustard. He was going to take them out the first good Saturday and wanted me to come along.

"I can't make it," I said, "my leg's worse this year than it was last."

The fifteenth of November was clear and so warm that we sat out on the porch till nine o'clock. It was still warm when we went to bed towards eleven. The change must have come in the middle of the night. I woke once, hearing the clock strike two, and felt the air cold on my face and thought before I went back to sleep that the weather had broken at last. When I woke again at dawn the cold air was slapping my face hard. I came wide awake, turned over in bed and looked out of the window.

There was a scaly-bark hickory tree growing on the east side of the house. You could see its upper branches from the bedroom window. The leaves had turned yellow a week ago. But yesterday evening when I walked out there in the yard they had still been flat with green streaks showing in them. Now they were curled up tight and a lot of leaves had fallen on to the ground.

I got out of bed quietly so as not to wake Molly, dressed and went down the back way over to the Thomas house. There was no one stirring but I knew which room Joe's was. The window was open and I could hear him snoring. I went up and stuck my head in.

"Hey," I said, "killing frost."

He opened his eyes and looked at me and then his eyes went shut. I reached my arm through the window and shook him. "Get up," I said, "we got to start right away."

He was awake now and out on the floor stretching. I told him to dress and be over at the house as quick as he could. I'd have breakfast ready for us both.

Aunt Martha had a way of leaving fire in the kitchen stove at night. There were red embers there now. I poked the ashes out and piled kindling on top of them. When the flames came up I put some heavier wood on, filled the coffee pot, and put some grease on in a skillet. By the time Joe got there I had coffee ready and some hoe cakes to go with our fried eggs. Joe had brought a thermos bottle. We put the rest of the coffee in it and I found a ham in the pantry and made some sandwiches.

While I was fixing the lunch Joe went down to the lot to hitch up. He was just driving Old Dick out of the stable when I came down the back steps. The dogs knew what was up, all right. They were whining and surging against the fence and Bob, the big dog, thrust his paw through and into the pocket of my hunting coat as I passed. While Joe was snapping on the leashes I got a few hand-fuls of straw from the rack and put it in the foot of the buggy. It was twelve miles where we were going; the dogs would need to ride warm coming back late.

Joe said he would drive. We got in the buggy and started out, up Seventh Street and on over to College and out through Scuff-town. When we got into the nigger section we could see what a killing frost it had been. A light shimmer over all the ground still and the weeds around the cabins dark and matted the way they are when the frost hits them hard and twists them.

We drove on over the Red River bridge and up into the open country. At Jim Gill's place the cows had come up and were stand-ing waiting to be milked but nobody was stirring yet from the house. I looked back from the top of the hill and saw that the frost mists still hung heavy in the bottom and thought it was a good sign. A day like this when the earth is warmer than the air currents is good for the hunter. Scent particles are borne on the warm air and birds will forage far on such a day.

It took us over an hour to get from Gloversville to Spring Creek. Joe wanted to get out as soon as we hit the big bottom there but I held him down and we drove on to the top of the ridge. We got out there, unhitched Old Dick and turned him into one of Rob Fayerlee's pastures—I thought how surprised Rob would be when he saw him grazing there—put our guns together, and started out, the dogs still on leash.

It was rough, broken ground, scrub oak, with a few gum trees and lots of buckberry bushes. One place a patch of corn ran clear up to the top of the ridge. As we passed along between the rows I could see the frost glistening on the north side of the stalks. I knew it was going to be a good day.

I walked over to the brow of the hill. From here you can see off over the whole valley—I've hunted every foot of it in my time—tobacco land, mostly. One or two patches of corn there on the side of the ridge. I thought we might start there and then I knew that wouldn't do. Quail will linger on the roost a cold day and feed in shelter during the morning. It is only in the afternoon that they will work out to the open.

The dogs were whining. Joe bent down and was about to slip their leashes. "Hey, boy," I said, "don't do that."

I turned around and looked down the other side of the ridge. It was better that way. The corn land of the bottoms ran high up on to the hill in several places there and where the corn stopped there were big patches of ironweed and buckberry. I knocked my pipe out on a stump.

"Let's go that way," I said.

Joe was looking at my old buckhorn whistle that I had slung around my neck. "I forgot to bring mine."

"All right," I said, "I'll handle 'em."

He unfastened their collars and cast off. They broke away, racing for the first hundred yards and barking, then suddenly swerved. The big dog took off to the right along the hillside. The bitch, Judy, skirted a belt of corn along the upper bottomlands. I kept my eye on the big dog. A dog that has bird sense will know cover when he sees it. This big Bob was an independent hunter, all right, I could see him moving fast through the scrub oaks, working his way down toward a patch of ironweed. He caught first scent just on the edge of the weed patch and froze with every indication of class, head up, nose stuck out, and tail straight in air. Judy, meanwhile, had been following the line of the corn field. A hundred yards away she caught sight of Bob's point and backed him.

We went up and flushed the birds. They got up in two bunches. I heard Joe's shot while I was in the act of raising my gun and I saw his bird fall not thirty paces from where I stood. I had covered the middle bird of the larger bunch—that's the one led by the boss cock—the way I usually do. He fell, whirling head over heels, driven a little forward by the impact. A well-centered shot. I could tell by the way the feathers fluffed as he tumbled.

The dogs were off through the grass. They had retrieved both birds. Joe stuck his in his pocket. He laughed. "I thought there for a minute you were going to let him get away."

I looked at him but I didn't say anything. It's a wonderful thing to be twenty years old.

The majority of the singles had flown straight ahead to settle in the rank grass that jutted out from the bottomland. Judy got down to work at once but the big dog broke off to the left, wanting to get footloose to find another covey. I thought of how Trecho, the best dog I ever had—the best dog any man ever had—used always to be wanting to do the same thing and I laughed.

"Naw, you don't," I said, "come back here, you scoundrel, and hunt these singles."

He stopped on the edge of a briar patch, looked at me and heeled up promptly. I clucked him out again. He gave me another look. I thought we were beginning to understand each other better. We got some nice points among those singles but we followed that valley along the creek bed and through two or three more corn fields without finding another covey. Joe was disappointed but I wasn't beginning to worry yet; you always make your bag in the afternoon.

It was twelve o'clock by this time, no sign of frost anywhere and the sun beating down steady on the curled-up leaves.

"Come on," I said, "let's go up to Buck's spring and eat."

We walked up the ravine whose bed was still moist with the fall rains and came out at the head of the hollow. They had cleared out some of the trees on the side of the ravine but the spring itself was the same: a deep pool welling up between the roots of an old sycamore. I unwrapped the sandwiches and the piece of cake and laid them on a stump. Joe got the thermos bottle out of his pocket. Something had gone wrong with it and the coffee was stone cold. We were about to drink it that way when Joe saw a good tin can flung down beside the spring. He made a trash fire and we put the coffee in the can and heated it to boiling.

It was warm in the ravine, sheltered from the wind, with the little fire burning. I turned my game leg so that the heat fell full on my knee. Joe had finished his last sandwich and was reaching for the cake.

"Good ham," he said.

"It's John Ferguson's," I told him.

He had got up and was standing over the spring. "Wonder how long this wood'll last, under water this way."

I looked at the sycamore root, green and slick where the thin stream of water poured over it, then my eyes went back to the dogs. They were tired, all right. Judy had gone off to lie down in a cool place at the side of the spring, but the big dog, Bob, lay there, his forepaws stretched out in front of him, never taking his eyes off our faces. I looked at him and thought how different he was from his mate and like some dogs I had known—and men too—who lived only for hunting and could never get enough no matter how long the day. There was something about his head and his markings that reminded one of another dog I used to hunt with a long time ago and I asked the boy who had trained him. He said the old fellow he bought the dogs from had been killed last spring, over in Trigg—Charley Morrison.

Charley Morrison! I remembered how he died, out hunting by himself and the gun had gone off, accidentally they said. Charley had called his dog to him, got blood over him and sent him home. The dog went, all right, but when they got there Charley was dead. Two years ago that was and now I was hunting the last dogs he'd ever trained. . . .

Joe lifted the thermos bottle. "Another cup?"

I held my cup out and he filled it. The coffee was still good and hot. I drank it, standing up, running my eye over the country in front of us. Afternoon is different from morning, more exciting. It isn't only as I say that you'll make your bag in the afternoon, but it takes more figuring. They're fed and rested and when they start out again they'll work in the open and over a wider range.

Joe was stamping out his cigarette: "Let's go."

The dogs were already out of sight but I could see the sedge grass ahead moving and I knew they'd be making for the same thing that took my eye: a spearhead of thicket that ran far out into this open field. We came up over a little rise. There they were,

Bob on a point and Judy backing him not fifty feet from the thicket. I saw it was going to be tough shooting. No way to tell whether the birds were between the dog and the thicket or in the thicket itself. Then I saw that the cover was more open along the side of the thicket and I thought that that was the way they'd go if they were in the thicket. But Joe had already broken away to the left. He got too far to the side. The birds flushed to the right and left him standing, flat-footed, without a shot.

He looked sort of foolish and grinned.

I thought I wouldn't say anything and then I found myself speaking: "Trouble with you, you try to out-think the dog."

There was nothing to do about it, though. The chances were that the singles had pitched in the trees below. We went down there. It was hard hunting. The woods were open, the ground everywhere heavily carpeted with leaves. Dead leaves make a tremendous rustle when the dogs surge through them. It takes a good nose to cut scent keenly in such noisy cover. I kept my eye on Bob. He never faltered, getting over the ground in big, springy strides but combing every inch of it. We came to an open place in the woods. Nothing but hickory trees and bramble thickets overhung with trailing vines. Bob passed the first thicket and came to a beautiful point. We went up. He stood perfectly steady but the bird flushed out fifteen or twenty steps ahead of him. I saw it swing to the right, gaining altitude very quickly—woods birds will always cut back to known territory—and it came to me how it would be.

I called to Joe: "Don't shoot yet."

He nodded and raised his gun, following the bird with the barrel. It was directly over the treetops when I gave the word and he shot, scoring a clean kill.

He laughed excitedly as he stuck the bird in his pocket. "My God, man, I didn't know you could take that much time!"

We went on through the open woods. I was thinking about a day I'd had years ago in the woods at Grassdale, with my uncle, James Morris, and his son, Julian. Uncle James had given Julian and me hell for missing just such a shot. I can see him now standing up against a big pine tree, his face red from liquor and his gray hair ruffling in the wind: "*Let him alone! Let him alone!* And establish your lead as he climbs."

Joe was still talking about the shot he'd made. "Lord, I wish I could get another one like that."

"You won't," I said, "we're getting out of the woods now."

We struck a path that led due west and followed it for half a mile. My leg was stiff from the hip down now and every time I brought it over, the pain would start in my knee, Zing! and travel up and settle in the small of my back. I walked with my head down, watching the light catch on the ridges of Joe's brown corduroy trousers and then shift and catch again. Sometimes he would get on ahead and then there would be nothing but the black tree trunks coming up out of the dead leaves.

Joe was talking about some wild land up on the Cumberland. We could get up there on an early train. Have a good day. Might even spend the night. When I didn't answer he turned around: "Man, you're sweating."

I pulled my handkerchief out and wiped my face. "Hot work," I said.

He had stopped and was looking about him. "Used to be a spring somewhere around here."

He had found the path and was off. I sat down on a stump and mopped my face some more. The sun was halfway down through the trees now, the whole west woods ablaze with the light. I sat there and thought that in another hour it would be good and dark and I wished that the day could go on and not end so soon and yet I didn't see how I could make it much farther with my leg the way it was.

Joe was coming up the path with his folding cup full of water. I hadn't thought I was thirsty but the cold water tasted good. We sat there awhile and smoked, then Joe said that we ought to be starting back, that we must be a good piece from the rig by this time.

We set out, working north through the edge of the woods. It was rough going and I was thinking that it would be all I could do to make it back to the rig when we climbed a fence and came out at one end of a long field that sloped down to a wooded ravine. Broken ground, badly gullied and covered with sedge everywhere except where sumac thickets had sprung up—as birdy a place as ever I saw. I looked it over and knew I had to hunt it, leg or no leg, but it would be close work, for me and the dogs too.

I blew them in a bit and we stood there watching them cut up the cover. The sun was down now; there was just enough light left to see the dogs work. The big dog circled the far wall of the basin and came up wind just off the drain, then stiffened to a point. We walked down to it. The birds had obviously run a bit into the scraggly sumac stalks that bordered the ditch. My mind was so much on the dogs I forgot Joe. He took one step too many. The fullest blown bevy of the day roared up through the tangle. It had to be fast work. I raised my gun and scored with the only barrel I had time to peg. Joe shouted; I knew he had got one too.

We stood there trying to figure out which way the singles had gone but they had fanned out too quick for us, excited as we were, and after beating around awhile we gave up and went on.

We came to the rim of the swale, eased over it, crossed the dry creek bed that was drifted thick with leaves, and started up the other side. I had blown in the dogs, thinking there was no use for them to run their heads off now we'd started home, but they didn't come. I walked on a little farther, then I looked back and saw Bob's white shoulders through a tangle of cinnamon vine.

Joe had turned around too. "They've pinned a single out of that last covey," he said.

I looked over at him quick. "Your shot."

He shook his head. "No, you take it."

I limped back and flushed the bird. It went skimming along the buckberry bushes that covered that side of the swale. In the fading light I could hardly make it out and I shot too quick. It swerved over the thicket and I let go with the second barrel. It staggered, then zoomed up. Up, up, up, over the rim of the hill and above the tallest hickories. It hung there for a second, its wings black against the gold light, before, wings still spread, it came whirling down, like an autumn leaf, like the leaves that were everywhere about us, all over the ground.

COMMENT

Like "Fifty Pounds," Miss Gordon's story is primarily concerned with character, but with this difference: here there is no moment of sudden revelation, and the action has fewer complications. It may even seem that there is no plot, that the story is little more than an anecdote of hunting. Yet the careful reader will discover that he has been reading something more than an account of a day's hunting. He has a very complete picture of the character of the narrator of the story—a picture of his strong personality, of his knowledge, of his observant nature, of his impulse to teach, of his philosophic cast of mind, of his stoicism. The student should find the actual passages which indicate these and other characteristics.

Again, the story may seem to have no conflict. There certainly is not the open opposition of wills that appears in the two preceding stories. But conflict may be internal as well as external. What are the conflicting forces in the narrator? Is conflict any the less real because it is played down rather than emphasized? How does the playing down enhance our sense of the narrator's character?

Finally, there is in a very real sense a conflict between the narrator and his companion, good friends though they are. This is not a conflict of irreconcilable purposes and objectives, but of the differences in human beings who may even be bound by a common purpose and mutual affection. Here there is the difference between youth and age, health and ill health, ignorance and experience, excitement and self-discipline. Note how these differences appear in almost every part of the action and how, quietly presented as they are, they help create tension. Note also how these differences are related to the conflict within the narrator.

In endeavoring to get hold of the whole meaning of the story, the reader should study especially the last sentence. Why does the author give us a final—and therefore very emphatic—picture of the falling bird and remind us at the same time of the "fading light" and the "autumn leaf"? Do they not all remind us of the situation of the narrator and thus become symbols? If this is true, the ending is a very rich and effective one.

Other points to observe: the quick exposition (the conveying of necessary information) in the first two pages of the story; the way in which all the activities of the day are made concrete; the use of a style suited to the narrator (in the main, short sentences, with the subjects and verbs coming mostly near the beginning of the sentences).

Eudora Welty

Eudora Welty was born in Mississippi in 1909, was educated at the University of Wisconsin and the Columbia School of Advertising, spent some time in advertising work, and is now living in Jackson, Mississippi. Her hobbies are water-coloring and photography. During the last decade her stories have been appearing regularly in various periodicals, and several volumes of her collected stories have been published. In 1942 she held a Guggenheim Fellowship. Her most recent volume, *The Golden Apples*, contains a number of stories about the characters in one town; taken together they constitute, in effect, a novel. The scenes of nearly all her stories are Southern, but this fact does not imply a limitation of either her interests or her point of view. In effect she ranges from a tough comic realism to the poetic and fantastic, and through her Southern materials she interprets human experience generally.

A Worn Path

I T WAS December—a bright frozen day in the early morning. Far out in the country there was an old Negro woman with her head tied in a red rag, coming along a path through the pinewoods. Her name was Phoenix Jackson. She was very old and small and she walked slowly in the dark pine shadows, moving a little from side to side in her steps, with the balanced heaviness and lightness of a pendulum in a grandfather clock. She carried a thin, small cane made from an umbrella, and with this she kept tapping the frozen earth in front of her. This made a grave and persistent noise in the still air, that seemed meditative like the chirping of a solitary little bird.

She wore a dark striped dress reaching down to her shoe tops, and an equally long apron of bleached sugar sacks, with a full pocket: all neat and tidy, but every time she took a step she might have fallen over her shoelaces, which dragged from her unlaced

A WORN PATH From *A Curtain of Green and Other Stories*, copyright, 1936, 1937, 1938, 1939, 1941, by Eudora Welty. Reprinted by permission of Harcourt, Brace and Company, Inc.

shoes. She looked straight ahead. Her eyes were blue with age. Her skin had a pattern all its own of numberless branching wrinkles and as though a whole little tree stood in the middle of her forehead, but a golden color ran underneath, and the two knobs of her cheeks were illumined by a yellow burning under the dark. Under the red rag her hair came down on her neck in the frailest of ringlets, still black, and with an odor like copper.

Now and then there was a quivering in the thicket. Old Phoenix said, "Out of my way, all you foxes, owls, beetles, jack rabbits, coons and wild animals! . . . Keep out from under these feet, little bob-whites. . . . Keep the big wild hogs out of my path. Don't let none of those come running my direction. I got a long way." Under her small black-freckled hand her cane, limber as a buggy whip, would switch at the brush as if to rouse up any hiding things.

On she went. The woods were deep and still. The sun made the pine needles almost too bright to look at, up where the wind rocked. The cones dropped as light as feathers. Down in the hollow was the mourning dove—it was not too late for him.

The path ran up a hill. "Seem like there is chains about my feet, time I get this far," she said, in the voice of argument old people keep to use with themselves. "Something always take a hold of me on this hill—pleads I should stay."

After she got to the top she turned and gave a full, severe look behind her where she had come. "Up through pines," she said at length. "Now down through oaks."

Her eyes opened their widest, and she started down gently. But before she got to the bottom of the hill a bush caught her dress.

Her fingers were busy and intent, but her skirts were full and long, so that before she could pull them free in one place they were caught in another. It was not possible to allow the dress to tear. "I in the thorny bush," she said. "Thorns, you doing your appointed work. Never want to let folks pass, no sir. Old eyes thought you was a pretty little *green* bush."

Finally, trembling all over, she stood free, and after a moment dared to stoop for her cane.

"Sun so high!" she cried, leaning back and looking, while the thick tears went over her eyes. "The time getting all gone here."

At the foot of this hill was a place where a log was laid across the creek.

"Now comes the trial," said Phoenix.

Putting her right foot out, she mounted the log and shut her eyes. Lifting her skirt, leveling her cane fiercely before her, like a festival figure in some parade, she began to march across. Then she opened her eyes and she was safe on the other side.

"I wasn't as old as I thought," she said.

But she sat down to rest. She spread her skirts on the bank around her and folded her hands over her knees. Up above her was a tree in a pearly cloud of mistletoe. She did not dare to close her eyes, and when a little boy brought her a plate with a slice of marble-cake on it she spoke to him. "That would be acceptable," she said. But when she went to take it there was just her own hand in the air.

So she left that tree, and had to go through a barbed-wire fence. There she had to creep and crawl, spreading her knees and stretching her fingers like a baby trying to climb the steps. But she talked loudly to herself: she could not let her dress be torn now, so late in the day, and she could not pay for having her arm or her leg sawed off if she got caught fast where she was.

At last she was safe through the fence and risen up out in the clearing. Big dead trees, like black men with one arm, were standing in the purple stalks of the withered cotton field. There sat a buzzard.

"Who you watching?"

In the furrow she made her way along.

"Glad this not the season for bulls," she said, looking sideways, "and the good Lord made his snakes to curl up and sleep in the winter. A pleasure I don't see no two-headed snake coming around that tree, where it come once. It took a while to get by him, back in the summer."

She passed through the old cotton and went into a field of dead corn. It whispered and shook and was taller than her head. "Through the maze now," she said, for there was no path.

Then there was something tall, black, and skinny there, moving before her.

At first she took it for a man. It could have been a man dancing in the field. But she stood still and listened, and it did not make a sound. It was as silent as a ghost.

"Ghost," she said sharply, "who be you the ghost of? For I have heard of nary death close by."

But there was no answer—only the ragged dancing in the wind. She shut her eyes, reached out her hand, and touched a sleeve. She found a coat and inside that an emptiness, cold as ice.

"You scarecrow," she said. Her face lighted. "I ought to be shut up for good," she said with laughter. "My senses is gone. I too old. I the oldest people I ever know. Dance, old scarecrow," she said, "while I dancing with you."

She kicked her foot over the furrow, and with mouth drawn down, shook her head once or twice in a little strutting way. Some husks blew down and whirled in streamers about her skirts.

Then she went on, parting her way from side to side with the cane, through the whispering field. At last she came to the end, to a wagon track where the silver grass blew between the red ruts. The quail were walking around like pullets, seeming all dainty and unseen.

"Walk pretty," she said. "This the easy place. This the easy going."

She followed the track, swaying through the quiet bare fields, through the little strings of trees silver in their dead leaves, past cabins silver from weather, with the doors and windows boarded shut, all like old women under a spell sitting there. "I walking in their sleep," she said, nodding her head vigorously.

In a ravine she went where a spring was silently flowing through a hollow log. Old Phoenix bent and drank. "Sweet-gum makes the water sweet," she said, and drank more. "Nobody know who made this well, for it was here when I was born."

The track crossed a swampy part where the moss hung as white as lace from every limb. "Sleep on, alligators, and blow your bubbles." Then the track went into the road.

Deep, deep the road went down between the high green-colored banks. Overhead the live-oaks met, and it was as dark as a cave.

A black dog with a lolling tongue came up out of the weeds by the ditch. She was meditating, and not ready, and when he came at her she only hit him a little with her cane. Over she went in the ditch, like a little puff of milkweed.

Down there, her senses drifted away. A dream visited her, and she reached her hand up, but nothing reached down and gave her a pull. So she lay there and presently went to talking. "Old woman," she said to herself, "that black dog come up out of the weeds to stall you off, and now there he sitting on his fine tail, smiling at you."

A white man finally came along and found her—a hunter, a young man, with his dog on a chain.

"Well, Granny!" he laughed. "What are you doing there?"

"Lying on my back like a June-bug waiting to be turned over, mister," she said, reaching up her hand.

He lifted her up, gave her a swing in the air, and set her down. "Anything broken, Granny?"

"No sir, them old dead weeds is springy enough," said Phoenix, when she had got her breath. "I thank you for your trouble."

"Where do you live, Granny?" he asked, while the two dogs were growling at each other.

"Away back yonder, sir, behind the ridge. You can't even see it from here."

"On your way home?"

"No sir, I going to town."

"Why, that's too far! That's as far as I walk when I come out myself, and I get something for my trouble." He patted the stuffed bag he carried, and there hung down a little closed claw. It was one of the bob-whites, with its beak hooked bitterly to show it was dead. "Now you go on home, Granny!"

"I bound to go to town, mister," said Phoenix. "The time come around."

He gave another laugh, filling the whole landscape. "I know you old colored people! Wouldn't miss going to town to see Santa Claus!"

But something held old Phoenix very still. The deep lines in her face went into a fierce and different radiation. Without warning, she had seen with her own eyes a flashing nickel fall out of the man's pocket onto the ground.

"How old are you, Granny?" he was saying.

"There is no telling, mister," she said, "no telling."

Then she gave a little cry and clapped her hands and said, "Git on away from here, dog! Look! Look at that dog!" She laughed as if in admiration. "He ain't scared of nobody. He a big black dog." She whispered, "Sic him!"

"Watch me get rid of that cur," said the man. "Sic him, Pete! Sic him!"

Phoenix heard the dogs fighting, and heard the man running and throwing sticks. She even heard a gunshot. But she was slowly bending forward by that time, further and further forward, the lids stretched down over her eyes, as if she were doing this in her sleep. Her chin was lowered almost to her knees. The yellow palm of her hand came out from the fold of her apron. Her fingers slid down and along the ground under the piece of money with the grace and care they would have in lifting an egg from under a setting hen. Then she slowly straightened up, she stood erect, and the nickel was in her apron pocket. A bird flew by. Her lips moved. "God watching me the whole time. I come to stealing."

The man came back, and his own dog panted about them. "Well, I scared him off that time," he said, and then he laughed and lifted his gun and pointed it at Phoenix.

She stood straight and faced him.

"Doesn't the gun scare you?" he said, still pointing it.

"No, sir, I seen plenty go off closer by, in my day, and for less than what I done," she said, holding utterly still.

He smiled, and shouldered the gun. "Well, Granny," he said, "you must be a hundred years old, and scared of nothing. I'd give you a dime if I had any money with me. But you take my advice and stay home, and nothing will happen to you."

"I bound to go on my way, mister," said Phoenix. She inclined her head in the red rag. Then they went in different directions, but she could hear the gun shooting again and again over the hill.

She walked on. The shadows hung from the oak trees to the road like curtains. Then she smelled wood-smoke, and smelled the river, and she saw a steeple and the cabins on their steep steps. Dozens of little black children whirled around her. There ahead was Natchez shining. Bells were ringing. She walked on.

In the paved city it was Christmas time. There were red and green electric lights strung and crisscrossed everywhere, and all turned on in the daytime. Old Phoenix would have been lost if she had not distrusted her eyesight and depended on her feet to know where to take her.

She paused quietly on the sidewalk where people were passing by. A lady came along in the crowd, carrying an armful of red-, green- and silver-wrapped presents; she gave off perfume like the red roses in hot summer, and Phoenix stopped her.

"Please, missy, will you lace up my shoe?" She held up her foot.

"What do you want, Grandma?"

"See my shoe," said Phoenix. "Do all right for out in the country, but wouldn't look right to go in a big building."

"Stand still then, Grandma," said the lady. She put her packages down on the sidewalk beside her and laced and tied both shoes tightly.

"Can't lace 'em with a cane," said Phoenix. "Thank you, missy. I doesn't mind asking a nice lady to tie up my shoe, when I gets out on the street."

Moving slowly and from side to side, she went into the big building, and into a tower of steps, where she walked up and around and around until her feet knew to stop.

She entered a door, and there she saw nailed up on the wall the document that had been stamped with the gold seal and framed in the gold frame, which matched the dream that was hung up in her head.

"Here I be," she said. There was a fixed and ceremonial stiffness over her body.

"A charity case, I suppose," said an attendant who sat at the desk before her.

But Phoenix only looked above her head. There was sweat on her face, the wrinkles in her skin shone like a bright net.

"Speak up, Grandma," the woman said. "What's your name? We must have your history, you know. Have you been here before? What seems to be the trouble with you?"

Old Phoenix only gave a twitch to her face as if a fly were bothering her.

"Are you deaf?" cried the attendant.

But then the nurse came in.

"Oh, that's just old Aunt Phoenix," she said. "She doesn't come for herself—she has a little grandson. She makes these trips just as regular as clockwork. She lives away back off the Old Natchez Trace." She bent down. "Well, Aunt Phoenix, why don't you just

take a seat? We won't keep you standing after your long trip."
She pointed.

The old woman sat down, bolt upright in the chair.

"Now, how is the boy?" asked the nurse.

Old Phoenix did not speak.

"I said, how is the boy?"

But Phoenix only waited and stared straight ahead, her face very
solemn and withdrawn into rigidity.

"Is his throat any better?" asked the nurse. "Aunt Phoenix, don't
you hear me? Is your grandson's throat any better since the last
time you came for the medicine?"

With her hands on her knees, the old woman waited, silent, erect
and motionless, just as if she were in armor.

"You mustn't take up our time this way, Aunt Phoenix," the nurse
said. "Tell us quickly about your grandson, and get it over. He
isn't dead, is he?"

At last there came a flicker and then a flame of comprehension
across her face, and she spoke.

"My grandson. It was my memory had left me. There I sat and
forgot why I made my long trip."

"Forgot?" The nurse frowned. "After you came so far?"

Then Phoenix was like an old woman begging a dignified forgiveness for waking up frightened in the night. "I never did go to
school, I was too old at the Surrender," she said in a soft voice.
"I'm an old woman without an education. It was my memory fail
me. My little grandson, he is just the same, and I forgot it in the
coming."

"Throat never heals, does it?" said the nurse, speaking in a loud,
sure voice to old Phoenix. By now she had a card with something
written on it, a little list. "Yes. Swallowed lye. When was it?—
January—two-three years ago—"

Phoenix spoke unasked now. "No, missy, he not dead, he just
the same. Every little while his throat begin to close up again,
and he not able to swallow. He not get his breath. He not able to
help himself. So the time come around, and I go on another trip
for the soothing medicine."

"All right. The doctor said as long as you came to get it, you
could have it," said the nurse. "But it's an obstinate case."

"My little grandson, he sit up there in the house all wrapped up, waiting by himself," Phoenix went on. "We is the only two left in the world. He suffer and it don't seem to put him back at all. He got a sweet look. He going to last. He wear a little patch quilt and peep out holding his mouth open like a little bird. I remembers so plain now. I not going to forget him again, no, the whole enduring time. I could tell him from all the others in creation."

"All right." The nurse was trying to hush her now. She brought her a bottle of medicine. "Charity," she said, making a check mark in a book.

Old Phoenix held the bottle close to her eyes, and then carefully put it into her pocket.

"I thank you," she said.

"It's Christmas time, Grandma," said the attendant. "Could I give you a few pennies out of my purse?"

"Five pennies is a nickel," said Phoenix stiffly.

"Here's a nickel," said the attendant.

Phoenix rose carefully and held out her hand. She received the nickel and then fished the other nickel out of her pocket and laid it beside the new one. She stared at her palm closely, with her head on one side.

Then she gave a tap with her cane on the floor.

"This is what come to me to do," she said. "I going to the store and buy my child a little windmill they sells, made out of paper. He going to find it hard to believe there such a thing in the world. I'll march myself back where he waiting, holding it straight up in this hand."

She lifted her free hand, gave a little nod, turned around, and walked out of the doctor's office. Then her slow step began on the stairs, going down.

COMMENT

Here is another study of age, and some of the details are like those in "The Last Day in the Field": the aged protagonist must make a long walk, the time is the end of the year, and there is also a contrast with youth. Yet the author has written a quite different kind of story. Unlike

Miss Gordon's hero, who is obviously a figure in his community, Old Phoenix is an unimportant person of another race, and so she must face not only the physical and mental difficulties of age, but poverty and a world which evokes many fears. The words of both the young hunter and the hospital attendants, although essentially kindly, make clear that Old Phoenix has a very lowly status. What words of the hunter suggest, also, that she hardly seems fit to go on her errand?

The author gives a very concrete picture of the hazards, real and imagined, which the old woman must face. The reader will observe the details of these hazards and notice how large they bulk in the story and how small any such element is in "The Last Day in the Field." He will also notice another sharp difference: the motivation of Old Phoenix's journey is quite different from that of the lame huntsman. She is going on an errand of mercy.

In view of these facts, it is clear that there was a great danger in these materials—the danger of overstressing the pathos of the situation and of producing a sentimental effect. This is a problem of tone. Miss Welty has successfully avoided the danger of a sentimental tone, and the reader will want to find the reasons why this is true. Perhaps the following questions are worth considering.

1. How might the story be different if we knew Old Phoenix's purpose from the start?

2. What is Old Phoenix's attitude toward herself? Does she exhibit self-pity?

3. Notice that the author keeps very strictly to Phoenix's point of view and does not throw in cue words of her own. What would be the effect of this kind of statement: "The fierce December wind cruelly pierced Old Phoenix's ragged garments as, with a picture of the little sufferer always before her, she forged ahead, her staunch old heart denying its age with every beat"?

4. What is the advantage of the author's throwing opportunities as well as hazards in the path of Old Phoenix? How do these amplify the picture of her character?

5. Does Old Phoenix have a sense of humor?

6. Notice that a frequent·element in Miss Welty's style is the comparison: "Over she went in the ditch, like a little puff of milkweed"; "Her fingers slid down . . . with the grace and care they would have in lifting an egg from under a setting hen"; ". . . the wrinkles in her skin shone like a bright net." Comparisons may sometimes be used to influence feelings in a certain way—to help induce pity, sorrow, and so forth. Are these and other comparisons (which the student should look up) used in this way? How are they used?

DIFFERENT POINTS
OF VIEW

William Faulkner

William Faulkner, regarded by many critics as the finest living writer of prose fiction in America, was born in Mississippi in 1897 and except for a few periods has lived there ever since, often making a living by nonliterary occupations such as being postmaster. During World War I he flew in the Canadian air force and was wounded; later he lived in New Orleans, sharing an apartment with Sherwood Anderson; and he has done some scenario work in Hollywood. He not only lives in the South but writes about it: a recurrent theme of his is the replacement of an older type of Southern life by a new calculating way of life represented by a family named Snopes. But there is a great deal of variety of theme in his dozen or more novels and volumes of short stories. Faulkner went without recognition for a number of years, but by the time of *Intruder in the Dust* (1948) he was a widely read writer. Among his most important novels are *Sound and Fury*, *The Hamlet*, and *Light in August*.

That Evening Sun

MONDAY is no different from any other weekday in Jefferson now. The streets are paved now, and the telephone and electric companies are cutting down more and more of the shade trees—the water oaks, the maples and locusts and elms— to make room for iron poles bearing clusters of bloated and ghostly and bloodless grapes, and we have a city laundry which makes the rounds on Monday morning, gathering the bundles of clothes into bright-colored, specially made motorcars: the soiled wearing of a whole week now flees apparitionlike behind alert and irritable electric horns, with a long diminishing noise of rubber and asphalt like tearing silk, and even the Negro women who still take in white people's washing after the old custom, fetch and deliver it in automobiles.

But fifteen years ago, on Monday morning the quiet, dusty, shady streets would be full of Negro women with, balanced on their steady, turbaned heads, bundles of clothes tied up in sheets, almost as large as cotton bales, carried so without touch of hand between the kitchen door of the white house and the blackened washpot beside a cabin door in Negro Hollow.

Nancy would set her bundle on the top of her head, then upon the bundle in turn she would set the black straw sailor hat which she wore winter and summer. She was tall, with a high, sad face sunken a little where her teeth were missing. Sometimes we would go a part of the way down the lane and across the pasture with her, to watch the balanced bundle and the hat that never bobbed nor wavered, even when she walked down into the ditch and up the other side and stooped through the fence. She would go down on her hands and knees and crawl through the gap, her head rigid, uptilted, the bundle steady as a rock or a balloon, and rise to her feet again and go on.

Sometimes the husbands of the washing women would fetch and deliver the clothes, but Jesus never did that for Nancy, even before Father told him to stay away from our house, even when Dilsey was sick and Nancy would come to cook for us.

And then about half the time we'd have to go down the lane to Nancy's cabin and tell her to come on and cook breakfast. We would stop at the ditch, because Father told us to not have anything to do with Jesus—he was a short black man, with a razor scar down his face—and we would throw rocks at Nancy's house until she came to the door, leaning her head around it without any clothes on.

"What yawl mean, chunking my house?" Nancy said. "What you little devils mean?"

"Father says for you to come on and get breakfast," Caddy said. "Father says it's over a half an hour now, and you've got to come this minute."

"I ain't studying no breakfast," Nancy said. "I going to get my sleep out."

"I bet you're drunk," Jason said. "Father says you're drunk. Are you drunk, Nancy?"

"Who says I is?" Nancy said. "I got to get my sleep out. I ain't studying no breakfast."

So after a while we quit chunking the cabin and went back home.

When she finally came, it was too late for me to go to school. So we thought it was whiskey until that day they arrested her again and they were taking her to jail and they passed Mr. Stovall. He was the cashier in the bank and a deacon in the Baptist church, and Nancy began to say:

"When you going to pay me, white man? When you going to pay me, white man? It's been three times now since you paid me a cent—" Mr. Stovall knocked her down, but she kept on saying, "When you going to pay me, white man? It's been three times now since—" until Mr. Stovall kicked her in the mouth with his heel and the marshal caught Mr. Stovall back, and Nancy lying in the street, laughing. She turned her head and spat out some blood and teeth and said, "It's been three times now since he paid me a cent."

That was how she lost her teeth, and all that day they told about Nancy and Mr. Stovall, and all that night the ones that passed the jail could hear Nancy singing and yelling. They could see her hands holding to the window bars, and a lot of them stopped along the fence, listening to her and to the jailer trying to make her stop. She didn't shut up until almost daylight, when the jailer began to hear a bumping and scraping upstairs and he went up there and found Nancy hanging from the window bar. He said that it was cocaine and not whiskey, because no nigger would try to commit suicide unless he was full of cocaine, because a nigger full of cocaine wasn't a nigger any longer.

The jailer cut her down and revived her; then he beat her, whipped her. She had hung herself with her dress. She had fixed it all right, but when they arrested her she didn't have on anything except a dress and so she didn't have anything to tie her hands with and she couldn't make her hands let go of the window ledge. So the jailer heard the noise and ran up there and found Nancy hanging from the window, stark naked, her belly already swelling out a little, like a little balloon.

When Dilsey was sick in her cabin and Nancy was cooking for us, we could see her apron swelling out; that was before Father told Jesus to stay away from the house. Jesus was in the kitchen, sitting behind the stove, with his razor scar on his black face like a piece of dirty string. He said it was a watermelon that Nancy had under her dress.

"It never come off of your vine, though," Nancy said.

"Off of what vine?" Caddy said.

"I can cut down the vine it did come off of," Jesus said.

"What makes you want to talk like that before these chillen?" Nancy said. "Whyn't you go on to work? You done et. You want Mr. Jason to catch you hanging around his kitchen, talking that way before these chillen?"

"Talking what way?" Caddy said. "What vine?"

"I can't hang around white man's kitchen," Jesus said. "But white man can hang around mine. White man can come in my house, but I can't stop him. When white man want to come in my house, I ain't got no house. I can't stop him, but he can't kick me outen it. He can't do that."

Dilsey was still sick in her cabin. Father told Jesus to stay off our place. Dilsey was still sick. It was a long time. We were in the library after supper.

"Isn't Nancy through in the kitchen yet?" Mother said. "It seems to me that she has had plenty of time to have finished the dishes."

"Let Quentin go and see," Father said. "Go and see if Nancy is through, Quentin. Tell her she can go on home."

I went to the kitchen. Nancy was through. The dishes were put away and the fire was out. Nancy was sitting in a chair, close to the cold stove. She looked at me.

"Mother wants to know if you are through," I said.

"Yes," Nancy said. She looked at me. "I done finished." She looked at me.

"What is it?" I said. "What is it?"

"I ain't nothing but a nigger," Nancy said. "It ain't none of my fault."

She looked at me, sitting in the chair before the cold stove, the sailor hat on her head. I went back to the library. It was the cold stove and all, when you think of a kitchen being warm and busy and cheerful. And with a cold stove and the dishes all put away, and nobody wanting to eat at that hour.

"Is she through?" Mother said.

"Yessum," I said.

"What is she doing?" Mother said.

"She's not doing anything. She's through."

"I'll go and see," Father said.

"Maybe she's waiting for Jesus to come and take her home," Caddy said.

"Jesus is gone," I said. Nancy told us how one morning she woke up and Jesus was gone.

"He quit me," Nancy said. "Done gone to Memphis, I reckon. Dodging them city *po*-lice for a while, I reckon."

"And a good riddance," Father said. "I hope he stays there."

"Nancy's scaired of the dark," Jason said.

"So are you," Caddy said.

"I'm not," Jason said.

"Scairy cat," Caddy said.

"I'm not," Jason said.

"You, Candace!" Mother said. Father came back.

"I am going to walk down the lane with Nancy," he said. "She says that Jesus is back."

"Has she seen him?" Mother said.

"No. Some Negro sent her word that he was back in town. I won't be long."

"You'll leave me alone, to take Nancy home?" Mother said. "Is her safety more precious to you than mine?"

"I won't be long," Father said.

"You'll leave these children unprotected, with that Negro about?"

"I'm going too," Caddy said. "Let me go, Father."

"What would he do with them, if he were unfortunate enough to have them?" Father said.

"I want to go, too," Jason said.

"Jason!" Mother said. She was speaking to Father. You could tell that by the way she said the name. Like she believed that all day Father had been trying to think of doing the thing she wouldn't like the most, and that she knew all the time that after a while he would think of it. I stayed quiet, because Father and I both knew that Mother would want him to make me stay with her if she just thought of it in time. So Father didn't look at me. I was the oldest. I was nine and Caddy was seven and Jason was five.

"Nonsense," Father said. "We won't be long."

Nancy had her hat on. We came to the lane. "Jesus always been good to me," Nancy said. "Whenever he had two dollars, one of them was mine." We walked in the lane. "If I can just get through the lane," Nancy said, "I be all right then."

The lane was always dark. "This is where Jason got scaired on Hallowe'en," Caddy said.

"I didn't," Jason said.

"Can't Aunt Rachel do anything with him?" Father said. Aunt Rachel was old. She lived in a cabin beyond Nancy's, by herself. She had white hair and she smoked a pipe in the door, all day long; she didn't work any more. They said she was Jesus' mother. Sometimes she said she was and sometimes she said she wasn't any kin to Jesus.

"Yes you did," Caddy said. "You were scairder than Frony. You were scairder than T.P. even. Scairder than niggers."

"Can't nobody do nothing with him," Nancy said. "He say I done woke up the devil in him and ain't but one thing going to lay it down again."

"Well, he's gone now," Father said. "There's nothing for you to be afraid of now. And if you'd just let white men alone."

"Let what white men alone?" Caddy said. "How let them alone?"

"He ain't gone nowhere," Nancy said. "I can feel him. I can feel him now, in this lane. He hearing us talk, every word, hid somewhere, waiting. I ain't seen him, and I ain't going to see him again but once more, with that razor in his mouth. That razor on that string down his back, inside his shirt. And then I ain't going to be even surprised."

"I wasn't scaired," Jason said.

"If you'd behave yourself, you'd have kept out of this," Father said. "But it's all right now. He's probably in Saint Louis now. Probably got another wife by now and forgot all about you."

"If he has, I better not find out about it," Nancy said. "I'd stand there right over them, and every time he wropped her, I'd cut that arm off. I'd cut his head off and I'd slit her belly and I'd shove—"

"Hush," Father said.

"Slit whose belly, Nancy?" Caddy said.

"I wasn't scaired," Jason said. "I'd walk right down this lane by myself."

"Yah," Caddy said. "You wouldn't dare to put your foot down in it if we were not here too."

II

Dilsey was still sick, so we took Nancy home every night until Mother said, "How much longer is this going on? I to be left alone in this big house while you take home a frightened Negro?"

We fixed a pallet in the kitchen for Nancy. One night we waked up, hearing the sound. It was not singing and it was not crying, coming up the dark stairs. There was a light in Mother's room and we heard Father going down the hall, down the back stairs, and Caddy and I went into the hall. The floor was cold. Our toes curled away from it while we listened to the sound. It was like singing and it wasn't like singing, like the sound that Negroes make.

Then it stopped and we heard Father going down the back stairs, and we went to the head of the stairs. Then the sound began again, in the stairway, not loud, and we could see Nancy's eyes halfway up the stairs, against the wall. They looked like cat's eyes do, like a big cat against the wall, watching us. When we came down the steps to where she was, she quit making the sound again, and we stood there until Father came back up from the kitchen, with his pistol in his hand. He went back down with Nancy and they came back with Nancy's pallet.

We spread the pallet in our room. After the light in Mother's room went off, we could see Nancy's eyes again. "Nancy," Caddy whispered, "are you asleep, Nancy?"

Nancy whispered something. It was oh or no, I don't know which. Like nobody had made it, like it came from nowhere and went nowhere, until it was like Nancy was not there at all; that I had looked so hard at her eyes on the stairs that they had got printed on my eyeballs, like the sun does when you have closed your eyes and there is no sun. "Jesus," Nancy whispered. "Jesus."

"Was it Jesus?" Caddy said. "Did he try to come into the kitchen?"

"Jesus," Nancy said. Like this: Jeeeeeeeeeeeeeeeesus, until the sound went out, like a match or a candle does.

"It's the other Jesus she means," I said.

"Can you see us, Nancy?" Caddy whispered. "Can you see our eyes too?"

"I ain't nothing but a nigger," Nancy said. "God knows. God knows."

"What did you see down there in the kitchen?" Caddy whispered. "What tried to get in?"

"God knows," Nancy said. We could see her eyes. "God knows."

Dilsey got well. She cooked dinner. "You'd better stay in bed a day or two longer," Father said.

"What for?" Dilsey said. "If I had been a day later, this place would be to rack and ruin. Get on out of here now, and let me get my kitchen straight again."

Dilsey cooked supper too. And that night, just before dark, Nancy came into the kitchen.

"How do you know he's back?" Dilsey said. "You ain't seen him."

"Jesus is a nigger," Jason said.

"I can feel him," Nancy said. "I can feel him laying yonder in the ditch."

"Tonight?" Dilsey said. "Is he there tonight?"

"Dilsey's a nigger too," Jason said.

"You try to eat something," Dilsey said.

"I don't want nothing," Nancy said.

"I ain't a nigger," Jason said.

"Drink some coffee," Dilsey said. She poured a cup of coffee for Nancy. "Do you know he's out there tonight? How come you know it's tonight?"

"I know," Nancy said. "He's there, waiting. I know. I done lived with him too long. I know what he is fixing to do fore he know it himself."

"Drink some coffee," Dilsey said. Nancy held the cup to her mouth and blew into the cup. Her mouth pursed out like a spreading adder's, like a rubber mouth, like she had blown all the color out of her lips with blowing the coffee.

"I ain't a nigger," Jason said. "Are you a nigger, Nancy?"

"I hellborn, child," Nancy said. "I won't be nothing soon. I going back where I come from soon."

III

She began to drink the coffee. While she was drinking, holding the cup in both hands, she began to make the sound again. She made the sound into the cup and the coffee sploshed out onto her hands and her dress. Her eyes looked at us and she sat there, her elbows on her knees, holding the cup in both hands, looking at us across the wet cup, making the sound.

"Look at Nancy," Jason said. "Nancy can't cook for us now. Dilsey's got well now."

"You hush up," Dilsey said. Nancy held the cup in both hands, looking at us, making the sound, like there were two of them: one looking at us and the other making the sound. "Whyn't you let Mr. Jason telefoam the marshal?" Dilsey said. Nancy stopped then, holding the cup in her long brown hands. She tried to drink some coffee again, but it sploshed out of the cup, onto her hands and her dress, and she put the cup down. Jason watched her.

"I can't swallow it," Nancy said. "I swallows but it won't go down me."

"You go down to the cabin," Dilsey said. "Frony will fix you a pallet and I'll be there soon."

"Won't no nigger stop him," Nancy said.

"I ain't a nigger," Jason said. "Am I, Dilsey?"

"I reckon not," Dilsey said. She looked at Nancy. "I don't reckon so. What you going to do, then?"

Nancy looked at us. Her eyes went fast, like she was afraid there wasn't time to look, without hardly moving at all. She looked at us, at all three of us at one time. "You member that night I stayed in yawls' room?" she said. She told about how we waked up early the next morning, and played. We had to play quiet, on her pallet, until Father woke up and it was time to get breakfast. "Go and ask your maw to let me stay here tonight," Nancy said. "I won't need no pallet. We can play some more."

Caddy asked Mother. Jason went too. "I can't have Negroes sleeping in the bedrooms," Mother said. Jason cried. He cried until Mother said he couldn't have any dessert for three days if he didn't stop. Then Jason said he would stop if Dilsey would make a chocolate cake. Father was there.

"Why don't you do something about it?" Mother said. "What do we have officers for?"

"Why is Nancy afraid of Jesus?" Caddy said. "Are you afraid of Father, Mother?"

"What could the officers do?" Father said. "If Nancy hasn't seen him, how could the officers find him?"

"Then why is she afraid?" Mother said.

"She says he is there. She says she knows he is there tonight."

"Yet we pay taxes," Mother said. "I must wait here alone in this big house while you take a Negro woman home."

"You know that I am not lying outside with a razor," Father said.

"I'll stop if Dilsey will make a chocolate cake," Jason said. Mother told us to go out and Father said he didn't know if Jason would get a chocolate cake or not, but he knew what Jason was going to get in about a minute. We went back to the kitchen and told Nancy.

"Father said for you to go home and lock the door, and you'll be all right," Caddy said. "All right from what, Nancy? Is Jesus mad at you?" Nancy was holding the coffee cup in her hands again, her elbows on her knees and her hands holding the cup between her knees. She was looking into the cup. "What have you done that made Jesus mad?" Caddy said. Nancy let the cup go. It didn't break on the floor, but the coffee spilled out, and Nancy sat there with her hands still making the shape of the cup. She began to make the sound again, not loud. Not singing and not unsinging. We watched her.

"Here," Dilsey said. "You quit that, now. You get aholt of yourself. You wait here. I going to get Versh to walk home with you." Dilsey went out.

We looked at Nancy. Her shoulders kept shaking, but she quit making the sound. We stood and watched her.

"What's Jesus going to do to you?" Caddy said. "He went away."

Nancy looked at us. "We had fun that night I stayed in yawls' room, didn't we?"

"I didn't," Jason said. "I didn't have any fun."

"You were asleep in Mother's room," Caddy said. "You were not there."

"Let's go down to my house and have some more fun," Nancy said.

"Mother won't let us," I said. "It's too late now."

"Don't bother her," Nancy said. "We can tell her in the morning. She won't mind."

"She wouldn't let us," I said.

"Don't ask her now," Nancy said. "Don't bother her now."

"She didn't say we couldn't go," Caddy said.

"We didn't ask," I said.

"If you go, I'll tell," Jason said.

"We'll have fun," Nancy said. "They won't mind, just to my house. I been working for yawl a long time. They won't mind."

"I'm not afraid to go," Caddy said. "Jason is the one that's afraid. He'll tell."

"I'm not," Jason said.

"Yes, you are," Caddy said. "You'll tell."

"I won't tell," Jason said. "I'm not afraid."

"Jason ain't afraid to go with me," Nancy said. "Is you, Jason?"

"Jason is going to tell," Caddy said. The lane was dark. We passed the pasture gate. "I bet if something was to jump out from behind that gate, Jason would holler."

"I wouldn't," Jason said. We walked down the lane. Nancy was talking loud.

"What are you talking so loud for, Nancy?" Caddy said.

"Who; me?" Nancy said. "Listen at Quentin and Caddy and Jason saying I'm talking loud."

"You talk like there was five of us here," Caddy said. "You talk like Father was here too."

"Who; me talking loud, Mr. Jason?" Nancy said.

"Nancy called Jason 'Mister,'" Caddy said.

"Listen how Caddy and Quentin and Jason talk," Nancy said.

"We're not talking loud," Caddy said. "You're the one that's talking like Father—"

"Hush," Nancy said; "hush, Mr. Jason."

"Nancy called Jason 'Mister' aguh—"

"Hush," Nancy said. She was talking loud when we crossed the ditch and stooped through the fence where she used to stoop through with the clothes on her head. Then we came to her house. We were going fast then. She opened the door. The smell of the house was like the lamp and the smell of Nancy was like the wick, like they were waiting for one another to begin to smell. She lit the lamp and closed the door and put the bar up. Then she quit talking loud, looking at us.

"What're we going to do?" Caddy said.

"What do yawl want to do?" Nancy said.

"You said we would have some fun," Caddy said.

There was something about Nancy's house; something you could smell besides Nancy and the house. Jason smelled it, even. "I don't want to stay here," he said. "I want to go home."

"Go home, then," Caddy said.

"I don't want to go by myself," Jason said.

"We're going to have some fun," Nancy said.

"How?" Caddy said.

Nancy stood by the door. She was looking at us, only it was like she had emptied her eyes, like she had quit using them. "What do you want to do?" she said.

"Tell us a story," Caddy said. "Can you tell a story?"

"Yes," Nancy said.

"Tell it," Caddy said. We looked at Nancy. "You don't know any stories."

"Yes," Nancy said. "Yes I do."

She came and sat in a chair before the hearth. There was a little fire there. Nancy built it up, when it was already hot inside. She built a good blaze. She told a story. She talked like her eyes looked, like her eyes watching us and her voice talking to us did not belong to her. Like she was living somewhere else, waiting somewhere else. She was outside the cabin. Her voice was inside and the shape of her, the Nancy that could stoop under a barbed wire fence with a bundle of clothes balanced on her head as though without weight, like a balloon, was there. But that was all. "And so this here queen come walking up to the ditch, where that bad man was hiding. She was walking up to the ditch, and she say, 'If I can just get past this here ditch,' was what she say . . ."

"What ditch?" Caddy said. "A ditch like that one out there? Why did a queen want to go into a ditch?"

"To get to her house," Nancy said. She looked at us. "She had to cross the ditch to get into her house quick and bar the door."

"Why did she want to go home and bar the door?" Caddy said.

IV

Nancy looked at us. She quit talking. She looked at us. Jason's legs stuck straight out of his pants where he sat on Nancy's lap. "I don't think that's a good story," he said. "I want to go home."

"Maybe we had better," Caddy said. She got up from the floor. "I bet they are looking for us right now." She went toward the door.

"No," Nancy said. "Don't open it." She got up quick and passed Caddy. She didn't touch the door, the wooden bar.

"Why not?" Caddy said.

"Come back to the lamp," Nancy said. "We'll have fun. You don't have to go."

"We ought to go," Caddy said. "Unless we have a lot of fun."
She and Nancy came back to the fire, the lamp.

"I want to go home," Jason said. "I'm going to tell."

"I know another story," Nancy said. She stood close to the lamp. She looked at Caddy, like when your eyes look up at a stick balanced on your nose. She had to look down to see Caddy, but her eyes looked like that, like when you are balancing a stick.

"I won't listen to it," Jason said. "I'll bang on the floor."

"It's a good one," Nancy said. "It's better than the other one."

"What's it about?" Caddy said. Nancy was standing by the lamp. Her hand was on the lamp, against the light, long and brown.

"Your hand is on that hot globe," Caddy said. "Don't it feel hot to your hand?"

Nancy looked at her hand on the lamp chimney. She took her hand away, slow. She stood there, looking at Caddy, wringing her long hand as though it were tied to her wrist with a string.

"Let's do something else," Caddy said.

"I want to go home," Jason said.

"I got some popcorn," Nancy said. She looked at Caddy and then at Jason and then at me and then at Caddy again. "I got some popcorn."

"I don't like popcorn," Jason said. "I'd rather have candy."

Nancy looked at Jason. "You can hold the popper." She was still wringing her hand; it was long and limp and brown.

"All right," Jason said. "I'll stay a while if I can do that. Caddy can't hold it. I'll want to go home again if Caddy holds the popper."

Nancy built up the fire. "Look at Nancy putting her hands in the fire," Caddy said. "What's the matter with you, Nancy?"

"I got popcorn," Nancy said. "I got some." She took the popper from under the bed. It was broken. Jason began to cry.

"Now we can't have any popcorn," he said.

"We ought to go home, anyway," Caddy said. "Come on, Quentin."

"Wait," Nancy said; "wait. I can fix it. Don't you want to help me fix it?"

"I don't think I want any," Caddy said. "It's too late now."

"You help me, Jason," Nancy said. "Don't you want to help me?"

"No," Jason said. "I want to go home."

"Hush," Nancy said; "hush. Watch. Watch me. I can fix it so Jason can hold it and pop the corn." She got a piece of wire and fixed the popper.

"It won't hold good," Caddy said.

"Yes it will," Nancy said. "Yawl watch. Yawl help me shell some corn."

The popcorn was under the bed too. We shelled it into the popper and Nancy helped Jason hold the popper over the fire.

"It's not popping," Jason said. "I want to go home."

"You wait," Nancy said. "It'll begin to pop. We'll have fun then."

She was sitting close to the fire. The lamp was turned up so high it was beginning to smoke. "Why don't you turn it down some?" I said.

"It's all right," Nancy said. "I'll clean it. Yawl wait. The popcorn will start in a minute."

"I don't believe it's going to start," Caddy said. "We ought to start home, anyway. They'll be worried."

"No," Nancy said. "It's going to pop. Dilsey will tell um yawl with me. I been working for yawl long time. They won't mind if yawl at my house. You wait, now. It'll start popping any minute now."

Then Jason got some smoke in his eyes and he began to cry. He dropped the popper into the fire. Nancy got a wet rag and wiped Jason's face, but he didn't stop crying.

"Hush," she said. "Hush." But he didn't hush. Caddy took the popper out of the fire.

"It's burned up," she said. "You'll have to get some more popcorn, Nancy."

"Did you put all of it in?" Nancy said.

"Yes," Caddy said. Nancy looked at Caddy. Then she took the popper and opened it and poured the cinders into her apron and began to sort the grains, her hands long and brown, and we watching her.

"Haven't you got any more?" Caddy said.

"Yes," Nancy said; "yes. Look. This here ain't burnt. All we need to do is—"

"I want to go home," Jason said. "I'm going to tell."

"Hush," Caddy said. We all listened. Nancy's head was already turned toward the barred door, her eyes filled with red lamplight. "Somebody is coming," Caddy said.

Then Nancy began to make that sound again, not loud, sitting there above the fire, her long hands dangling between her knees; all of a sudden water began to come out on her face in big drops, running down her face, carrying in each one a little turning ball of firelight like a spark until it dropped off her chin. "She's not crying," I said.

"I ain't crying," Nancy said. Her eyes were closed. "I ain't crying. Who is it?"

"I don't know," Caddy said. She went to the door and looked out. "We've got to go now," she said. "Here comes Father."

"I'm going to tell," Jason said. "Yawl made me come."

The water still ran down Nancy's face. She turned in her chair. "Listen. Tell him. Tell him we going to have fun. Tell him I take good care of yawl until in the morning. Tell him to let me come home with yawl and sleep on the floor. Tell him I won't need no pallet. We'll have fun. You member last time how we had so much fun?"

"I didn't have fun," Jason said. "You hurt me. You put smoke in my eyes. I'm going to tell."

V

Father came in. He looked at us. Nancy did not get up.

"Tell him," she said.

"Caddy made us come down here," Jason said. "I didn't want to."

Father came to the fire. Nancy looked up at him. "Can't you go to Aunt Rachel's and stay?" he said. Nancy looked up at Father, her hands between her knees. "He's not here," Father said. "I would have seen him. There's not a soul in sight."

"He in the ditch," Nancy said. "He waiting in the ditch yonder."

"Nonsense," Father said. He looked at Nancy. "Do you know he's there?"

"I got the sign," Nancy said.

"What sign?"

"I got it. It was on the table when I come in. It was a hogbone, with blood meat still on it, laying by the lamp. He's out there When yawl walk out that door, I gone."

"Gone where, Nancy?" Caddy said.

"I'm not a tattletale," Jason said.

"Nonsense," Father said.

"He out there," Nancy said. "He looking through that window this minute, waiting for yawl to go. Then I gone."

"Nonsense," Father said. "Lock up your house and we'll take you on to Aunt Rachel's."

" 'Twon't do no good," Nancy said. She didn't look at Father now, but he looked down at her, at her long, limp, moving hands. "Putting it off won't do no good."

"Then what do you want to do?" Father said.

"I don't know," Nancy said. "I can't do nothing. Just put it off. And that don't do no good. I reckon it belong to me. I reckon what I going to get ain't no more than mine."

"Get what?" Caddy said. "What's yours?"

"Nothing," Father said. "You all must get to bed."

"Caddy made me come," Jason said.

"Go on to Aunt Rachel's," Father said.

"It won't do no good," Nancy said. She sat before the fire, her elbows on her knees, her long hands between her knees. "When even your own kitchen wouldn't do no good. When even if I was sleeping on the floor in the room with your chillen, and the next morning there I am, and blood—"

"Hush," Father said. "Lock the door and put out the lamp and go to bed."

"I scaired of the dark," Nancy said. "I scaired for it to happen in the dark."

"You mean you're going to sit right here with the lamp lighted?" Father said. Then Nancy began to make the sound again, sitting before the fire, her long hands between her knees. "Ah, damnation," Father said. "Come along, chillen. It's past bedtime."

"When yawl go home, I gone," Nancy said. She talked quieter now, and her face looked quiet, like her hands. "Anyway, I got my coffin money saved up with Mr. Lovelady." Mr. Lovelady was a short, dirty man who collected the Negro insurance, coming around to the cabins or the kitchens every Saturday morning, to collect fifteen cents. He and his wife lived at the hotel. One morning his wife committed suicide. They had a child, a little girl. He and the child went away. After a week or two he came back alone. We would see him going along the lanes and the back streets on Saturday mornings.

"Nonsense," Father said. "You'll be the first thing I'll see in the kitchen tomorrow morning."

"You'll see what you'll see, I reckon," Nancy said. "But it will take the Lord to say what that will be."

VI

We left her sitting before the fire.

"Come and put the bar up," Father said. But she didn't move. She didn't look at us again, sitting quietly there between the lamp and the fire. From some distance down the lane we could look back and see her through the open door.

"What, Father?" Caddy said. "What's going to happen?"

"Nothing," Father said. Jason was on Father's back, so Jason was the tallest of all of us. We went down into the ditch. I looked at it, quiet. I couldn't see much where the moonlight and the shadows tangled.

"If Jesus *is* hid here, he can see us, can't he?" Caddy said.

"He's not there," Father said. "He went away a long time ago."

"You made me come," Jason said, high; against the sky it looked like Father had two heads, a little one and a big one. "I didn't want to."

We went up out of the ditch. We could still see Nancy's house and the open door, but we couldn't see Nancy now, sitting before the fire with the door open, because she was tired. "I just done got tired," she said. "I just a nigger. It ain't no fault of mine."

But we could hear her, because she began just after we came up out of the ditch, the sound that was not singing and not unsinging. "Who will do our washing now, Father?" I said.

"I'm not a nigger," Jason said, high and close above Father's head.

"You're worse," Caddy said, "you are a tattletale. If something was to jump out, you'd be scairder than a nigger."

"I wouldn't," Jason said.

"You'd cry," Caddy said.

"Caddy," Father said.

"I wouldn't!" Jason said.

"Scairy cat," Caddy said.

"Candace!" Father said.

COMMENT

"That Evening Sun" is an example of a more complicated type of story than has appeared in this volume so far. It is roughly like Miss Welty's story in that its central figure is a Negro woman who is facing difficulty and danger alone. But this single resemblance only serves to underscore the major differences between the stories. As a character, Nancy is differently conceived from Old Phoenix, and she is placed in a far more involved situation. Although the focus of the story is nearly always on Nancy, Faulkner has introduced so many other characters and attitudes that he is virtually writing what is sometimes called the multiplicity story. Nancy herself is not oversimplified: her terrified hallucination involves a sense of both her personal fate and her situation as a Negro; and her attitude to Jesus, as the last half dozen paragraphs in Section I show, is compounded of more than fear. Besides her own view of things, we are shown that of Dilsey and that of Jesus, who acts also not only in terms of individual character but also in terms of his sense of a racial situation. We see Nancy not only in her relationship to Jesus, but in several kinds of relationship to the whole community—that which is represented in the episode with Mr. Stovall, that represented in the jail scene, and that which appears in the more stable dealings with the white family for whom she works. Within this family itself we see different attitudes toward Nancy—that of the mother, whose neurotic self-centeredness makes her want to ignore the problem entirely; that of the father, who at once blames, sympathizes with, and tries to help Nancy, and finally gives her up in despair; and that of the children who talk about all that is going on and that is talked about by their elders but still are essentially uncomprehending.

One of the results of this method of telling a story—of introducing numerous points of view—is to suggest the many-sidedness of actual existence, the co-existence of many different worlds that in part coincide but in many ways remain independent. Yet it is clear that Faulkner does not want merely to give an impression of a chaotic world. For one thing, he suggests relationships among the different worlds by using patterns of repeated experience: for instance, Nancy is terrified, the mother uses a pretense of fear as a device for securing attention, and the children are often scared, or pretending not to be scared, or arguing as to who is more scared. It might be said that the different worlds are unified by fright. Again, there are problems of status between the races, among members of the family, and even within the limited chil-

dren's world. Such variations on a theme suggest the presence of a common element and thus have a unifying effect. But more important, Faulkner does not tell the story now from one point of view, now from another, but sticks to one point of view—that of the children. We see and hear directly only what they see and hear. The main effects of the story lie in the ironic discrepancy between the facts themselves, which the reader understands, and the limited perception of these facts by the children. The children miss the problem of sex; in their acceptance of entertainment from Nancy they do not know that what is for them a not very successful game is for her a life-and-death matter; they see her hand getting burnt, but see it simply as another everyday fact; Quentin records, without sensing their meaning, the fatalistic remarks of Nancy. In so far as the adult world is accessible to the children, they echo it in a fragmentary form: the race problem is reflected only in Jason's "I'm not a nigger," repeated with unconscious cruelty in the presence of the Negroes. Once Nancy is out of sight, the larger world is shut off, and the child world narrows down to its own inner clashes, the note on which the story closes.

The fact that the children do not fully record a grown-up world, or else replay adult drama in their own terms, is one of the facts of the story, one of the things that we perceive. Yet it is not entirely an end in itself. For the partial perceptiveness of the children is one of the ways of stimulating the imagination of the reader and compelling him to re-create for himself the meanings which the author conveys by suggestion. The ironic disparity between perceiver and perceived is one of the ways of establishing the drama for the reader.

Mark Schorer

Mark Schorer is one of a fairly large number of contemporary writers who are also professional teachers. He has taught at Wisconsin, Dartmouth, and Harvard, and is now in charge of advanced writing classes at the University of California in Berkeley. Born in Wisconsin in 1908, he took both his A.B. and his Ph.D. degrees at the University of Wisconsin. He was twice awarded a Guggenheim Fellowship to work on a book length study of William Blake, which appeared in 1946. He has written two novels, *A House Too Old* and *The Hermit Place*. His short stories have appeared in numerous magazines, and thirty-two of them have been collected in a volume entitled *The State of Mind*.

What We Don't Know Hurts Us

THE MIDAFTERNOON winter sun burned through the high California haze. Charles Dudley, working with a mattock in a thicket of overgrowth, felt as steamy and as moldy as the black adobe earth in which his feet kept slipping. Rain had fallen for five days with no glimmer of sunshine, and now it seemed as if the earth, with fetid animation, like heavy breath, were giving all that moisture back to the air. The soil, or the broom which he was struggling to uproot, had a disgusting, acrid odor, as if he were tussling with some obscene animal instead of with a lot of neglected vegetation, and suddenly an overload of irritations—the smell, the stinging sweat in his eyes, his itching skin, his blistering palms—made him throw the mattock down and come diving out of the thicket into the clearing he had already achieved.

"Is it hard?"

He looked up and saw Josephine, his wife, sitting on the railing of the balcony onto which the french doors of their bedroom opened. She was holding a dust mop, and a tea towel was wrapped

WHAT WE DON'T KNOW HURTS US From *The State of Mind* by Mark Schorer. Reprinted by permission of the publishers, Houghton Mifflin Company.

around her head, and her face seemed pallid and without character, as it always did to Charles when she neglected to wear lipstick.

He snorted instead of replying, and wiped his muddy hands on the seat of his stiff new levis. Then he walked over to the short flight of steps that led up to the balcony from the garden, and lit a cigarette.

"It looks as though the ground levels out up there where you're working," Josephine said.

"Yes, it does. Somebody once had a terrace up there. It's full of overgrown geraniums that are more like snakes, and a lot of damned rose vines."

"You've got the pepper tree almost free. It's going to be very nice, isn't it?"

He looked up at the pepper tree, with its delicate, drooping branches and the long gray tendrils that hung down from the branches to the ground. He had chopped out the broom as far up the incline as the tree, and now he could see that a big branch of the eucalyptus at the very edge of the property had forced the top of the pepper tree to grow out almost horizontally from the main portion of its trunk. "Look at the damned thing!" he said.

"It's charming, like a Japanese print."

"I'm going to hate this house long before it's livable," he said.

"Oh, Charles!"

"I didn't want to buy a house. I never wanted to own any house. I certainly never wanted to own a miserable, half-ruined imitation of a Swiss chalet built on an incline that was meant for goats." Vehemently he flipped his cigarette up into the pile of brush he had accumulated.

Josephine stood up and shook out the dust mop. "Let's not go into all that again. There was no choice. It's no pleasure for me, either, living the way we are, nor is it for the children." She paused, and then she added a cold supplement. "I sometimes think that your disinclination to own anything is a form of irresponsibility." She turned swiftly and went into the house.

He stood staring after her, frowning a little, for it seemed momentarily that with studied intent she had cracked the bland habit of her amiability. But in a minute she reappeared in the doorway and said matter-of-factly, "I heard on the radio that Boston has had eighteen inches of snow." Then she went back inside.

"Are you trying to make me homesick?" he asked of no one as he started back up the incline, and he remembered the frozen river, snow blowing over the Esplanade, and city lights faint in a blizzard.

He began again to chop at the roots of the broom. All right, he told himself, so he was being unpleasant. He did not like the idea of being pinned down by a mortgage to a place his firm had picked for him. He did not even like the idea of being pinned down by a mortgage. To own something was, to that extent, to be owned, and he did not like the feeling. His idea of a good way to live was in a duplex apartment owned by someone else, in Charles River Square, or, better than that but always less likely, in a duplex apartment owned by someone else, on the East River. He connected happiness with a certain luxury, and, probably, sexuality with elegance and freedom. These were not noble associations, he was aware, and he knew that it was foolish to let impossibilities, as they faded, become forms of minor torture. This knowledge made him chop more angrily than ever at the broom.

It was vegetation with which Charles felt that he had a peculiar intimacy, perhaps the only thing in California which, in the several weeks they had lived there, he had really come to know. And he loathed it with a violence which he recognized as quite undue, and which, now, made him feel childish and curiously guilty. Yet he could not laugh away his loathing. The stuff was ubiquitous, and sprang up anywhere at all the minute the ground was neglected. If it grew up in a patch, it began a foolish competition with itself, and the thin, naked stalks shot ten and twelve and fourteen feet into the air, all stretching up to the sun for the sake of a plume of paltry foliage at the top. Then the foliage tangled together in a thatch, and when you had managed to chop out the shallow roots of the tree, you still had to extricate its trivial but tenacious branches from those of all its neighbors to get it out of the clump. Once it was out, the wood was good for nothing, but dried up into a kind of bamboo stalk so insubstantial that it did not make even decent kindling. As a tree it was a total fraud, and in spite of the nuisance of its numbers, and of its feminine air of lofty self-importance, it was, with its shallow roots in this loose soil, very vulnerable to attack. Charles beat away at it in an angry frenzy, as if he were overwhelming, after a long struggle, some bitter foe.

He did not hear his son come up the incline behind him, and the boy stood quietly watching until his father turned to toss a stalk up on the pile in the clearing. Then the boy said, "Hi." He said it tentatively, almost shyly, as though his father's responses were unpredictable.

"Hi, Gordon."

"What're you doing?"

"Can't you see? How was school?"

"It stinks," he answered doggedly, his dark eyes half-averted and sorrowful.

Charles felt a twinge of pain for him. "Cheer up. Give it time. You'll get to like it after a while."

"I'll never like it," Gordon said stubbornly.

Charles took up his mattock again. "Sure you will," he said as he began to swing it.

"Nobody likes me."

Charles let the mattock come to rest and, turning once more to the boy, he spoke with an impatient excess of patience. "You say that every day. I've told you it isn't true. You're a new boy in the school, and you came in the middle of the term, and there's never yet been a new boy who entered a school late and made friends right away. You're nearly nine, and you can understand that. Anyway, I'm tired of explaining it to you."

"When can I get a paper route?"

Charles laughed without humor. "My God, boy! Give us a chance to get settled."

"I need money."

"You get an allowance."

"I need more money," the boy insisted. "I want a paper route. How do kids get them?"

"You can work for me. You can get in there with a hedge shears and cut out all those vines."

The boy looked at his father despairingly and shook his head. "No, I need a lot of money."

"You can earn a lot of money working for me," Charles said, swinging his mattock.

"I need a dollar," Gordon said faintly.

His father did not hear him, and he did not turn from his work again until presently he heard his daughter calling him shrilly from the foot of the hill on which the house stood.

"What is it?" he called back. She was climbing the path, and he saw that she had a white envelope in her hand.

Then Gordon broke into rapid, desperate speech. "I need a dollar. I'll pay it back out of my allowance. Remember yesterday I told you about that dollar I found? I have to pay it back."

Charles stared at him. "What dollar?"

Gordon glanced wildly over his shoulder. His sister, holding the menacing white envelope in one hand and her workman's tin lunch box in the other, was halfway up the hill, coming along the side of the house. Pleadingly, Gordon looked back at his father. "The dollar. Remember? I told you I found it. You wanted to know what I did with it."

"What dollar?"

He sighed. "You didn't listen! You never listen!"

Charles patted his shoulder. "Now take it easy. Don't get excited. Tell me again. I don't think you told me anything about a dollar yesterday."

"The dollar I found. You asked me what I did with it, and I told you I gave it to Crow, and you said I should have brought it home to you."

"That Crow! I thought you were joking."

Penelope, the six-year-old, was behind him now, and Gordon's shoulders sagged in despair. "I wasn't joking," he said almost wearily as Penelope handed his father the letter. "You never really listen."

Charles read the precise handwriting on the envelope. "Mr. or Mrs. Dudley," it said, and in the lower left-hand corner, "Courtesy of Penelope." He opened the envelope and read the message:

Dear Mr. and Mrs. Dudley,

Gordon became involved in some difficulty about a dollar today, and I wish you would help me. The dollar was lunch money belonging to a girl who says she left it deep in her coat pocket, in the cloakroom, yesterday. When I brought it up with Gordon, he immediately said that he did not steal it. He says that he found it on the floor, and he also says that he told his father about it yesterday and that his father said he should have brought it home to him, and now he is fixed in his confusions. He gave it to an older boy named Will Crow, who spent it, and I have told Gordon that he will have to return a dollar to the girl tomorrow. Gordon is a very worth-while little personality, but I do not think he has been entirely happy here at the Crestview School, and therefore, if you can help me straighten this out to his own best interest, I will be ever so grateful.

Sincerely yours,

GERTRUDE GRANDJENT,
Principal.

Charles groaned in exasperation. "My God, why did you have to drag me into it? What will that woman think?"

Gordon's lips were trembling. "You remember? I did tell you, didn't I?"

"Yes, I remember now. I remember very clearly that you told me you found it on the way to school, and when I asked you what you did with it, and you said you gave it to Crow, naturally I said you should have brought it home. *Listen,* Gordon—" The very simplicity of the boy's strategy infuriated Charles, and it was with an effort that he controlled his temper. He said, "Penny, you go in now and tell your mother you're home."

Penny was staring at her brother. "What did Gordon do?"

"Run along, Penny, as I told you."

She went down the incline reluctantly, staring back over her shoulder, and when she had gone into the house, Charles turned to Gordon again and said, "Sit down."

They sat down side by side on the damp slope. Gordon said, "Will you lend me a dollar and keep my allowance until it's made up? I have to take it back tomorrow."

"We'll talk about that later." Charles tapped the letter with his muddy hand. "Why did you tell me you found it in the street?"

Gordon looked away but answered promptly. "I knew if I told you I found it in school, you'd have said I should have taken it to the office."

"So you lied to me instead. That was better?"

Gordon did not answer.

"Answer me."

"Yes."

"Yes, what?"

"I lied."

That was that. Charles started over. "Why did you tell Miss Grandjent that you did not steal it when she hadn't even said that you had?"

"I knew that's what she thought."

"How did you know?"

"I just knew."

Charles hesitated. When he spoke again, his voice was warmer, friendly, almost confidential. "What's the little girl's name, Gordon?"

"She's not little. She's in high fourth."

"What's her name?"

"I don't know. Joan, I guess."

"What color is her coat?"

Gordon glanced at his father sharply. "I don't know. I never noticed it."

Charles bit his lip in exasperation and stood up. "Let's go inside." He led the way in.

Josephine was standing on a chair in the middle of the living room. She was dusting the hideous chandelier of dark metal and colored glass which hung from the center of the ceiling. It was only one of many distasteful features in the house which the Dudleys hoped to rid it of, but it was hard to find men to do all the necessary work, and none would promise to do it quickly. An electrician had torn away a good deal of plaster and lathing, and a carpenter had ripped out some bookshelves and ugly mantels and taken down most of a wall between the dining room and a useless hallway, but neither had returned, and painters, plasterers, paper hangers had not yet come at all. The Dudleys had decided to leave most of their belongings in storage until the work was done, and to bring nothing out of storage that they cared about. The result was that the house was almost fantastically disordered and bleak and squalid, and while Josephine managed to keep an even temper under these conditions, Charles, who found them very trying, did not.

He stood in the doorway of the living room now and said to her, "Why do you bother?"

"The light was so dim," she said, and then, seeing his expression, asked quickly, "What's wrong?"

"Another problem." He came heavily into the living room and gave her the letter. She read it standing on the chair, her face expressionless. Then she stepped down and went out into the hall where Gordon was lurking and said, "Come in, dear."

There was one old sofa in the room, and Josephine sat down there with Gordon. Charles sat facing them on the single straight chair. Josephine took Gordon's hands and said, "Now tell me everything, Gordon, just the way it happened."

The boy's face was composed in a kind of stolid determination, but when he raised his moody eyes from the bare floor to his father, his chin began to tremble, his eyelids fluttered, and suddenly the dogged expression broke in despair, his body sagged, his head fell back against the sofa, and he burst into harsh sobs. Josephine put her arm around his shoulders and held him close while he cried, and she shook her head sharply at Charles as he jumped up impatiently. He sat down again. Finally Gordon stopped crying, almost as abruptly as he had begun.

"How did it happen, Gordon?" his mother asked.

He straightened up and stared at the floor again. "Nothing happened. I just came in the cloakroom and saw it on the floor. I took it and put it in my pocket, and at recess I gave it to Crow."

"Didn't anyone see you pick it up?"

"There wasn't anyone else there."

"In the cloakroom? Before school? Why not?"

"I was late."

"Late? But why? You left here in plenty of time."

"I stopped on the way and played with a cat."

Josephine frowned. "So there was no one else there at all to see you?" she asked meaningfully.

"No."

Josephine glanced at Charles. He drew his lips apart and, with a heavy satiric edge, said, "Well, Gordon, that's too bad! If there'd been someone else there, you could prove that you hadn't—"

Josephine broke in. "Tell me just where the dollar was, Gordon," she said softly, and her voice had no relation to the look in her eyes as she glanced at Charles.

"On the floor."

"But exactly where? Was it near the little girl's coat?"

"She isn't little."

"Was it near her coat?"

"I don't know which coat is hers."

"Was it near any coat?"

"It was on the floor, near all of them. They hang on a rack, and it was on the floor near them."

Josephine paused, and Gordon wriggled his shoulders out from under her arm and slumped in the corner of the sofa, away from her. "When can I get out of here?" he asked.

"When you start answering our questions," his father said sharply. "You insist that you didn't steal it?"

Gordon raised his lids slowly, as if they were very heavy, and stared out at his father from under his brows. "I found it on the floor."

Josephine spoke brightly. "Very well. We have settled that. But, Gordon, surely you don't think that because you found it on the floor, it belonged to you? Don't you see that it was just as much stealing it as if you had really taken it from the pocket of the person it belonged to?"

"Not as much," Gordon said.

"But it wasn't *yours!* You knew that."

The boy nodded.

"Well, then—"

"Someone else would have found it!"

"But would someone else have kept it?"

"I didn't keep it."

Charles leaped up from his chair. "That's the point! Why in God's name did you give it to that Crow rat?"

"He's my friend," Gordon said with simple defiance, and then he slid off the sofa and lay on the floor.

"Your friend! A fine friend!" Charles shouted in disgust, standing over him. "Get up!"

Gordon did not make any effort to move, and Josephine grasped Charles's arm. "Let me," she said quietly. "Sit down."

"Nonsense!" he cried angrily at her, and pulled his arm free of her touch. "I'll take over now." He seized the boy by the shoulders and pulled him up on the sofa. The jerk which he gave his body made the boy's head bob back and forward like a doll's, and he slumped against the sofa back almost as if he had been injured, dull eyes staring out of his pale face. "Now listen to me, Gordon.

I don't know if you took that money out of someone's pocket or not, but it looks, from the way you're behaving, as if you did. Anyway, you took it. It didn't belong to you, you knew that, and yet you took it. Do you see that there is no difference between the floor and the pocket as long as you kept it?"

"I didn't keep it," Gordon repeated, but almost listlessly.

"Oh, my God!" Charles ran his hand through his hair, and the rumpled hair gave him a sudden wild look. "Listen," he said as quietly as he could, "we are all having a very hard time here. We are trying to live in a house that isn't fit to live in. I am trying to get used to a new office. Your mother—"

Josephine said, "Don't bother about me."

"I will bother! We are all having a tough time, and Gordon can't think of anything better to do than to get into this mess at school. Of all the friends you could pick, you pick that nasty Crow brat, who is too old for you by three years and is a snide little—"

"Charles!"

Gordon lay back on the sofa. He looked ill and defeated.

"Will you admit that you stole that dollar? That taking it from the floor was just as much stealing it as if you had taken it from the pocket?"

"Yes," he answered faintly.

"Speak up!"

"Yes, I *do!*" Gordon cried, and turned his face away.

Then the room was very still. Josephine stood stiffly beside the couch, her eyes fixed on Charles with dismay. Charles sagged a little, as if he, too, were defeated. And Gordon might have been asleep or dreaming, so remote had he suddenly become. Then they all heard a sly noise at the door, and Charles and Josephine swung toward it. Penelope stood there, embarrassed to have been caught. She giggled and said, "Why did Gordon steal money?"

"Go away," Charles said.

"Go to your room, dear," Josephine said, "or go outside."

"But why did Gordon steal money?"

Charles walked to the girl, gave her a little push, and closed the door on her face. Then he came back to the sofa. He sat down next to Gordon, and when he spoke, his voice was nearly lifeless. "You want to earn that dollar. All right, you can, Gordon. First go to your room and write your five sentences. Do them quickly for a change, and then go out into that patch of broom with the hedge shears and cut down all the vines you can find in it. You have an hour left before it gets dark."

Gordon's eyes dreamed over his father's face, and then he slowly got up and left the room. His parents watched him go, and when he had closed the door softly behind him, Charles broke out. "What is it, what stubbornness, that makes that boy so impenetrable? Did he steal that money or not? I haven't the slightest idea. All I could do was force him to admit that there was no difference between the two things."

Josephine was looking at him with studied appraisal.

"Well?" he challenged her.

"You forced his admission. Did that gain anything? And what did it lose? How much did it hurt him? Is it of very great importance whether he stole it or not?"

"I don't know what's more important."

"No, I really think you don't."

"Well?"

"What's more important is why he took it, and what he did with it, and why he did that. What's more important is that he's a miserable little boy, and that you haven't made the slightest effort to understand *that*. All you've done is played the heavy parent, shown him that you don't trust him or believe him, and left him with a nice new layer of solidified guilt, and what is he supposed to do with *that?*"

"Let's skip the psychology for a change," Charles said. "There is an old-fashioned principle of honesty and dishonesty."

"There's a more old-fashioned one of simple perception!" Josephine's face was red with anger. She stood in the middle of the bare room and looked rapidly around her, as if she felt a sudden desperate need, a hunger, for objects. But there was only the sofa, the chair, and Charles. Her eyes came back to him.

"Have you thought of his difficulties at all? Just the simple matter of his writing, for example? He came from a school where the children printed, and he printed as well as anyone. He comes here where the children do cursive writing, and of course he's made to feel like a fool, and he has to practice at home to learn it when other boys are playing. Or have you once helped him with that?

Have you even suggested a sentence he might write? No. All you've
done is to give him the extremely comforting bit of information
that new boys, especially if they enter school late, have a hard
time making friends! The one friend he has made you deride.
No, don't interrupt. I know he's a horrid boy. I don't want Gordon
playing with him either. But you haven't the sense to see that what
has brought them together is that they are both pariahs. I think
Gordon's giving that dollar to that dreadful boy is one of the most
touching things I've ever heard of!"

"If what you've told me about Crow is true," Charles said quietly,
"I won't have Gordon playing with him, and that's that."

"Because Crow taught him some nasty words and told him some
nasty, mistaken things about sex! You're perfectly right. But you
can't just stand there and say no to him! If you were half a father,
you would have told him yourself. *You* should be his friend! You're
the one who should be giving him a decent attitude toward those
things. You *are* his father, after all."

"Oh, listen— He's not even nine!"

"All right. But he's getting it, isn't he? And all wrong?" And then,
without warning, she sat down heavily on the single chair and
began to sob, her reddened face lifted, her mouth twisted in sorrow, tears streaming down over her cheeks. "All *wrong!*" she wailed.

Charles went to her quickly and, half standing, half kneeling
beside the chair, awkwardly put his arms around her. "Josephine,
listen—"

"Oh, I know!" she sobbed. "We all get in your way. We're all a
nuisance that you're saddled with! We all just *bother* you! I know!
It just isn't your idea of the way to live. You really hate it, don't
you?"

His arms tightened. "Darling," he said, "don't be a damned fool.
Listen, I love you, I love the kids. Why, little Penny, I—"

"Oh, yes. Penny, sure! She's tractable! She doesn't raise any problems. That's different!"

"You're crazy. Gordon, too. You. Maybe I'm not much good with
him, but that doesn't mean . . . And listen . . . I'll try. I'll go out
there now."

She dug in her pocket for a piece of Kleenex. She blew her nose
and wiped her eyes. She pulled the tea towel off her head and
shook out her hair. Then she blew her nose again. "I'm all right

now," she said, getting up. She picked up the dustcloth which she had flung over the back of the chair, and she said, "It's probably just this awful house, the way we have to camp. I'm going to get cleaned up and dress, and I'm going to find a tablecloth, and we'll have dinner at a table tonight, instead of sitting on the floor with plates in our laps."

He said, "Good girl! I'll go and fix it up with Gordon."

Charles went into Gordon's room. It was empty. He glanced at the table where Gordon worked and saw that there was a sheet of writing there. Then he looked out of the window and saw the boy on his hands and knees in among the remaining broom. He crossed the hall to the bedroom where Josephine was dressing. "I may not be very subtle with him, but I seem to get results," he said. She merely glanced up at him, and as he went out on the balcony, down the steps, and up the slippery incline, he felt no satisfaction whatever in his remark.

"How's it going?" he asked the boy.

Gordon glanced over his shoulder. "All right," he said, and turned at once to his job. The hedge shears made a busy, innocent sound.

Charles found his mattock where he had dropped it, and began to chop at the edge of the overgrowth again. Immediately his nostrils filled with the poisonous smell he had noticed before, his hands began to chafe, and even though the heat of the sun had gone in the late afternoon, sweat broke out with a prickling sensation all over his face and body. Once more he was tense with irritation, and he said, "That awful smell! What is it?"

"I don't know," Gordon replied without looking up.

"Like something decaying."

The boy did not answer, and Charles chopped angrily away at a root. When it came free, he shook the earth off and tossed the slim tree down the slope. "This crazy, piddling stuff!" he shouted, and then reminded himself that it was only a kind of exaggerated weed, a thing that grew everywhere, so futile that it could not even send down a decent root and was hardly designed as a personal affront to him. Or was it? He laughed and started to chop at the next root, but stopped at once. "I'm quitting for today," he said. "Come on, let's go in."

Gordon said, "No, I'll work a while. I want to earn the money."

"Oh, let it go. We'll fix that up."

Gordon stared at him. "I want to earn it," he said, and went on clipping at the rose vines.

"All right," Charles said, "but come in soon. You'll have to wash up thoroughly to get that muck off."

He went back into the house by way of the bedroom, but Josephine was no longer there. He went into Gordon's room, but she was not there, either. On the table lay the white sheet of ruled paper covered with the boy's writing, his five sentences in their hasty, uncertain, and very large cursive characters. Charles picked it up. The first sentence was, "I am going to cut vins." The second was, "I am going to ern mony." The third was, "The sun is shining." The fourth was, "When it rains here it rains hard." The last, which seemed to have been written with greater care, with a kind of precision and flourish which his writing had never shown before, was, "You hate me and I hate you."

Charles took a sharp breath and held it, then sagged. After a moment he walked to the window and put his forehead against the cool glass. He stared out into the desolate garden, at the bare earth and the darkening tangle, and tried to think. When he heard Josephine moving on high heels somewhere in the rugless house, he began to fold the sheet of paper, and he folded it again and again, until it was a small hard square. This he stuffed deep into his pocket.

He came into the hall and saw Josephine standing in the center of the barren living room. She looked tall in an old but still handsome black housecoat, a straight, severe garment which hung from the tightly belted waist in heavy folds, and was without ornament or color anywhere. Her hair was pulled tautly away from her face, and her face was smooth and white, and her mouth was painted dark red.

She was detached from the room, from the house, and utterly from him—remote and beautiful, cold in resolution. Never in the ten years he had known her had she appeared so wonderfully in possession of herself. And, helplessly, Charles turned away.

He went into the boy's room again, and looked out to see the boy. But twilight had obscured the garden now, shadows hung about it like veils, and Charles could hardly see into the trees. Then he thought that he saw Gordon's shape, hunched on the ground among the slim trunks, and he went out quickly to find him. Perhaps, even now, after everything, it was the boy who, somehow, could help.

COMMENT

Here is another story in which an important part is played by children. But the method differs from Faulkner's in that the author uses the father's point of view. A further difference is that the interest does not draw primarily upon the contrast between the greater and lesser understanding of the two generations: here we have rather an open conflict between two generations, complicated by a clash between the parents themselves. The conventional situation in which the father is all-wise is ironically reversed, for Charles is presented as having very little more understanding than his son, and the son as having an almost precociously sharp understanding of older people, especially his father.

At a first reading of the story, the student may be somewhat puzzled as to what attitude he is expected to take toward the participants in the quarrel. This initial difficulty is perhaps traceable to a technical device of Mr. Schorer: he holds very rigidly to Charles's point of view and, although he permits the reader to see over Charles's head, he does not directly make anything clearer to the reader than it is to Charles himself. It would of course be easy to make explanations. But to tell the story as it is told is to avoid all simplification and to compel the reader to feel directly the complexity of the situation, to experience it rather than to read about it. There are real difficulties in Gordon's personality; Charles's moral convictions may be right, but he applies them with so little understanding that he is likely to secure results opposite those which he intends; Josephine's psychological understanding is admirable, but she is not made entirely into a heroine.

In a story in which the conflict is as overt as here, we are likely to feel called upon to take sides. Actually we are not asked to do that so much as we are asked to have a full awareness of all the ingredients in the situation; if a story leads us to be strongly partisan, it is likely to have the structure of melodrama, in which there is usually a clear-cut opposition of good and evil. By carefully avoiding this type of over-simplification, Mr. Schorer compels us to look for less obvious meanings.

His ending is significant. We should note that he does not promise an easy reconciliation, a popular cliché which would be untrue to the characters as presented and developed. Are we then to assume that this *latest effort of Charles will simply widen the breach with his son? Probably not. For one thing, Charles now comes as a person in need rather than as a person in command. But more important than that: the ending serves to pull together various subtle suggestions of a basic similarity between Charles and Gordon. Gordon has had problems of adjustment at school, his father in his own new surroundings (we have seen how exasperated he is by the difficulties). Each of them has acted with thoughtless good intentions, and has found his actions recoiling upon him. Just as the boy found misunderstanding at school, so the father has now found animosity in both his child and wife. Just as the father has cut off his son, he has now been cut off by his wife. The final effect of this story, then, may be said to be not a sense of the gap between the generations, but an ironic equating of the generations.*

Josephine's earlier remark about Charles's "irresponsibility" is related to this point. Is the remark to be taken entirely literally? Are there other evidences that Charles does not always act maturely? Is it merely the business of the story to characterize Charles as immature? Does our attitude toward him change in the course of the story?

The author is very careful to describe the physical conditions of the house and of the backyard in which Charles is working. Is there any evidence that these conditions are to be taken in a symbolic as well as in a literal sense?

Jessamyn West

As the contents of many of her stories suggest, Jessamyn West is a Quaker. The stories collected in the volume *The Friendly Persuasion* (1946), which was her first book, are based on the life of a Quaker family in Indiana, which is the author's native state. However, she has spent most of her life in California, where she now lives. She graduated from Whittier College and did graduate work at the University of California; illness prevented her from completing a doctor's degree. She has done a great deal of magazine writing and has collaborated in the authorship of a musical comedy.

Shivaree Before Breakfast

ELIZA always said Labe never put a foot out of bed until he heard her start to scrape the gravy skillet. "Thee won't see Labe," she'd say fondly, "until he hears that sound—knows the gravy's going on the breakfast table." Labe was harum-scarum and Eliza had a tenderness for her son's easy-going ways.

But that morning in September the big cast-iron skillet was still hanging on its nail behind the stove, a light spot if anything in the early morning darkness. There wasn't a smell in the house of dried beef frizzling for gravy, nor of the birchwood smoke which always seeped out a little around the second joint of the kitchen stovepipe. The starling still slept in his wooden cage by the front door, as if the sun were just lost behind the west rim of hills, not almost ready to push his head above the eastern wood lot. And Labe had both feet out of bed.

He wasn't completely awake yet and he was mumbling and complaining—but he was out of bed. His brother Joshua, who was three years older though scarcely any bigger, stood in front of him talking fiercely. But Joshua almost always talked to him fiercely, about

SHIVAREE BEFORE BREAKFAST From *The Friendly Persuasion*, copyright, 1940, 1943, 1944, 1945, by Jessamyn West. Reprinted by permission of Harcourt, Brace and Company, Inc.

something he hadn't done right, so Labe sat on the edge of the bed and swayed back and forth with sleep still as warm and cozy about him as a nest. He didn't want to hear what Josh was saying, be snatched out of the nest, find himself sitting in his unbleached muslin nightgown, the cold September air touching him like little pieces of iron.

Josh was buttoning his last suspender loop to his pants. "Labe," he said, "thee makes me sick. Thee just about turns my stomach. This was thy idea. Thee said to do it. And it's just like always. I'm ready and thee's so dilly-dallyish, it'll be too late. Old Alf Applegate'll be up and out to work before we get there."

Josh sounded the way he felt—as if he'd like to give Labe a good sound smack—but he knew better. Labe would bawl like a bay steer, and their mother would be in, and then there wouldn't be any shivareeing Old Alf now, or any morning.

"I'm going down and wash," he said, "and get the horse fiddle and go on without thee."

Labe knew then he'd have to wake up; Josh would more than likely do what he said. His nightshirt was over his head, and one leg was in his knickerbockers, before Josh was half way down the back stairs.

Labe tip-toed down the front stairs. Josh had gone the back way so's he could wash, but Labe didn't see any sense washing. Nobody'd see him but Josh and Alf, and Old Alf'd be too excited about his new wife to notice such things.

His hand slid along the cool bannister, his feet went slowly along the stairs into the gray room as if into water. Labe always loved the first morning sight of the big sitting-room—to creep up on it when the furniture wasn't ready yet for human eyes. Chair still turned toward chair, clock and grate saying who knows what to each other with tick and tock and little clunks of falling coals.

It was just light enough to see outlines—pa's shoes by the grate, mother's shawl over the back of the rocker, Mattie's knitting where she'd left it on the newel post. It's like a ship, he thought, where the crew'd got the plague and all died in their bunks, with everything left just as they'd last touched it. He stood on the steps, the first man to view that sorry scene after the disaster.

Josh put his head in the front door. "It's almost sunup," he whispered like a hornet, ready to sting. Labe forgot the plague-stricken ship and ran out to shivaree Old Alf.

Josh was washed clean as a pebble and his fine black hair had a part down it straight as a pike. He had the horse fiddle in one hand, and a lard can with pebbles in it for Labe to shake in the other. "Thee carry thy own stuff," he said to Labe.

"Sure," Labe said. "Want me to take the fiddle, too?"

Josh gave him a sharp look out of his black, green-flecked eyes—but Labe didn't know enough to be sarcastic. He was saying something to Ebony, the starling, like he always did before he went any place.

The early hour, the grayness, their secret made them keep their voices low. "I bet thee dreamed it," Josh said. "I bet it was one of thy daydreams, that Old Alf got married and was talking to a woman."

They were cutting across the west forty. From there on they could follow the pike direct to Applegate's. The corn stubble raked the skin rough on their bare feet, but they were used to that. Beyond the river bend, behind the sycamores, the sky that had been gray was getting yellow. A crow slanted in from the woods lot to the open fields ready to start his morning work. The pebbles in Labe's lard can rattled a little as he walked.

"No, sir, Josh," he said, his round face so serious he looked as if he might cry. "No, Josh, honest, I didn't. I heard him. I told thee it was the morning pa took me fishing. And I got tired and sat down on a stump by Alf's place—and then's when I heard him."

"What'd he say?" Josh asked. He knew—Labe had told him a half dozen times—but every time he thought of those words coming out of Alf Applegate's old hickory-nut face, he was so tickled he couldn't wait until he'd heard them again. "What was it he said?"

"First, I could just hear him talking—but not what he was saying. It kind of sounded like he's talking to a baby, at first. Then he said, 'Time to get up, Molly darling. Time to tie up your beautiful black hair, Molly darling. Night's over—time for day and work.' Maybe that ain't it exactly," Labe added conscientiously, "but as far as I can remember, it is."

Josh shook his head. "'Molly darling, Molly darling.' Did you hear anything—that sounded like—kissing, Labe?" Josh's face burned a little to be asking such a question.

Labe said, "Thee think I'm soft? Sit on a stump and listen to Old Alf Applegate kissing? 'Smack, smack, smack.' Who'd listen to that?"

Josh didn't say what he'd have done. "If he'd got a wife," he said, "why don't our folks know it? Why's he hiding her?"

"Cause he's ashamed to be getting married, he's so old. He's scared folks'll laugh at him."

Labe suddenly stopped. "I got to go to the privy, Josh," he said.

"Thee always has to go to the privy the minute we start any place," Josh said bitterly. "Thee can just go here."

"No," he said, "I'm going back. Thee go on and I'll catch up with thee," and back he ran across the cornfield at a great clip, the stones rattling in his lard pail like hail on a roof.

"Set thy pail down," Josh called after him. "Thee'll wake the dead."

I'll go off and leave him, Josh thought. I'll run and get there first and the shivaree will be over before Labe comes. But as he watched Labe covering the field like a hound with long easy lopes he knew it wasn't any use. He could run until his legs stung like nettles, and the back of his mouth tasted as if he had swallowed a lump of sulphur, and Labe would still catch up with him, breathing easy and talking, even, as he ran. It never seemed fair to Josh. Labe washed about once a week, a rat could live in his white curly hair for all Labe would ever disturb it with a comb; his shirt-tail was always out and his pants flapped almost to his ankles. He was just plain dirty and messy and everybody loved him.

Josh turned and tramped on fast, climbed the snake fence and went at a trot down the pike. Goldenrod and farewell-summer and iron weed bloomed at the pike's edge. The yellow sky was reddening; the dry sharp morning air, just waking up, sent a flurry of maple leaves across the road. Josh trotted right through them, thinking hard. He liked to be clean and neat, to put away things people had left about, to set the chairs in orderly rows, to pull the blinds so they all hung level. And that was right. Cleanliness was next to godliness, he thought stoutly, his pipestem legs methodically measuring off the pike—and he had both—and it was beyond him how Labe, who wasn't any of one, and not so's you could notice it of the other, was always being petted and forgiven. Even by his mother, who was a Quaker preacher and ought to be as fair as God. Maybe God Himself wasn't so awfully fair, he thought bitterly as he heard Labe's bare feet come slapping up the pike behind him, his lard pail rattling.

"I didn't take long, did I?" Labe called cheerfully. Josh looked at him somberly. "Thee set thy hand to the plow, and then thee turned back."

Labe didn't say anything. He was thinking how surprised Old Alf and his wife were going to be when they heard him and Josh outside their window playing the horse fiddle and shaking the lard pail.

"Thee would be salt, now," Josh went on, "if thee was Lot's wife. And thee would be dirty salt, too, because thee don't ever wash."

"How could I be a wife?" Labe asked.

Josh wasn't stumped, "God could do it for a miracle."

But Labe wasn't interested in miracles. "Josh," he asked, "does thee think Old Alf's got some candy on hand ready to give the shivaree-ers?"

"No," Josh said scornfully. "He don't think anyone knows he's married, so why would he be fixed for a shivaree?"

They were almost there. Josh took out his handkerchief and put it in with the stones so they wouldn't rattle and give them away. Old Alf's house set to the left of the pike on a little rise at the end of a long and cypress-framed lane. Not many people went up the lane now that Alf's old English mother was dead, except to use it as a short cut to the fishing pools in the creek which lay behind the house.

When Josh and Labe turned into the lane they began to talk in whispers again. "We ain't too late," Labe said. "No smoke from the chimney, yet. They're still in bed."

"No credit to thee, we ain't," Josh whispered back.

"I'll show thee the window where I heard the talk coming from."

They tip-toed round the old house that had once been white, but was gray now with age. They walked through flower beds that no longer stayed within their border, and tried to lift their feet above the piles of drifted leaves.

"There it is," Labe whispered, pointing to a window at the back of the house. They pressed themselves along the edge of the house until they stood under the window.

Labe's face was sparkling. Cautiously he got Josh's handkerchief out from around the pebbles. "Thee ready?" he asked, pail poised for action.

"Sh," Josh said, pinching his arm. "Sh. Let's listen to them talk first." They stood there listening, hearing only their own heartbeats. There wasn't another sound to be heard except a scratching in the leaves made by a sparrow celebrating sunup.

Then they heard Old Alf say something. Something they couldn't catch, something in a low soft voice that sounded the way Labe had said—as if he might be talking to a baby. Finally his voice was louder and they could hear what he was saying.

"Molly darling," he said, "I'd ought to get up and light the fire for you. You're a sweet girl to say you'll do it for me—a sweet girl, with your long black hair. But you're plain spoiling me, Molly darling. That's what you are."

There was a pause. "They're kissing now," Josh said. Labe looked at Josh with respect.

Old Alf went on. "I always did say, Molly, there's no sight so pretty as a woman combing out her hair. And when her hair's as black and her arms as white as yours, Molly, it's a pure feast for the eyes. A pure feast." The old fellow sighed contentedly. Labe was getting restive. He wanted to start the shivaree, but Josh gave him another pinch.

"A woman as good as you and as pretty as you, Molly, is more than any man deserves—but that you should be from Tewkesbury —can talk old times with me—" He sounded as if he was going to cry. "Lord, my cup runneth over."

Then he got cheerful again. "Flannel cakes for breakfast, did you say? Flannel cakes and treacle and tea strong enough for a mouse to trot over. That's my girl, Molly. That's the breakfast to get."

"I can't hear her talk," Labe complained.

"Maybe she's dumb," Josh whispered. "Maybe that's the reason he's keeping her a secret."

They heard the cornhusk mattress rustle, the old man's bare feet hit the floor boards. "I'll be downstairs, Molly," he called, "before the cake's on."

"Now," Josh whispered, "now," and he turned the handle of his horse fiddle so that it sounded like a cat with its tail caught in a door. Labe shook his lard pail so hard and fast every inch of space was packed with sound waves. He hopped up and down while he shook it, like an Indian brave. This was what they'd planned and waited for and here they were doing it. Pretty soon Old Alf would bring his wife to the window, and make a little speech, and maybe give them some candy.

But Old Alf didn't bring his wife. He came to the window alone, his nightcap still tied under his sharp brown chin, his striped nightshirt hanging from his bony shoulders. He peered out as if he didn't know what his eyes might light on. When he saw the boys under his window he said with more wonderment than anger, "What's the meaning of this racket? This time of day? Under my window? You Birdwell boys taken leave of your senses?"

Labe spoke up. Shivareeing was a polite and thoughtful thing to do. It was a disgrace if you got married and no one shivaree-ed you. So Labe felt proud and honorable about the enterprise. "We was shivareeing thee and thy new wife," he said. "Thee and Molly," he explained as Old Alf continued to stare at them.

"What's that?" the old man said, and he had the same look in his eyes Labe had seen in the eyes of a cotton-tail he had run into a fence corner. For the first time Labe felt a little uncertain about what he was doing.

Josh said, "It's a shivaree for thee and Molly. We found out thy secret and got ahead of everybody else."

"My secret," the old man said, and looked as if his bony shoulders kind of folded up inside his nightshirt.

"We heard thee talking to her," Labe said, "and knowed thee was married."

"Talking to her," repeated Old Alf, and seemed to wake up for the first time. "You heard me talking to her?" He stood there at the window for a long time looking at them. Then he said, "Go round to the back and come in, boys. Door's unlocked. I'll be right down."

The old man was downstairs by the time Josh and Labe opened the kitchen door. "Come in and sit, boys," he said, but the boys felt better standing. He had taken off his nightcap and pulled a pair of pants on over his nightshirt but his feet were still bare. Labe tried to keep his eyes off the bristle of black hair on his big knobby toes. Old Alf kept pinching his lower lip together, and his sad brown eyes still had the rabbit-in-the-fence-corner look.

"Boys," he said, "I ain't married." He went over to the bucket where he kept his corncobs soaking in coal-oil, took a half dozen and put them in the cook-stove.

Labe didn't know what to think. Josh thought, That ain't no way to be talking to a hired girl. He said, "We heard thee talking. Talking to Molly darling," he added.

Old Alf got his fire going before he said any more. Then he settled himself in a rocking chair and put one bare foot on top of the other.

"How old're you boys?"

"Thirteen," said Josh.

"Ten," said Labe.

"Six or seven of you Birdwells, ain't there?"

"Six," Josh said. "Sarah died."

"Six," the old man repeated. "You don't ever get lonesome over there, do you?" He rocked back and forth and rubbed his bare feet together.

"Neither did I while ma was alive. You boys remember ma?" They nodded. Little dried-up old lady who always came out to talk to them when they cut across the Applegate place to go fishing.

"While she was alive," Old Alf said, "I didn't know the meaning of the word. Ma was a great talker. Nothing she wasn't interested in. She'd call out to me before she got up what'd I think the weather'd be like. Loved to talk about how high the river was—or how much the corn had growed. Didn't matter what it was, she'd have something to say about it. I used to get a little tired of it. Yes, I did," he told the staring boys. "Then after she'd been dead awhile didn't seem as if I could stand it. Getting up and not a sound in the house. Not a sound," he said, and rubbed his feet slowly and sadly together. "Not a single sound," he repeated, and leaned toward the boys trying to make them see how bad it had been.

Josh and Labe backed toward the door.

"Then's when I started talking to Molly," he told them.

Josh asked in a dry voice he couldn't seem to dampen by swallowing. "Who is Molly? Is she," he asked, knowing his Bible, "thy concubine?"

"No," Old Alf said, and sighed. "No, she ain't. She ain't nobody. She don't exist. I just made her up. I talk to her—just to hear my own voice. I just pretend she's my wife. There ain't no harm in it —or none I can see anyways, and besides I never figured anybody'd hear me."

The stove was drawing good now and the kitchen was warming, but Josh felt cold—he felt as if all his blood had got stuck in his heart and made it heavy as a bucket of lead. He looked at Old Alf as if he were part of a nightmare he was dreaming.

But Labe was smiling. Everything was clear to him now.

"Thee got anyone else?" he asked.

It was the old man's turn to stare. "Eh?" he asked.

"Thee got anyone else thee talks to? Besides Molly," he explained.

"No," Alf said shortly, "just Molly. I ain't no Mormon."

Labe knew about them. "Thee could have children," he said.

"No," Old Alf insisted. "There's just Molly. At my age children would rile me."

Josh felt his heart getting smaller and smaller, and heavier and heavier. "Thee's crazy," he said. "Thee's gone soft in the head." He had to believe that—not that this was what growing up meant for everyone—for him too. Growing up meant not being worried or scared any more. Meant having things just as they ought to be, the way you liked them, everything neat and happy—at last. If it didn't, what was the use of being alive—taking the trouble to grow up? If you just got scareder and lonesomer—like Old Alf? No, he was loony, crazy as a bedbug.

Old Alf was nodding his head and giving his lip a pull at each nod. "That's what folk'll be saying all right. No misdoubting that. If they get wind of this, 'Old Alf's gone off his head,' they'll say. Not though," he said, "if you boys could manage to keep mum. Hold your tongues. I ain't asking you to. But," he added, "I don't know's your ma, or pa either, for that matter, would much cotton to the idea of you boys eavesdropping. The way you was. And you know yourselves I ain't any more cracked than you are."

Labe was only an inch or two from Alf's bare toes now. Cracked? He'd never seen a grownup act so smart. "I won't tell a living soul, Mr. Applegate," he said. "And don't thee say anything to mother." A hand of bones and leather went round Labe's and gave it a shake.

Old Alf looked at Josh. Josh was flat against the kitchen door;

his black eyes seemed to have flowed to points. "Well, Joshua?" he asked.

"Thee's crazy," Josh said, "but thee needn't worry. I won't tell anyone." He turned and flashed out the door.

Labe watched him race round the corner of the house. "I guess I'd better go," he said. "Breakfast'll be over." But he kind of hated to go. The sun was shining through the dusty windows, the teakettle was humming, a cat had crawled out of the woodbox. Old Alf was rocking away, his eyes on something Labe couldn't see.

"Good-bye," Labe said.

Old Alf roused himself, and for a long minute the old man and the boy looked at each other.

"Come back again," Old Alf said, smiling.

"Thank thee," Labe answered, "I will," and off he loped after Josh, his lard pail rattling.

COMMENT

In Miss West's story we again find the children's point of view, as in Faulkner's story, but here the materials are organized differently: the children, instead of being mere auditors and observers on the edge of a situation which primarily involves adults, are themselves the chief actors in a situation which they create. Thus the usual irony of children's failure to understand is heightened in this story; here the children not only mistake the facts but also, in planning the shivaree (from charivari, serenade), act in terms of their mistake.

Perhaps the most interesting aspect of the story is the way in which the climax—the revelation that Old Alf does not have a wife—is managed. Miss West is careful to avoid stressing the pathos of the old man's solitude; it is clear that it is not her chief intention to make us feel sorry for him. Instead of directly describing Old Alf's feelings, she has him engage in what is, in effect, a game of wits with the boys; thus she maintains tension instead of permitting the relaxation that is characteristic of sentimental effects. She also develops the humorous possibilities of the situation. Yet she does not let the whole thing evaporate in a trivial joke. On the contrary, she makes it meaningful by keeping the emphasis upon the way in which the boys respond to their unexpected discovery. Here she uses very effectively the contrast between them which she has developed throughout the story. Labe is the more flexible and easygoing of the boys; he is still within the realm of make-believe games, and he falls immediately into the style of Old Alf's fantasy and even suggests some elaborations of it. Because he adjusts easily to the situation, he is reluctant to go, and the author appropriately has him stay longer. Josh is stiffer and is inclined to judge life by rules; but he is older and more reflective, and instead of participating in Old Alf's game, he sees immediately its implications. In other words, he is no longer the child who does not understand, and in so far as the story is about him, it is about the shock of the child's first insight into the adult world. Since he fights against his own recognition, the final scene is complicated by the conflict within him. Should this conflict have been developed more fully?

The student should observe the management of the exposition in the early part of the story. What are the means by which the necessary facts are indirectly or inconspicuously made known?

The story has some good examples of imagery—of words that appeal directly to the senses. How many of the senses are appealed to? What is the advantage of words of this kind?

Sidney Alexander

A native of New York City, Sidney Alexander was born in 1913. He spent three years in the army in World War II, part of the time as a radio operator and part of the time in the division of public relations. For several years he was a welfare worker in Harlem. He has done considerable writing of different kinds—drama, verse, and stories. He has written for radio, and several of his verse plays have been broadcast. He has published two volumes of poems, *The Man on the Queue* and *Tightrope in the Dark*. His stories have appeared in many magazines, and several of them have won prizes.

Part of the Act

To THE adult eye, it was just the prosaic and none-too-tidy arcade leading into Madison Square Garden. But to the bright-eyed little girl of seven bounding up the slight incline with her uncle, the doors ahead of them were gateways to magic, portals to never-never land. She had never been to a circus before; and for two weeks now (ever since her uncle had told her), the anticipation of it had tinted her days with an unreal glow, and peopled her nights with motley visitors of fancy.

Oh, why does he walk so slowly? she thought; how could this tall, usually playful uncle of hers be so deliberate? She began tugging at his sleeve, urging him forward, and he glanced down at her and gently smiled. Then he clasped her eager little hand as a side current in the throng threatened to separate them. But he did not quicken his steps and it seemed an hour to Helen before they reached the red-faced guard who performed the magic ritual of ripping their tickets in half and returning the stubs, thereby permitting them to pass through the gate.

"Stay close by me, honey," the man said as the little girl began

PART OF THE ACT Reprinted from *Story* by permission of the author and Story Magazine, Inc.

to wander off into the buzzing crowd. "You'll get lost and then your mother will have my head."

She laughed and squeezed his big hand in hers. Why should mother want Paul's head? What a silly idea! But then this uncle of hers was given to queer statements; sometimes he didn't talk like a grownup at all; he built fantasies in the air, knocked them down, concocted the weirdest stories that floated vaguely in all directions like the blue smoke from his pipe.

Now he was standing still for a moment, taking his bearings. The lobby was jammed with children adorned with tasseled sombreros, snapping circus whips, laughing, crying out with piping voices, dragging their heavy-footed parents after them.

It was their world today, he reflected, gay as their floating balloons, raucous as their tin horns, as it had been his world so many years before. When was it . . . fifteen years since he had last been to the circus? But now, as he stood with Helen in the swirling crowd, the years were rolling further back than that, and he was with his father in the old Garden, and Poppa was saying, "Now stay in your seats. I'll be right back." Then he had gone to the men's room, leaving the two children alone in the terraced balcony. And after five minutes Paul was certain Poppa was never coming back; oh, they were lost forever and soon a policeman would come to take them away to the station house or wherever abandoned children were taken. And he was crying bitterly, hysterically, and a motherly woman was saying "There, there . . ." and Sister was trying desperately not to cry because she was braver than he was, even in thunderstorms. Of course, Poppa had returned to laugh at him.

But that was long ago. The Garden had changed as he had changed. Somehow it seemed much smaller than the Garden of his childhood, though in reality it was much larger. So had his grandfather once loomed ten feet high, his head in the clouds. . . .

He was back in Madison Square Garden, that was the important thing. He was going to see what he had seen as a child, but through Helen's eyes as well as his own. She was tugging him this way and that, crying out in eagerness. The varnish of good and evil would be stripped from events, the clean, fresh colors would emerge . . . and yet, the varnish would be there all the time. That was why he liked to go places with Helen. The double vision intrigued him.

He looked down at the child. She was trembling with anticipation. Her hazel eyes were darting about the lobby. "Oh Paul, buy me a sombrero!" she cried as they passed a vendor's stand. "Buy me a whip!"

"Later," Paul said, patting her head. No, she is not beautiful, he thought, looking down at her, she's certainly no bisque doll. Her hair was nondescript brown, her features rather ordinary. But what wonderful vitality in her chunky, firm-fleshed body, what gaiety in the quick eyes, what roguishness in the trill of laughter. She wore a starched summery pinafore that flared out from her straight hips. She was always dancing in his vision.

The years melted away when he was with Helen. In contrast to her childish energy, his own movements seemed sluggish, old—older than his thirty-odd years. Sometimes when he sat on a rock in Central Park and watched her cavorting on the grass, he felt a pleasant sense of melancholy, a quietistic acceptance of childhood gone.

But always he descended from this aloof eminence, tumbled to the lawn himself, fell to her world, shared her games, became a child with her. At such times, an ant crawling through the grass was an elephant crashing through a heavy jungle; a precarious pile of dominoes was a skyscraper toppled by the giant hand of Helen or the whirlwind blown from Helen's mouth. It was a wonderful world—this world of Helen's—a world with no cause and no effect, no news and no newspapers; and his ability to enter into it without reluctance—as a child-citizen rather than an adult interloper—was the chief bond of their love.

"We have almost an hour before the circus starts," he said to her. "Let's go down to the side show."

"Oh!" she sighed ecstatically. It was one of those long-drawn-out "ohs" that bespeak everything—wonderment, thanks, ineffable joy. She held his hand tightly as they wedged through the cackling, perspiring crowd down the spiral staircase to the basement.

The side shows disgusted him.

Was it possible that he had once, like Helen now, shrieked with joy at the sight of such monstrosities? As he stood packed there amidst the gaping crowd, looking up at those abominations on the platform, he felt sticky beads of sweat rolling down his armpits and he longed for escape to clean, fresh air.

But Helen was crying, "Lift me! Lift me!" She could not see because of the mob; so he hoisted her upon his shoulders where she sat, with her satiny cool thighs brushing his cheeks, ogling the freaks.

They were standing in front of the Tallest Couple in the World. The Tallest Couple were dressed in cowboy and cowgirl clothes, their sombreros as big around the rim as auto wheels. They were selling "wedding rings"—good-luck charms made of lead—for twenty-five cents.

Paul managed to work his way forward to the platform, where dozens of children were stretching forth their thin stalks of arms for the thrill of shaking hands with the giants.

He gave Helen a quarter and she, too, leaned forward, holding him about the neck with one hand and handing the quarter to the seven-foot girl with the other. The giantess smiled and slipped the good-luck ring over two of Helen's fingers and the child screamed with delight, "Oh, I can put two fingers in it! Look, Paul! Oh, look at the ring! It's the biggest ring in the world! Look at my ring, Paul! I have *two* fingers in it!"

As she waved her "wedding ring" before his eyes, there arose unbidden in Paul's mind, like murky underwater growths, images of the giant couple in bed: he heard the titanic threshings and whippings of their love fury, the clinchings of leviathans. . . . And that Lilliputian couple—the next attraction—waiting so sourly on the platform as the side-show barkers waved the crowd on—was their love-making accomplished with mouselike whimpers, sharp nipping of the teeth?

The images persisted, the slimy underwater growths billowed on the ocean floor of his consciousness, and he felt uncomfortable, indecent, that such thoughts should well up in him while he was with Helen. Her thighs were brushing his cheeks, cool and pure.

The midget with the squashed-in face was playing a tune very badly on a midget piano while his wife tap-danced like a marionette. They bowed stiffly, forcing their lips apart in stage smiles, and then retired from the scene.

"She has no arms or legs!" Helen suddenly shouted in Paul's ear. She was bouncing up and down on his shoulders, pointing to the stage next to the midgets. A torso woman was sitting there in a specially built chair; deep, lined with red velvet, and with high side arms to contain her truncated body.

"Shhh . . ." Paul whispered. "That's not very nice. You might hurt her feelings."

A blond woman near by heard his admonition and laughed crudely. "Augh, she don't care 'bout them remarks. That's what she's gettin' paid for."

"And now, Ladees and Gentlemen!" the barker cried, "this *charming* little lady will *deemonstrate* the power of the *yooman* will. As you can see—just draw a little closer there—that's right—let *everybody* see—Miss Sanbras was born without arms or legs"—and he waved his own perfectly good arms toward the charming little lady who was looking at the crowd with the one-eyed somnolence of a cat— ". . . by sheer indom-inable will . . . overcame her handicaps."

"I can't see," Helen whimpered. He had put her down, his shoulders aching, and now she was stretching on tiptoes trying vainly to get a glimpse at the magic platform. In her down world, all she saw were backs and feet.

"All right," Paul sighed wearily, and he hoisted the little girl upon his shoulders again.

A typewriter on a portable table was rolled out, and then to the hand-clapping glee of the spectators, the lady who was just a torso began to peck at the keys with her nose.

"Just like a woodpecker!" the little girl exclaimed, pinching Paul's cheeks in her excitement.

The barker unrolled the paper from the machine and held it aloft for the spectators to see the perfect typing. Meanwhile the torso lady reclined with a bored expression on her pinched, pale face.

Paul was happy when they left her for the sword swallower. The sight of the living torso made his gorge rise in disgust, and he felt an overwhelming surge of sadness for all the truncated people of the world, the half-men and parts of men. . . . He realized already that this visit to the circus would not be a success. Try as he would, he could not look upon these horrors with the eyes of Helen. Too many overtones echoed beyond the walls of Madison Square Garden, the world outside reflected here in a distorted mirror.

But meanwhile, the sword swallower had inserted a wiggly blade like a long bread knife down his gullet, and then withdrawn it, smacking his lips as if he had just devoured a delicious steak.

"Look! look!" Helen cried out as the sword swallower ran his tongue over his lips in anticipation of his next meal. "He *likes* the taste of swords! He thinks they're *delicious!*" And she broke into a foamy spill of laughter, pleased with her sense of mischief, tickled at the incongruity of feeding upon swords.

Now the sword swallower bent his head back and thrust a lighted blue-white neon tube down his extraordinary esophagus, and the lights on the platform were dimmed to reveal the neon tube shining reddishly through the living scabbard of his flesh. The line of pale light traced upward from the pit of his stomach to his mouth, from which projected—like some mockery of a crucifixion—the cross hilt of the neon sword.

But it was especially when they went to see the elephant that Paul realized what time had done to him, the associations from which he could not free himself but of which the child was free, looking innocently as she did, like Eve before the temptation, at this monstrous garden of freaks.

Hundreds of children with their adult overseers lined the rail behind which, in a malodorous straw-sprinkled enclosure, stood the great beasts, lumbering with heavy grace upon gray tree-trunk feet, their skins the color of fossil rock, folded and creased and pitted like oversized garments on their enormous frames. Their little eyes shone intelligently as they waved their trunks over the rail, begging for peanuts.

Next to Helen, a little boy was throwing peanuts at the elephants, throwing them with a kind of desperation as he backed away from the approaching trunk. It was wonderful the way the great beast would sniff among the straw, find the peanut and loop it back to his mysterious hidden mouth. And then he would be waving his trunk in the little boy's face again, and the boy would cringe and throw another nut at the pink-fleshed opening at the tip of the coil.

It was these bifurcated nostrils—wet, pinkish, quivering, sucking all in—that disturbed Paul. But Helen was not disturbed. He had purchased a bag of peanuts for her, and she was smiling at the sight of these enormous beggars behind the rail, their fat rumps bumping playfully, their ridiculous noses. And here was Helen, courageously feeding them, calmly holding her place as the motile thing reached forward in a begging arc, the delicate pink tips fluttering like a butterfly's wings. Unlike the little boy, she did not shrink away in fright. Instead, she neatly dropped the peanuts into place—one in each nostril—as if she were sorting them into compartments.

And she did this with such assurance while the beast waited, fixing his greedy little eyes at her paper bag, that Paul felt proud. And yet he could not overcome his distaste, and he stood impatiently by as Helen, slowly and with a craftsman's precision, bedded two peanuts at a time into the bifurcated nostrils.

"Kids are sure funny," remarked a stout, shirt-sleeved man to Paul. He had been observing the little girl and the boy, the contrasts in their behavior. He wiped his pale pink shining forehead with a dirty handkerchief, and grinned. "You never know what they're likely to do. That one's scared as hell. But that kid of yours . . . she don't seem afraid of nothing. Prob'ly ride on the elephant's back if you'd let her."

Helen paused in her feeding. She looked up and remarked calmly, without vanity, "I'm not afraid of elephants."

"We can see that, dear," Paul said, while the fat man burst out laughing. "But you shouldn't brag about it."

"I'm not bragging," she said. "I like elephants. I think they're funny."

"I tell you, them kids are simply wonderful!" exploded the fat man, loosening the sticky shirt under his armpits. "Your daughter?"

"Not mine," Paul said. "My sister-in-law's. I think she's kind of wonderful too."

"Hey, Pat! C'mere! Lookit this!" a strident voice called, and the fat man disappeared in the milling throng.

Paul glanced at his watch. "You'd better finish the rest of the peanuts yourself," he told Helen. "We ought to go up and take our seats soon."

Reluctantly she left the beggars' row of pachyderms, and clasping hands, they crossed to have a look at Gargantua before going upstairs for the main show. As they buffeted their way through the kaleidoscopic crowd, they passed the giraffes. High above the gaping, gabbling mob, their little heads balanced on still precise necks, they looked down upon the people with the aloof Olympian coolness of gods, dwellers of mountain tops, creatures of a higher world.

"Ooh, give me the peanuts!" Helen cried, reaching for the paper bag which he was carrying.

"You're not allowed," Paul said, pointing to a sign on the bars behind which the lady-footed speckled giraffes stood, motionless as painted statues.

"*For-bid-den to feed the gi-raffes,*" Helen read in a loud voice, spelling out the syllables. She was thoughtful a moment, then looked at her uncle with that bright flash of roguery in her eyes. "I know why."

"You know why what?"

"I know why you can't feed the giraffes."

"Why?"

"Because," she said gravely, extending one foot and hopping over it with the other, "their heads are too high to reach." And she burst out into another trill of laughter, immensely pleased at her little joke.

"Well, if you can't reach *them*, why couldn't they reach *you?*" Paul asked with mock gravity. "Why couldn't they just bend their heads down?"

"Oh *you!*" said the little girl. "I was only fooling."

"Oh . . ." said Paul, acting very surprised.

"You *knew* I was fooling."

"No, I didn't," he said solemnly. "I thought you really meant it."

"You did not!" she insisted, troubled now by his apparent naïveté, and he looked upon her upturned sweet face, suddenly so serious, and he laughed loudly and bent to kiss her. "Of course, silly, I knew it all the time. Come, we've got to hurry."

There was a large crowd before the glass-enclosed cage of Mr. and Mrs. Gargantua. As Paul and Helen approached, they heard little ripples of laughter now and then, or sudden exclamations, or breathy gusts of "ahs" as the beasts performed some feat that delighted their watchers.

As they reached the buzzing rim of the crowd, Paul peered over the many bobbing heads into the electric-lighted, air-conditioned, glass-enclosed cage. The two gorillas were squatting on the floor like a couple of bundles of fur. Feces dotted the floor. A trapeze was swinging idly.

"I can't see," sounded Helen's familiar complaint from below, and again he had to lift her to his shoulders.

Impudently, Gargantua was staring at the people through the close-knit bars that prevented him from smashing the glass with a blow of his hairy fist. His black barrel chest was slowly heaving, and his tiny eyes were almost invisible behind the mat of hair, the squashed-up nose, the overhanging beetling brow.

Suddenly Mrs. Gargantua—smaller, but no more delicate than her mate—stood up and waddled to the other corner of the cage. As she passed her huge partner, he slapped her playfully behind the ears. The crowd roared, and the she-gorilla pushed her husband away and then scuttled with an ungainly hop to the other corner where she plumped down, her back disdainful to the audience, and began to search for fleas.

"By God," breathed a sharp-faced little man who, like Paul, was staggeringly serving as the scaffold for a child. "They're just like humans, ain't they?"

"Yeah," said the man's blousy, gum-chewing wife, "I wonder what they think sometimes, having people stare at 'em all day. What a life! No privacy at all," she added with a sly chuckle.

"Aw, they love it," said a young woman, entering the conversation. "They love to show off. See, there he goes again."

With a catlike bound, surprising for a creature of his weight, Gargantua had leaped onto the swinging trapeze and now he was performing miracles of acrobatics: dangling by one arm, doubling in and out, swinging head downward.

His wife paid no attention to all this, but the crowd was delighted, and Paul found himself being pressed closer and closer to the cage, while Helen clapped her hands in glee.

All of a sudden, the beast leaped from the trapeze and waddled forward, looking with an arrogant expression at the great crowd he had collected by his exhibition. And then, slowly, he bared his teeth in a foul grin, and spat, and they cringed back, momentarily forgetting that between their civilized selves and this uncomfortable reminder of their ancestry there was the saving glass, down which the ugly spittle of his disdain was slowly flowing.

"Let's go, honey," Paul said, shaking his niece's ankle to distract her attention from the cage.

"Oh, wait a minute!" Helen exclaimed, fresh wonderment in her voice.

As if the spitting were not enough, the ugly beast had now begun to commit an abomination. Slowly, deliberately, with an obscene glaze in his eyes, he continued working in full view of them all, as if by this latest outrage he wished not so much to gratify himself as to indicate his utter contempt for all humanity.

There was a titter of embarrassment among the adults. The thin-faced man next to Paul abruptly lifted his son down from his shoulders and, with his blushing wife, hurriedly walked away. Here and there in the crowd Paul heard complaining cries of children who were being dragged away from this scene of infamy. There was no sound from Helen. Her hands gripped his shoulders.

"Let's go," he said abruptly. "It's time for the show to start."

She made no protest when he put her down. Her face was silent, thoughtful. As they made their way toward the spiral staircase, she twisted around for one last, backward glance. A man laughed gruffly in Paul's face.

After he had watched for what seemed the hundredth time a dizzying procession of white and brown horses prancing round and round in a wooden ring while agile riders leaped upon their bare bobbing backs or somersaulted from one horse to another, Paul fought no more against the ravages of time. For once he, too, like Helen, had been unable to keep his seat for wonder, and had stood as she was standing now, clutching the cold iron guardrail of the balcony, utterly fascinated by the spinning, whirling, pirouetting three-ringed saturnalia of the circus. Now, he was falling asleep.

For the first half hour she did not speak at all. Her silence was broken only by throaty gurgles of delight, tiny exclamations, spontaneous uncontrolled flutters of the hands.

But Paul was quickly bored at the ever-changing and yet change-less spectacle in the three rings below—the maneuvers of dogs, the dancing elephants, the knotty-calfed acrobats, in sparkling rhine-stone tights, the flamboyant showman who caught rubber balls thrown out from the audience upon a peg clenched in his teeth and finally juggled three flaming torches in the darkened arena, while, flanking him, a geometric ballet of half-naked girls (the modern touch) wrote upon the darkness with phosphorescent pencils.

Soon Paul found himself looking less upon the circus than upon the reflections of it in his niece's face. Her emotions were written there like clouds upon a still pool, the blue and green and orange beams of light danced in miniature in her eyes, her mouth opened in round O's of amazement, her lips tightened with anxiety for some daring performer.

He looked upon Helen's face as upon the face of his lost childhood. And now she had broken sufficiently from the spell of rapture to notice her uncle's moonlike observation and she breathed ecstatically, "Oh, Paul! Isn't it *wonderful?* Only I don't know what to look at first. There's *so* much going on."

"Look at the seals," he suggested, pointing. "There . . . in the middle ring. He's going to play a song."

"Does he take piano lessons, too? Like me?"

"No," Paul said. "He's a natural-born musician." The little girl laughed appreciatively. "But watch. . . ."

The star performer of the seals was waddling to the center of the ring, while all his comrades of the act rested their sleek blubbery bodies upon encircling stools, their flippers dangling. Some were still munching chunks of fish which had been awarded them for their virtuosities in balancing red-and-white striped balls upon their noses.

Oily in the spotlight which followed his clumsy progress across the ring, the star seal put his pointy mouth to one of the horns in a rack before him, and suddenly let loose a blast that echoed all over the Garden. Immediately all the seals began furiously flapping their flippers together in applause, and the audience roared.

"They clap too! Just like people!" Helen said.

"Just like people," nodded Paul.

But the ringmaster was not satisfied. He was snapping his fingers angrily, summoning the seal back to the rack of horns, and now the seal's head was poised like a cobra ready to strike, and he began to blow first one and then another of the horns, darting back and forth faster and faster until Paul recognized a weirdly distorted version of "My Country, 'Tis of Thee," *prestissimo.*

Again, all the seals clapped their flippers, some of them banging upon the stools like a paid claque. Paul half expected one of them to shout, "Bravo!"

"Bettuh sit back in yo' seat," a Negro man said to Helen, who.

was leaning in her excitement far out over the guardrail. She drew back at the man's gentle restraining touch, never taking her eyes from the spectacle below.

"Thanks," Paul murmured, silently reproaching himself.

"These kids . . ." the Negro said with a confiding sigh. "Yuh gotta watch 'em like hawks."

Like Paul, like almost all the elders in the Garden, he was chaperoning a child—a handsome little boy about Helen's age, with eggshell-brown skin and eyes of an Oriental cast, shining as porcelain.

"Well," said Paul, "I suppose the circus excites them more than it does us."

"You ain't kiddin'."

Meanwhile, the two children were looking at each other with the sniffing, tremulous curiosity of strange dogs. And then Helen laughed and the little Negro boy laughed too, and in a twinkling they were comrades, sharing the delight of the strange world below.

Somehow Paul sensed that the Negro, like himself, felt a twinge of envy and sadness and bitterness at the instant blooming of this friendship, destined to wither at the touch of time. He saw them (and he knew the Negro man saw them too) many years hence, when their innocence would have fled, when speech between them would be a guarded mailed joust, a play of swords, implications, punctilio. He knew (and the Negro man knew) that this innocent clasping of hands, pink in eggshell brown, would not survive many more years, and perhaps it was this realization that lent an undertone of sadness to the wary speech between the two men, between all adult whites and adult blacks.

Simultaneously, the children cried, "The clowns! Oooh, look at the clowns!" and bursting from the doors at each end of the arena came the extravagant shapes of fancy in a long procession.

Oh, the beloved clowns! Paul thought with a lift of his spirit. His boredom was gone. He forgot the Negro man; he forgot Helen; he could not take his eyes from the wonderful clowns performing all the tricks he had seen so many years ago. He was glad the tricks had not changed.

There was the ancient wheeze of the automobile with thirty passengers (the last one out being the Tallest Man in the World with the sour-faced midget on his shoulder). There was the inevitable clown who piled table upon table twenty feet high and then sat on a chair atop the precarious scaffolding, smoking a cigar as he nonchalantly rocked back and forth to the delighted screams of Helen, back and forth until he toppled with a terrific crash, harmlessly. There were magician clowns who waved bull-fight cloths over their colleagues who thereby were transformed into jackasses or goats. There was the prestidigitator clown pulling eggs out of his ears. There was the usual mad scramble at the bargain counter—with the riot call, the frantic whistling, the wig-pulling, the stereotyped chase, the deafening noise of blank cartridges fired by bluehelmeted cops.

There was the Sambo clown whose head suddenly shot off ten feet into the air, to Paul's needless embarrassment, for his Negro friend laughed uproariously.

And most delightful of all, to Paul's freshly awakened eyes, was the red-wigged baggy-trousered clown who walked on mincing feet, while he delicately fluttered a fan that kept a fragile yellow paper butterfly in the air. Every so often, he would stop fanning and softly catch the falling butterfly in his outstretched derby.

Around and around the track he went, performing the same wistful little stunt.

But aside from the innocent interludes of the clowns, Paul's afternoon proved a misery. His boredom had given way to terror. By the time the aerialists began their act, he was emotionally spent. In imagination he had flirted with death too many times that afternoon.

When the incredible Chinese tied his feet in a gunny sack and slid blindfolded down the inclined wire the entire length of the arena, Paul had turned his face away. When one obstreperous tiger refused to be prodded by pole or chair, onto his perch, and lunged and roared at the brave man in the cage, Paul completed in imagination the leap, the torn flesh, the blood. No, not even Helen's presence could help him, the wheel had turned too far, not even Helen. . . . As she gaped and gurgled with delight, he winced and sweated out every act. He had begun to doze off from sheer nervous exhaustion when the marvelous aerialists began their flights.

Helen was tugging at his sleeve. "Paul! how can you sleep? Look what they're doing!"

He knew what they were doing. They were swinging from

trapeze to trapeze, somersaulting, gripping the oncoming wrists at the last moment, twisting and diving and turning in a wondrous poetry of motion. All the same, Paul was grateful for the net. And when one of the girls missed and the crowd gasped and she fell deeply into the net and bounced to her feet, he was not even aware that he had averted his face until Helen asked him why.

"Why what?"

"Why did you turn your face away when the girl fell?"

"Oh, did I?"

"Yes." She was grinning at him, making fun of his fear.

"I don't know," Paul said. "I guess I thought she might get hurt."

"Oh, she couldn't get hurt," the little girl said blandly. "She fell on purpose . . . didn't she?" What had begun as a statement ended as a question, as she read some doubt in her uncle's face.

"Sho' she fell on purpose," said the Negro man, winking to Paul. "It's just part of the act."

"Of course," said Paul. "Still I'm glad they've got a net."

"Well, even if they didn't have a net," persisted Helen, "they'd do a flip-flop and land right on their feet, wouldn't they?"

"Yeah," laughed the Negro. "They got springs in their heels."

The aerialists were gone, the wonderful aerialists, who had swooped and dived like birds in the smoky upper reaches of the Garden, had folded their wings, their nests were dismantled, the long afternoon was reaching its climax. And now the band flared up in brassy fanfare, and the metallic voice of the announcer cried, "The Gallos! Death-defying artists of the High Wire!"

Six figures bounded into the spotlighted circle and bowed deeply. There were three men and three women. Their bodies magnificently proportioned: the V-tapering chests and slim waists of the men, the small breasts and firm flat buttocks of the women were clearly defined in identical tights of Lincoln green.

Swiftly they were hoisted to their platforms, more than one hundred feet above the hard board floor. Between the platforms stretched a tightrope almost at eye level with the balcony where Paul and Helen sat. And then began a series of exploits that paled everything that they had seen that afternoon, a performance so audacious that Paul could not bear to look upon it steadily.

O God, where are the nets? he thought, why don't they bring out the nets? But there were no nets. There was nothing between that high wire and the hard floor. The only concession the acrobats made to safety were long flexible balancing poles. And as the gossamer glint of wire trembled with its load of green figures, Helen dwelt ecstatically upon them; but Paul kept turning away, finding relief in the terraced row of spectators, the solid sanity of the iron girders of the Garden.

"Jesus . . ." murmured the Negro.

Paul glanced again, sucked in his breath. Somehow he felt angry at these Gallos, the indecency of what they were doing, the indecency of holding life so cheaply. For what had begun excruciatingly enough when the first girl inched her away across that wire so high above the floor, continued to mount in intensity, horror piled upon horror, as the Gallos developed new complications in their stunts, just as a composer begins with a simple theme, then introduces a second theme, and weaves and embroiders, inverts and develops until he has achieved a shining fabric of emotional intensity.

So the Gallos wove their themes of danger and courage to the pitch where Paul's brow was dewed with sweat, and he had twisted his handkerchief into a tight grimy ball.

The Chinese who had slid so madly down the wire had stabbed him with fear. But this was worse. This was far worse. For the other fear had been over in a moment, like a flare of lightning, and then there had been the welcome sighs of relief, the laughing, bowing little figure in the distance, the blessed applause.

But this torture was slow, excruciating, endless. As the green figures moved warily across the wire, as man and woman passed each other on that aerial sidewalk attenuated beyond belief, as they mounted on each other's shoulders—they seemed to be deliberately performing all their deeds in slow motion to prolong the agony, to make each feat seem the limit of human courage, only to be superseded by another act even more daring.

No matter how often Paul forbore to look, he found himself returning again and again to the vision of those figures on the wire, staring at them with the fascinated revulsion of a voyeur.

Now they were taxing the very limits of credulity, and Helen clutched her uncle's wet hand and cried, "Oh, Paul! Look what they're doing now! Do you think they'll fall?"

"Shhh . . ." Paul whispered as if her loud words would blow them from the wire.

The Negro was leaning forward in his seat, his mouth open, the shadows purplish on his temples. He whistled with disbelief and shook his head.

For two of the Gallos had inched out upon the high wire and hoisted a bar with halters upon their shoulders. And now a girl was cautiously climbing up one of the young men's backs, slowly straddling his neck, creeping tremulously out upon the bar. The silvery wire vibrated like a piano string as she did a split upon the bar, and then she was climbing down, warily down, while the crowd held its breath and all three had slithered back to the platforms.

An audible sigh, a tremendous crackling of applause.

"Phew!" exclaimed the Negro, wiping his forehead as he turned to Paul. "I'm sure glad that's over."

"Can you do that, Daddy?" asked the little boy.

"Naw," he grinned. "What do you think I am—crazy?"

"I bet my Uncle Paul can do it," Helen said with competitive pride.

"I bet he can't," said Paul without a trace of humor. "I bet he wouldn't even if he could."

But he had no chance to say more. The trumpets were blowing, the lights were dimming. Soon the entire Garden was in darkness save for the smoke-laden convergence of beams upon the glint of wire. The Gallos had reached the climax of their act.

"Don't tell me they're going to ride out on those *bicycles!*" said a woman's voice behind Paul.

"Aw, that's easier than walkin'," scoffingly replied a man.

"Yeah, wise guy, let's see you do it."

"Well, that's a damnfool thing to say. . . ."

From both platforms a cyclist had already begun to ride out on that unbelievable roadway, the long balancing poles swaying on the handle bars. And now the four other members of the troupe were slithering out on foot. It was the first time all six had been on the wire at the same time, and the wire tightened with the weight, its slack taken up in a tense arc.

Precariously balanced there in space in their Lincoln green tights and with their long flexible poles, they looked like six strange insects—huge Martian insects—waving their antennae in the air. Slowly the two pairs, a man and woman from each side, inched their way toward the two cyclists in the center. The wire trembled.

Paul was hunched forward in his seat. The roof of his mouth was dry. For the hundredth time during their act, he resented what the Gallos were doing, resented courage expended on so trivial a goal, and he was crying to himself over and over, Why don't they use a net? Why don't the damn fools use a net?

"Look, Paul," Helen suddenly said, pointing down below. "Just like firemen."

Holding a small jump net no more than ten feet in diameter, were a group of assistants, straining their heads upward at the contemptuous Gallos, following their slow green progress across the wire.

Why this fake concession to safety? Paul thought bitterly. Whom are they trying to fool? They were only dramatizing the danger, slapping him harder in the face. The net was obviously inadequate.

But he had no time to reason further. A mounting drum roll heightened tension as the insectlike figures converged. A bar was slung from one cyclist's shoulders to the other; two acrobats were balancing themselves upon the bar. And then the living pyramid of green began to shimmer in Paul's eyes as with disbelief he saw another bar slung across the shoulders of the topmost figures, and the two remaining girls were climbing on their comrades' shoulders, up, up, up, until they stood upon the second bar, slowly swaying in the balance of the twenty-foot poles. It was absolutely incredible— two upon two—the cyclists, the men upon them, the girls upon them—all swaying on that spider strand a hundred and fifty feet above the floor.

And as they stood so, bathed in the rainbow-colored floodlights, a human pyramid of defiance, the crowd roared its approval, the mounting drum roll was punctuated by a cymbal crash, the men holding the fire net strained their tense faces upward, and then the Gallos began slowly to dismount.

When they fell, Paul wasn't surprised. It was logical that they should fall. It was the only possible culmination to the forebodings he had felt all afternoon. Yes, when the woman behind him screamed with such agony, when the Negro gurgled, "Ahhh," like a death rattle, and the great crowd gasped like a wounded dinosaur, Paul knew what had happened before his eyes saw it. Yes, it was inevitable that the Gallos should fall at the very pinnacle of their defiance, at the moment of dismounting—it was his childhood that was falling; his faith, his innocence tumbling from the wire in a bizarre conglomeration of green limbs and whirling bicycles.

He heard a rapid succession of sickening thuds—one, two, three, four—as the Gallos hit the floor. One woman landed on her back in the small net which had scurried frantically back and forth beneath the falling green flashes in a pathetic attempt to catch them all.

Another had hit one of the bearers of the net, and the two of them sat on the floor staring into each other's faces with dazed, surprised expressions. The acrobat's green legs were twisted grotesquely backward like a frog's.

But all the other Gallos had smashed upon the boards. Some lay still. Others were twitching in their green tights like grasshoppers squashed under a heel. In the center of the ring, a girl had landed on her back—her head awry, her tights split open at the bosom so that her pink naked breasts lay exposed like the soft flesh within the green shell of a sea creature. Blood was trickling from her mouth.

One body was entangled in the twisted spokes of a wheel. The other cyclist was draped ungracefully across the wooden rim of the center ring. At his feet, a close-cropped dark-haired girl was moaning, her arms reaching upward, her fingers clenching and unclenching in indescribable convulsions.

And now the crowd recovered from its first shock, and Paul felt himself rocking in a litany of mourners—the singsong of hysteria, the Negro crying over and over, "Jesus Christ! Jesus Christ!", the woman behind him screaming mechanically like a car horn out of order, the herdlike trampling of panicky feet as exodus began, the young man puking on the stony stairs.

Below them in the pit of horror, stretcher bearers had appeared. Doctors were bending over the green broken insects. The mauled parts of the bicycles were being gathered together; tarpaulins covered the pools of blood.

Then all at once, the incongruous blare of the band sounded, playing an exit march. The circus was over. Paul shook Helen's shoulder and said softly, "Come, darling, the show is over."

She was still staring silently down at the pit. She had not moved or spoken once since the Gallos fell. Her little hands tightly gripped the guardrail. Paul tapped her shoulder again. She turned around and stared at him. Her eyes were wide open, perplexed, but she said nothing as he repeated, "Come, darling. It's all over now."

As they made their way down the steps, stifled in a crowd of solemn adults and squeaking children, Helen suddenly broke her silence. She looked up at her uncle's face with a suddenly radiant smile, as if she had just thought of something. "It was all part of the act, wasn't it, Paul?"

"What?"

"Their falling down. . . . They did it on purpose, didn't they?"

He heard a splutter of cruel laughter near by. A motherly-looking woman glanced at Paul with tear-pinked pitying eyes. *"Oy, Gott! Gott!"* she moaned in Yiddish, her palm flat against her cheek, *"Was weis'n sie, die kinder?"* Paul's lips tightened.

They were out of the Garden at last, standing at the northeast corner of Forty-ninth Street and Eighth Avenue, waiting for the traffic lights to change.

An excited crowd still poured, black and molten, from the front gate, swirled around them, siphoned off down the side streets. Paul stared at the passing figures without comprehension. He could catch scraps of conversation, but even without this he would have known by their gestures what they were talking about. He thought he saw his Negro friend and the little boy crossing the street. He felt drugged, sick with memory. How could they talk so much? Helen's voice shocked him awake: "You didn't answer me, Paul."

"What, dear?"

He stooped over her; solicitous, henlike, feeling her small in the shadow of his wings.

"They weren't *really* hurt, were they?" Her hazel eyes were pleading now.

"No," he said abruptly.

"They fell on purpose, didn't they?" Her birdlike voice trailed off—shreds of questions, of answers, of innocence ravaged by the event. "It was all part of the act, wasn't it?"

He stared down Eighth Avenue. The afternoon had turned gray. The city was without bulk, one-dimensional. Drizzle hung in the air like dots of a newspaper photograph. In the middle distance he could see the McGraw-Hill Building, dull green against the misty sky. Something was . . . He turned away. At the intersection of

Forty-ninth and Eighth, a clown cop was directing traffic. Every time the lights changed, his head·shot ten feet into the air. In the neon blaze of a bar, a legless-armless girl was selling pencils on the sidewalk. Gargantua leered from a cheap hotel. From one green parapet of the McGraw-Hill Building, tiny figures appeared, walking on air. The invisible tightrope stretched river to river. The sky grew dark. The acrobats were tottering. . . .

"Of course," Paul said.

COMMENT

This story differs primarily from the others that use both a child's and a grownup's point of view by developing both points of view very fully and centering our attention upon the fully portrayed contrast between them. But there is a subtler and still more important difference: whereas stories with children are likely to stress the child's inability to grasp the adult point of view (an element which is also present here), "Part of the Act" puts more emphasis upon the adult's inability to share the child's point of view. The two points of view qualify each other.

Mr. Alexander spends the first several pages contrasting Paul's and Helen's different ways of looking at things and yet establishing the fact that in many things Paul is able to share her world. Thus he accounts for their going to the circus together, and at the same time sets up a background for the ironic new development in Paul—his discovery that the circus is a game which he cannot play in Helen's terms. In fact, at the few places where he can take it wholly in her terms, he is inclined to be bored. The author is skillful in his choice of the circus and in making us sharply aware of its contradictory values—the possibility of its being seen and comprehended by the girl entirely as a game, and its symbolic possession of serious meanings for the man. In fact, the last long paragraph makes it unmistakable that the circus is really a symbol for life itself, which for the child is a harmless game but for the adult contains a large share of terror and evil. The child can see a thing in its superficial, picturesque aspects; the adult must see it in all its meaningfulness, and must evaluate it.

The reader should hunt out all those passages in which details of the side show and circus have for Paul some bearing upon human nature and experience generally. He will then see that the story can be read as a kind of parable about life. And yet it is not a parable in the sense that the secondary meaning tends to blot out the primary, literal mean-ing. The side shows and main shows are not shadowy and abstract like the parts of an allegory. Rather they are very concretely presented; and the story can be read entirely in its literal terms. But to miss the impli-cations is to miss a good deal.

The story presents one problem of structure: Is it unified, or does it break down into a series of episodes? In arriving at an answer to this question, the reader might consider such matters as the effect of the theme in holding the parts together, the effect of tension between the contrasted points of view, the climactic arrangement of the parts, and the varying length of the different parts.

Could it be said that the experience of Josh in "Shivaree Before Breakfast" is the germ of Paul's experience in "Part of the Act"?

CONTRASTS IN METHOD AND THEME

James Joyce

The most radical literary experimenter of the twentieth century, James Joyce (1882-1941) for a time considered the priesthood, medicine, and music as careers. In 1903 he left his native Dublin permanently. He supported himself for a while by teaching languages, of which he had an extraordinary knowledge, but he had already found his essential occupation in writing. *Dubliners,* his volume of short stories, portrays Dublin life in a restrained, objective manner. *A Portrait of the Artist As a Young Man,* which has its origins in autobiography, takes on a more symbolic manner: it is in effect a definition of the artist as type. *Ulysses* is a strikingly original portrayal of a day in Dublin, the various episodes finding analogies in different parts of the *Odyssey. Finnegans Wake,* the last and most controversial of Joyce's works, endeavors to include the whole of man's experience by the use of the subconscious, the cyclic theory of history, and other devices.

A Little Cloud

EIGHT years before he had seen his friend off at the North Wall and wished him godspeed. Gallaher had got on. You could tell that at once by his travelled air, his well-cut tweed suit, and fearless accent. Few fellows had talents like his and fewer still could remain unspoiled by such success. Gallaher's heart was in the right place and he had deserved to win. It was something to have a friend like that.

Little Chandler's thoughts ever since lunchtime had been of his meeting with Gallaher, of Gallaher's invitation and of the great city London where Gallaher lived. He was called Little Chandler because, though he was but slightly under the average stature, he gave one the idea of being a little man. His hands were white and small, his frame was fragile, his voice was quiet and his manners were refined. He took the greatest care of his fair silken hair and moustache and used perfume discreetly on his handkerchief. The half-moons of his nails were perfect and when he smiled you caught a glimpse of a row of childish white teeth.

As he sat at his desk in the King's Inns he thought what changes those eight years had brought. The friend whom he had known under a shabby and necessitous guise had become a brilliant figure on the London Press. He turned often from his tiresome writing to gaze out of the office window. The glow of a late autumn sunset covered the grass plots and walks. It cast a shower of kindly golden dust on the untidy nurses and decrepit old men who drowsed on the benches; it flickered upon all the moving figures— on the children who ran screaming along the gravel paths and on everyone who passed through the gardens. He watched the scene and thought of life; and (as always happened when he thought of life) he became sad. A gentle melancholy took possession of him. He felt how useless it was to struggle against fortune, this being the burden of wisdom which the ages had bequeathed to him.

He remembered the books of poetry upon his shelves at home. He had bought them in his bachelor days and many an evening, as he sat in the little room off the hall, he had been tempted to take one down from the bookshelf and read out something to his wife. But shyness had always held him back; and so the books had remained on their shelves. At times he repeated lines to himself and this consoled him.

When his hour had struck he stood up and took leave of his desk and of his fellow-clerks punctiliously. He emerged from under the feudal arch of the King's Inns, a neat modest figure, and walked swiftly down Henrietta Street. The golden sunset was waning and the air had grown sharp. A horde of grimy children populated the street. They stood or ran in the roadway or crawled up the steps before the gaping doors or squatted like mice upon the thresholds. Little Chandler gave them no thought. He picked his way deftly through all that minute vermin-like life and under the shadow of the gaunt spectral mansions in which the old nobility of Dublin had roystered. No memory of the past touched him, for his mind was full of a present joy.

He had never been in Corless's but he knew the value of the name. He knew that people went there after the theatre to eat oysters and drink liqueurs; and he had heard that the waiters there spoke French and German. Walking swiftly by at night he had seen cabs drawn up before the door and richly dressed ladies, escorted by cavaliers, alight and enter quickly. They wore noisy dresses and many wraps. Their faces were powdered and they caught up their dresses, when they touched earth, like alarmed Atalantas. He had always passed without turning his head to look. It was his habit to walk swiftly in the street even by day and whenever he found himself in the city late at night he hurried on his way apprehensively and excitedly. Sometimes, however, he courted the causes of his fear. He chose the darkest and narrowest streets and, as he walked boldly forward, the silence that was spread about his footsteps troubled him, the wandering, silent figures troubled him; and at times a sound of low fugitive laughter made him tremble like a leaf.

He turned to the right towards Capel Street. Ignatius Gallaher on the London Press! Who would have thought it possible eight years before? Still, now that he reviewed the past, Little Chandler could remember many signs of future greatness in his friend. People used to say that Ignatius Gallaher was wild. Of course, he did mix with a rakish set of fellows at that time, drank freely and borrowed money on all sides. In the end he had got mixed up in some shady affair, some money transaction: at least, that was one version of his flight. But nobody denied him talent. There was always a certain . . . something in Ignatius Gallaher that impressed you in spite of yourself. Even when he was out at elbows and at his wits' end for money he kept up a bold face. Little Chandler remembered (and the remembrance brought a slight flush of pride to his cheek) one of Ignatius Gallaher's sayings when he was in a tight corner:

"Half time now, boys," he used to say lightheartedly. "Where's my considering cap?"

That was Ignatius Gallaher all out; and, damn it, you couldn't but admire him for it.

Little Chandler quickened his pace. For the first time in his life he felt himself superior to the people he passed. For the first time his soul revolted against the dull inelegance of Capel Street. There was no doubt about it: if you wanted to succeed you had to go away. You could do nothing in Dublin. As he crossed Grattan Bridge he looked down the river towards the lower quays and pitied the poor stunted houses. They seemed to him a band of tramps, huddled together along the river-banks, their old coats covered with dust and soot, stupefied by the panorama of sunset and waiting for the first chill of night to bid them arise, shake themselves and begone. He wondered whether he could write a poem to express his idea. Perhaps Gallaher might be able to get it into some London paper for him. Could he write something original? He was not sure what idea he wished to express but the thought that a poetic moment had touched him took life within him like an infant hope. He stepped onward bravely.

Every step brought him nearer to London, farther from his own sober inartistic life. A light began to tremble on the horizon of his mind. He was not so old—thirty-two. His temperament might be said to be just at the point of maturity. There were so many different moods and impressions that he wished to express in verse. He felt them within him. He tried to weigh his soul to see if it was a poet's soul. Melancholy was the dominant note of his temperament, he thought, but it was a melancholy tempered by recurrences of faith and resignation and simple joy. If he could give expression to it in a book of poems perhaps men would listen. He would never be popular: he saw that. He could not sway the crowd but he might appeal to a little circle of kindred minds. The English critics, perhaps, would recognise him as one of the Celtic school by reason of the melancholy tone of his poems; besides that, he would put in allusions. He began to invent sentences and phrases from the notice which his book would get. "*Mr. Chandler has the gift of easy and graceful verse.*" . . . "*A wistful sadness pervades these poems.*" . . . "*The Celtic note.*" It was a pity his name was not more Irish-looking. Perhaps it would be better to insert his mother's name before the surname: Thomas Malone Chandler, or better still: T. Malone Chandler. He would speak to Gallaher about it.

He pursued his revery so ardently that he passed his street and had to turn back. As he came near Corless's his former agitation began to overmaster him and he halted before the door in indecision. Finally he opened the door and entered.

The light and noise of the bar held him at the doorways for a few moments. He looked about him, but his sight was confused by the shining of many red and green wine-glasses. The bar seemed to him to be full of people and he felt that the people were observing him curiously. He glanced quickly to right and left (frowning slightly to make his errand appear serious), but when his sight cleared a little he saw that nobody had turned to look at him: and there, sure enough, was Ignatius Gallaher leaning with his back against the counter and his feet planted far apart.

"Hallo, Tommy, old hero, here you are! What is it to be? What will you have? I'm taking whisky: better stuff than we get across the water. Soda? Lithia? No mineral? I'm the same. Spoils the flavour. . . . Here, *garçon*, bring us two halves of malt whisky, like a good fellow. . . . Well, and how have you been pulling along since I saw you last? Dear God, how old we're getting! Do you see any signs of aging in me—eh, what? A little grey and thin on the top—what?"

Ignatius Gallaher took off his hat and displayed a large closely cropped head. His face was heavy, pale and clean-shaven. His eyes, which were of bluish slate-colour, relieved his unhealthy pallor and shone out plainly above the vivid orange tie he wore. Between these rival features the lips appeared very long and shapeless and colourless. He bent his head and felt with two sympathetic fingers the thin hair at the crown. Little Chandler shook his head as a denial. Ignatius Gallaher put on his hat again.

"It pulls you down," he said, "press life. Always hurry and scurry, looking for copy and sometimes not finding it: and then, always to have something new in your stuff. Damn proofs and printers, I say, for a few days. I'm deuced glad, I can tell you, to get back to the old country. Does a fellow good, a bit of a holiday. I feel a ton better since I landed again in dear dirty Dublin. . . . Here you are, Tommy. Water? Say when."

Little Chandler allowed his whisky to be very much diluted.

"You don't know what's good for you, my boy," said Ignatius Gallaher. "I drink mine neat."

"I drink very little as a rule," said Little Chandler modestly. "An odd half-one or so when I meet any of the old crowd: that's all."

"Ah, well," said Ignatius Gallaher, cheerfully, "here's to us and to old times and old acquaintance."

They clinked glasses and drank the toast.

"I met some of the old gang today," said Ignatius Gallaher. "O'Hara seems to be in a bad way. What's he doing?"

"Nothing," said Little Chandler. "He's gone to the dogs."

"But Hogan has a good sit, hasn't he?"

"Yes; he's in the Land Commission."

"I met him one night in London and he seemed to be very flush. . . . Poor O'Hara! Boose, I suppose?"

"Other things, too," said Little Chandler shortly.

Ignatius Gallaher laughed.

"Tommy," he said, "I see you haven't changed an atom. You're the very same serious person that used to lecture me on Sunday mornings when I had a sore head and a fur on my tongue. You'd want to knock about a bit in the world. Have you never been anywhere even for a trip?"

"I've been to the Isle of Man," said Little Chandler.

Ignatius Gallaher laughed.

"The Isle of Man!" he said. "Go to London or Paris: Paris, for choice. That'd do you good."

"Have you seen Paris?"

"I should think I have! I've knocked about there a little."

"And is it really so beautiful as they say?" asked Little Chandler.

He sipped a little of his drink while Ignatius Gallaher finished his boldly.

"Beautiful?" said Ignatius Gallaher, pausing on the word and on the flavour of his drink. "It's not so beautiful, you know. Of course, it is beautiful. . . . But it's the life of Paris; that's the thing. Ah, there's no city like Paris for gaiety, movement, excitement. . . ."

Little Chandler finished his whisky and, after some trouble, succeeded in catching the barman's eye. He ordered the same again.

"I've been to the Moulin Rouge," Ignatius Gallaher continued when the barman had removed their glasses, "and I've been to all the Bohemian cafés. Hot stuff! Not for a pious chap like you, Tommy."

Little Chandler said nothing until the barman returned with two glasses: then he touched his friend's glass lightly and reciprocated the former toast. He was beginning to feel somewhat disillusioned. Gallaher's accent and way of expressing himself did not please him. There was something vulgar in his friend which he had not observed before. But perhaps it was only the result of living in London amid the bustle and competition of the Press. The old personal charm was still there under this new gaudy manner. And, after all, Gallaher had lived, he had seen the world. Little Chandler looked at his friend enviously.

"Everything in Paris is gay," said Ignatius Gallaher. "They believe in enjoying life—and don't you think they're right? If you
want to enjoy yourself properly you must go to Paris. And, mind
you, they've a great feeling for the Irish there. When they heard
I was from Ireland they were ready to eat me, man."

Little Chandler took four or five sips from his glass.

"Tell me," he said, "is it true that Paris is so . . . immoral as they
say?"

Ignatius Gallaher made a catholic gesture with his right arm.

"Every place is immoral," he said. "Of course you do find spicy
bits in Paris. Go to one of the students' balls, for instance. That's
lively, if you like, when the *cocottes* begin to let themselves loose.
You know what they are, I suppose?"

"I've heard of them," said Little Chandler.

Ignatius Gallaher drank off his whisky and shook his head.

"Ah," he said, "you may say what you like. There's no woman
like the Parisienne—for style, for go."

"Then it is an immoral city," said Little Chandler, with timid
insistence—"I mean, compared with London or Dublin?"

"London!" said Ignatius Gallaher. "It's six of one and half-a-dozen
of the other. You ask Hogan, my boy. I showed him a bit about
London when he was over there. He'd open your eye. . . . I say,
Tommy, don't make punch of that whisky: liquor up."

"No, really. . . ."

"O, come on, another one won't do you any harm. What is it?
The same again, I suppose?"

"Well . . . all right."

"*François*, the same again. . . . Will you smoke, Tommy?"

Ignatius Gallaher produced his cigar-case. The two friends lit
their cigars and puffed at them in silence until their drinks were
served.

"I'll tell you my opinion," said Ignatius Gallaher, emerging after
some time from the clouds of smoke in which he had taken refuge,
"it's a rum world. Talk of immorality! I've heard of cases—what
am I saying?—I've known them: cases of . . . immorality. . . ."

Ignatius Gallaher puffed thoughtfully at his cigar and then, in
a calm historian's tone, he proceeded to sketch for his friend some
pictures of the corruption which was rife abroad. He summarised
the vices of many capitals and seemed inclined to award the palm

to Berlin. Some things he could not vouch for (his friends had told him), but of others he had had personal experience. He spared neither rank nor caste. He revealed many of the secrets of religious houses on the Continent and described some of the practices which were fashionable in high society and ended by telling, with details, a story about an English duchess—a story which he knew to be true. Little Chandler was astonished.

"Ah, well," said Ignatius Gallaher, "here we are in old jog-along Dublin where nothing is known of such things."

"How dull you must find it," said Little Chandler, "after all the other places you've seen!"

"Well," said Ignatius Gallaher, "it's a relaxation to come over here, you know. And, after all, it's the old country, as they say, isn't it? You can't help having a certain feeling for it. That's human nature. . . . But tell me something about yourself. Hogan told me you had . . . tasted the joys of connubial bliss. Two years ago, wasn't it?"

Little Chandler blushed and smiled.

"Yes," he said. "I was married last May twelve months."

"I hope it's not too late in the day to offer my best wishes," said Ignatius Gallaher. "I didn't know your address or I'd have done so at the time."

He extended his hand, which Little Chandler took.

"Well, Tommy," he said, "I wish you and yours every joy in life, old chap, and tons of money, and may you never die till I shoot you. And that's the wish of a sincere friend, an old friend. You know that?"

"I know that," said Little Chandler.

"Any youngsters?" said Ignatius Gallaher.

Little Chandler blushed again.

"We have one child," he said.

"Son or daughter?"

"A little boy."

Ignatius Gallaher slapped his friend sonorously on the back.

"Bravo," he said, "I wouldn't doubt you, Tommy."

Little Chandler smiled, looked confusedly at his glass and bit his lower lip with three childishly white front teeth.

"I hope you'll spend an evening with us," he said, "before you go back. My wife will be delighted to meet you. We can have a little music and—"

"Thanks awfully, old chap," said Ignatius Gallaher, "I'm sorry we didn't meet earlier. But I must leave tomorrow night."

"Tonight, perhaps . . . ?"

"I'm awfully sorry, old man. You see I'm over here with another fellow, clever young chap he is too, and we arranged to go to a little card-party. Only for that. . . ."

"O, in that case. . . ."

"But who knows?" said Ignatius Gallaher considerately. "Next year I may take a little skip over here now that I've broken the ice. It's only a pleasure deferred."

"Very well," said Little Chandler, "the next time you come we must have an evening together. That's agreed now, isn't it?"

"Yes, that's agreed," said Ignatius Gallaher. "Next year if I come, *parole d'honneur.*"

"And to clinch the bargain," said Little Chandler, "we'll just have one more now."

Ignatius Gallaher took out a large gold watch and looked at it.

"Is it to be the last?" he said. "Because you know, I have an a.p."

"O, yes, positively," said Little Chandler.

"Very well, then," said Ignatius Gallaher, "let us have another one as a *deoc an doruis*—that's good vernacular for a small whisky, I believe."

Little Chandler ordered the drinks. The blush which had risen to his face a few moments before was establishing itself. A trifle made him blush at any time: and now he felt warm and excited. Three small whiskies had gone to his head and Gallaher's strong cigar had confused his mind, for he was a delicate and abstinent person. The adventure of meeting Gallaher after eight years, of finding himself with Gallaher in Corless's surrounded by lights and noise, of listening to Gallaher's stories and of sharing for a brief space Gallaher's vagrant and triumphant life, upset the equipoise of his sensitive nature. He felt acutely the contrast between his own life and his friend's, and it seemed to him unjust. Gallaher was his inferior in birth and education. He was sure that he could do something better than his friend had ever done, or could ever do, something higher than mere tawdry journalism if he only got the chance. What was it that stood in his way? His unfortunate timidity! He wished to vindicate himself in some way, to assert his manhood. He saw behind Gallaher's refusal of his invitation. Gallaher was only patronising him by his friendliness just as he was patronising Ireland by his visit.

The barman brought their drinks. Little Chandler pushed one glass towards his friend and took up the other boldly.

"Who knows?" he said, as they lifted their glasses. "When you come next year I may have the pleasure of wishing long life and happiness to Mr. and Mrs. Ignatius Gallaher."

Ignatius Gallaher in the act of drinking closed one eye expressively over the rim of his glass. When he had drunk he smacked his lips decisively, set down his glass and said:

"No blooming fear of that, my boy. I'm going to have my fling first and see a bit of life and the world before I put my head in the sack—if I ever do."

"Some day you will," said Little Chandler calmly.

Ignatius Gallaher turned his orange tie and slate-blue eyes full upon his friend.

"You think so?" he said.

"You'll put your head in the sack," repeated Little Chandler stoutly, "like everyone else if you can find the girl."

He had slightly emphasised his tone and he was aware that he had betrayed himself; but, though the colour had heightened in his cheek, he did not flinch from his friend's gaze. Ignatius Gallaher watched him for a few moments and then said:

"If ever it occurs, you may bet your bottom dollar there'll be no mooning and spooning about it. I mean to marry money. She'll have a good fat account at the bank or she won't do for me."

Little Chandler shook his head.

"Why, man alive," said Ignatius Gallaher, vehemently, "do you know what it is? I've only to say the word and tomorrow I can have the woman and the cash. You don't believe it? Well, I know it. There are hundreds—what am I saying?—thousands of rich Germans and Jews, rotten with money, that'd only be too glad. . . . You wait a while, my boy. See if I don't play my cards properly. When I go about a thing I mean business, I tell you. You just wait."

He tossed his glass to his mouth, finished his drink and laughed loudly. Then he looked thoughtfully before him and said in a calmer tone:

"But I'm in no hurry. They can wait. I don't fancy tying myself up to one woman, you know."

He imitated with his mouth the act of tasting and made a wry face.

"Must get a bit stale, I should think," he said.

. . . .

Little Chandler sat in the room off the hall, holding a child in his arms. To save money they kept no servant but Annie's young sister Monica came for an hour or so in the morning and an hour or so in the evening to help. But Monica had gone home long ago. It was a quarter to nine. Little Chandler had come home late for tea and, moreover, he had forgotten to bring Annie home the parcel of coffee from Bewley's. Of course she was in a bad humour and gave him short answers. She said she would do without any tea but when it came near the time at which the shop at the corner closed she decided to go out herself for a quarter of a pound of tea and two pounds of sugar. She put the sleeping child deftly in his arms and said:

"Here. Don't waken him."

A little lamp with a white china shade stood upon the table and its light fell over a photograph which was enclosed in a frame of crumpled horn. It was Annie's photograph. Little Chandler looked at it, pausing at the thin tight lips. She wore the pale blue summer blouse which he had brought her home as a present one Saturday. It had cost him ten and elevenpence; but what an agony of nervousness it had cost him! How he had suffered that day, waiting at the shop door until the shop was empty, standing at the counter and trying to appear at his ease while the girl piled ladies' blouses before him, paying at the desk and forgetting to take up the odd penny of his change, being called back by the cashier, and finally, striving to hide his blushes as he left the shop by examining the parcel to see if it was securely tied. When he brought the blouse home Annie kissed him and said it was very pretty and stylish; but when she heard the price she threw the blouse on the table and said it was a regular swindle to charge ten and elevenpence for it. At first she wanted to take it back but when she tried it on she was delighted with it, especially with the make of the sleeves, and kissed him and said he was very good to think of her.

Hm! . . .

He looked coldly into the eyes of the photograph and they answered coldly. Certainly they were pretty and the face itself was pretty. But he found something mean in it. Why was it so unconscious and ladylike? The composure of the eyes irritated him. They repelled him and defied him: there was no passion in them, no rapture. He thought of what Gallaher had said about rich Jewesses. Those dark Oriental eyes, he thought, how full they are of passion, of voluptuous longing! . . . Why had he married the eyes in the photograph?

He caught himself up at the question and glanced nervously round the room. He found something mean in the pretty furniture which he had bought for his house on the hire system. Annie had chosen it herself and it reminded him of her. It too was prim and pretty. A dull resentment against his life awoke within him. Could he not escape from his little house? Was it too late for him to try to live bravely like Gallaher? Could he go to London? There was the furniture still to be paid for. If he could only write a book and get it published, that might open the way for him.

A volume of Byron's poems lay before him on the table. He opened it cautiously with his left hand lest he should waken the child and began to read the first poem in the book:

> "Hushed are the winds and still the evening gloom,
>   Not e'en a Zephyr wanders through the grove,
> Whilst I return to view my Margaret's tomb
>   And scatter flowers on the dust I love."

He paused. He felt the rhythm of the verse about him in the room. How melancholy it was! Could he, too, write like that, express the melancholy of his soul in verse? There were so many things he wanted to describe: his sensation of a few hours before on Grattan Bridge, for example. If he could get back again into that mood. . . .

The child awoke and began to cry. He turned from the page and tried to hush it: but it would not be hushed. He began to rock it to and fro in his arms but its wailing cry grew keener. He rocked it faster while his eyes began to read the second stanza:

"Within this narrow cell reclines her clay,
        That clay where once . . ."

It was useless. He couldn't read. He couldn't do anything. The wailing of the child pierced the drum of his ear. It was useless, useless! He was a prisoner for life. His arms trembled with anger and suddenly bending to the child's face he shouted:

"Stop!"

The child stopped for an instant, had a spasm of fright and began to scream. He jumped up from his chair and walked hastily up and down the room with the child in his arms. It began to sob piteously, losing its breath for four or five seconds, and then bursting out anew. The thin walls of the room echoed the sound. He tried to soothe it but it sobbed more convulsively. He looked at the contracted and quivering face of the child and began to be alarmed. He counted seven sobs without a break between them and caught the child to his breast in fright. If it died! . . .

The door was burst open and a young woman ran in, panting.

"What is it? What is it?" she cried.

The child, hearing its mother's voice, broke out into a paroxysm of sobbing.

"It's nothing, Annie . . . it's nothing. . . . He began to cry . . ."

She flung her parcels on the floor and snatched the child from him.

"What have you done to him?" she cried, glaring into his face.

Little Chandler sustained for one moment the gaze of her eyes and his heart closed together as he met the hatred in them. He began to stammer:

"It's nothing. . . . He . . . he began to cry. . . . I couldn't . . . I didn't do anything. . . . What?"

Giving no heed to him she began to walk up and down the room, clasping the child tightly in her arms and murmuring:

"My little man! My little mannie! Was 'ou frightened, love? . . . There now, love! There now! . . . Lambabaun! Mamma's little lamb of the world! . . . There now!"

Little Chandler felt his cheeks suffused with shame and he stood back out of the lamplight. He listened while the paroxysm of the child's sobbing grew less and less; and tears of remorse started to his eyes.

COMMENT

In moving from Alexander's story to Joyce's we continue with a contrast of points of view—here, of course, the points of view of two adults. It is the first of the stories in this book in which such a contrast is used directly as the chief method. Yet the presentation of the contrast itself is not the final business of the story. If we examine the proportion of the story, we find that Chandler and Gallaher are shown together for only about half the length; in the first one-fourth we see Chandler, in his office and on the street, anticipating his meeting with Gallaher, and in the final fourth he is shown at home in relation to his wife and child. The effect of this arrangement is, of course, to make us study Chandler more thoroughly and give us a fuller sense of his character. How can we account for this choice by the author? In what way is Chandler, an inexperienced stay-at-home, fundamentally more interesting than Gallaher? In making Chandler the more interesting, Joyce is reversing what conventional expectations?

The contrast between points of view finally becomes, of course, a contrast of the characters themselves. In such a situation an author has several options: he may simply present the different characters, like a master of ceremonies, without making a value-judgment or even implying that such a judgment may be made; or the details of his narrative may suggest the existence of real distinctions which will incline the reader to approve of one more than the other. What does Joyce do here? Does Joyce so weight the story as to make the reader more sympathetic with one character than the other? If so, does he do this at the cost of not presenting the favored character fully, that is, of glossing over his less admirable traits? Or does he maintain his detachment—inclining the reader to yield his sympathy to one character and yet keeping him entirely aware of the character's shortcomings?

Does the contrast between the men ever develop into a kind of conflict? In this connection, note Chandler's prediction that Gallaher will marry and Gallaher's insistence that, if he does, he will marry for money. What is each man really asserting?

In contrasts between points of view, we often find the story turning upon the fact that the possessor of one point of view does not understand another. Is that the case here? Or is there evidence that each understands the other, or at least feels that he does?

Chandler resents Gallaher's "patronizing." Yet Joyce presents Gallaher as having a very powerful influence upon Chandler; a considerable part *of the story is devoted to tracing this influence. In this respect the story really turns upon a paradox—that even in the Gallaher whom in one way he rejects, Chandler in another way sees the embodiment of some of his own aspirations. Perhaps, therefore, we may read the story as contrasting two different ways of life and implying that both have some part in, or even contend for mastery of, man's life. In this connection, note Chandler's conflicts at home.*

Are we always to take Chandler's estimate of himself at face value? Consider, for instance, his thoughts about writing poetry.

James Thurber

James Thurber, who is equally well known for his humorous writing and his humorous drawing, was born in Ohio in 1894 and educated at the Ohio State University. The loss of an eye in a childhood accident frustrated his effort to join the army in World War I. After 1919 he was a newspaperman in Columbus, Ohio, and in Paris. In the late '20's he began a connection with *The New Yorker* that has lasted until the present day; at one time he was managing editor. He has collaborated in writing a successful play, *The Male Animal*. As an artist he is known primarily for his cartoons. He also has illustrated many books, both his own and those of other authors. He writes fables, essays, parodies, stories, and autobiography of a very original flavor.

The Secret Life of Walter Mitty

W E'RE going through!" The Commander's voice was like thin ice breaking. He wore his full-dress uniform, with the heavily braided white cap pulled down rakishly over one cold gray eye. "We can't make it, sir. It's spoiling for a hurricane, if you ask me." "I'm not asking you, Lieutenant Berg," said the Commander. "Throw on the power light! Rev her up to 8,500! We're going through!" The pounding of the cylinders increased: ta-pocketa-pocketa-pocketa-*pocketa-pocketa*. The Commander stared at the ice forming on the pilot window. He walked over and twisted a row of complicated dials. "Switch on No. 8 auxiliary!" he shouted. "Switch on No. 8 auxiliary!" repeated Lieutenant Berg. "Full strength in No. 3 turret!" shouted the Commander. "Full strength in No. 3 turret!" The crew, bending to their various tasks in the huge, hurtling eight-engined Navy hydroplane, looked at each other and grinned. "The Old Man'll get us through," they said to one another. "The Old Man ain't afraid of Hell!" . . .

"Not so fast! You're driving too fast!" said Mrs. Mitty. "What are you driving so fast for?"

"Hmm?" said Walter Mitty. He looked at his wife, in the seat beside him, with shocked astonishment. She seemed grossly unfamiliar, like a strange woman who had yelled at him in a crowd. "You were up to fifty-five," she said. "You know I don't like to go more than forty. You were up to fifty-five." Walter Mitty drove on toward Waterbury in silence, the roaring of the SN202 through the worst storm in twenty years of Navy flying fading in the remote, intimate airways of his mind. "You're tensed up again," said Mrs. Mitty. "It's one of your days. I wish you'd let Dr. Renshaw look you over."

Walter Mitty stopped the car in front of the building where his wife went to have her hair done. "Remember to get those overshoes while I'm having my hair done," she said. "I don't need overshoes," said Mitty. She put her mirror back into her bag. "We've been all through that," she said, getting out of the car. "You're not a young man any longer." He raced the engine a little. "Why don't you wear your gloves? Have you lost your gloves?" Walter Mitty reached in a pocket and brought out the gloves. He put them on, but after she had turned and gone into the building and he had driven on to a red light, he took them off again. "Pick it up, brother!" snapped a cop as the light changed, and Mitty hastily pulled on his gloves and lurched ahead. He drove around the streets aimlessly for a time, and then he drove past the hospital on his way to the parking lot.

. . . "It's the millionaire banker, Wellington McMillan," said the pretty nurse. "Yes?" said Walter Mitty, removing his gloves slowly. "Who has the case?" "Dr. Renshaw and Dr. Benbow, but there are two specialists here, Dr. Remington from New York and Dr. Pritchard-Mitford from London. He flew over." A door opened down a long, cool corridor and Dr. Renshaw came out. He looked distraught and haggard. "Hello, Mitty," he said. "We're having the devil's own time with McMillan, the millionaire banker and close personal friend of Roosevelt. Obstreosis of the ductal tract. Tertiary. Wish you'd take a look at him." "Glad to," said Mitty.

In the operating room there were whispered introductions: "Dr. Remington, Dr. Mitty. Dr. Pritchard-Mitford, Dr. Mitty." "I've read your book on streptothricosis," said Pritchard-Mitford, shaking hands. "A brilliant performance, sir." "Thank you," said Walter Mitty. "Didn't know you were in the States, Mitty," grumbled Remington. "Coals to Newcastle, bringing Mitford and me up here for a tertiary." "You are very kind," said Mitty. A huge, complicated machine, connected to the operating table, with many tubes and wires, began at this moment to go pocketa-pocketa-pocketa. "The new anaesthetizer is giving away!" shouted an interne. "There is no one in the East who knows how to fix it!" "Quiet, man!" said Mitty, in a low, cool voice. He sprang to the machine, which was now going pocketa-pocketa-queep-pocketa-queep. He began fingering delicately a row of glistening dials. "Give me a fountain pen!" he snapped. Someone handed him a fountain pen. He pulled a faulty piston out of the machine and inserted the pen in its place. "That will hold for ten minutes," he said. "Get on with the operation." A nurse hurried over and whispered to Renshaw, and Mitty saw the man turn pale. "Coreopsis has set in," said Renshaw nervously. "If you would take over, Mitty?" Mitty looked at him and at the craven figure of Benbow, who drank, and at the grave, uncertain faces of the two great specialists. "If you wish," he said. They slipped a white gown on him; he adjusted a mask and drew on thin gloves; nurses handed him shining . . .

"Back it up, Mac! Look out for that Buick!" Walter Mitty jammed on the brakes. "Wrong lane, Mac," said the parking-lot attendant, looking at Mitty closely. "Gee. Yeh," muttered Mitty. He began cautiously to back out of the lane marked "Exit Only." "Leave her sit there," said the attendant. "I'll put her away." Mitty got out of the car. "Hey, better leave the key." "Oh," said Mitty, handing the man the ignition key. The attendant vaulted into the car, backed it up with insolent skill, and put it where it belonged.

They're so damn cocky, thought Walter Mitty, walking along Main Street; they think they know everything. Once he had tried to take his chains off, outside New Milford, and he had got them wound around the axles. A man had had to come out in a wrecking car and unwind them, a young, grinning garageman. Since then Mrs. Mitty always made him drive to a garage to have the chains taken off. The next time, he thought, I'll wear my right arm in a sling; they won't grin at me then. I'll have my right arm in a sling and they'll see I couldn't possibly take the chains off myself. He kicked at the slush on the sidewalk. "Overshoes," he said to himself, and he began looking for a shoe store.

When he came out into the street again, with the overshoes in a box under his arm, Walter Mitty began to wonder what the other thing was his wife had told him to get. She had told him, twice before they set out from their house for Waterbury. In a way he hated these weekly trips to town—he was always getting something wrong. Kleenex, he thought, Squibb's, razor blades? No. Toothpaste, toothbrush, bicarbonate, carborundum, initiative and referendum? He gave it up. But she would remember it. "Where's the what's-its-name?" she would ask. "Don't tell me you forgot the what's-its-name." A newsboy went by shouting something about the Waterbury trial.

. . . "Perhaps this will refresh your memory." The District Attorney suddenly thrust a heavy automatic at the quiet figure on the witness stand. "Have you ever seen this before?" Walter Mitty took the gun and examined it expertly. "This is my Webley-Vickers 50.80," he said calmly. An excited buzz ran around the courtroom. The Judge rapped for order. "You are a crack shot with any sort of firearms, I believe?" said the District Attorney, insinuatingly. "Objection!" shouted Mitty's attorney. "We have shown that the defendant could not have fired the shot. We have shown that he wore his right arm in a sling on the night of the fourteenth of July." Walter Mitty raised his hand briefly and the bickering attorneys were stilled. "With any known make of gun," he said evenly, "I could have killed Gregory Fitzhurst at three hundred feet *with my left hand.*" Pandemonium broke loose in the courtroom. A woman's scream rose above the bedlam and suddenly a lovely, dark-haired girl was in Walter Mitty's arms. The District Attorney struck at her savagely. Without rising from his chair, Mitty let the man have it on the point of the chin. "You miserable cur!" . . .

"Puppy biscuit," said Walter Mitty. He stopped walking and the buildings of Waterbury rose up out of the misty courtroom and surrounded him again. A woman who was passing laughed. "He said 'Puppy biscuit,'" she said to her companion. "That man said 'Puppy biscuit' to himself." Walter Mitty hurried on. He went into an A. & P., not the first one he came to but a smaller one farther up the street. "I want some biscuit for small, young dogs," he said to the clerk. "Any special brand, sir?" The greatest pistol shot in the world thought a moment. "It says 'Puppies Bark for It' on the box," said Walter Mitty.

His wife would be through at the hairdresser's in fifteen minutes, Mitty saw in looking at his watch, unless they had trouble drying it; sometimes they had trouble drying it. She didn't like to get to the hotel first; she would want him to be there waiting for her as usual. He found a big leather chair in the lobby, facing a window, and he put the overshoes and the puppy biscuit on the floor beside it. He picked up an old copy of *Liberty* and sank down into the chair. "Can Germany Conquer the World Through the Air?" Walter Mitty looked at the pictures of bombing planes and of ruined streets.

. . . "The cannonading has got the wind up in young Raleigh, sir," said the sergeant. Captain Mitty looked up at him through tousled hair. "Get him to bed," he said wearily, "with the others. I'll fly alone." "But you can't, sir," said the sergeant anxiously. "It takes two men to handle that bomber and the Archies are pounding hell out of the air. Von Richtman's circus is between here and Saulier." "Somebody's got to get that ammunition dump," said Mitty. "I'm going over. Spot of brandy?" He poured a drink for the sergeant and one for himself. War thundered and whined around the dugout and battered at the door. There was a rending of wood and splinters flew through the room. "A bit of a near thing," said Captain Mitty carelessly. "The box barrage is closing in," said the sergeant. "We only live once, Sergeant," said Mitty, with his faint, fleeting smile. "Or do we?" He poured another brandy and tossed it off. "I never see a man could hold his brandy like you, sir," said the sergeant. "Begging your pardon, sir." Captain Mitty stood up and strapped on his huge Webley-Vickers automatic. "It's forty kilometres through hell, sir,". said the sergeant. Mitty finished one last brandy. "After all," he said softly, "what isn't?" The pounding of the cannon increased; there was the rat-tat-tatting of machine guns, and from somewhere came the menacing pocketa-pocketa-pocketa of the new flame-throwers. Walter Mitty walked to the door of the dugout humming "Auprès de Ma Blonde." He turned and waved to the sergeant. "Cheerio!" he said. . . .

Something struck his shoulder. "I've been looking all over this hotel for you," said Mrs. Mitty. "Why do you have to hide in this old chair? How did you expect me to find you?" "Things close in," said Walter Mitty vaguely. "What?" Mrs. Mitty said. "Did you get the what's-its-name? The puppy biscuits? What's in that box?" "Overshoes," said Mitty. "Couldn't you have put them on in the store?" "I was thinking," said Walter Mitty. "Does it ever occur to you that I am sometimes thinking?" She looked at him. "I'm going to take your temperature when I get you home," she said.

They went out through the revolving doors that made a faintly derisive whistling sound when you pushed them. It was two blocks to the parking lot. At the drugstore on the corner she said, "Wait here for me. I forgot something. I won't be a minute." She was more than a minute. Walter Mitty lighted a cigarette. It began to rain, rain with sleet in it. He stood up against the wall of the drugstore, smoking. . . . He put his shoulders back and his heels together. "To hell with the handkerchief," said Walter Mitty scornfully. He took one last drag on his cigarette and snapped it away. Then, with that faint, fleeting smile playing about his lips, he faced the firing squad; erect and motionless, proud and disdainful, Walter Mitty the Undefeated, inscrutable to the last.

COMMENT

Like "A Little Cloud," Thurber's "The Secret Life of Walter Mitty" presents the discrepancy between the actual life of the protagonist and the life which he can imagine himself to be living. But out of very similar material Joyce and Thurber have made wholly different stories. The difference may be described as one of tone: Thurber's story is essentially comic. How, we may ask, do the two authors secure such diverse effects?

In part, the effects result from selection. Thurber leaves out entirely certain matters which are emphasized in Joyce's story—the drabness of the protagonist's surroundings, the monotony of his life, the commonplaceness of his home—which are not conducive to comic tone. There is no suggestion that Walter Mitty is a misfit or a failure or condemned to a dreary existence. Further, Thurber does not show Walter as suffering from anguish or revulsion, whereas Joyce selects for special demonstration the bitterness which Chandler can feel and does feel on at least one occasion. Again, Joyce pictures a wife only in her capacity to be rather disagreeable; Walter Mitty's wife is not especially charming either, but her sharpness accompanies a concern for her husband's welfare that seems rooted in a sound understanding of him. Finally, there is a sharp difference in characterization: Little Chandler has some keenness of mind and great sensitiveness, but in Walter we are shown no quality which can exact serious attention or respect.

The point is that all these differences do not occur accidentally, but are the result of choices by authors aiming at one kind of effect or another. Joyce introduces materials that call forth a kind of emotion or seriousness incompatible with comic form (although comedy may have its own kind of serious intention).

The management of proportion is also significant. In Joyce's story we spend most of our time seeing a bleak actuality, and only peep briefly into a better life which Chandler can imagine. In Thurber's story we spend most of our time in Walter's cozy dreams, and only briefly glance at a real world which is not very hard after all. As far as the stories are concerned, Walter is a happy man, and Chandler an unhappy one. Then there is the quality of the dreams themselves. Chandler thinks of an achievement which is, so to speak, possible: there is the pathos of actual failure. But Walter soars off into grandiose visions that are ludicrously inconsistent with any recognizable possibilities.

With regard to Walter's dreams, the reader should note several things: the way in which, sometimes at both beginning and end, they are related to some aspect or other of the everyday world; the details which indicate that the dreams are specifically compensatory; and the way in which, in most of the dreams, real virtues—i.e., courage, self-possession, professional skill, philosophic acceptance of destiny—are made to seem comic. In arriving at an answer to the last-named problem the reader might explore the following questions:

1. Would the effect be different if Walter were imagining the virtues as belonging to someone else?

2. Would the effect be different if the virtues were not exhibited in such trite situations and if the participants did not speak in such a stereotyped style?

In the third paragraph we suggested that comedy may have its own kind of seriousness. Does Thurber's story, with its comic manner, "say" something "serious"? In other words, does it stop at the level of an entertaining joke, or does it suggest a general truth of some kind?

As a last point: What is the irony of the word inscrutable *in the final paragraph of the story?*

Kay Boyle

Kay Boyle was born in St. Paul in 1903, attended schools in various parts of the country, including the Conservatory of Music in Cincinnati, and in 1922 went to Europe for what turned out to be a residence of almost twenty years. After the conquest of France she and her family returned to the United States, and she now lives in New York. Her early writing was published in *avant-garde* magazines, but with the growth of her reputation her work has been very widely published. She has written a number of volumes of short stories, and her collected poems appeared in 1938. Some of her best-known stories grew out of the political tensions of Europe during the 1930's.

Effigy of War

THE BARMAN at the big hotel on the sea front had been an officer in the Italian army during the last war, and somehow or other the rumor began to get around. Whether it was that he said too much to people who spoke his own language with him, saying late at night that the vines in Italy were like no other vines and the voices more musical and the soldiers as good as any others, no matter what history had to say about them, or whether it got around in some other way, it was impossible to know. But the story came to the director of the hotel (Cannes, it was, and the people just as gaudily dressed as other years, and the shops on the Croisette as fancy), and because of the feeling that ran high against the foreigner and against the name of Italy, the director stepped into the lounge bar about eleven one morning to tell the barman what he'd better do. He was a dressy, expensive-looking little man, the director, who could speak four languages with ease, and he had been a Russian once, a White Russian, so that France was the only country left to him now. He came into the bar at a quiet hour, just before the idle would begin wandering in out of the eternally springtime sun, and he jerked his cuffs inside his morning coat and screwed the soft, sagging folds of his throat from his collar wings and started speaking quietly over the mahogany-colored bar.

"Maestro," he said to the barman who had been ten years with them, "with all this trouble going on the management would quite understand your wanting to go back to Italy."

"Italy?" the barman said, and it might have been Siberia he was pronouncing as a destination and the look in his eyes was as startled. He stopped whatever it was he had been doing, setting the glasses straight or putting the ash trays out or the olives, and he looked at the director. He was a slight, dark man and his face was as delicate-boned as a monkey's, and the hair was oiled down flat upon his monkey-fragile skull.

"A lot of Italians are going back," the director said, and he swung himself up onto the stool as elegantly and lightly as a dwarf dressed up for a public appearance, the flesh hairless and pink, and the hand on the wood of the bar as plump as a child's. "Give me a glass of milk," he said, and he went on saying in a lower voice: "In times like these everyone wants to avoid all the trouble they can. Everybody likes to feel he's in his own country." He said it with a slight Russian accent, and the barman waited while the director took the cigarette out of the silver case, and then the barman snapped the lighter open and held the flame to the end of the cigarette in his dark, monkey-nervous hand. "We're perfectly willing to discuss things with you," the director said, and as the first bluish breath of smoke drifted between them, their eyes met for a moment across it, and the director was the first to look away.

"Ah, if we should all go back to the places we belong to!" the barman said as he put the lighter into the pocket of his starched white coat. He turned aside to take the bottle of milk off the ice, and he went on saying in strangely poetic sorrow: "If we all returned to the waters of our own seas and the words of our own languages, France would be left a wilderness—"

"Of course, there are some national exceptions," the director added quickly. "There are some nationalities which cannot go back." He took a swallow of milk and looked rather severely at the barman. "In countries where there have been revolutions, economic upheavals," he went on, his hand with the cigarette in it making the vague, comprehensive gestures of unrest. "But with Italians," he said, and the barman suddenly leaned forward and laid his small bony hands down flat upon the bar.

"Well, me," he said, "I've been fifteen years in this country. I'm too old to go back now. For me, Mussolini was an economic up-heaval," he said. He picked up the bottle of milk again and filled the director's glass, pouring it out a little too quickly. "I've never gone back, not since fifteen years," he said, the words spoken sharply and rapidly, almost breathlessly across the bar. "I'm like a refugee, like a political refugee," he said. "I haven't the right to go back."

"That can be taken care of," the director said, and he took out his folded handkerchief and dabbed at the drops of milk on his upper lip. "The management would advance you what you needed to get back, write you a good testimonial—"

"I haven't done military service for them," the barman said, and he was smiling in something like pain at the director, the grin pulled queer and ancient as a monkey's across his face. "I can't go back," he said. "This is my country by now. If I can't go on working here I can't work anywhere. I wouldn't leave this country no matter what anybody said to me or no matter what they did to me."

"You never did very much about getting any papers out," said the director. He was looking straight ahead at the small silk flags of all the nations and at his own immaculately preserved reflection in the glass. "You never did much about trying to change your nationality," he said, and he took another discreet swallow of milk. "You should have thought of that before."

"I might have been a Frenchman today if it hadn't been for my wife," the barman said, and his tongue ran eagerly out along his lip. "My wife—" he said, and he leaned closer, the starched sleeves, with the hairy, bony little wrists showing, laid on the bar. "I haven't seen her for fifteen years," he said, and the director looked at the glass of milk and shrugged his shoulders. "She's in Italy, and she wouldn't sign the papers. She wouldn't do that one thing," he said, the eyes dark and bright, and the face lit suddenly, like a poet's, with eagerness and pain. "Not that she wanted me," he said. "It wasn't that. But women like that, Italian women, they're as soft and beautiful as flowers and as stubborn as weeds." He said it in abrupt poetic violence, and the director stirred a little uneasily and finished the milk in his glass.

"Now, you take a run up to the Italian Consul this afternoon and have a talk with him," he said, and he wiped his upper lip with his folded handkerchief again. "Tell him you're thinking of going back. Put Raymond on duty for the afternoon. And another thing, Maestro," he said as he got down off the bar stool, "don't keep that *Corriere della Sera* out there where everybody can see it. Put it in your pocket and read it when you get home," he said.

It might have passed off quietly enough like that if the Dane hadn't come into it. He was a snub-nosed, sun-blacked, blond-headed little man who gave swimming lessons in one of the bathing establishments on the beach. He had been a long time there, walking season after season tough and cocky up and down the beach with his chest high and his thumbs hooked into the white belt of his bathing trunks. He wore a bright clean linen cap down to his yellow brows, and royal-blue swimming shorts, and the muscles in his shoulders and arms were as thick and smooth as taffy. But after the war came, he didn't parade up and down the esplanade in the same way in the sun, but stayed hour after hour in the water or else in a corner of the beach café. He still gave lessons, but he let the pupils seek him out in the shade of the café, as if the eyes of the mobilized and the uniformed and the envious could see him less distinctly there.

The one who started it all was the Greek waiter in the big hotel who had got his French naturalization papers eight months before and was leaving for training camp in a week or two. He'd lean over the diners—what was left of the English and the American colony, and the dukes and duchesses, and the Spanish who had got their jewels and their pelts and their money out of Spain—and he'd say:

"What nationality do you think I am, eh? What country would you say I come from?" showing his teeth in pride and pleasure at them as he slipped the dishes of *filets de soles bonne femme* or *champignons à la Reine d'Angleterre* down before them, provided the maître d'hôtel was looking the other way. Sometimes the guests would say he looked one thing, and sometimes another: Italian, Rumanian, or even Argentine, and he'd smile like a prima donna at them, leaning almost on their shoulders, with his eyes shining and the serviette flung rather wildly over his arm.

"No, no, oh, *mon dieu*, no!" he'd say. "I'm pure French. What do you think of that? In another two or three months you'll see me coming in here with gold stripes on my sleeve, ordering everything like everybody else has to eat." And then he'd take out his mobilization order and show it to them, balancing the *homard à l'américaine* on its platter in the other hand as he opened out the stamped, signed paper. "I'm French," he'd say, with the garlic hanging on his breath. "I'm going right into the French army to fight. I'm going to fight for everybody sitting here having dinner to-night," he'd say, and he'd give the people at the next table their salad, holding his mobilization order open in his hand.

The Greek waiter had never liked the look of the Dane, and now that he had his military orders he couldn't so much as stand the sight of the cold-eyed, golden little man. In the hours he had off in the afternoons, he took the habit of walking out on the esplanade and stopping just above the bathing place to call the names down to him. There he would be, the Dane, with his white cap on and his royal-blue bathing trunks, talking half naked to the half-naked girls or women on the beach, war or no war, and going on making money just the same.

"*Sale étranger!*" the Greek would call down, with a fine Greek accent to it, and "*Crapule!*," with his voice ringing out like an opera singer's across the sand and the striped bathing houses and the sea. "France for the French!" he'd roar over the railing, and the little Dane in his bathing suit would go quietly on with his swimming lessons, or if he were alone he'd turn and go into the beach café and sit down out of sight in the shade. There was a week ahead still before the Greek waiter would go, and all those days in the afternoons he'd stand on the esplanade and call the names down. In the end he appealed to the French themselves, exhorting them to rise. "The French for the French!" he'd shout down through the funnel of his hands. "Don't employ foreigners! Give a French-man the job!"

The last night of the week the little Dane came into the lounge bar for a drink before he went to bed; coming late, in discretion, when no one else was there. The two of them were talking there together, the Dane sitting on the stool with the glass of beer before him, and the Italian on the other side with his starched jacket on and the wisps of his monkey hair slicked flat across his skull, and in a few minutes the barman would have taken the bottles down and locked the safes and turned the lights out, and then nothing would have occurred. But now the barman was leaning on the counter, speaking the French tongue in a low, rather grievous voice to the swimming teacher, his thin hand rocking from side to side like a little boat as he talked.

"Drinking has ceased," he was saying in faultless pentameter, "in the old way it has ceased. Even before September there was a difference, as if the thirst of man had been slaked at last. To any sensitive eye, the marks of death were to be seen for years on the façades of casinos, palace hotels, luxury restaurants, and on the terraces of country clubs and vast private estates. Even the life of the big bars has been dying," he said. "For years now that I can remember, the lounge bar has been passing through the agonies of death." He made a tragic and noble gesture toward the empty leather armchairs in the half-darkened room, and he said in a low, dreamy voice: "All this is finished. There is no more place in the hearts of men for this kind of thing. The race that insisted on this atmosphere of redundance for its pleasure, that demanded this futility, is vanishing, dying—"

"War levels the ranks," the Dane said quietly. His sun-blacked, sun-withered face under the bright light thatch of hair was as immobile as if carved from wood.

"Ah, before the war even," the barman said softly, and then he stopped, for the men had come into the bar. The Greek waiter walked a little ahead of the others, wearing a gray jersey and a cap pulled down, and they both of them knew him; it was the others behind him they had never seen before.

"Get that one, the one on the stool," the Greek waiter said, and one of the other men stepped past him and walked toward the bar. Just before he got there he lifted his right arm and hit the swimming teacher on the chin. The little, light-crowned head and the strong, small body rose clear of the stool an instant, like a piece of paper lifted and spun sidewise by the wind, and then it sailed into the corner and collapsed there, bent double, by the leather chair. "That's the kind of language he understands," the Greek said, and he crossed the length of thick, soft carpet, jerking his cap up on his forehead. He was smiling with delight when he kicked the swimming teacher's body into another shape. "Walking up and down out there on the beach," the Greek said, and he turned back to the others and the Italian barman behind the bar. "Giving lessons just like men weren't bleeding their guts out for him and people like him—"

"He volunteered. I tell you that man volunteered," the barman began saying, and his bones were shaking like a monkey's in his skin. "I've seen the paper he got. I know he volunteered to fight like anybody else would—" And when he jumped for the bell the Greek waiter reached over and took him by the collar of his starched white coat and dragged him out across the plates of potato chips and the empty beer bottle and the glass the Dane had been drinking and slung him across the elegant little glass-topped tables into the other corner of the room.

"Pick him up and take him along too," the Greek said. "I know all about him I need to know. He was an officer last war, officer in the Italian army, so you'll know what side he'll fight on this time. Take them both out," he said. "This country's not good enough for them, not good enough for either of them."

They did it by moonlight, taking the two men's clothes off on the sand and shingles by the Mediterranean water, and giving it to them in fiercely accelerating violence. They broke the swimming teacher's jaw, and they snapped the arms of the barman behind him like firewood, beating the breath and the life from them with whatever fell under their hands. The Greek carried over an armful of folding iron chairs from the bathing establishment's darkened, abandoned porch and, with these as weapons, they battered the two men's heads down and drove their mouths into the sand.

"So now repeat this after me, foreigners," the Greek began saying in wild holy passion as he kneeled beside them. He had taken the flag out of his jersey and was shaking out its folds. "So now repeat what I'm going to tell you," he said in violent religious fervor against the pulsing and murmuring of the water, and his hands were trembling as he laid the flag out where their mouths could bleed upon the tricolor emblem, the cotton stuff transformed now to the exigencies of a nation and a universe.

COMMENT

As the title indicates, the story is about war; the references to "the last war" make clear that the time is the beginning of World War II. But the author is not very specific about time and immediate circumstances; from this very indefiniteness we may conclude that the story is less about a specific war than about war in general. The second aspect of her method is that she finds her materials, not in front lines or army life, but among civilians at a quiet seaside resort. But she makes an interpretation of the war spirit by showing the conduct of people when they are under the influence of that spirit.

On the face of it the story is rather simple: a mob of hoodlums beat up a pair of perfectly innocent civilians. The action is told directly and quickly: it is almost as if we in the audience were following a newsreel camera as it recorded a tight little sequence of scenes following straightforwardly one upon another. But if we look more closely, we find that the author has chosen to do something more difficult than at first appears. She has taken, as the victims with whom we sympathize, two types who in wartime are likely to get very little sympathy—the civilian who seems not to be entering the "war effort," and the "national of an alien country." The reader should hunt out the details of the means by which she secures the reader's sympathy for them; in general, of course, her method is to treat them as individuals rather than types. On the other hand, the author takes, as the leader of her brutal assailants, a type who is likely to be a popular hero in wartime—the man who loudly asserts his nationality and goes off to fight. In the last paragraph he and his followers go through a familiar ritual of patriotism: they attack "foreigners" and use the flag as a symbol—with "holy passion" and "religious fervor." The author is really turning upside down the usual expectations; she is in effect compelling the reader to identify himself with the mob and to re-examine his premises. Note, in this connection, the use of the adjectives wild and violent in the last paragraph.

That the satire is intended to be general is shown by the last word in the story, which says, in effect, "This is the way all wars are." The mingling of different nationals in a land where none of them have been born is an ironic comment on the nationalism which plays so large a part in modern wars. The fact that the scene is in France perhaps has a special point, for traditionally France has been hospitable to people of foreign birth. Placing the action at a seaside resort makes possible the sharpest contrast between the standards of peace and war. The eighth paragraph *from the end of the story develops the irony in a very original way: large and comfortable drinking places are virtually made into symbols of an amiable way of life that is gone.*

In making his final estimate of the story the reader should remember the meaning of effigy: "a sculptured or pictured likeness . . . ; often, a crude image or picture of one who is the object of odium."

Irwin Shaw

Irwin Shaw was born in Brooklyn in 1913 and was writing by the time he attended high school and Brooklyn College, where he also played football. When he was only twenty-three, his antiwar play *Bury the Dead* was a great theatrical success. A few years later, when the United States entered World War II, he enlisted as a private. In addition to holding various nonliterary jobs he has written various plays and many stories and done writing for both radio and movies. His stories have appeared in numerous magazines and have been collected in three volumes—*Sailor off the Bremen, Welcome to the City,* and *Act of Faith.*

Sailor off the Bremen

THEY sat in the small white kitchen, Ernest and his brother Charlie and Preminger and Dr. Slater, all bunched around the porcelain-topped table, so that the kitchen seemed to be overflowing with men. Sally stood at the stove turning griddlecakes over thoughtfully, listening to what Preminger was saying.

"So everything was excellent. The Comrades arrived, dressed in evening gowns and—what do you call them?"

"Tuxedos," Charlie said.

"Tuxedos." Preminger nodded. "Very handsome people," he said, his English precise and educated, but with a definite German accent. "Mixing with all the other handsome people who came to say good-bye to their friends on the boat, everybody very gay, everybody with a little whiskey on the breath, nobody would suspect they were Party members, they were so clean and upperclass." He laughed at his own joke. With his crew-cut hair and his straight nose and blue eyes, he looked like a young boy from a Middle-Western college. His laugh was a little high and short and he talked fast, as though he wanted to get a great many words out

SAILOR OFF THE BREMEN Reprinted by permission of Random House, Inc. Copyright 1939 by Irwin Shaw. And also: Reprinted from *The New Yorker* by permission of the author.

to beat a certain deadline, but otherwise being a Communist in Germany and a deck officer on the Bremen had not left any mark on him. "It is a wonderful thing," he said, "how many pretty girls there are in the Party in the United States."

They all laughed, even Ernest, who put his hand up to cover the empty spaces in his front teeth. His hand covered his mouth and the fingers cupped around the neat black patch over his eye, and he smiled at his wife behind that concealment, getting his merriment over with swiftly so he could take his hand down and compose his face. Sally watched him from the stove. "Here," she said, dumping three griddlecakes onto a plate and putting them before Preminger. "Better than Childs restaurant."

"Wonderful," Preminger said, dousing the cakes with syrup. "Each time I come to America, I feast on these. There is nothing like it in the whole continent of Europe."

"All right," Charlie said. He leaned across the kitchen table, practically covering it because he was so big. "Finish the story."

"So I gave the signal," Preminger said, waving his fork, "when everything was nice and ready, everybody having a good time, stewards running this way, that way, with champagne, and we had a very nice little demonstration. Nice signs, good, loud yelling, the Nazi flag cut down one, two, three from the pole, the girls standing together singing like angels, everybody running there from all parts of the ship." He smeared butter methodically on the top cake. "So then the rough business. Expected. Naturally. After all, we all know it is no cocktail party for Lady Astor." He squinted at his plate. "A little pushing, expected. Maybe a little crack over the head here and there, expected. Justice comes with a headache these days, we all know that. But my people, the Germans, you must always expect the worst from them. They organize like lightning. Method. How to treat a riot on a ship. Every steward, every oiler, every sailor was there in a minute and a half. Two men would hold a Comrade, another would beat him. Nothing left to accident."

"What's the sense in going over the whole thing again?" Ernest said. "It's all over."

"Shut up," Charlie said.

"Two stewards got hold of Ernest," Preminger said softly, "and another one did the beating. Stewards are worse than sailors. All day long they take orders, they hate the world. Ernest was unlucky. The steward who beat him up is a member of the Nazi party. He is an Austrian. He is not a normal man."

"Sally," Ernest said, "give Mr. Preminger some more milk."

"He kept hitting Ernest," Preminger said, tapping on the porcelain top with his fork. "And he kept laughing and laughing."

"You're sure you know who he is?" Charlie asked.

"I know who he is. He is twenty-five years old, very dark and good-looking, and he sleeps with at least two ladies a voyage." Preminger slopped his milk around in the bottom of his glass. "His name is Lueger. He spies on the crew for the Nazis. He has sent two men already to concentration camps. He knew what he was doing when he kept hitting Ernest in the eye. I tried to get to him, but I was in the middle of a thousand people screaming and running. If something happens to that Lueger, it will be a very good thing."

"Have a cigar," Ernest said, pulling two out of his pocket.

"Something'll happen to him," Charlie said. He took a deep breath and leaned back from the table.

"What do you prove if you beat up one stupid sailor?" Ernest said.

"I don't prove anything," Charlie said. "I'm just going to have a good time with the boy that knocked my brother's eye out. That's all."

"It's not a personal thing," Ernest said in a tired voice. "It's the movement of Fascism. You don't stop Fascism with a personal crusade against one German. If I thought it would do some good, I'd say sure, go ahead."

"My brother, the Communist," Charlie said bitterly. "He goes out and gets ruined and still he talks dialectics. The Red saint with the long view. The long view gives me a pain. I'm taking a very short view of Mr. Lueger."

"Speaking as a Party member," Preminger said, "I approve of your brother's attitude, Charlie. Speaking as a man, please put Lueger on his back for at least six months. Where is that cigar, Ernest?"

Dr. Slater spoke up in his polite, dentist's voice. "As you know," he said, "I'm not the type for violence." Dr. Slater weighed a hundred and thirty-three pounds and it was almost possible to see through his wrists, he was so frail. "But as Ernest's friend, I think there'd be a definite satisfaction for all of us, including Ernest, if this Lueger was taken care of. You may count on me for anything within my powers." His voice was even drier than usual, and he spoke as if he had reasoned the whole thing out slowly and carefully and had decided to disregard the fear, the worry, the possible great damage. "That's my opinion," he said.

"Sally," Ernest said, "talk to these damn fools."

"I think," Sally said, looking at her husband's face, which was stiffly composed now, like a corpse's face, "I think they know what they're talking about."

Ernest shrugged. "Emotionalism. A large, useless gesture. You're all tainted by Charlie's philosophy. He's a football player, he has a football player's philosophy. Somebody knocks you down, you knock him down, everything is fine."

"Please shut up, Ernest." Charlie stood up and banged on the table. "I've got my stomach full of Communist tactics. I'm acting strictly in the capacity of your brother. If you'd had any brains, you'd have stayed away from that lousy boat. You're a painter, an artist, you make water colors. What the hell is it your business if lunatics're running Germany? But you go and get your eye beat out. O.K. Now I step in. Purely personal. None of your business. Please go and lie down in the bedroom. We have arrangements to make here."

Ernest stood up, hiding his mouth, which was twitching, and walked into the bedroom, closed the door, and lay down on the bed in the dark, with his eye open.

The next day, Charlie and Dr. Slater and Sally went down to the Bremen an hour before sailing time and boarded the ship on different gangplanks. They stood separately on the A deck, up forward, waiting for Preminger. Eventually he appeared, very boyish and crisp in his blue uniform. He walked past them, touched a steward on the arm—a dark, good-looking young steward—said something to him, and went aft. Charlie and Dr. Slater examined the steward closely, so that when the time came, on a dark street, there would be no mistake. Then they went home, leaving Sally there, smiling at Lueger.

"Yes," Sally said two weeks later, "it is very clear. I'll have dinner with him, and I'll go to a movie with him and get him to take at least two drinks, and I'll tell him I live on West Twelfth Street, near West Street. There's a whole block of apartment houses there. I'll get him down to West Twelfth Street between a quarter to one and one in the morning, and you'll be waiting—you and Slater—on Greenwich Street, at the corner, under the Ninth Avenue 'L.' And you'll say, 'Pardon me, can you direct me to Sheridan Square?' and I'll start running."

"That's right," Charlie said. "That's fine." He blew reflectively on his huge hands. "That's the whole story for Mr. Lueger. You'll go through with it now, Sally? You're sure you can manage it?"

"I'll go through with it," Sally said. "I had a long talk with him today when the boat came in. He's very—anxious. He likes small girls like me, he says, with black hair."

"What's Ernest going to do tonight?" Dr. Slater asked. In the two weeks of waiting his throat had become so dry he had to swallow desperately every five or six words. "Somebody ought to take care of Ernest tonight."

"He's going to Carnegie Hall," Sally said. "They're playing Brahms and Debussy."

"That's a good way to spend an evening," Charlie said. He opened his collar and pulled down his tie. "The only place I can go with Ernest these days is the movies. It's dark, so I don't have to look at him."

"He'll pull through," Dr. Slater said professionally. "I'm making him new teeth. He won't be so self-conscious. He'll adjust himself."

"He hardly paints any more," Sally said. "He just sits around the house and looks at his old pictures."

"He used to be a very merry man," Slater said. "Always laughing. Always sure of what he was saying. Before he was married we used to go out together all the time and all the time the girls—my girl and his girl, no matter who they were—would give all their attention to him. All the time. I didn't mind. I love your brother Ernest as if he was my younger brother. I could cry when I see him sitting now, covering his eye and his teeth, not saying anything, just listening to what other people have to say."

"Mr. Lueger," Charlie said. "Our pal, Mr. Lueger."

"He carries a picture of Hitler," Sally said. "In his watch. He showed me. He says he's lonely."

"I have a theory," Slater said. "My theory is that when Ernest finds out what happens to this Lueger, he'll pick up. It'll be a kind of springboard to him. It's my private notion of the psychology of the situation." He swallowed nervously. "How big is this Lueger?"

"He's a large, strong man," Sally said.

"I think you ought to have an instrument of some kind, Charlie," Slater said. "Really I do."

Charlie laughed. He extended his two hands, palms up, the fingers curved a little, broad and muscular. "I want to take care of Mr. Lueger with my bare fists."

"There is no telling what—"

"Don't worry, Slater," Charlie said. "Don't worry one bit."

At twelve that night, Sally and Lueger walked down Eighth Avenue from the Fourteenth Street subway station. Lueger held Sally's arm as they walked, his fingers moving up and down, occasionally grasping the loose cloth of her coat.

"I like you," he said, walking very close to her. "You are a good girl. You are made excellent. I am happy to accompany you home. You are sure you live alone?"

"Don't worry," Sally said. "I'd like a drink."

"Aaah," Lueger said. "Waste time."

"I'll pay for it," Sally said. She had learned a lot about him in the evening. "My own money. Drinks for you and me."

"If you say so," Lueger said, steering her into a bar. "One drink, because we have something to do tonight." He pinched her playfully and laughed, looking obliquely into her eyes with a kind of technical suggestiveness.

Under the Ninth Avenue "L" at Twelfth Street, Charlie and Dr. Slater leaned against an Elevated pillar, in deep shadow.

"I wonder if they're coming," Slater said finally, in a flat, high whisper.

"They'll come," Charlie said, keeping his eyes on the little triangular park up Twelfth Street where it joins Eighth Avenue. "That Sally has guts. That Sally loves my dumb brother like he was the President of the United States. As if he was a combination of Lenin and Michelangelo. And he had to go and get his eye batted out."

"He's a very fine man," Slater said, "your brother Ernest. A man with true ideals. I am very sorry to see what has happened to his character since—is that them?"

"No," Charlie said. "It's two girls from the Y.W.C.A. on the corner."

"He used to be a very happy man," Slater said. "Always laughing."

"Yeah," Charlie said. "Yeah. Why don't you keep quiet, Slater?"

"Excuse me," Slater said. "I don't like to bother you. But I must talk. Otherwise, if I just stand here keeping still, I will suddenly start running and I'll run right up to Forty-second Street. I can't keep quiet at the moment, excuse me."

"Go ahead and talk then," Charlie said, patting him on the shoulder. "Shoot your mouth right off, all you want."

"I am only doing this because I think it will help Ernest," Slater said, leaning hard against the pillar, in the shadow, to keep his knees straight. The Elevated was like a dark roof stretching all the way across from building line to building line. "We should have brought an instrument with us, though. A club, a knife, brass knuckles." Slater put his hands in his pockets, holding them tight against the cloth to keep them from trembling. "It will be very bad if we mess this up. Won't it be very bad, Charlie?"

"Sh-h-h," Charlie said.

Slater looked up the street. "That's them. That's Sally, that's her coat."

"Sh-h-h, Slater. Sh-h-h."

"I feel very cold, Charlie. Do you feel cold? It's a warm night but I—"

"For Christ's sake, shut up!"

"We'll fix him," Slater whispered. "Yes, Charlie, I'll shut up. Sure, I'll shut up, depend on me, Charlie."

Sally and Lueger walked slowly down Twelfth Street. Lueger had his arm around Sally's waist. "That was a very fine film tonight," he was saying. "I enjoy Deanna Durbin. Very young, fresh, sweet. Like you." He grinned at Sally in the dark and held tighter to her waist. "A small young maid. You are just the kind I like." When he tried to kiss her, Sally turned her head away.

"Let's walk fast," she said, watching Charlie and Slater move out from the "L" shadow. "Let's not waste time."

Lueger laughed happily. "That's it. That's the way a girl should talk."

They walked swiftly toward the Elevated, Lueger laughing, his hand on her hip in certainty and possession.

"Pardon me," Slater said. "Could you direct me to Sheridan Square?"

"Well," said Sally, stopping, "it's—"

Charlie swung, and Sally started running as soon as she heard the wooden little noise a fist makes on a man's face. Charlie held Lueger up with one hand and chopped the lolling head with the other. Then he carried Lueger back into the shadows against a high iron fence. He hung Lueger by his overcoat against one of the iron points, so he could use both hands on him. Slater watched for a moment, then turned and looked up at Eighth Avenue.

Charlie worked very methodically, getting his two hundred pounds behind short, accurate, smashing blows that made Lueger's head jump and loll and roll against the iron pikes. Charlie hit him in the nose three times, squarely, using his fist the way a carpenter uses a hammer. Each time Slater heard the sound of bone breaking, cartilage tearing. When Charlie got through with the nose, he went after the mouth, hooking along the side of the jaws with both hands until teeth fell out and the jaw hung open, smashed, loose with the queer looseness of flesh that is no longer moored to solid bone. Charlie started crying, the tears running down into his mouth, the sobs shaking him as he swung his fists. Even then Slater didn't turn around. He just put his hands to his ears and looked steadfastly at Eighth Avenue.

Charlie was talking. "You bastard!" he was saying. "Oh you dumb, mean, skirt-chasing, sonofabitch bastard!" And he kept hitting with fury and deliberation at the shattered face.

A car came up Twelfth Street from the waterfront and slowed down at the corner. Slater jumped on the running board. "Keep moving," he said, very tough, "if you know what's good for you."

Then he jumped off the running board and watched the car speed away.

Charlie, still sobbing, pounded Lueger in the chest and belly. With each blow, Lueger slammed against the iron fence with a noise like a carpet being beaten until his coat ripped off the pike and he slid to the sidewalk. Charlie stood back then, his fists swaying, the sweat running down his face inside his collar, his clothes stained with blood. "O.K.," he said. "O.K., you bastard." He walked swiftly uptown under the "L" in the shadows, and Slater hurried after him.

Much later, in the hospital, Preminger stood over the bed in which Lueger lay unconscious, in splints and bandages.

"Yes," he said to the detective and the doctor, "that's our man. Lueger. A steward. The papers on him are correct."

"Who do you think done it?" the detective asked in a routine voice. "Did he have any enemies?"

"Not that I know of," Preminger said. "He was a very popular boy. Especially with the ladies."

The detective started out of the ward. "Well," he said, "he won't be a very popular boy when he gets out of here."

Preminger shook his head. "You must be very careful in a strange city," he said to the interne, and went back to his ship.

COMMENT

Although the action takes place before World War II, "Sailor off the Bremen" can be included in the war-story category in that it concerns a conflict between two powerful political forces and because the conflict leads to violence. The story has excellent suspense—first in the flashback episode in which we learn what happened to Ernest, then in the working out of the plan for revenge, and then in the carrying out of the revenge. In a story in which there is so much physical violence, and in which the characters act with high emotional intensity, suspense is rather readily created. The careful reader, however, will want to see what the story offers besides enjoyment of suspense, what meaning is attached to the conflict presented. In this story the problem may be put in this fashion: What attitude is the reader to take toward the beat-

ing up of Lueger? The danger here is one that we have seen in other stories—the danger of a purely melodramatic situation in which the reader can simply and wholeheartedly identify himself with an entirely good agent contending with an entirely bad agent.

The story does a number of things which make it easy to adopt Charlie's point of view without question, and to accept him as a simple bringer of justice. Ernest is presented as virtually an innocent victim, whose life has been seriously damaged; the revengers are apparently motivated only by loyal devotion; Lueger is described as evil in more ways than one, and given no saving grace. At first glance, then, the revenge may seem a necessary and even noble-minded retribution.

Perhaps the author was satisfied to leave it at that; if so, we would have to decide that he had not fully explored all the implications of his materials. But there is considerable evidence that we are not to accept the beating of Lueger in the same simple way in which Charlie talks about it and plans it. Before the event Ernest makes a critical judgment of his brother: "He's a football player, he has a football player's philosophy. Somebody knocks you down, you knock him down, everything is fine." Dr. Slater and Charlie himself are hardly presented as happy and glorious conquerors. Dr. Slater is terrified and revolted, and Charlie's sobbing apparently indicates a deep conflict within himself. By means of these elements the story makes a critique of the revenge at the same time that it presents understandingly the feelings which led to the revenge. Finally, the imagery used by the author in describing Charlie's attack on Lueger is such as to make the scene a bestial rather than a triumphant one.

What, then, does the story as a whole say? Is it not stating dramatically that violence is the source of violence, that in times of vast political upheaval forces are released which drive men on despite themselves and lead only to primitive behavior? Is there any evidence in the story that even Ernest, whose mind appears to have a large share in controlling his conduct, is partly mastered by the feelings to which the others are subject?

In view of the very serious issue which has been raised, the ending seems somewhat trivial. We see only the implied satisfaction of Preminger, who has helped stimulate the revenge but who has been entirely outside the suffering of the others. How might Ernest have been used, in a final scene, to pull the story together? Recall, in this connection, that Dr. Slater had worked himself up to the revenge by prophesying that it would be of great psychological value to Ernest.

William March

William Edward March Campbell was born in Alabama in 1894. He began writing didactic poetry and stories when he was scarcely more than a boy. The son of a sawmill operator, he began work in a lumber mill at 14, later took a business course, attended college for a year, and spent some time in the University of Alabama law school. When World War I began he enlisted in the marines, was gassed and severely wounded, and received several decorations. For many years he worked for a steamship company, being stationed for a while at Hamburg and at London. He did not begin writing regularly for publication until the 1930's, when he published several volumes of short stories and several novels. His stories have a wide range, moving between farce on the one hand and serious psychological and moral studies on the other.

Personal Letter

Hamburg, Germany,
December 17th, 1932.

DEAR MR. TYLER:

I wrote you a long, official letter last week and forwarded same via the S.S. *Manhattan.* That letter, which should be in your hands by the time you receive this, contained information you wanted regarding berthing facilities, pilotage in and out, tug hire, stevedoring costs, etc., etc. If I failed to cover any point that you had in mind, or if any part of my report is not detailed enough, please let me know, and I'll remedy the situation promptly.

As you will remember, you also asked me to drop you a line under private cover regarding my personal impression of this country, and that is what I would like to do in this letter. I have thought a good deal about the best way to accomplish this, and have come to the conclusion that the easiest way to do it is to simply recount a little incident which happened the other night in a cafe.

PERSONAL LETTER From *Trial Balance*, copyright, 1945, by William March. Reprinted by permission of Harcourt, Brace and Company, Inc.

First, let me say again that the agents you have in mind for representing us here are very efficient and have co-operated with me at all times. Herr Voelker, director of the agency, has been especially helpful. He is an intelligent and highly educated man. A few nights ago, he asked me to have dinner with him and attend the opera later, which I did. After that, he suggested we take in a beer cafe that he knew of, and so we went there, too. This place was pretty well filled up when we arrived, mostly with men in storm trooper uniforms. I won't explain who they are, as I covered that point in my first letter under the heading of Political Situation and Future Outlook, to which I refer you.

Well, Herr Voelker and I went to the basement bar and ordered our drinks, talking together all the time. We were speaking in English and discussing business matters and things in general, and at first I didn't notice that a group of these storm troopers had closed around us, shutting us off from the others at the bar.

To make a long story short, the leader of the group touched me on the shoulder and told me that I was in Germany now, and that while I was in Germany I would speak German or nothing at all. Most of these North Germans speak English very well indeed, since they have eight years of it in school, and so, naturally, this fellow spoke English, too.

I twisted around and looked these boys over, but they only held their backs stiffer, threw out their chests and frowned, just like something out of the opera I'd just seen. I still couldn't believe I'd heard correctly, and so I said, "Were you speaking to me?" And this leader answered in a voice which trembled with anger, "I repeat for the last time. When you are in Germany, you are to speak German. If you cannot speak German, you are to remain silent. Is that clear? We will endure no further insults from foreigners."

By that time I was sure it was some sort of a gag which Herr Voelker and his boys had cooked up for me. You know the sort of thing I mean, don't you? Like the time at the Traffic Association dinner when they played that joke on Oscar Wilcoxon. If you remember now, a girl with a baby in her arms burst into the dining-room just before the speeches began. She asked if there was a man present named Oscar Wilcoxon, and when the master of ceremonies said that there was, she demanded that he marry her, like he had promised to do, and give a name to his child.

Everybody was in on the stunt except Oscar himself, and it got a lot of laughs. Oscar kept trying to explain that somebody else must have been using his name illegally, because he'd never seen the young lady before in his life; but this girl had been carefully coached in her part, and the more Oscar tried to explain matters, the worse things got. I kept thinking to myself at the time that if anybody pulled a trick like that on me, I'd fall right in with the gag and say yes, I was the father of the baby all right, but I couldn't be sure about the mother because it was always so dark in the alley back of the pickle works where we met.

Well, when the storm trooper said what he did about not speaking English in Germany, I wanted to laugh, it struck me as so comical, but I didn't. I'd already decided to play it their way and pretend to take the whole thing seriously. So I kept a straight face and said, "You gentlemen would like others to believe that you are real Germans, but you are not real Germans at all. If a real German heard what you have just said, he'd cover his face with shame."

I waited a moment and then added, "If you were real Germans, like you pretend to be, you'd realize that since I'm not a German, but an American, that I'm not as bright as you are. You'd know that Americans haven't got your culture, and that we haven't had your natural advantages. Americans think slowly," I said. "They don't master languages the way you do." Then I sighed and turned back to Herr Voelker, as if the subject was ended, as far as I was concerned.

The storm troopers seemed nonplused at my attitude, and they went into a huddle at one end of the bar. My German isn't the best in the world, but I could understand most of what they said without any trouble. The gist of it was that I was right, and that they were wrong; that even though I was a foreigner, I had the true philosophy. Well, I let them talk it over for a while, and then suddenly I wheeled around and gave them the other barrel. "A true German doesn't expect the same perfection from inferior people that he expects from himself," I said. "I thought that was something everybody knew by this time."

I said all this in a quick, stern voice, Mr. Tyler, and the troopers straightened up and stood at attention while I gave them a thorough dressing down. At the end of my speech, I said, "So you see? If you were true Germans, and believed in your mission, you wouldn't humiliate me before my friends. Oh, no, you wouldn't do that at all! Instead, you'd come to me as a teacher and say, 'Let me instruct you in our beautiful language! Let me explain to you our wonderful way of life!'" I waited a moment and then said sadly, "No. No, you are not true Germans. You only pretend to be. And now go away please before I lose the last of my illusions."

I nudged Herr Voelker with my elbow and winked behind my hand, but he only raised his eyes and stared at me over the edge of his glass. By that time there were tears in the eyes of the leader of the troopers. He wanted to buy me a drink, to prove that everything was all right, but I thought I'd keep the thing going a little longer, and played hard to butter up. Finally, I did let him buy me a drink, and then I bought him one in return. I thought, then, that the joke would break, and the laughter and the explanations come, but that didn't happen, and I began to feel a little uneasy.

Not long afterwards, Herr Voelker and I got up to leave. When we were outside, Herr Voelker said he was sorry such an unpleasant incident had occurred, and that he would have prevented it if he had been able to do so. He said he thought I had acted with rare presence of mind in being frank and aboveboard with the storm troopers, instead of trying to lie my way out of the situation. I was so astonished that I stood still on the pavement and said, "Did you think I meant what I said? An intelligent, educated man like yourself? Did you really believe I was in earnest?"

And, before God, Mr. Tyler, Herr Voelker drew himself up haughtily and said, "Why shouldn't I think you meant it? Every point you made was logical and entirely true."

Mr. Tyler, I've often read in books about an icy hand which clutched at somebody-or-other's heart. I never before took the words seriously, thinking it was just a phrase that writers used, but now I know that it's a true expression. That's exactly the way I felt as I walked along with Herr Voelker until we reached the taxi rank on the corner, and I got into a cab alone, and went back to my hotel.

Now, maybe there isn't anything important in the incident, but I think there is. There's something going on beneath the surface here as sure as you're a foot high. I don't quite know what it is so far, but I do know that it's something horrible.

This turned out to be a long letter, didn't it? I suppose you'll be receiving it during the Christmas holidays, so let me take this opportunity of wishing you a happy Christmas and a prosperous New Year. People here celebrate Christmas in a big way. They gather together in groups, sing songs about the Christ child, and weep over the loved ones who are far away. It is the season of love, goodwill, and the renewal of old affections, or so Herr Voelker tells me. He invited me, as a special compliment, to spend the day in the bosom of his own family, so I could see first hand what a German Christmas is really like; but I expressed my regrets, and said that business obligations made it necessary for me to be in Paris on that day. To tell you the truth, Mr. Tyler, everybody here frightens me a little—they are all so full of sentiment and fury.

With best regards, and again wishing you the compliments of the season, I remain,

Sincerely yours,

ROBERT B. McINTOSH.

COMMENT

March's story resembles Shaw's in finding its material in explosive political attitudes that can lead to war. Shaw's story, however, pictures the actual reciprocal violence which is, in effect, war, whereas March is primarily interested in the basic attitudes and in the shock which accompanies recognition of these attitudes. In other ways, too, he organizes his material differently. Instead of presenting a clash between two kinds of political forces, he uses the point of view of a virtually nonpolitical man and lets us feel the discrepancy between his assumptions and the facts which he discovers.

The characterization of Mr. McIntosh bears significantly upon the effect of the story. It is important that he is not a conscious representative of political democracy, who speaks for one form of politics against another and who thus might create a simple melodrama of good and evil. Rather he is a businessman who seems to have no very formal political ideas; he is obviously a trusted, dependable representative of his firm, but at the same time a hard-bitten man of the world who enjoys and can carry through practical jokes. He is not the sort of person, therefore, who is likely to burst into an obvious kind of political oratory. The author does not use denunciation to secure his effect, but relies rather upon the incredulity of the observer to suggest the nature of what is going on.

The reader should notice, too, that this incredulity is in the main expressed dramatically rather than by direct assertion. The storm troopers seem "like something out of the opera" and "comical"; their demands seem exactly like a painfully obvious "gag" at a professional dinner; Mr. McIntosh replies in the same spirit, talking nonsense that seems appropriate; then, in an ironic climax, he finds that he has been taken literally. All this is a way of saying that the experience is a "bad joke." But now, by having Mr. Voelker in the story, the author is able to have a very effective second climax. Why is this second climax more important to the meaning of the story than the first one? What is implied by the fact that Mr. Voelker agrees with the storm troopers? How is Mr. Voelker characterized earlier in the story?

Mr. McIntosh does make several comments in the last three paragraphs. Notice that in the main he uses understatement, not intemperate exclamations: it is as if he were still meditating on what he has seen. Analyze the effect of the paragraph in which he thinks over the cliché "an icy hand." What is the effect of the description of the Christmas celebration? Why does Mr. McIntosh not join the Voelkers for Christmas?

The next to the last sentence of the story contains one phrase which is perhaps too brilliant to be used by Mr. McIntosh—"full of sentiment and fury." This phrase is paradoxical in that it contains an implied contradiction; a paradox compels the reader to think through the relationship of the apparently inconsistent terms. Would this phrase seem to be equally applicable to the situations described in the stories by Kay Boyle and Irwin Shaw? If this is true, may we not feel that the phrase is a very good one to describe an explosive situation, whatever the nation? Such a conclusion would permit us to regard Mr. McIntosh's story as being, not merely a record of an old historical situation, but a very economical account of a universal pattern of disorder.

Katherine Anne Porter

Born in Texas in 1894, Katherine Anne Porter has traveled widely; she has lived in various European countries, in Bermuda, in Mexico, and in different parts of the United States. In recent years she has done a tour of duty in Hollywood. Perhaps this constant movement suggests that she inherits some of the traits of the ancestor from whom she is directly descended, Daniel Boone. In the course of her travels she has supported herself by all sorts of journalistic work. She has been writing short stories for many years but has published a relatively small number of them; she is a meticulous craftsman and has thrown away more pages than she has sent to the printer. The scenes of her stories are varied, but for materials she returns frequently to Mexico and to Texas and Louisiana, where she spent her childhood. *Flowering Judas, The Leaning Tower,* and *Pale Horse, Pale Rider* are her best-known volumes.

Flowering Judas

BRAGGIONI sits heaped upon the edge of a straight-backed chair much too small for him, and sings to Laura in a furry, mournful voice. Laura has begun to find reasons for avoiding her own house until the latest possible moment, for Braggioni is there almost every night. No matter how late she is, he will be sitting there with a surly, waiting expression, pulling at his kinky yellow hair, thumbing the strings of his guitar, snarling a tune under his breath. Lupe the Indian maid meets Laura at the door, and says with a flicker of a glance towards the upper room, "He waits."

Laura wishes to lie down, she is tired of her hairpins and the feel of her long tight sleeves, but she says to him, "Have you a new song for me this evening?" If he says yes, she asks him to sing it. If he says no, she remembers his favorite one, and asks him to sing it again. Lupe brings her a cup of chocolate and a plate of rice,

FLOWERING JUDAS From *Flowering Judas and Other Stories,* copyright, 1930, 1935, by Katherine Anne Porter. Reprinted by permission of Harcourt, Brace and Company, Inc.

and Laura eats at the small table under the lamp, first inviting Braggioni, whose answer is always the same: "I have eaten, and besides, chocolate thickens the voice."

Laura says, "Sing, then," and Braggioni heaves himself into song. He scratches the guitar familiarly as though it were a pet animal, and sings passionately off key, taking the high notes in a prolonged painful squeal. Laura, who haunts the markets listening to the ballad singers, and stops every day to hear the blind boy playing his reed-flute in Sixteenth of September Street, listens to Braggioni with pitiless courtesy, because she dares not smile at his miserable performance. Nobody dares to smile at him. Braggioni is cruel to everyone, with a kind of specialized insolence, but he is so vain of his talents, and so sensitive to slights, it would require a cruelty and vanity greater than his own to lay a finger on the vast cureless wound of his self-esteem. It would require courage, too, for it is dangerous to offend him, and nobody has this courage.

Braggioni loves himself with such tenderness and amplitude and eternal charity that his followers—for he is a leader of men, a skilled revolutionist, and his skin has been punctured in honorable warfare—warm themselves in the reflected glow, and say to each other: "He has a real nobility, a love of humanity raised above mere personal affections." The excess of this self-love has flowed out, inconveniently for her, over Laura, who, with so many others, owes her comfortable situation and her salary to him. When he is in a very good humor, he tells her, "I am tempted to forgive you for being a *gringa. Gringita!*" and Laura, burning, imagines herself leaning forward suddenly, and with a sound back-handed slap wiping the suety smile from his face. If he notices her eyes at these moments he gives no sign.

She knows what Braggioni would offer her, and she must resist tenaciously without appearing to resist, and if she could avoid it she would not admit even to herself the slow drift of his intention. During these long evenings which have spoiled a long month for her, she sits in her deep chair with an open book on her knees, resting her eyes on the consoling rigidity of the printed page when the sight and sound of Braggioni singing threaten to identify themselves with all her remembered afflictions and to add their weight to her uneasy premonitions of the future. The gluttonous bulk of Braggioni has become a symbol of her many disillusions, for a revolutionist should be lean, animated by heroic faith, a vessel of abstract virtues. This is nonsense, she knows it now and is ashamed of it. Revolution must have leaders, and leadership is a career for energetic men. She is, her comrades tell her, full of romantic error, for what she defines as cynicism in them is merely "a developed sense of reality." She is almost too willing to say, "I am wrong, I suppose I don't really understand the principles," and afterward she makes a secret truce with herself, determined not to surrender her will to such expedient logic. But she cannot help feeling that she has been betrayed irreparably by the disunion between her way of living and her feeling of what life should be, and at times she is almost contented to rest in this sense of grievance as a private store of consolation. Sometimes she wishes to run away, but she stays. Now she longs to fly out of this room, down the narrow stairs, and into the street where the houses lean together like conspirators under a single mottled lamp, and leave Braggioni singing to himself.

Instead she looks at Braggioni, frankly and clearly, like a good child who understands the rules of behavior. Her knees cling together under sound blue serge, and her round white collar is not purposely nun-like. She wears the uniform of an idea, and has renounced vanities. She was born Roman Catholic, and in spite of her fear of being seen by someone who might make a scandal of it, she slips now and again into some crumbling little church, kneels on the chilly stone, and says a Hail Mary on the gold rosary she bought in Tehuantepec. It is no good and she ends by examining the altar with its tinsel flowers and ragged brocades, and feels tender about the battered doll-shape of some male saint whose white, lace-trimmed drawers hang limply around his ankles below the hieratic dignity of his velvet robe. She has encased herself in a set of principles derived from her early training, leaving no detail of gesture or of personal taste untouched, and for this reason she will not wear lace made on machines. This is her private heresy, for in her special group the machine is sacred, and will be the salvation of the workers. She loves fine lace, and there is a tiny edge of fluted cobweb on this collar, which is one of twenty precisely alike, folded in blue tissue paper in the upper drawer of her clothes chest.

Braggioni catches her glance solidly as if he had been waiting for it, leans forward, balancing his paunch between his spread knees, and sings with tremendous emphasis, weighing his words. He has, the song relates, no father and no mother, nor even a friend to console him; lonely as a wave of the sea he comes and goes, lonely as a wave. His mouth opens round and yearns side-ways, his balloon cheeks grow oily with the labor of song. He bulges marvelously in his expensive garments. Over his lavender collar, crushed upon a purple necktie, held by a diamond hoop: over his ammunition belt of tooled leather worked in silver, buckled cruelly around his gasping middle: over the tops of his glossy yellow shoes Braggioni swells with ominous ripeness, his mauve silk hose stretched taut, his ankles bound with the stout leather thongs of his shoes.

When he stretches his eyelids at Laura she notes again that his eyes are the true tawny yellow cat's eyes. He is rich, not in money, he tells her, but in power, and this power brings with it the blameless ownership of things, and the right to indulge his love of small luxuries. "I have a taste for the elegant refinements," he said once, flourishing a yellow silk handkerchief before her nose. "Smell that? It is Jockey Club, imported from New York." Nonetheless he is wounded by life. He will say so presently. "It is true everything turns to dust in the hand, to gall on the tongue." He sighs and his leather belt creaks like a saddle girth. "I am disappointed in everything as it comes. Everything." He shakes his head. "You, poor thing, you will be disappointed too. You are born for it. We are more alike than you realize in some things. Wait and see. Some day you will remember what I have told you, you will know that Braggioni was your friend."

Laura feels a slow chill, a purely physical sense of danger, a warning in her blood that violence, mutilation, a shocking death, wait for her with lessening patience. She has translated this fear into something homely, immediate, and sometimes hesitates before crossing the street. "My personal fate is nothing, except as the testimony of a mental attitude," she reminds herself, quoting from some forgotten philosophic primer, and is sensible enough to add, "Anyhow, I shall not be killed by an automobile if I can help it."

"It may be true I am as corrupt, in another way, as Braggioni," she thinks in spite of herself, "as callous, as incomplete," and if this is so, any kind of death seems preferable. Still she sits quietly, she does not run. Where could she go? Uninvited she has promised herself to this place; she can no longer imagine herself as living in another country, and there is no pleasure in remembering her life before she came here.

Precisely what is the nature of this devotion, its true motives, and what are its obligations? Laura cannot say. She spends part of her days in Xochimilco, near by, teaching Indian children to say in English, "The cat is on the mat." When she appears in the classroom they crowd about her with smiles on their wise, innocent, clay-colored faces, crying, "Good morning, my titcher!" in immaculate voices, and they make of her desk a fresh garden of flowers every day.

During her leisure she goes to union meetings and listens to busy important voices quarreling over tactics, methods, internal politics. She visits the prisoners of her own political faith in their cells, where they entertain themselves with counting cockroaches, repenting of their indiscretions, composing their memoirs, writing out manifestoes and plans for their comrades who are still walking about free, hands in pockets, sniffing fresh air. Laura brings them food and cigarettes and a little money, and she brings messages disguised in equivocal phrases from the men outside who dare not set foot in the prison for fear of disappearing into the cells kept empty for them. If the prisoners confuse night and day, and complain, "Dear little Laura, time doesn't pass in this infernal hole, and I won't know when it is time to sleep unless I have a reminder," she brings them their favorite narcotics, and says in a tone that does not wound them with pity, "Tonight will really be night for you," and though her Spanish amuses them, they find her comforting, useful. If they lose patience and all faith, and curse the slowness of their friends in coming to their rescue with money and influence, they trust her not to repeat everything, and if she inquires, "Where do you think we can find money, or influence?" they are certain to answer, "Well, there is Braggioni, why doesn't he do something?"

She smuggles letters from headquarters to men hiding from firing squads in back streets in mildewed houses, where they sit in tumbled beds and talk bitterly as if all Mexico were at their heels, when Laura knows positively they might appear at the band concert in the Alameda on Sunday morning, and no one would notice them. But Braggioni says, "Let them sweat a little. The next time they may be careful. It is very restful to have them out of the way for a while." She is not afraid to knock on any door in any street after midnight, and enter in the darkness, and say to one of these men who is really in danger: "They will be looking for you—seriously—tomorrow morning after six. Here is some money from Vicente. Go to Vera Cruz and wait."

She borrows money from the Roumanian agitator to give to his bitter enemy the Polish agitator. The favor of Braggioni is their disputed territory, and Braggioni holds the balance nicely, for he can use them both. The Polish agitator talks love to her over café tables, hoping to exploit what he believes is her secret sentimental preference for him, and he gives her misinformation which he begs her to repeat as the solemn truth to certain persons. The Roumanian is more adroit. He is generous with his money in all good causes, and lies to her with an air of ingenuous candor, as if he were her good friend and confidant. She never repeats anything they may say. Braggioni never asks questions. He has other ways to discover all that he wishes to know about them.

Nobody touches her, but all praise her gray eyes, and the soft, round under lip which promises gayety, yet is always grave, nearly always firmly closed: and they cannot understand why she is in Mexico. She walks back and forth on her errands, with puzzled eyebrows, carrying her little folder of drawings and music and school papers. No dancer dances more beautifully than Laura walks, and she inspires some amusing, unexpected ardors, which cause little gossip, because nothing comes of them. A young captain who had been a soldier in Zapata's army attempted, during a horseback ride near Cuernavaca, to express his desire for her with the noble simplicity befitting a rude folk-hero: but gently, because he was gentle. This gentleness was his defeat, for when he alighted, and removed her foot from the stirrup, and essayed to draw her down into his arms, her horse, ordinarily a tame one, shied fiercely, reared and plunged away. The young hero's horse careered blindly after his stable-mate, and the hero did not return to the hotel until rather late that evening. At breakfast he came to her table in full charro dress, gray buckskin jacket and trousers with strings of silver buttons down the leg, and he was in a humorous, careless mood. "May I sit with you?" and "You are a wonderful rider. I was terrified that you might be thrown and dragged. I should never have forgiven myself. But I cannot admire you enough for your riding!"

"I learned to ride in Arizona," said Laura.

"If you will ride with me again this morning, I promise you a horse that will not shy with you," he said. But Laura remembered that she must return to Mexico City at noon.

Next morning the children made a celebration and spent their playtime writing on the blackboard, "We lov ar ticher," and with tinted chalks they drew wreaths of flowers around the words. The young hero wrote her a letter: "I am a very foolish, wasteful, impulsive man. I should have first said I love you, and then you would not have run away. But you shall see me again." Laura thought, "I must send him a box of colored crayons," but she was trying to forgive herself for having spurred her horse at the wrong moment.

A brown, shock-haired youth came and stood in her patio one night and sang like a lost soul for two hours, but Laura could think of nothing to do about it. The moonlight spread a wash of gauzy silver over the clear spaces of the garden, and the shadows were cobalt blue. The scarlet blossoms of the Judas tree were dull purple, and the names of the colors repeated themselves automatically in her mind, while she watched not the boy, but his shadow, fallen like a dark garment across the fountain rim, trailing in the water. Lupe came silently and whispered expert counsel in her ear: "If you will throw him one little flower, he will sing another song or two and go away." Laura threw the flower, and he sang a last song and went away with the flower tucked in the band of his hat. Lupe said, "He is one of the organizers of the Typographers Union, and before that he sold corridos in the Merced market, and before that, he came from Guanajuato, where I was born. I would not trust any man, but I trust least those from Guanajuato."

She did not tell Laura that he would be back again the next night, and the next, nor that he would follow her at a certain fixed distance around the Merced market, through the Zócolo, up Francisco I. Madero Avenue, and so along the Paseo de la Reforma to Chapultepec Park, and into the Philosopher's Footpath, still with that flower withering in his hat, and an indivisible attention in his eyes.

Now Laura is accustomed to him, it means nothing except that he is nineteen years old and is observing a convention with all propriety, as though it were founded on a law of nature, which in the end it might well prove to be. He is beginning to write poems which he prints on a wooden press, and he leaves them stuck like handbills in her door. She is pleasantly disturbed by the abstract, unhurried watchfulness of his black eyes which will in time turn easily towards another object. She tells herself that throwing the flower was a mistake, for she is twenty-two years old and knows better; but she refuses to regret it, and persuades herself that her negation of all external events as they occur is a sign that she is gradually perfecting herself in the stoicism she strives to cultivate against that disaster she fears, though she cannot name it.

She is not at home in the world. Every day she teaches children who remain strangers to her, though she loves their tender round hands and their charming opportunist savagery. She knocks at unfamiliar doors not knowing whether a friend or a stranger shall answer, and even if a known face emerges from the sour gloom of that unknown interior, still it is the face of a stranger. No matter what this stranger says to her, nor what her message to him, the very cells of her flesh reject knowledge and kinship in one monotonous word. No. No. No. She draws her strength from this one holy talismanic word which does not suffer her to be led into evil. Denying everything, she may walk anywhere in safety, she looks at everything without amazement.

No, repeats this firm unchanging voice of her blood; and she looks at Braggioni without amazement. He is a great man, he wishes to impress this simple girl who covers her great round breasts with thick dark cloth, and who hides long, invaluably beautiful legs under a heavy skirt. She is almost thin except for the incomprehensible fullness of her breasts, like a nursing mother's, and Braggioni, who considers himself a judge of women, speculates again on the puzzle of her notorious virginity, and takes the liberty of speech which she permits without a sign of modesty, indeed, without any sort of sign, which is disconcerting.

"You think you are so cold, *gringita!* Wait and see. You will surprise yourself some day! May I be there to advise you!" He stretches his eyelids at her, and his ill-humored cat's eyes waver in a separate glance for the two points of light marking the opposite ends of a smoothly drawn path between the swollen curve of her breasts. He is not put off by that blue serge, nor by her resolutely fixed gaze. There is all the time in the world. His cheeks are bellying with the wind of song. "O girl with the dark eyes," he sings, and reconsiders. "But yours are not dark. I can change all that. O girl with the green eyes, you have stolen my heart away!" Then his mind wanders to the song, and Laura feels the weight of his attention being shifted elsewhere. Singing thus, he seems harmless, he is quite harmless, there is nothing to do but sit patiently and say "No," when the moment comes. She draws a full breath, and her mind wanders also, but not far. She dares not wander too far.

Not for nothing has Braggioni taken pains to be a good revolutionist and a professional lover of humanity. He will never die of it. He has the malice, the cleverness, the wickedness, the sharpness of wit, the hardness of heart, stipulated for loving the world profitably. *He will never die of it.* He will live to see himself kicked out from his feeding trough by other hungry world-saviors. Traditionally he must sing in spite of his life which drives him to bloodshed, he tells Laura, for his father was a Tuscany peasant who drifted to Yucatan and married a Maya woman: a woman of race, an aristocrat. They gave him the love and knowledge of music, thus: and under the rip of this thumbnail, the strings of the instrument complain like exposed nerves.

Once he was called Delgadito by all the girls and married women who ran after him; he was so scrawny all his bones showed under his thin cotton clothing, and he could squeeze his emptiness to the very backbone with his two hands. He was a poet and the revolution was only a dream then; too many women loved him and sapped away his youth, and he could never find enough to eat anywhere, anywhere! Now he is a leader of men, crafty men who whisper in his ear, hungry men who wait for hours outside his office for a word with him, emaciated men with wild faces who waylay him at the street gate with a timid, "Comrade, let me tell you . . ." and they blow the foul breath from their empty stomachs in his face.

He is always sympathetic. He gives them handfuls of small coins from his own pocket, he promises them work, there will be demonstrations, they must join the unions and attend the meetings, above all they must be on the watch for spies. They are closer to him than his own brothers, without them he can do nothing—until tomorrow, comrade!

Until tomorrow. "They are stupid, they are lazy, they are treacherous, they would cut my throat for nothing," he says to Laura. He has good food and abundant drink, he hires an automobile and drives in the Paseo on Sunday morning, and enjoys plenty of sleep in a soft bed beside a wife who dares not disturb him; and he sits pampering his bones in easy billows of fat, singing to Laura, who knows and thinks these things about him. When he was fifteen, he tried to drown himself because he loved a girl, his first love, and she laughed at him. "A thousand women have paid for that," and his tight little mouth turns down at the corners. Now he perfumes his hair with Jockey Club, and confides to Laura: "One woman is really as good as another for me, in the dark. I prefer them all."

His wife organizes unions among the girls in the cigarette factories, and walks in picket lines, and even speaks at meetings in the evening. But she cannot be brought to acknowledge the benefits of true liberty. "I tell her I must have my freedom, net. She does not understand my point of view." Laura has heard this many times. Braggioni scratches the guitar and meditates. "She is an instinctively virtuous woman, pure gold, no doubt of that. If she were not, I should lock her up, and she knows it."

His wife, who works so hard for the good of the factory girls, employs part of her leisure lying on the floor weeping because there are so many women in the world, and only one husband for her, and she never knows where nor when to look for him. He told her: "Unless you can learn to cry when I am not here, I must go away for good." That day he went away and took a room at the Hotel Madrid.

It is this month of separation for the sake of higher principles that has been spoiled not only for Mrs. Braggioni, whose sense of reality is beyond criticism, but for Laura, who feels herself bogged in a nightmare. Tonight Laura envies Mrs. Braggioni, who is alone, and free to weep as much as she pleases about a concrete wrong. Laura has just come from a visit to the prison, and she is waiting for tomorrow with a bitter anxiety as if tomorrow may not come, but time may be caught immovably in this hour, with herself transfixed, Braggioni singing on forever, and Eugenio's body not yet discovered by the guard.

Braggioni says: "Are you going to sleep?" Almost before she can shake her head, he begins telling her about the May-day disturbances coming on in Morelia, for the Catholics hold a festival in honor of the Blessed Virgin, and the Socialists celebrate their martyrs on that day. "There will be two independent processions, starting from either end of town, and they will march until they meet, and the rest depends . . ." He asks her to oil and load his pistols. Standing up, he unbuckles his ammunition belt, and spreads it laden across her knees. Laura sits with the shells slipping through the cleaning cloth dipped in oil, and he says again he cannot understand why she works so hard for the revolutionary idea unless she loves some man who is in it. "Are you not in love with some-one?" "No," says Laura. "And no one is in love with you?" "No." "Then it is your own fault. No woman need go begging. Why, what is the matter with you? The legless beggar woman in the Alameda has a perfectly faithful lover. Did you know that?"

Laura peers down the pistol barrel and says nothing, but a long, slow faintness rises and subsides in her; Braggioni curves his swollen fingers around the throat of the guitar and softly smothers the music out of it, and when she hears him again he seems to have forgotten her, and is speaking in the hypnotic voice he uses when talking in small rooms to a listening, close-gathered crowd. Some day this world, now seemingly so composed and eternal, to the edges of every sea shall be merely a tangle of gaping trenches, of crashing walls and broken bodies. Everything must be torn from its accustomed place where it has rotted for centuries, hurled sky-ward and distributed, cast down again clean as rain, without sep-arate identity. Nothing shall survive that the stiffened hands of poverty have created for the rich and no one shall be left alive except the elect spirits destined to procreate a new world cleansed of cruelty and injustice, ruled by benevolent anarchy: "Pistols are good, I love them, cannon are even better, but in the end I pin my faith to good dynamite," he concludes, and strokes the pistol lying in her hands. "Once I dreamed of destroying this city, in case it offered resistance to General Ortíz, but it fell into his hands like an overripe pear."

He is made restless by his own words, rises and stands waiting. Laura holds up the belt to him: "Put that on, and go kill some-body in Morelia, and you will be happier," she says softly. The presence of death in the room makes her bold. "Today, I found Eugenio going into a stupor. He refused to allow me to call the prison doctor. He had taken all the tablets I brought him yesterday. He said he took them because he was bored."

"He is a fool, and his death is his own business," says Braggioni, fastening his belt carefully.

"I told him if he had waited only a little while longer, you would have got him set free," says Laura. "He said he did not want to wait."

"He is a fool and we are well rid of him," says Braggioni, reaching for his hat.

He goes away. Laura knows his mood has changed, she will not see him any more for a while. He will send word when he needs her to go on errands into strange streets, to speak to the strange faces that will appear, like clay masks with the power of human speech, to mutter their thanks to Braggioni for his help. Now she is free, and she thinks, I must run while there is time. But she does not go.

Braggioni enters his own house where for a month his wife has spent many hours every night weeping and tangling her hair upon her pillow. She is weeping now, and she weeps more at the sight of him, the cause of all her sorrows. He looks about the room. Nothing is changed, the smells are good and familiar, he is well acquainted with the woman who comes toward him with no reproach except grief on her face. He says to her tenderly: "You are so good, please don't cry any more, you dear good creature." She says, "Are you tired, my angel? Sit here and I will wash your feet." She brings a bowl of water, and kneeling, unlaces his shoes, and when from her knees she raises her sad eyes under her blackened lids, he is sorry for everything, and bursts into tears. "Ah, yes, I am hungry, I am tired, let us eat something together," he says, between sobs. His wife leans her head on his arm and says, "Forgive me!" and this time he is refreshed by the solemn, endless rain of her tears.

Laura takes off her serge dress and puts on a white linen nightgown and goes to bed. She turns her head a little to one side, and lying still, reminds herself that it is time to sleep. Numbers tick in her brain like little clocks, soundless doors close of themselves around her. If you would sleep, you must not remember anything, the children will say tomorrow, good morning, my teacher, the poor prisoners who come every day bringing flowers to their jailor.

1-2-3-4-5—it is monstrous to confuse love with revolution, night with day, life with death—ah, Eugenio!

The tolling of the midnight bell is a signal, but what does it mean? Get up, Laura, and follow me: come out of your sleep, out of your bed, out of this strange house. What are you doing in this house? Without a word, without fear she rose and reached for Eugenio's hand, but he eluded her with a sharp, sly smile and drifted away. This is not all, you shall see—Murderer, he said, follow me, I will show you a new country, but it is far away and we must hurry. No, said Laura, not unless you take my hand, no; and she clung first to the stair rail, and then to the topmost branch of the Judas tree that bent down slowly and set her upon the earth, and then to the rocky ledge of a cliff, and then to the jagged wave of a sea that was not water but a desert of crumbling stone. Where are you taking me, she asked in wonder but without fear. To death, and it is a long way off, and we must hurry, said Eugenio. No, said Laura, not unless you take my hand. Then eat these flowers, poor prisoner, said Eugenio in a voice of pity, take and eat: and from the Judas tree he stripped the warm bleeding flowers, and held them to her lips. She saw that his hand was fleshless, a cluster of small white petrified branches, and his eye sockets were without light, but she ate the flowers greedily for they satisfied both hunger and thirst. Murderer! said Eugenio, and Cannibal! This is my body and my blood. Laura cried No! and at the sound of her own voice, she awoke trembling, and was afraid to sleep again.

COMMENT

Like the three preceding writers, Miss Porter uses political raw materials, but she makes a far more elaborate use of them. The other writers really abstract the political from the whole of life, but Miss Porter actually emphasizes the way in which the political and the other aspects of life become enmeshed. We see Braggioni as much in his private as in his political life; we have an account of Laura's political work, but we learn also of her teaching, of her religious background, of her differences with her colleagues in political work, of her relations with various men. In a sense, her political life is left vague; her party is not named. The author uses a general phrase, "prisoners of her own political faith," as if to eliminate all partisan points of view and thus to present Laura's situation as one possible to a follower of any political creed. Indeed, we see less of Laura's political emotions than of her ethical concern (she evaluates Braggioni on moral rather than political grounds, and she wonders whether she is "as corrupt, as callous, as incomplete" as he) and of her psychological state (her essential withdrawal from the others, her constant undefined fears). All these issues are finally presented in terms of private understanding and conviction: we see almost everything as Laura sees it, remembers it, or reflects upon it. (In Virginia Woolf's "The New Dress," which comes later, the reader will see a still more rigid staying within a woman's mind, and an almost total exclusion of the outer realities which are quite important in this story.)

At one level the story derives its tension from the contrast between a novice who engages in political work idealistically, and an experienced professional politician who, though he seems to be actuated entirely by love of humanity, is a calculating and ruthless leader with little sympathy for followers in trouble. The irony of this contrast is amplified by another more subtle irony: despite his resentment and self-pity and claims of unhappiness, Braggioni feels no serious inner clash, and even his one-sided relationship with his wife seems more or less satisfactory to both; whereas Laura, with her doubts and self-criticisms, is the victim of severe inner conflict. She feels "betrayed irreparably by the disunion between her way of life and her feeling of what life should be." Aspirations and actuality conflict. She is assiduous in her work, despite the disillusions symbolized by the "gluttonous bulk of Braggioni." She thinks of flight but stays on, as if "bogged in a nightmare." Mexico and all the people remain strange, yet she apparently has nowhere else to go.

Here there is much more than the political; in Laura's experiences there is really dramatized a very general conflict between the ideal and the actual. Now the ideal is very likely to become intangible and abstract and therefore not real at all, which the author must avoid above all things. In giving a concrete form to the ideal, Miss Porter uses a very interesting device, to identify which we must read the text very closely; she borrows a number of very suggestive images and terms from religion. Although Laura can no longer find satisfaction in the practices of the Church, her dress is "nun-like"; her present life is a "devotion" with certain "obligations"; most important, she is said to be "not at home in the world," the phrase "the world" being a traditional one to denote the worldly as opposed to the spiritual life. Her reiterated "No. No. No." is again in effect a religious rejection of the secular world. The reader who is interested will find other examples of this subtle but persistent pattern of language which has a strong influence on the meaning of the story.

It is such passages as these, as well as the earlier introduction of the Judas tree (so called because of the legend that Judas had hanged himself on it), that lead up to the dream which concludes the story. Miss Porter uses the now familiar psychology of dreams to give a final vivid expression to the feelings of Laura that have here, with the disappearance of Braggioni, become the undisputed center of the story. Various elements in the Christian story which have lain dormant in Laura's mind now rise up to give a symbolic expression to the emotions aroused by the political life in which she has been participating. The main theme in her nightmare is betrayal. We need not seek precise allegorical equivalents for all parts of the dream, but it is at least clear that she regards herself as implicated in a great betrayal. What this episode says is, in effect, that her present life is a bad dream. In setting forth her terror in vivid images, the nightmare ends the story very effectively. And since it throws stress upon the private problem of guilt, it shows how far from the bare political starting point the author's methods of development have taken the story.

A further way of seeing how individually Miss Porter has developed her story is to recognize the existence of a relationship between the two main characters which is very familiar in fiction: Laura has to put up with Braggioni's advances because he controls her job. This could easily become the melodramatic conflict of the courageous girl and the unwelcome lover. Note how far the author is from any such organization of her materials.

A recurrent element in the author's style is the paradox: "the vast cureless wound of his self-esteem," "this sense of grievance as a private store of consolation," "ominous ripeness," and other examples which the reader should find. Each such expression should be analyzed carefully. Does the use of a series of paradoxes contribute to the tone or meaning of the story?

Katherine Mansfield

Kathleen Mansfield Beauchamp, the daughter of a banker, was born in New Zealand in 1888. She published her first story at the age of nine. After spending five years at school in England, she found life in New Zealand unhappy, and in 1908 she returned to England to live. Although she had become an excellent cellist while in school, she now substituted a literary for a musical career. Her first collected volume of stories, entitled *In a German Pension,* was published in 1911. In 1912 she began collaborating with John Middleton Murry, the critic, in the editing of several literary magazines. They were married in 1913. Pursued constantly by ill health, she moved to various places in Europe in search of better climate and medical care. She died suddenly in France in 1923. She was a conscientious craftsman who kept striving for greater precision and refinement in the setting forth of her ironic perceptions of human conduct.

Bliss

ALTHOUGH Bertha Young was thirty she still had moments like this when she wanted to run instead of walk, to take dancing steps on and off the pavement, to bowl a hoop, to throw something up in the air and catch it again, or to stand still and laugh at—nothing—at nothing, simply.

What can you do if you are thirty and, turning the corner of your own street, you are overcome, suddenly, by a feeling of bliss —absolute bliss!—as though you'd suddenly swallowed a , bright piece of that late afternoon sun and it burned in your bosom, sending out a little shower of sparks into every particle, into every finger and toe? . . .

Oh, is there no way you can express it without being "drunk and disorderly"? How idiotic civilization is! Why be given a body if you have to keep it shut up in a case like a rare, rare fiddle?

"No, that about the fiddle is not quite what I mean," she thought,

BLISS From *Short Stories of Katherine Mansfield.* Reprinted by permission of Alfred A. Knopf, Inc. Copyright 1920, 1937, by Alfred A. Knopf, Inc.

running up the steps and feeling in her bag for the key—she'd forgotten it, as usual—and rattling the letter-box. "It's not what I mean,
because— Thank you, Mary"—she went into the hall. "Is nurse
back?"

"Yes, M'm."

"And has the fruit come?"

"Yes, M'm. Everything's come."

"Bring the fruit up to the dining-room, will you? I'll arrange it
before I go upstairs."

It was dusky in the dining-room and quite chilly. But all the
same Bertha threw off her coat; she could not bear the tight clasp
of it another moment, and the cold air fell on her arms.

But in her bosom there was still that bright glowing place—that
shower of little sparks coming from it. It was almost unbearable.
She hardly dared to breathe for fear of fanning it higher, and yet
she breathed deeply, deeply. She hardly dared to look into the cold
mirror—but she did look, and it gave her back a woman, radiant,
with smiling, trembling lips, with big, dark eyes and an air of
listening, waiting for something . . . divine to happen . . . that
she knew must happen . . . infallibly.

Mary brought in the fruit on a tray and with it a glass bowl, and
a blue dish, very lovely, with a strange sheen on it as though it
had been dipped in milk.

"Shall I turn on the light, M'm?"

"No, thank you. I can see quite well."

There were tangerines and apples stained with strawberry pink.
Some yellow pears, smooth as silk, some white grapes covered with
a silver bloom and a big cluster of purple ones. These last she had
bought to tone in with the new dining-room carpet. Yes, that did
sound rather far-fetched and absurd, but it was really why she had
bought them. She had thought in the shop: "I must have some
purple ones to bring the carpet up to the table." And it had seemed
quite sense at the time.

When she had finished with them and had made two pyramids
of these bright round shapes, she stood away from the table to get
the effect—and it really was most curious. For the dark table seemed
to melt into the dusky light and the glass dish and the blue bowl
to float in the air. This, of course in her present mood, was so
incredibly beautiful. . . . She began to laugh.

"No, no. I'm getting hysterical." And she seized her bag and coat and ran upstairs to the nursery.

Nurse sat at a low table giving Little B her supper after her bath. The baby had on a white flannel gown and a blue woollen jacket, and her dark, fine hair was brushed up into a funny little peak. She looked up when she saw her mother and began to jump.

"Now, my lovey, eat it up like a good girl," said Nurse, setting her lips in a way that Bertha knew, and that meant she had come into the nursery at another wrong moment.

"Has she been good, Nanny?"

"She's been a little sweet all the afternoon," whispered Nanny. "We went to the park and I sat down on a chair and took her out of the pram and a big dog came along and put its head on my knee and she clutched its ear, tugged it. Oh, you should have seen her."

Bertha wanted to ask if it wasn't rather dangerous to let her clutch at a strange dog's ear. But she did not dare to. She stood watching them, her hands by her side, like the poor little girl in front of the rich little girl with the doll.

The baby looked up at her again, stared, and then smiled so charmingly that Bertha couldn't help crying:

"Oh, Nanny, do let me finish giving her her supper while you put the bath things away."

"Well, M'm, she oughtn't to be changed hands while she's eating," said Nanny, still whispering. "It unsettles her; it's very likely to upset her."

How absurd it was. Why have a baby if it has to be kept—not in a case like a rare, rare fiddle—but in another woman's arms?

"Oh, I must!" said she.

Very offended, Nanny handed her over.

"Now, don't excite her after her supper. You know you do, M'm. And I have such a time with her after!"

Thank heaven! Nanny went out of the room with the bath towels.

"Now I've got you to myself, my little precious," said Bertha, as the baby leaned against her.

She ate delightfully, holding up her lips for the spoon and then waving her hands. Sometimes she wouldn't let the spoon go; and sometimes, just as Bertha had filled it, she waved it away to the four winds.

When the soup was finished Bertha turned round to the fire.

"You're nice—you're very nice!" said she, kissing her warm baby. "I'm fond of you. I like you."

And, indeed, she loved Little B so much—her neck as she bent forward, her exquisite toes as they shone transparent in the firelight—that all her feeling of bliss came back again, and again she didn't know how to express it—what to do with it.

"You're wanted on the telephone," said Nanny, coming back in triumph and seizing *her* Little B.

Down she flew. It was Harry.

"Oh, is that you, Ber? Look here. I'll be late. I'll take a taxi and come along as quickly as I can, but get dinner put back ten minutes —will you? All right?"

"Yes, perfectly. Oh, Harry!"

"Yes?"

What had she to say? She'd nothing to say. She only wanted to get in touch with him for a moment. She couldn't absurdly cry: "Hasn't it been a divine day!"

"What is it?" rapped out the little voice.

"Nothing. *Entendu*," said Bertha, and hung up the receiver, thinking how more than idiotic civilization was.

They had people coming to dinner. The Norman Knights—a very sound couple—he was about to start a theatre, and she was awfully keen on interior decoration, a young man, Eddie Warren, who had just published a little book of poems and whom everybody was asking to dine, and a "find" of Bertha's called Pearl Fulton. What Miss Fulton did, Bertha didn't know. They had met at the club and Bertha had fallen in love with her, as she always did fall in love with beautiful women who had something strange about them.

The provoking thing was that, though they had been about together and met a number of times and really talked, Bertha couldn't yet make her out. Up to a certain point Miss Fulton was rarely, wonderfully frank, but the certain point was there, and beyond that she would not go.

Was there anything beyond it? Harry said "No." Voted her

dullish, and "cold like all blond women, with a touch, perhaps, of anæmia of the brain." But Bertha wouldn't agree with him: not yet, at any rate.

"No, the way she has of sitting with her head a little on one side, and smiling, has something behind it, Harry, and I must find out what that something is."

"Most likely it's a good stomach," answered Harry.

He made a point of catching Bertha's heels with replies of that kind . . . "liver frozen, my dear girl," or "pure flatulence," or "kidney disease,". . . and so on. For some strange reason Bertha liked this, and almost admired it in him very much.

She went into the drawing-room and lighted the fire; then, picking up the cushions, one by one, that Mary had disposed so carefully, she threw them back on to the chairs and the couches. That made all the difference; the room came alive at once. As she was about to throw the last one she surprised herself by suddenly hugging it to her, passionately, passionately. But it did not put out the fire in her bosom. Oh, on the contrary!

The windows of the drawing-room opened on to a balcony overlooking the garden. At the far end, against the wall, there was a tall, slender pear tree in fullest, richest bloom; it stood perfect, as though becalmed against the jade-green sky. Bertha couldn't help feeling, even from this distance, that it had not a single bud or a faded petal. Down below, in the garden beds, the red and yellow tulips, heavy with flowers, seemed to lean upon the dusk. A grey cat, dragging its belly, crept across the lawn, and a black one, its shadow, trailed after. The sight of them, so intent and so quick, gave Bertha a curious shiver.

"What creepy things cats are!" she stammered, and she turned away from the window and began walking up and down. . . .

How strong the jonquils smelled in the warm room. Too strong? Oh, no. And yet, as though overcome, she flung down on a couch and pressed her hands to her eyes.

"I'm too happy—too happy!" she murmured.

And she seemed to see on her eyelids the lovely pear tree with its wide open blossoms as a symbol of her own life.

Really—really—she had everything. She was young. Harry and she were as much in love as ever, and they got on together splendidly and were really good pals. She had an adorable baby. They didn't have to worry about money. They had this absolutely satisfactory house and garden. And friends—modern, thrilling friends, writers and painters and poets or people keen on social questions—just the kind of friends they wanted. And then there were books, and there was music, and she had found a wonderful little dressmaker, and they were going abroad in the summer, and their new cook made the most superb omelettes. . . .

"I'm absurd. Absurd!" She sat up; but she felt quite dizzy, quite drunk. It must have been the spring.

Yes, it was the spring. Now she was so tired she could not drag herself upstairs to dress.

A white dress, a string of jade beads, green shoes and stockings. It wasn't intentional. She had thought of this scheme hours before she stood at the drawing-room window.

Her petals rustled softly into the hall, and she kissed Mrs. Norman Knight, who was taking off the most amusing orange coat with a procession of black monkeys round the hem and up the fronts.

". . . Why! Why! Why is the middle-class so stodgy—so utterly without a sense of humour! My dear, it's only by a fluke that I am here at all—Norman being the protective fluke. For my darling monkeys so upset the train that it rose to a man and simply ate me with its eyes. Didn't laugh—wasn't amused—that I should have loved. No, just stared—and bored me through and through."

"But the cream of it was," said Norman, pressing a large tortoise-shell-rimmed monocle into his eye, "you don't mind me telling this, Face, do you?" (In their home and among their friends they called each other Face and Mug.) "The cream of it was when she, being full fed, turned to the woman beside her and said: 'Haven't you ever seen a monkey before?'"

"Oh, yes!" Mrs. Norman Knight joined in the laughter. "Wasn't that too absolutely creamy?"

And a funnier thing still was that now her coat was off she did look like a very intelligent monkey—who had even made that yellow silk dress out of scraped banana skins. And her amber earrings; they were like little dangling nuts.

"This is a sad, sad fall!" said Mug, pausing in front of Little B's perambulator. "When the perambulator comes into the hall—" and he waved the rest of the quotation away.

The bell rang. It was lean, pale Eddie Warren (as usual) in a state of acute distress.

"It *is* the right house, *isn't* it?" he pleaded.

"Oh, I think so—I hope so," said Bertha brightly.

"I have had such a *dreadful* experience with a taxi-man; he was *most* sinister. I couldn't get him to *stop*. The *more* I knocked and called the *faster* he went. And *in* the moonlight this *bizarre* figure with the *flattened* head *crouching* over the *lit-tle* wheel. . . ."

He shuddered, taking off an immense white silk scarf. Bertha noticed that his socks were white, too—most charming.

"But how dreadful!" she cried.

"Yes, it really was," said Eddie, following her into the drawing-room. "I saw myself *driving* through Eternity in a *timeless* taxi."

He knew the Norman Knights. In fact, he was going to write a play for N. K. when the theatre scheme came off.

"Well, Warren, how's the play?" said Norman Knight, dropping his monocle and giving his eye a moment in which to rise to the surface before it was screwed down again.

And Mrs. Norman Knight: "Oh, Mr. Warren, what happy socks!"

"I *am* so glad you like them," said he, staring at his feet. "They seem to have got so *much* whiter since the moon rose." And he turned his lean sorrowful young face to Bertha. "There *is* a moon, you know."

She wanted to cry: "I am sure there is—often—often!"

He really was a most attractive person. But so was Face, crouched before the fire in her banana skins, and so was Mug, smoking a cigarette and saying as he flicked the ash: "Why doth the bridegroom tarry?"

"There he is, now."

Bang went the front door open and shut. Harry shouted: "Hullo, you people. Down in five minutes." And they heard him swarm up the stairs. Bertha couldn't help smiling; she knew how he loved doing things at high pressure. What, after all, did an extra five minutes matter? But he would pretend to himself that they mattered beyond measure. And then he would make a great point of coming into the drawing-room, extravagantly cool and collected.

Harry had such a zest for life. Oh, how she appreciated it in him. And his passion for fighting—for seeking in everything that came up against him another test of his power and of his courage

—that, too, she understood. Even when it made him just occasionally, to other people, who didn't know him well, a little ridiculous perhaps. . . . For there were moments when he rushed into battle where no battle was. . . . She talked and laughed and positively forgot until he had come in (just as she had imagined) that Pearl Fulton had not turned up.

"I wonder if Miss Fulton has forgotten?"

"I expect so," said Harry. "Is she on the 'phone?"

"Ah! There's a taxi, now." And Bertha smiled with that little air of proprietorship that she always assumed while her women finds were new and mysterious. "She lives in taxis."

"She'll run to fat if she does," said Harry coolly, ringing the bell for dinner. "Frightful danger for blond women."

"Harry—don't," warned Bertha, laughing up at him.

Came another tiny moment, while they waited, laughing and talking, just a trifle too much at their ease, a trifle too unaware. And then Miss Fulton, all in silver, with a silver fillet binding her pale blond hair, came in smiling, her head a little on one side.

"Am I late?"

"No, not at all," said Bertha. "Come along." And she took her arm and they moved into the dining-room.

What was there in the touch of that cool arm that could fan—fan—start blazing—blazing—the fire of bliss that Bertha did not know what to do with?

Miss Fulton did not look at her; but then she seldom did look at people directly. Her heavy eyelids lay upon her eyes and the strange half smile came and went upon her lips as though she lived by listening rather than seeing. But Bertha knew, suddenly, as if the longest, most intimate look had passed between them—as if they had said to each other: "You, too?"—that Pearl Fulton, stirring the beautiful red soup in the grey plate, was feeling just what she was feeling.

And the others? Face and Mug, Eddie and Harry, their spoons rising and falling—dabbing their lips with their napkins, crumbling bread, fiddling with the forks and glasses and talking.

"I met her at the Alpha show—the weirdest little person. She'd not only cut off her hair, but she seemed to have taken a dreadfully good snip off her legs and arms and her neck and her poor little nose as well."

"Isn't she very *liée* with Michael Oat?"

"The man who wrote *Love in False Teeth?*"

"He wants to write a play for me. One act. One man. Decides to commit suicide. Gives all the reasons why he should and why he shouldn't. And just as he has made up his mind either to do it or not to do it—curtain. Not half a bad idea."

"What's he going to call it—'Stomach Trouble'?"

"I *think* I've come across the *same* idea in a lit-tle French review, *quite* unknown in England."

No, they didn't share it. They were dears—dears—and she loved having them there, at her table, and giving them delicious food and wine. In fact, she longed to tell them how delightful they were, and what a decorative group they made, how they seemed to set one another off and how they reminded her of a play by Tchekof!

Harry was enjoying his dinner. It was part of his—well, not his nature, exactly, and certainly not his pose—his—something or other —to talk about food and to glory in his "shameless passion for the white flesh of the lobster" and "the green of pistachio ices—green and cold like the eyelids of Egyptian dancers."

When he looked up at her and said: "Bertha, this is a very admirable *soufflée!*" she almost could have wept with child-like pleasure.

Oh, why did she feel so tender towards the whole world tonight? Everything was good—was right. All that happened seemed to fill again her brimming cup of bliss.

And still, in the back of her mind, there was the pear tree. It would be silver now, in the light of poor dear Eddie's moon, silver as Miss Fulton, who sat there turning a tangerine in her slender fingers that were so pale a light seemed to come from them.

What she simply couldn't make out—what was miraculous—was how she should have guessed Miss Fulton's mood so exactly and so instantly. For she never doubted for a moment that she was right, and yet what had she to go on? Less than nothing.

"I believe this does happen very, very rarely between women. Never between men," thought Bertha. "But while I am making the coffee in the drawing-room perhaps she will 'give a sign.'"

What she meant by that she did not know, and what would happen after that she could not imagine.

While she thought like this she saw herself talking and laughing. She had to talk because of her desire to laugh.

"I must laugh or die."

But when she noticed Face's funny little habit of tucking some-thing down the front of her bodice—as if she kept a tiny, secret hoard of nuts there, too—Bertha had to dig her nails into her hands —so as not to laugh too much.

It was over at last. And: "Come and see my new coffee machine," said Bertha.

"We only have a new coffee machine once a fortnight," said Harry. Face took her arm this time; Miss Fulton bent her head and followed after.

The fire had died down in the drawing-room to a red, flickering "nest of baby phœnixes," said Face.

"Don't turn up the light for a moment. It is so lovely." And down she crouched by the fire again. She was always cold . . . "without her little red flannel jacket, of course," thought Bertha.

At that moment Miss Fulton "gave the sign."

"Have you a garden?" said the cool, sleepy voice.

This was so exquisite on her part that all Bertha could do was to obey. She crossed the room, pulled the curtains apart, and opened those long windows.

"There!" she breathed.

And the two women stood side by side looking at the slender, flowering tree. Although it was so still it seemed, like the flame of a candle, to stretch up, to point, to quiver in the bright air, to grow taller and taller as they gazed—almost to touch the rim of the round, silver moon.

How long did they stand there? Both, as it were, caught in that circle of unearthly light, understanding each other perfectly, crea-tures of another world, and wondering what they were to do in this one with all this blissful treasure that burned in their bosoms and dropped, in silver flowers, from their hair and hands?

For ever—for a moment? And did Miss Fulton murmur: "Yes. Just *that.*" Or did Bertha dream it?

Then the light was snapped on and Face made the coffee and Harry said: "My dear Mrs. Knight, don't ask me about my baby. I never see her. I shan't feel the slightest interest in her until she has a lover," and Mug took his eye out of the conservatory for a moment and then put it under glass again and Eddie Warren drank his coffee and set down the cup with a face of anguish as though he had drunk and seen the spider.

"What I want to do is to give the young men a show. I believe London is simply teeming with first-chop, unwritten plays. What I want to say to 'em is: 'Here's the theatre. Fire ahead.'"

"You know, my dear, I am going to decorate a room for the Jacob Nathans. Oh, I am so tempted to do a fried-fish scheme, with the backs of the chairs shaped like frying pans and lovely chip potatoes embroidered all over the curtains."

"The trouble with our young writing men is that they are still too romantic. You can't put out to sea without being seasick and wanting a basin. Well, why won't they have the courage of those basins?"

"A *dreadful* poem about a *girl* who was *violated* by a beggar *without* a nose in a lit-tle wood. . . ."

Miss Fulton sank into the lowest, deepest chair and Harry handed round the cigarettes.

From the way he stood in front of her shaking the silver box and saying abruptly: "Egyptian? Turkish? Virginian? They're all mixed up," Bertha realized that she not only bored him; he really disliked her. And she decided from the way Miss Fulton said: "No, thank you, I won't smoke," that she felt it, too, and was hurt.

"Oh, Harry, don't dislike her. You are quite wrong about her. She's wonderful, wonderful. And, besides, how can you feel so differently about someone who means so much to me. I shall try to tell you when we are in bed tonight what has been happening. What she and I have shared."

At those last words something strange and almost terrifying darted into Bertha's mind. And this something blind and smiling whispered to her: "Soon these people will go. The house will be quiet—quiet. The lights will be out. And you and he will be alone together in the dark room—the warm bed. . . ."

She jumped up from her chair and ran over to the piano.

"What a pity someone does not play!" she cried. "What a pity somebody does not play."

For the first time in her life Bertha Young desired her husband.

Oh, she'd loved him—she'd been in love with him, of course, in every other way, but just not in that way. And, equally, of course, she'd understood that he was different. They'd discussed it so often. It had worried her dreadfully at first to find that she was so cold, but after a time it had not seemed to matter. They were so frank with each other—such good pals. That was the best of being modern.

But now—ardently! ardently! The word ached in her ardent body! Was this what that feeling of bliss had been leading up to? But then—then—

"My dear," said Mrs. Norman Knight, "you know our shame. We are the victims of time and train. We live in Hampstead. It's been so nice."

"I'll come with you into the hall," said Bertha. "I loved having you. But you must not miss the last train. That's so awful, isn't it?"

"Have a whisky, Knight, before you go?" called Harry.

"No, thanks, old chap."

Bertha squeezed his hand for that as she shook it.

"Good night, good-bye," she cried from the top step, feeling that this self of hers was taking leave of them for ever.

When she got back into the drawing-room the others were on the move.

". . . Then you can come part of the way in my taxi."

"I shall be so thankful not to have to face another drive alone after my dreadful experience."

"You can get a taxi at the rank just at the end of the street. You won't have to walk more than a few yards."

"That's a comfort. I'll go and put on my coat."

Miss Fulton moved towards the hall and Bertha was following when Harry almost pushed past.

"Let me help you."

Bertha knew that he was repenting his rudeness—she let him go. What a boy he was in some ways—so impulsive—so—simple.

And Eddie and she were left by the fire.

"I wonder if you have seen Bilks' new poem called Table d'Hôte," said Eddie softly. "It's so wonderful. In the last Anthology. Have you got a copy? I'd so like to show it to you. It begins with an incredibly beautiful line: 'Why Must it Always be Tomato Soup?'"

"Yes," said Bertha. And she moved noiselessly to a table opposite the drawing-room door and Eddie glided noiselessly after her. She picked up the little book and gave it to him; they had not made a sound.

While he looked it up she turned her head towards the hall. And she saw . . . Harry with Miss Fulton's coat in his arms and Miss Fulton with her back turned to him and her head bent. He tossed the coat away, put his hands on her shoulders and turned her violently to him. His lips said: "I adore you," and Miss Fulton laid her moonbeam fingers on his cheeks and smiled her sleepy smile. Harry's nostrils quivered; his lips curled back in a hideous grin while he whispered: "Tomorrow," and with her eyelids Miss Fulton said: "Yes."

"Here it is," said Eddie. " 'Why Must it Always be Tomato Soup?' It's so *deeply* true, don't you feel? Tomato soup is so *dreadfully* eternal."

"If you prefer," said Harry's voice, very loud, from the hall, "I can phone you a cab to come to the door."

"Oh, no. It's not necessary," said Miss Fulton, and she came up to Bertha and gave her the slender fingers to hold.

"Good-bye. Thank you so much."

"Good-bye," said Bertha.

Miss Fulton held her hand a moment longer.

"Your lovely pear tree!" she murmured.

And then she was gone, with Eddie following, like the black cat following the grey cat.

"I'll shut up shop," said Harry, extravagantly cool and collected.

"Your lovely pear tree—pear tree—pear tree!"

Bertha simply ran over to the long windows.

"Oh, what is going to happen now?" she cried.

But the pear tree was as lovely as ever and as full of flower and as still.

COMMENT

In one sense William March's "Personal Letter" might be called an atmosphere story, for its main action involves the recording of a certain atmosphere by the letter writer. But the term atmosphere story is applicable to "Bliss" in a far more inclusive sense, for the effect of Miss Mansfield's story depends largely upon the success with which the reader has been made to feel the special mood that has become the total reality of Bertha's day. It is neither ideas nor overt actions which give Bertha her central position; rather it is the particular tone that her life has taken on. There are two main ironies in the story: Bertha's realization that her admired Miss Fulton shares her own unique bliss, and then her discovery that the shared mood has the same origin for each—love for Harry. In terms of the structure of the story, however, we see that the author is not merely basing her effect upon the familiar irony of a husband's infidelity, or even on the less familiar irony that he is carrying on an affair with his wife's latest friend. For Miss Mansfield devotes most of her space to a dramatic portrayal of the tone of Bertha's day. What happens at the end, then, is less a disclosure of a fact than an interruption of her special mood, a dissolving of her own unique experience in her new knowledge. The final events depend upon the careful building-up of a particular tone throughout the story.

The creation of an atmosphere of ecstasy is difficult; if the author depends merely upon abstract assertions, the whole thing will fall flat. Miss Mansfield is always concrete. In the first paragraph Bertha's feelings are shown in terms of her impulses to different kinds of action. In the second paragraph there is the original, startling image—"swallowed a bright piece of that . . . sun and it burned in your bosom." The room is chilly, but she takes off her coat. There is especial excitement in arranging the fruit, in taking the baby from the nurse, in talking to Harry on the phone, in anticipating the guests, in recalling Harry's witticisms about Miss Fulton. After the guests come, the author skillfully contrasts two kinds of atmosphere: there is Bertha's own private excitement, her own sense of wonderful things to come, shown by direct description of her inner remarks, sensations, and imaginings; these parts are balanced against the gay, superficial chatter of the guests, whom we see only externally as social personalities—in Bertha's words, "a decorative group."

The reader should look for other ways in which the atmosphere is produced—for other specific images and actions that objectify feeling. Is the sentence structure of any significance here? What is the effect of a general use of rather short sentences, of breaking sentences up into phrases, of introducing many expressions between dashes?

Does the disclosure of the affair between Harry and Miss Fulton come entirely as a surprise, or has the reader been prepared for it in any way?

Why does the author constantly use italics in the speeches of Eddie Warren?

Why is it appropriate for both women to find a special focus of their feelings in the garden? Does it have any symbolic value?

Bertha consciously finds in the pear tree a symbol of her own life. The meaning of Miss Fulton's admiration of the pear tree is clear enough. But what is the meaning of the final sentence of the story? Does it imply that nothing is changed? Or is it implied that in the face of her shock Bertha can find some support in the tree? Or is there some other meaning?

Aldous Huxley

Aldous Huxley was born in England in 1894, was educated at Eton and Oxford, and spent a number of years writing an exhausting number of reviews, criticism, and other articles for different magazines. A descendant of Thomas Huxley and of Matthew Arnold, he has exhibited the scientific interests of the one and the critical bent of the other; in more recent years his thought has developed new philosophic turns. He has written many volumes of poetry, short stories, essays, and novels. In earlier years he wrote satirical fiction; his *Point Counter Point* of 1928, with its experimental form and well-dramatized ideas, has become a modern classic; his subsequent novels, however, often bow under their philosophical weight. Mr. Huxley has traveled in various parts of the world. In recent years his home has been in California.

The Gioconda Smile

"Miss spence will be down directly, sir."

"Thank you," said Mr. Hutton, without turning round. Janet Spence's parlormaid was so ugly, ugly on purpose, it always seemed to him, malignantly, criminally ugly, that he could not bear to look at her more than was necessary. The door closed. Left to himself, Mr. Hutton got up and began to wander round the room, looking with meditative eyes at the familiar objects it contained.

Photographs of Greek statuary, photographs of the Roman Forum, colored prints of Italian masterpieces, all very safe and well known. Poor, dear Janet, what a prig—what an intellectual snob! Her real taste was illustrated in that water color by the pavement artist, the one she had paid half a crown for (and thirty-five shillings for the frame). How often he had heard her tell the story, how often expatiated on the beauties of that skillful imitation of an oleograph! "A real Artist in the streets," and you could hear the capital A in

Artist as she spoke the words. She made you feel that part of his glory had entered into Janet Spence when she tendered him that half-crown for the copy of the oleograph. She was implying a compliment to her own taste and penetration. A genuine Old Master for half a crown. Poor, dear Janet!

Mr. Hutton came to a pause in front of a small oblong mirror. Stooping a little to get a full view of his face, he passed a white, well-manicured finger over his mustache. It was as curly, as freshly auburn as it had been twenty years ago. His hair still retained its color, and there was no sign of baldness yet—only a certain elevation of the brow. "Shakespearean," thought Mr. Hutton, with a smile, as he surveyed the smooth and polished expanse of his forehead.

Others abide our question, thou art free. . . . Footsteps in the sea . . . Majesty . . . Shakespeare, thou shouldst be living at this hour. No, that was Milton, wasn't it? Milton, the Lady of Christ's. There was no lady about him. He was what the women would call a manly man. That was why they liked him—for the curly auburn mustache and the discreet redolence of tobacco. Mr. Hutton smiled again; he enjoyed making fun of himself. Lady of Christ's? No, no. He was the Christ of Ladies. Very pretty, very pretty. The Christ of Ladies. Mr. Hutton wished there were somebody he could tell the joke to. Poor, dear Janet wouldn't appreciate it, alas!

He straightened himself up, parted his hair, and resumed his peregrination. Damn the Roman Forum; he hated those dreary photographs.

Suddenly he became aware that Janet Spence was in the room, standing near the door. Mr. Hutton started, as though he had been taken in some felonious act. To make these silent and spectral appearances was one of Janet Spence's peculiar talents. Perhaps she had been there all the time, and seen him looking at himself in the mirror. Impossible! But, still, it was disquieting.

"Oh, you gave me such a surprise," said Mr. Hutton, recovering his smile and advancing with outstretched hand to meet her.

Miss Spence was smiling too: her Gioconda smile, he had once called it in a moment of half-ironical flattery. Miss Spence had taken the compliment seriously, and always tried to live up to the Leonardo standard. She smiled on in silence while Mr. Hutton shook hands; that was part of the Gioconda business.

"I hope you're well," said Mr. Hutton. "You look it."

What a queer face she had! That small mouth pursed forward by the Gioconda expression into a little snout with a round hole in the middle, as though for whistling, was like a penholder seen from the front. Above the mouth a well-shaped nose, finely aquiline. Eyes large, lustrous, and dark, with the largeness, luster, and darkness that seem to invite sties and an occasional bloodshot suffusion. They were fine eyes, but unchangingly grave. The penholder might do its Gioconda trick, but the eyes never altered in their earnestness. Above them, a pair of boldly arched, heavily penciled black eyebrows lent a surprising air of power, as of a Roman matron, to the upper portion of the face. Her hair was dark and equally Roman; Agrippina from the brows upward.

"I thought I'd just look in on my way home," Mr. Hutton went on. "Ah, it's good to be back here—" he indicated with a wave of his hand the flowers in the vases, the sunshine and greenery beyond the windows—"it's good to be back in the country after a stuffy day of business in town."

Miss Spence, who had sat down, pointed to a chair at her side.

"No, really, I can't sit down," Mr. Hutton protested. "I must get back to see how poor Emily is. She was rather seedy this morning." He sat down, nevertheless. "It's these wretched liver chills. She's always getting them. Women—" He broke off and coughed, so as to hide the fact that he had uttered. He was about to say that women with weak digestions ought not to marry; but the remark was too cruel, and he didn't really believe it. Janet Spence, moreover, was a believer in eternal flames and spiritual attachments. "She hopes to be well enough," he added, "to see you at luncheon tomorrow. Can you come? Do?" He smiled persuasively. "It's my invitation too, you know."

She dropped her eyes, and Mr. Hutton almost thought that he detected a certain reddening of the cheek. It was a tribute; he stroked his mustache.

"I should like to come if you think Emily's really well enough to have a visitor."

"Of course. You'll do her good. You'll do us both good. In married life three is often better company than two."

"Oh, you're cynical."

Mr. Hutton always had a desire to say "Bow-wow-wow" whenever that last word was spoken. It irritated him more than any other word in the language. But instead of barking he made haste to protest.

"No, no. I'm only speaking a melancholy truth. Reality doesn't always come up to the ideal, you know. But that doesn't make me believe any the less in the ideal. Indeed, I believe in it passionately: the ideal of a matrimony between two people in perfect accord. I think it's realizable. I'm sure it is."

He paused significantly and looked at her with an arch expression. A virgin of thirty-six, but still unwithered; she had her charms. And there was something really rather enigmatic about her. Miss Spence made no reply, but continued to smile. There were times when Mr. Hutton got rather bored with the Gioconda. He stood up.

"I must really be going now. Farewell, mysterious Gioconda." The smile grew intenser, focused itself, as it were, in a narrower snout. Mr. Hutton made a Cinquecento gesture, and kissed her extended hand. It was the first time he had done such a thing; the action seemed not to be resented. "I look forward to tomorrow."

"Do you?"

For answer Mr. Hutton once more kissed her hand, then turned to go. Miss Spence accompanied him to the porch.

"Where's your car?" she asked.

"I left it at the gate of the drive."

"I'll come and see you off."

"No, no." Mr. Hutton was playful, but determined. "You must do no such thing. I simply forbid you."

"But I should like to come," Miss Spence protested, throwing a rapid Gioconda at him.

Mr. Hutton held up his hand. "No," he repeated, and then, with a gesture that was almost the blowing of a kiss, he started to run down the drive, lightly, on his toes, with long, bounding strides like a boy's. He was proud of that run; it was quite marvelously youthful. Still, he was glad the drive was no longer. At the last bend, before passing out of sight of the house, he halted and turned round. Miss Spence was still standing on the steps, smiling her smile. He waved his hand, and this time quite definitely and overtly wafted a kiss in her direction. Then, breaking once more into his magnificent canter, he rounded the last dark promontory of trees. Once out of sight of the house he let his high paces decline to a trot, and finally to a walk. He took out his handkerchief and began wiping his neck inside his collar. What fools, what fools! Had there ever been such an ass as poor, dear Janet Spence? Never, unless it was himself. Decidedly he was the more malignant fool, since he, at least, was aware of his folly and still persisted in it. Why did he persist? Ah, the problem that was himself, the problem that was other people . . .

He had reached the gate. A large, prosperous-looking motor was standing at the side of the road.

"Home, M'Nab." The chauffeur touched his cap. "And stop at the crossroads on the way, as usual," Mr. Hutton added, as he opened the door of the car. "Well?" he said, speaking into the obscurity that lurked within.

"Oh, Teddy Bear, what an age you've been!" It was a fresh and childish voice that spoke the words. There was the faintest hint of Cockney impurity about the vowel sounds.

Mr. Hutton bent his large form and darted into the car with the agility of an animal regaining his burrow.

"Have I?" he said, as he shut the door. The machine began to move. "You must have missed me a lot if you found the time so long." He sat back in the low seat; a cherishing warmth enveloped him.

"Teddy Bear . . ." and with a sigh of contentment a charming little head declined onto Mr. Hutton's shoulder. Ravished, he looked down sideways at the round, babyish face.

"Do you know, Doris, you look like the pictures of Louise de Kerouaille." He passed his fingers through a mass of curly hair.

"Who's Louise de Kera-whatever-it-is?" Doris spoke from remote distances.

"She was, alas! *Fuit*. We shall all be 'was' one of these days. Meanwhile . . ."

Mr. Hutton covered the babyish face with kisses. The car rushed smoothly along. M'Nab's back through the front window was stonily impassive, the back of a statue.

"Your hands," Doris whispered. "Oh, you mustn't touch me. They give me electric shocks."

Mr. Hutton adored her for the virgin imbecility of the words. How late in one's existence one makes the discovery of one's body!

"The electricity isn't in me, it's in you." He kissed her again, whispering her name several times: Doris, Doris, Doris. The scientific appellation of the sea mouse, he was thinking as he kissed the throat she offered him, white and extended like the throat of a victim awaiting the sacrificial knife. The sea mouse was a sausage with iridescent fur: very peculiar. Or was Doris the sea cucumber, which turns itself inside out in moments of alarm? He would really have to go to Naples again, just to see the aquarium. These sea creatures were fabulous, unbelievably fantastic.

"Oh, Teddy Bear!" (More zoology; but he was only a land animal. His poor little jokes!) "Teddy Bear, I'm so happy."

"So am I," said Mr. Hutton. Was it true?

"But I wish I knew if it were right. Tell me, Teddy Bear, is it right or wrong?"

"Ah, my dear, that's just what I've been wondering for the last thirty years."

"Be serious, Teddy Bear. I want to know if this is right; if it's right that I should be here with you and that we should love one another, and that it should give me electric shocks when you touch me."

"Right? Well, it's certainly good that you should have electric shocks rather than sexual repressions. Read Freud; repressions are the devil."

"Oh, you don't help me. Why aren't you ever serious? If only you knew how miserable I am sometimes, thinking it's not right. Perhaps, you know, there is a hell, and all that. I don't know what to do. Sometimes I think I ought to stop loving you."

"But could you?" asked Mr. Hutton, confident in the powers of his seduction and his mustache.

"No, Teddy Bear, you know I couldn't. But I could run away, I could hide from you, I could lock myself up and force myself not to come to you."

"Silly little thing!" He tightened his embrace.

"Oh, dear. I hope it isn't wrong. And there are times when I don't care if it is."

Mr. Hutton was touched. He had a certain protective affection for this little creature. He laid his cheek against her hair and so, interlaced, they sat in silence, while the car, swaying and pitching a little as it hastened along, seemed to draw in the white road and the dusty hedges toward it devouringly.

"Good-by, good-by."

The car moved on, gathered speed, vanished round a curve, and Doris was left standing by the signpost at the crossroads, still dizzy and weak with the languor born of those kisses and the electrical touch of those gentle hands. She had to take a deep breath, to draw herself up deliberately, before she was strong enough to start her homeward walk. She had half a mile in which to invent the necessary lies.

Alone, Mr. Hutton suddenly found himself the prey of an appalling boredom.

Mrs. Hutton was lying on the sofa in her boudoir, playing patience. In spite of the warmth of the July evening a wood fire was burning on the hearth. A black Pomeranian, extenuated by the heat and the fatigues of digestion, slept before the blaze.

"Phew! Isn't it rather hot in here?" Mr. Hutton asked as he entered the room.

"You know I have to keep warm, dear." The voice seemed breaking on the verge of tears. "I get so shivery."

"I hope you're better this evening."

"Not much, I'm afraid."

The conversation stagnated. Mr. Hutton stood leaning his back against the mantelpiece. He looked down at the Pomeranian lying at his feet, and with the toe of his right boot he rolled the little dog over and rubbed its white-flecked chest and belly. The creature lay in an inert ecstasy. Mrs. Hutton continued to play patience. Arrived at an *impasse,* she altered the position of one card, took back another, and went on playing. Her patiences always came out.

"Dr. Libbard thinks I ought to go to Llandrindod Wells this summer."

"Well, go, my dear, go, most certainly."

Mr. Hutton was thinking of the events of the afternoon: how they had driven, Doris and he, up to the hanging wood, had left the car to wait for them under the shade of the trees, and walked together out into the windless sunshine of the chalk down.

"I'm to drink the waters for my liver, and he thinks I ought to have massage and electric treatment, too."

Hat in hand, Doris had stalked four blue butterflies that were dancing together round a scabious flower with a motion that was like the flickering of blue fire. The blue fire burst and scattered into whirling sparks; she had given chase, laughing and shouting like a child.

"I'm sure it will do you good, my dear."

"I was wondering if you'd come with me, dear."

"But you know I'm going to Scotland at the end of the month."

Mrs. Hutton looked up at him entreatingly. "It's the journey," she said. "The thought of it is such a nightmare. I don't know if I can manage it. And you know I can't sleep in hotels. And then there's the luggage and all the worries. I can't go alone."

"But you won't be alone. You'll have your maid with you." He spoke impatiently. The sick woman was usurping the place of the healthy one. He was being dragged back from the memory of the sunlit down and the quick, laughing girl, back to this unhealthy, overheated room and its complaining occupant.

"I don't think I shall be able to go."

"But you must, my dear, if the doctor tells you to. And, besides, a change will do you good."

"I don't think so."

"But Libbard thinks so, and he knows what he's talking about."

"No, I can't face it. I'm too weak. I can't go alone." Mrs. Hutton pulled a handkerchief out of her black-silk bag and put it to her eyes.

"Nonsense, my dear, you must make the effort."

"I had rather be left in peace to die here." She was crying in earnest now.

"O Lord! Now do be reasonable. Listen now, please." Mrs. Hutton only sobbed more violently. "Oh, what is one to do?" He shrugged his shoulders and walked out of the room.

Mr. Hutton was aware that he had not behaved with proper patience; but he could not help it. Very early in his manhood he had discovered that not only did he not feel sympathy for the poor, the weak, the diseased, and deformed; he actually hated them. Once, as an undergraduate, he spent three days at a mission in the East End. He had returned, filled with a profound and ineradicable disgust. Instead of pitying, he loathed the unfortunate. It was not, he knew, a very comely emotion, and he had been ashamed of it at first. In the end he had decided that it was temperamental, inevitable, and had felt no further qualms. Emily had been healthy and beautiful when he married her. He had loved her then. But now—was it his fault that she was like this?

Mr. Hutton dined alone. Food and drink left him more benevolent than he had been before dinner. To make amends for his show of exasperation he went up to his wife's room and offered to read to her. She was touched, gratefully accepted the offer, and Mr. Hutton, who was particularly proud of his accent, suggested a little light reading in French.

"French? I am so fond of French." Mrs. Hutton spoke of the language of Racine as though it were a dish of green peas.

Mr. Hutton ran down to the library and returned with a yellow volume. He began reading. The effort of pronouncing perfectly absorbed his whole attention. But how good his accent was! The fact of its goodness seemed to improve the quality of the novel he was reading.

At the end of fifteen pages an unmistakable sound aroused him. He looked up; Mrs. Hutton had gone to sleep. He sat still for a little while, looking with a dispassionate curiosity at the sleeping face. Once it had been beautiful; once, long ago, the sight of it, the recollection of it, had moved him with an emotion profounder, perhaps, than any he had felt before or since. Now it was lined and cadaverous. The skin was stretched tightly over the cheek-bones, across the bridge of the sharp, birdlike nose. The closed eyes were set in profound bone-rimmed sockets. The lamplight striking on the face from the side emphasized with light and shade its cavities and projections. It was the face of a dead Christ by Morales.

> *Le squelette était invisible*
> *Au temps heureux de l'art païen.*

He shivered a little, and tiptoed out of the room.

On the following day Mrs. Hutton came down to luncheon. She had had some unpleasant palpitations during the night, but she was feeling better now. Besides, she wanted to do honor to her guest. Miss Spence listened to her complaints about Llandrindod Wells, and was loud in sympathy, lavish with advice. Whatever she said was always said with intensity. She leaned forward, aimed, so to speak, like a gun, and fired her words. Bang! the charge in her soul was ignited, the words whizzed forth at the narrow barrel of her mouth. She was a machine gun riddling her hostess with sympathy. Mr. Hutton had undergone similar bombardments, mostly of a literary or philosophic character, bombardments of Maeterlinck, of Mrs. Besant, of Bergson, of William James. Today the missiles were medical. She talked about insomnia, she expatiated on the virtues of harmless drugs and beneficent specialists. Under the bombardment Mrs. Hutton opened out, like a flower in the sun.

Mr. Hutton looked on in silence. The spectacle of Janet Spence evoked in him an unfailing curiosity. He was not romantic enough to imagine that every face masked an interior physiognomy of beauty or strangeness, that every woman's small talk was like a vapor hanging over mysterious gulfs. His wife, for example, and Doris; they were nothing more than what they seemed to be. But with Janet Spence it was somehow different. Here one could be sure that there was some kind of a queer face behind the Gioconda smile and the Roman eyebrows. The only question was: What exactly was there? Mr. Hutton could never quite make out.

"But perhaps you won't have to go to Llandrindod after all," Miss Spence was saying. "If you get well quickly Dr. Libbard will let you off."

"I only hope so. Indeed, I do really feel rather better today."

Mr. Hutton felt ashamed. How much was it his own lack of sympathy that prevented her from feeling well every day? But he comforted himself by reflecting that it was only a case of feeling, not of being better. Sympathy does not mend a diseased liver or a weak heart.

"My dear, I wouldn't eat those red currants if I were you," he said, suddenly solicitous. "You know that Libbard has banned everything with skins and pips."

"But I am so fond of them," Mrs. Hutton protested, "and I feel so well today."

"Don't be a tyrant," said Miss Spence, looking first at him and then at his wife. "Let the poor invalid have what she fancies; it will do her good." She laid her hand on Mrs. Hutton's arm and patted it affectionately two or three times.

"Thank you, my dear." Mrs. Hutton helped herself to the stewed currants.

"Well, don't blame me if they make you ill again."

"Do I ever blame you, dear?"

"You have nothing to blame me for," Mr. Hutton answered playfully. "I am the perfect husband."

They sat in the garden after luncheon. From the island of shade under the old cypress tree they looked out across a flat expanse of lawn, in which the parterres of flowers shone with a metallic brilliance.

Mr. Hutton took a deep breath of the warm and fragrant air. "It's good to be alive," he said.

"Just to be alive," his wife echoed, stretching one pale, knot-jointed hand into the sunlight.

A maid brought the coffee; the silver pots and the little blue cups were set on a folding table near the group of chairs.

"Oh, my medicine!" exclaimed Mrs. Hutton. "Run in and fetch it, Clara, will you? The white bottle on the sideboard."

"I'll go," said Mr. Hutton. "I've got to go and fetch a cigar in any case."

He ran in toward the house. On the threshold he turned round for an instant. The maid was walking back across the lawn. His wife was sitting up in her deck chair, engaged in opening her white parasol. Miss Spence was bending over the table, pouring out the coffee. He passed into the cool obscurity of the house.

"Do you like sugar in your coffee?" Miss Spence inquired.

"Yes, please. Give me rather a lot. I'll drink it after my medicine to take the taste away."

Mrs. Hutton leaned back in her chair, lowering the sunshade over her eyes so as to shut out from her vision the burning sky.

Behind her, Miss Spence was making a delicate clinking among the coffee cups.

"I've given you three large spoonfuls. That ought to take the taste away. And here comes the medicine."

Mr. Hutton had reappeared, carrying a wineglass, half full of a pale liquid.

"It smells delicious," he said, as he handed it to his wife.

"That's only the flavoring." She drank it off at a gulp, shuddered, and made a grimace. "Ugh, it's so nasty. Give me my coffee."

Miss Spence gave her the cup; she sipped at it. "You've made it like syrup. But it's very nice, after that atrocious medicine."

At half-past three Mrs. Hutton complained that she did not feel as well as she had done, and went indoors to lie down. Her husband would have said something about the red currants, but checked himself; the triumph of an "I told you so" was too cheaply won. Instead, he was sympathetic and gave her his arm to the house.

"A rest will do you good," he said. "By the way, I shan't be back till after dinner."

"But why? Where are you going?"

"I promised to go to Johnson's this evening. We have to discuss the war memorial, you know."

"Oh, I wish you weren't going." Mrs. Hutton was almost in tears. "Can't you stay? I don't like being alone in the house."

"But, my dear, I promised, weeks ago." It was a bother having to lie like this. "And now I must get back and look after Miss Spence."

He kissed her on the forehead and went out again into the garden. Miss Spence received him aimed and intense.

"Your wife is dreadfully ill," she fired off at him.

"I thought she cheered up so much when you came."

"That was purely nervous, purely nervous. I was watching her closely. With a heart in that condition and her digestion wrecked— yes, wrecked—anything might happen."

"Libbard doesn't take so gloomy a view of poor Emily's health." Mr. Hutton held open the gate that led from the garden into the drive; Miss Spence's car was standing by the front door.

"Libbard is only a country doctor. You ought to see a specialist."

He could not refrain from laughing. "You have a macabre passion for specialists."

Miss Spence held up her hand in protest. "I am serious. I think poor Emily is in a very bad state. Anything might happen—at any moment."

He handed her into the car and shut the door. The chauffeur started the engine and climbed into his place, ready to drive off.

"Shall I tell him to start?" He had no desire to continue the conversation.

Miss Spence leaned forward and shot a Gioconda in his direction. "Remember, I expect you to come and see me again soon."

Mechanically he grinned, made a polite noise, and, as the car moved forward, waved his hand. He was happy to be alone.

A few minutes afterward Mr. Hutton himself drove away. Doris was waiting at the crossroads. They dined together twenty miles from home, at a roadside hotel. It was one of those bad, expensive meals which are only cooked in country hotels frequented by motorists. It revolted Mr. Hutton, but Doris enjoyed it. She always enjoyed things. Mr. Hutton ordered a not very good brand of champagne. He was wishing he had spent the evening in his library.

When they started homeward Doris was a little tipsy and extremely affectionate. It was very dark inside the car, but looking forward, past the motionless form of M'Nab, they could see a bright and a narrow universe of forms and colors scooped out of the night by the electric head lamps.

It was after eleven when Mr. Hutton reached home. Dr. Libbard met him in the hall. He was a small man with delicate hands and well-formed features that were almost feminine. His brown eyes were large and melancholy. He used to waste a great deal of time sitting at the bedside of his patients, looking sadness through those eyes and talking in a sad, low voice about nothing in particular. His person exhaled a pleasing odor, decidedly antiseptic but at the same time suave and discreetly delicious.

"Libbard?" said Mr. Hutton in surprise. "You here? Is my wife ill?"

"We tried to fetch you earlier," the soft, melancholy voice replied. "It was thought you were at Mr. Johnson's, but they had no news of you there."

"No, I was detained. I had a breakdown," Mr. Hutton answered irritably. It was tiresome to be caught out in a lie.

"Your wife wanted to see you urgently."

"Well, I can go now." Mr. Hutton moved toward the stairs.

Dr. Libbard laid a hand on his arm. "I am afraid it's too late."

"Too late?" He began fumbling with his watch; it wouldn't come out of his pocket.

"Mrs. Hutton passed away half an hour ago."

The voice remained even in its softness, the melancholy of the eyes did not deepen. Dr. Libbard spoke of death as he would speak of a local cricket match. All things were equally vain and equally deplorable.

Mr. Hutton found himself thinking of Janet Spence's words. At any moment, at any moment. She had been extraordinarily right.

"What happened?" he asked. "What was the cause?"

Dr. Libbard explained. It was heart failure brought on by a violent attack of nausea, caused in its turn by the eating of something of an irritant nature. Red currants? Mr. Hutton suggested. Very likely. It had been too much for the heart. There was chronic valvular disease: something had collapsed under the strain. It was all over; she could not have suffered much.

"It's a pity they should have chosen the day of the Eton and Harrow match for the funeral," old General Grego was saying as he stood up, his top hat in his hand, under the shadow of the lich gate, wiping his face with his handkerchief.

Mr. Hutton overheard the remark and with difficulty restrained a desire to inflict grievous bodily pain on the General. He would have liked to hit the old brute in the middle of his big red face. Monstrous great mulberry, spotted with meal! Was there no respect for the dead? Did nobody care? In theory he didn't much care; let the dead bury their dead. But here, at the graveside, he had found himself actually sobbing. Poor Emily, they had been pretty happy once. Now she was lying at the bottom of a seven-foot hole. And here was Grego complaining that he couldn't go to the Eton and Harrow match.

Mr. Hutton looked round at the groups of black figures that were drifting slowly out of the churchyard toward the fleet of cabs and motors assembled in the road outside. Against the brilliant background of the July grass and flowers and foliage, they had a horribly alien and unnatural appearance. It pleased him to think that all these people would soon be dead too.

That evening Mr. Hutton sat up late in his library reading the life of Milton. There was no particular reason why he should have chosen Milton; it was the book that first came to hand, that was all. It was after midnight when he had finished. He got up from his armchair, unbolted the French windows, and stepped out onto the little paved terrace. The night was quiet and clear. Mr. Hutton looked at the stars and at the holes between them, dropped his eyes to the dim lawns and hueless flowers of the garden, and let them wander over the farther landscape, black and gray under the moon.

He began to think with a kind of confused violence. There were the stars, there was Milton. A man can be somehow the peer of stars and night. Greatness, nobility. But is there seriously a difference between the noble and the ignoble? Milton, the stars, death, and himself, himself. The soul, the body; the higher and the lower nature. Perhaps there was something in it, after all. Milton had a god on his side and righteousness. What had he? Nothing, nothing whatever. There were only Doris's little breasts. What was the point of it all? Milton, the stars, death, and Emily in her grave, Doris and himself—always himself . . .

Oh, he was a futile and disgusting being. Everything convinced him of it. It was a solemn moment. He spoke aloud: "I will, I will." The sound of his own voice in the darkness was appalling; it seemed to him that he had sworn that infernal oath which binds even the gods: "I will, I will." There had been New Year's Days and solemn anniversaries in the past, when he had felt the same contritions and recorded similar resolutions. They had all thinned away, these resolutions, like smoke, into nothingness. But this was a greater moment and he had pronounced a more fearful oath. In the future it was to be different. Yes, he would live by reason, he would be industrious, he would curb his appetites, he would devote his life to some good purpose. It was resolved and it would be so.

In practice he saw himself spending his mornings in agricultural pursuits, riding round with the bailiff, seeing that his land was farmed in the best modern way, silos and artificial manures and continuous cropping, and all that. The remainder of the day should be devoted to serious study. There was that book he had been intending to write for so long: *The Effect of Diseases on Civilization.*

Mr. Hutton went to bed humble and contrite, but with a sense that grace had entered into him. He slept for seven and a half hours, and woke to find the sun brilliantly shining. The emotions of the evening before had been transformed by a good night's rest into his customary cheerfulness. It was not until a good many seconds after his return to conscious life that he remembered his resolution, his Stygian oath. Milton and death seemed somehow different in the sunlight. As for the stars, they were not there. But the resolutions were good; even in the daytime he could see that. He had his horse saddled after breakfast, and rode round the farm with the bailiff. After luncheon he read Thucydides on the plague at Athens. In the evening he made a few notes on malaria in Southern Italy. While he was undressing he remembered that there was a good anecdote in Skelton's jestbook about the Sweating Sickness.

He would have made a note of it if only he could have found a pencil.

On the sixth morning of his new life Mr. Hutton found among his correspondence an envelope addressed in that peculiarly vulgar handwriting which he knew to be Doris's. He opened it, and began to read. She didn't know what to say, words were so inadequate. His wife dying like that, and so suddenly—it was too terrible. Mr. Hutton sighed, but his interest revived somewhat as he read on:

"Death is so frightening, I never think of it when I can help it. But when something like this happens, or when I am feeling ill or depressed, then I can't help remembering it is there so close, and I think about all the wicked things I have done and about you and me, and I wonder what will happen, and I am so frightened. I am so lonely, Teddy Bear, and so unhappy, and I don't know what to do. I can't get rid of the idea of dying, I am so wretched and help-less without you. I didn't mean to write to you; I meant to wait till you were out of mourning and could come and see me again, but I was so lonely and miserable, Teddy Bear, I had to write. I couldn't help it. Forgive me, I want you so much; I have nobody in the world but you. You are so good and gentle and understand-ing; there is nobody like you. I shall never forget how good and kind you have been to me, and you are so clever and know so much, I can't understand how you ever came to pay any attention to me, I am so dull and stupid, much less like me and love me, because you do love me a little, don't you, Teddy Bear?"

Mr. Hutton was touched with shame and remorse. To be thanked like this, worshiped for having seduced the girl, it was too much. It had just been a piece of imbecile wantonness. Imbecile, idiotic: there was no other way to describe it. For, when all was said, he had derived very little pleasure from it. Taking all things together, he had probably been more bored than amused. Once upon a time he had believed himself to be a hedonist. But to be a hedonist implies a certain process of reasoning, a deliberate choice of known pleasures, a rejection of known pains. This had been done without reason, against it. For he knew beforehand—so well, so well—that there was no interest or pleasure to be derived from these wretched affairs. And yet each time the vague itch came upon him he succumbed, involving himself once more in the old stupidity. There had been Maggie, his wife's maid, and Edith, the girl on the farm, and Mrs. Pringle, and the waitress in London, and others—there seemed to be dozens of them. It had all been so stale and boring. He knew it would be; he always knew. And yet, and yet . . . Experience doesn't teach.

Poor little Doris! He would write to her kindly, comfortingly, but he wouldn't see her again. A servant came to tell him that his horse was saddled and waiting. He mounted and rode off. That morning the old bailiff was more irritating than usual.

Five days later Doris and Mr. Hutton were sitting together on the pier at Southend; Doris, in white muslin with pink garnishings, radiated happiness; Mr. Hutton, legs outstretched and chair tilted, had pushed the panama back from his forehead and was trying to feel like a tripper. That night, when Doris was asleep, breathing and warm by his side, he recaptured, in this moment of darkness and physical fatigue, the rather cosmic emotion which had possessed him that evening, not a fortnight ago, when he had made his great resolution. And so his solemn oath had already gone the way of so many other resolutions. Unreason had triumphed; at the first itch of desire he had given way. He was hopeless, hopeless.

For a long time he lay with closed eyes, ruminating his humiliation. The girl stirred in her sleep. Mr. Hutton turned over and looked in her direction. Enough faint light crept in between the half-drawn curtains to show her bare arm and shoulder, her neck, and the dark tangle of hair on the pillow. She was beautiful, desirable. Why did he lie there moaning over his sins? What did it matter? If he were hopeless, then so be it; he would make the best of his hopelessness. A glorious sense of irresponsibility suddenly filled him. He was free, magnificently free. In a kind of exaltation he drew the girl toward him. She woke, bewildered, almost frightened under his rough kisses.

The storm of his desire subsided into a kind of serene merriment. The whole atmosphere seemed to be quivering with enormous silent laughter.

"Could anyone love you as much as I do, Teddy Bear?" The question came faintly from distant worlds of love.

"I think I know somebody who does," Mr. Hutton replied. The

submarine laughter was swelling, rising, ready to break the surface of silence and resound.

"Who? Tell me. What do you mean?" The voice had come very close; charged with suspicion, anguish, indignation, it belonged to this immediate world.

"Ah!"

"Who?"

"You'll never guess." Mr. Hutton kept up the joke until it began to grow tedious, and then pronounced the name: "Janet Spence."

Doris was incredulous. "Miss Spence of the Manor? That old woman?" It was too ridiculous. Mr. Hutton laughed too.

"But it's quite true," he said. "She adores me." Oh, the vast joke! He would go and see her as soon as he returned, see and conquer. "I believe she wants to marry me," he added.

"But you wouldn't . . . you don't intend . . ."

The air was fairly crepitating with humor. Mr. Hutton laughed aloud. "I intend to marry you," he said. It seemed to him the best joke he had ever made in his life.

When Mr. Hutton left Southend he was once more a married man. It was agreed that, for the time being, the fact should be kept secret. In the autumn they would go abroad together, and the world should be informed. Meanwhile he was to go back to his own house and Doris to hers.

The day after his return he walked over in the afternoon to see Miss Spence. She received him with the old Gioconda.

"I was expecting you to come."

"I couldn't keep away," Mr. Hutton gallantly replied.

They sat in the summerhouse. It was a pleasant place—a little old stucco temple bowered among dense bushes of evergreen. Miss Spence had left her mark on it by hanging up over the seat a blue-and-white Della Robbia plaque.

"I am thinking of going to Italy this autumn," said Mr. Hutton. He felt like a ginger-beer bottle, ready to pop with bubbling humorous excitement.

"Italy. . . ." Miss Spence closed her eyes ecstatically. "I feel drawn there too."

"Why not let yourself be drawn?"

"I don't know. One somehow hasn't the energy and initiative to set out alone."

"Alone. . . ." Ah, sound of guitars and throaty singing! "Yes, traveling alone isn't much fun."

Miss Spence lay back in her chair without speaking. Her eyes were still closed. Mr. Hutton stroked his mustache. The silence prolonged itself for what seemed a very long time.

Pressed to stay to dinner, Mr. Hutton did not refuse. The fun had hardly started. The table was laid in the loggia. Through its arches they looked out onto the sloping garden, to the valley below and the farther hills. Light ebbed away; the heat and silence were oppressive. A huge cloud was mounting up the sky, and there were distant breathings of thunder. The thunder drew nearer, a wind began to blow, and the first drops of rain fell. The table was cleared. Miss Spence and Mr. Hutton sat on in the growing darkness.

Miss Spence broke a long silence by saying meditatively: "I think everyone has a right to a certain amount of happiness, don't you?"

"Most certainly." But what was she leading up to? Nobody makes generalizations about life unless they mean to talk about themselves. Happiness: he looked back on his own life, and saw a cheerful, placid existence disturbed by no great griefs or discomforts or alarms. He had always had money and freedom; he had been able to do very much as he wanted. Yes, he supposed he had been happy, happier than most men. And now he was not merely happy; he had discovered in irresponsibility the secret of gaiety. He was about to say something about his happiness when Miss Spence went on speaking.

"People like you and me have a right to be happy some time in our lives."

"Me?" said Mr. Hutton, surprised.

"Poor Henry! Fate hasn't treated either of us very well."

"Oh, well, it might have treated me worse."

"You're being cheerful. That's brave of you. But don't think I can't see behind the mask."

Miss Spence spoke louder and louder as the rain came down more and more heavily. Periodically the thunder cut across her utterances. She talked on, shouting against the noise.

"I have understood you so well and for so long."

A flash revealed her, aimed and intent, leaning toward him. Her eyes were two profound and menacing gun barrels. The darkness re-engulfed her.

"You were a lonely soul seeking a companion soul. I could sympathize with you in your solitude. Your marriage . . ."

The thunder cut short the sentence. Miss Spence's voice became audible once more with the words:

". . . could offer no companionship to a man of your stamp. You needed a soul mate."

A soul mate—he! A soul mate! It was incredibly fantastic. "Georgette Leblanc, the ex-soul mate of Maurice Maeterlinck." He had seen that in the paper a few days ago. So it was thus that Janet Spence had painted him in her imagination—as a soul-mater. And for Doris he was a picture of goodness and the cleverest man in the world. And actually, really, he was what? Who knows?

"My heart went out to you. I could understand; I was lonely, too." Miss Spence laid her hand on his knee. "You were so patient." Another flash. She was still aimed, dangerously. "You never complained. But I could guess, I could guess."

"How wonderful of you!" So he was an *âme incomprise.* "Only a woman's intuition . . ."

The thunder crashed and rumbled, died away, and only the sound of the rain was left. The thunder was his laughter, magnified, externalized. Flash and crash, there it was again, right on top of them.

"Don't you feel that you have within you something that is akin to this storm?" He could imagine her leaning forward as she uttered the words. "Passion makes one the equal of the elements."

What was his gambit now? Why, obviously, he should have said, "Yes," and ventured on some unequivocal gesture. But Mr. Hutton suddenly took fright. The ginger beer in him had gone flat. The woman was serious—terribly serious. He was appalled.

Passion? "No," he desperately answered. "I am without passion."

But his remark was either unheard or unheeded, for Miss Spence went on with a growing exaltation, speaking so rapidly, however, and in such a burningly intimate whisper that Mr. Hutton found it very difficult to distinguish what she was saying. She was telling him, as far as he could make out, the story of her life. The lightning was less frequent now, and there were long intervals of darkness. But at each flash he saw her still aiming toward him, still yearning forward with a terrifying intensity. Darkness, the rain, and then flash! her face was there, close at hand. A pale mask, greenish white; the large eyes, the narrow barrel of the mouth, the heavy eyebrows. Agrippina, or wasn't it rather—yes, wasn't it rather George Robey?

He began devising absurd plans for escaping. He might suddenly jump up, pretending he had seen a burglar—Stop thief! stop thief! —and dash off into the night in pursuit. Or should he say that he felt faint, a heart attack, or that he had seen a ghost—Emily's ghost —in the garden? Absorbed in his childish plotting, he had ceased to pay any attention to Miss Spence's words. The spasmodic clutching of her hand recalled his thoughts.

"I honored you for that, Henry," she was saying.

Honored him for what?

"Marriage is a sacred tie, and your respect for it, even when the marriage was, as it was in your case, an unhappy one, made me respect you and admire you, and—shall I dare say the word?—"

Oh, the burglar, the ghost in the garden! But it was too late.

". . . yes, love you, Henry, all the more. But we're free now, Henry."

Free? There was a movement in the dark, and she was kneeling on the floor by his chair.

"Oh, Henry, Henry, I have been unhappy too."

Her arms embraced him, and by the shaking of her body he could feel that she was sobbing. She might have been a suppliant crying for mercy.

"You mustn't, Janet," he protested. Those tears were terrible, terrible. "Not now, not now! You must be calm; you must go to bed." He patted her shoulder, then got up, disengaging himself from her embrace. He left her still crouching on the floor beside the chair on which he had been sitting.

Groping his way into the hall, and without waiting to look for his hat, he went out of the house, taking infinite pains to close the front door noiselessly behind him. The clouds had blown over, and the moon was shining from a clear sky. There were puddles all along the road, and a noise of running water rose from the gutters and ditches. Mr. Hutton splashed along, not caring if he got wet.

How heart-rendingly she had sobbed! With the emotions of pity and remorse that the recollection evoked in him there was a certain resentment: why couldn't she have played the game that he was playing, the heartless, amusing game? Yes, but he had known all the time that she wouldn't, she couldn't, play that game; he had known and persisted.

What had she said about passion and the elements? Something absurdly stale, but true, true. There she was, a cloud black-bosomed and charged with thunder, and he, like some absurd little Benjamin Franklin, had sent up a kite into the heart of the menace. Now he was complaining that his toy had drawn the lightning.

She was probably still kneeling by that chair in the loggia, crying.

But why hadn't he been able to keep up the game? Why had his irresponsibility deserted him, leaving him suddenly sober in a cold world? There were no answers to any of his questions. One idea burned steady and luminous in his mind, the idea of flight. He must get away at once.

"What are you thinking about, Teddy Bear?"

"Nothing."

There was a silence. Mr. Hutton remained motionless, his elbows on the parapet of the terrace, his chin in his hands, looking down over Florence. He had taken a villa on one of the hilltops to the south of the city. From a little raised terrace at the end of the garden one looked down a long fertile valley on to the town and beyond it to the bleak mass of Monte Morello and, eastward of it, to the peopled hill of Fiesole, dotted with white houses. Everything was clear and luminous in the September sunshine.

"Are you worried about anything?"

"No, thank you."

"Tell me, Teddy Bear."

"But, my dear, there's nothing to tell." Mr. Hutton turned round, smiled, and patted the girl's hand. "I think you'd better go in and have your siesta. It's too hot for you here."

"Very well, Teddy Bear. Are you coming too?"

"When I've finished my cigar."

"All right. But do hurry up and finish it, Teddy Bear." Slowly, reluctantly, she descended the steps of the terrace and walked toward the house.

Mr. Hutton continued his contemplation of Florence. He had need to be alone. It was good sometimes to escape from Doris and the restless solicitude of her passion. He had never known the pains of loving hopelessly, but he was experiencing now the pains of being loved. These last weeks had been a period of growing discomfort. Doris was always with him, like an obsession, like a guilty conscience. Yes, it was good to be alone.

He pulled an envelope out of his pocket and opened it, not without reluctance. He hated letters; they always contained something unpleasant, nowadays, since his second marriage. This was from his sister. He began skimming through the insulting home-truths of which it was composed. The words "indecent haste," "social suicide," "scarcely cold in her grave," "person of the lower classes," all occurred. They were inevitable now in any communication from a well-meaning and right-thinking relative. Impatient, he was about to tear the stupid letter to pieces when his eye fell on a sentence at the bottom of the third page. His heart beat with uncomfortable violence as he read it. It was too monstrous! Janet Spence was going about telling everyone that he had poisoned his wife in order to marry Doris. What damnable malice! Ordinarily a man of the suavest temper, Mr. Hutton found himself trembling with rage. He took the childish satisfaction of calling names—he cursed the woman.

Then suddenly he saw the ridiculous side of the situation. The notion that he should have murdered anyone in order to marry Doris! If they only knew how miserably bored he was. Poor, dear Janet! She had tried to be malicious; she had only succeeded in being stupid.

A sound of footsteps aroused him; he looked round. In the garden below the little terrace the servant girl of the house was picking fruit. A Neapolitan, strayed somehow as far north as Florence, she was a specimen of the classical type a little debased. Her profile might have been taken from a Sicilian coin of a bad period. Her features, carved floridly in the grand tradition, expressed an almost perfect stupidity. Her mouth was the most beautiful thing about her; the calligraphic hand of nature had richly curved it into an expression of mulish bad temper. Under her hideous black clothes, Mr. Hutton divined a powerful body, firm and massive. He had looked at her before with a vague interest and curiosity. Today the curiosity defined and focused itself into a desire. An idyll of Theocritus. Here was the woman; he, alas, was not precisely like a goatherd on the volcanic hills. He called to her.

"Armida!"

The smile with which she answered him was so provocative, attested so easy a virtue, that Mr. Hutton took fright. He was on the brink once more—on the brink. He must draw back, oh! quickly, quickly, before it was too late. The girl continued to look up at him.

"*Ha chiamato?*" she asked at last.

Stupidity or reason? Oh, there was no choice now. It was imbecility every time.

"*Scendo,*" he called back to her. Twelve steps led from the garden to the terrace. Mr. Hutton counted them. Down, down, down, down. . . . He saw a vision of himself descending from one circle of the inferno to the next, from a darkness full of wind and hail to an abyss of stinking mud.

For a good many days the Hutton case had a place on the front page of every newspaper. There had been no more popular murder trial since George Smith had temporarily eclipsed the European War by drowning in a warm bath his seventh bride. The public imagination was stirred by this tale of a murder brought to light months after the date of the crime. Here, it was felt, was one of those incidents in human life, so notable because they are so rare, which do definitely justify the ways of God to man. A wicked man had been moved by an illicit passion to kill his wife. For months he had lived in sin and fancied security, only to be dashed at last more horribly into the pit he had prepared for himself. "Murder will out," and here was a case of it. The readers of the newspapers were in a position to follow every movement of the hand of God. There had been vague, but persistent rumors in the neighborhood; the police had taken action at last. Then came the exhumation order, the post-mortem examination, the inquest, the evidence of the experts, the verdict of the coroner's jury, the trial, the condemnation. For once Providence had done its duty, obviously, grossly, didactically, as in a melodrama. The newspapers were right in making of the case the staple intellectual food of a whole season.

Mr. Hutton's first emotion when he was summoned from Italy to give evidence at the inquest was one of indignation. It was a monstrous, a scandalous thing that the police should take such idle, malicious gossip seriously. When the inquest was over he would bring an action for malicious prosecution against the Chief Constable; he would sue the Spence woman for slander.

The inquest was opened; the astonishing evidence unrolled itself. The experts had examined the body, and had found traces of arsenic; they were of opinion that the late Mrs. Hutton had died of arsenic poisoning.

Arsenic poisoning . . . Emily had died of arsenic poisoning? After that, Mr. Hutton learned with surprise that there was enough arsenicated insecticide in his greenhouses to poison an army.

It was now, quite suddenly, that he saw it: there was a case against him. Fascinated, he watched it growing, growing, like some monstrous tropical plant. It was enveloping him, surrounding him; he was lost in a tangled forest.

When was the poison administered? The experts agreed that it must have been swallowed eight or nine hours before death. About lunchtime? Yes, about lunchtime. Clara, the parlormaid, was called. Mrs. Hutton, she remembered, had asked her to go and fetch her medicine. Mr. Hutton had volunteered to go instead; he had gone alone. Miss Spence—ah, the memory of the storm, the white face, the horror of it all!—Miss Spence confirmed Clara's statement, and added that Mr. Hutton had come back with the medicine already poured out in a wineglass, not in the bottle.

Mr. Hutton's indignation evaporated. He was dismayed, frightened. It was all too fantastic to be taken seriously, and yet this nightmare was a fact, it was actually happening.

M'Nab had seen them kissing, often. He had taken them for a drive on the day of Mrs. Hutton's death. He could see them reflected in the wind screen, sometimes out of the tail of his eye.

The inquest was adjourned. That evening Doris went to bed with a headache. When he went to her room after dinner, Mr. Hutton found her crying.

"What's the matter?" He sat down on the edge of her bed and began to stroke her hair. For a long time she did not answer, and he went on stroking her hair mechanically, almost unconsciously; sometimes, even, he bent down and kissed her bare shoulder. He had his own affairs, however, to think about. What had happened? How was it that the stupid gossip had actually come true? Emily had died of arsenic poisoning. It was absurd, impossible. The order of things had been broken, and he was at the mercy of an irresponsibility. What had happened, what was going to happen? He was interrupted in the midst of his thoughts.

"It's my fault, it's my fault!" Doris suddenly sobbed out. "I shouldn't have loved you; I oughtn't to have let you love me. Why was I ever born?"

Mr. Hutton didn't say anything, but looked down in silence at the abject figure of misery lying on the bed.

"If they do anything to you I shall kill myself."

She sat up, held him for a moment at arm's length, and looked at him with a kind of violence, as though she were never to see him again.

"I love you, I love you, I love you." She drew him, inert and passive, toward her, clasped him, pressed herself against him. "I didn't know you loved me as much as that, Teddy Bear. But why did you do it, why did you do it?"

Mr. Hutton undid her clasping arms and got up. His face became very red. "You seem to take it for granted that I murdered my wife," he said. "It's really too grotesque. What do you all take me for? A cinema hero?" He had begun to lose his temper. All the exasperation, all the fear and bewilderment of the day, was transformed into a violent anger against her. "It's all such damned stupidity. Haven't you any conception of a civilized man's mentality? Do I look the sort of man who'd go about slaughtering people? I suppose you imagined I was so insanely in love with you that I could commit any folly. When will you women understand that one isn't insanely in love? All one asks for is a quiet life, which you won't allow one to have. I don't know what the devil ever induced me to marry you. It was all a damned stupid, practical joke. And now you go about saying I'm a murderer. I won't stand it."

Mr. Hutton stamped toward the door. He had said horrible things, he knew, odious things that he ought speedily to unsay. But he wouldn't. He closed the door behind him.

"Teddy Bear!" He turned the handle; the latch clicked into place. "Teddy Bear!" The voice that came to him through the closed door was agonized. Should he go back? He ought to go back. He touched the handle, then withdrew his fingers and quickly walked away. When he was halfway down the stairs he halted. She might try to do something silly—throw herself out of the window or God knows what! He listened attentively; there was no sound. But he pictured her very clearly, tiptoeing across the room, lifting the sash as high as it would go, leaning out into the cold night air. It was raining a little. Under the window lay the paved terrace. How far below? Twenty-five or thirty feet? Once, when he was walking along Piccadilly, a dog had jumped out of a third-story window of the Ritz. He had seen it fall; he had heard it strike the pavement. Should he go back? He was damned if he would; he hated her.

He sat for a long time in the library. What had happened? What was happening? He turned the question over and over in his mind and could find no answer. Suppose the nightmare dreamed itself out to its horrible conclusion. Death was waiting for him. His eyes filled with tears; he wanted so passionately to live. "Just to be alive." Poor Emily had wished it too, he remembered: "Just to be alive." There were still so many places in this astonishing world unvisited, so many queer delightful people still unknown, so many lovely women never so much as seen. The huge white oxen would still be dragging their wains along the Tuscan roads, the cypresses would still go up, straight as pillars, to the blue heaven; but he would not be there to see them. And the sweet southern wines— Tears of Christ and Blood of Judas—others would drink them, not he. Others would walk down the obscure and narrow lanes between the bookshelves in the London Library, sniffing the dusty perfume of good literature, peering at strange titles, discovering unknown names, exploring the fringes of vast domains of knowledge. He would be lying in a hole in the ground. And why, why? Confusedly he felt that some extraordinary kind of justice was being done. In the past he had been wanton and imbecile and irresponsible. Now Fate was playing as wantonly, as irresponsibly, with him. It was tit for tat, and God existed after all.

He felt that he would like to pray. Forty years ago he used to kneel by his bed every evening. The nightly formula of his childhood came to him almost unsought from some long-unopened chamber of the memory. "God bless Father and Mother, Tom and Cissie and the Baby, Mademoiselle and Nurse, and everyone that I love, and make me a good boy. Amen." They were all dead now, all except Cissie.

His mind seemed to soften and dissolve; a great calm descended upon his spirit. He went upstairs to ask Doris's forgiveness. He found her lying on the couch at the foot of the bed. On the floor beside her stood a blue bottle of liniment, marked NOT TO BE TAKEN; she seemed to have drunk about half of it.

"You didn't love me," was all she said when she opened her eyes to find him bending over her.

Dr. Libbard arrived in time to prevent any very serious consequences. "You mustn't do this again," he said while Mr. Hutton was out of the room.

"What's to prevent me?" she asked defiantly.

Dr. Libbard looked at her with his large, sad eyes. "There's nothing to prevent you," he said. "Only yourself and your baby. Isn't it rather bad luck on your baby, not allowing it to come into the world because you want to go out of it?"

Doris was silent for a time. "All right," she whispered, "I won't."

Mr. Hutton sat by her bedside for the rest of the night. He felt himself now to be indeed a murderer. For a time he persuaded himself that he loved this pitiable child. Dozing in his chair, he woke up, stiff and cold, to find himself drained dry, as it were, of every emotion. He had become nothing but a tired and suffering carcass. At six o'clock he undressed and went to bed for a couple of hours' sleep. In the course of the same afternoon the coroner's jury brought in a verdict of "Willful Murder," and Mr. Hutton was committed for trial.

Miss Spence was not at all well. She had found her public appearances in the witness box very trying, and when it was all over she had something that was very nearly a breakdown. She slept badly, and suffered from nervous indigestion. Dr. Libbard used to call every other day. She talked to him a great deal, mostly about the Hutton case. Her moral indignation was always on the boil. Wasn't it appalling to think that one had had a murderer in one's house? Wasn't it extraordinary that one could have been for so long mistaken about the man's character? (But she had had an inkling from the first.) And then the girl he had gone off with—so low class, so little better than a prostitute. The news that the second Mrs. Hutton was expecting a baby, the posthumous child of a condemned and executed criminal, revolted her; the thing was shocking, an obscenity. Dr. Libbard answered her gently and vaguely, and prescribed bromide.

One morning he interrupted her in the midst of her customary tirade. "By the way," he said in his soft, melancholy voice, "I suppose it was really you who poisoned Mrs. Hutton."

Miss Spence stared at him for two or three seconds with enormous eyes, and then quietly said, "Yes." After that she started to cry.

"In the coffee, I suppose."

She seemed to nod assent. Dr. Libbard took out his fountain pen, and in his neat, meticulous calligraphy wrote out a prescription for a sleeping draught.

COMMENT

A comparison of Huxley's story with Miss Mansfield's shows to what different ends the theme of marital infidelity may be used. Miss Mansfield takes the wife's, Mr. Huxley the husband's, point of view; Miss Mansfield stops with the discovery of conduct apparently recent in origin; Mr. Huxley records a long series of infidelities. More important, Miss Mansfield uses the discovery less for itself than as a verification of a strange correspondence of moods, of which her management is rather subtle, whereas Mr. Huxley depends in part upon the far less subtle technique of the mystery story. A situation is described in such a way that either of two people may have administered poison; the fact that poison has been administered comes as a surprise; the reader's suspicion is directed at the wrong person; the suspected person's actions, if not his words, seem to justify the accusation; there is an omnipresent "understanding" character—the doctor; and then the revelation of the truth is made in a surprise ending or twist ending. The reader of "whodunits" will easily recognize all these devices.

But to describe these conventions of structure is to fall far short of telling what the story does. The ending, for instance, is not used altogether conventionally; at least it does not include a melodramatic denunciation or belated court action, nor does it even make a comment upon the irony of legal injustice. In fact, the real surprise of the surprise ending is that it is managed so quietly. The almost casual way in which the fact is told indicates that the intention is less to shock the reader than to give a final emphasis to a point that has already been set forth in the body of the story. It is perhaps debatable whether the concluding section is entirely successful in this or whether it deflects attention from the main character, who is Mr. Hutton.

For the story is Mr. Hutton's, and the major point concerns him. His character is developed almost entirely by means of his relationships with various women. The element which is common to them is that they take him very seriously, even love him passionately; the element common to all his relationships with women is that he cannot have any deep feeling for them, and is indeed bored or even terrified by pressing or intense devotion. He is a dilettante, subject only to vanity or impulse or idle curiosity, and in love and other aspects of life is incapable of sustained attention and devotion. The basic irony of the story is the contrast between his own triviality and the strength of feeling he evokes in women, two of whom are willing to commit murder because of him. Thus the concluding section should enlarge our sense of this contrast with its evidence on how far Janet Spence could go in her passion for Mr. Hutton.

As we have seen, the story does not raise the issue of Mr. Hutton's fate at the hands of the law. Does that mean that in its presentation of ironies of character it is indifferent to problems of justice? Or is it suggested that there is an ironic justice in Mr. Hutton's fate? In considering this question, the student should trace out the theme of "irresponsibility." Has Miss Spence, though unpunished, received a comparable sort of justice?

Mr. Hutton likes to play "the heartless, amusing game"; the women are incapable of doing so. This description of the story might suggest that Mr. Hutton is a villain, and the others his victims. Does Huxley interpret his characters in this way? Does he side with Janet and Doris, presenting them as entirely admirable characters? Or is there evidence that he regards them with the same detachment with which he views Mr. Hutton?

The tone of the story is essentially that of satiric comedy. Mr. Hutton's infidelities are presented less as immoral than as ridiculous, the expressions of a ludicrously immature personality. Miss Spence is really a comic version of a rather familiar romantic type; the title suggests the comic incongruity between her exterior, with its conscious suggestion of a special, elusive personality, and the actual triteness of her feelings and ideas. What is there in the treatment of Doris and Mr. Hutton which belongs essentially to comedy?

Graham Greene

Graham Greene, an English writer who was born in 1904, in recent years has evoked a great deal of controversial discussion. He was educated at Oxford and has been at different times an editor of the London *Times* and film critic for *The Spectator*. In his 20's he began writing a series of novels which were primarily popular in appeal but which have resulted, rather unusually, in the author's receiving critical consideration as a serious writer. For, although Greene modestly applies the term "entertainments" to his mystery and detective stories, they have a profound psychological interest. His interest in the religious theme is explicit in *The Heart of the Matter* (1948). His short stories in *Nineteen Stories* (1949) range from the playful comedy to the mature psychological study of "The Basement Room."

The Basement Room

WHEN the front door had shut them out and the butler Baines had turned back into the dark heavy hall, Philip began to live. He stood in front of the nursery door, listening until he heard the engine of the taxi die out along the street. His parents were gone for a fortnight's holiday; he was "between nurses," one dismissed and the other not arrived; he was alone in the great Belgravia house with Baines and Mrs. Baines.

He could go anywhere, even through the green baize door to the pantry or down the stairs to the basement living-room. He felt a stranger in his home because he could go into any room and all the rooms were empty.

You could only guess who had once occupied them: the rack of pipes in the smoking-room beside the elephant tusks, the carved wood tobacco jar; in the bedroom the pink hangings and pale perfumes and the three-quarter finished jars of cream which Mrs. Baines had not yet cleared away; the high glaze on the never-opened piano in the drawing-room, the china clock, the silly little tables and the silver: but here Mrs. Baines was already busy, pulling down the curtains, covering the chairs in dust-sheets.

"Be off out of here, Master Philip," and she looked at him with her hateful peevish eyes, while she moved round, getting everything in order, meticulous and loveless and doing her duty.

Philip Lane went downstairs and pushed at the baize door; he looked into the pantry, but Baines was not there, then he set foot for the first time on the stairs to the basement. Again he had the sense: this is life. All his seven nursery years vibrated with the strange, the new experience. His crowded busy brain was like a city which feels the earth tremble at a distant earthquake shock. He was apprehensive, but he was happier than he had ever been. Everything was more important than before.

Baines was reading a newspaper in his shirt-sleeves. He said: "Come in, Phil, and make yourself at home. Wait a moment and I'll do the honours," and going to a white cleaned cupboard he brought out a bottle of ginger-beer and half a Dundee cake. "Half-past eleven in the morning," Baines said. "It's opening time, my boy," and he cut the cake and poured out the ginger-beer. He was more genial than Philip had ever known him, more at his ease, a man in his own home.

"Shall I call Mrs. Baines?" Philip asked, and he was glad when Baines said no. She was busy. She liked to be busy, so why interfere with her pleasure?

"A spot of drink at half-past eleven," Baines said, pouring himself out a glass of ginger-beer, "gives an appetite for chop and does no man any harm."

"A chop?" Philip asked.

"Old Coasters," Baines said, "call all food chop."

"But it's not a chop?"

"Well, it might be, you know, cooked with palm oil. And then some paw-paw to follow."

Philip looked out of the basement window at the dry stone yard, the ash-can and the legs going up and down beyond the railings.

"Was it hot there?"

"Ah, you never felt such heat. Not a nice heat, mind, like you get in the park on a day like this. Wet," Baines said, "corruption." He cut himself a slice of cake. "Smelling of rot," Baines said, rolling his eyes round the small basement room, from clean cupboard to clean cupboard, the sense of bareness, of nowhere to hide a man's secrets. With an air of regret for something lost he took a long draught of ginger-beer.

"Why did father live out there?"

"It was his job," Baines said, "same as this is mine now. And it was mine then too. It was a man's job. You wouldn't believe it now, but I've had forty niggers under me, doing what I told them to."

"Why did you leave?"

"I married Mrs. Baines."

Philip took the slice of Dundee cake in his hand and munched it round the room. He felt very old, independent and judicial; he was aware that Baines was talking to him as man to man. He never called him Master Philip as Mrs. Baines did, who was servile when she was not authoritative.

Baines had seen the world; he had seen beyond the railings, beyond the tired legs of typists, the Pimlico parade to and from Victoria. He sat there over his ginger pop with the resigned dignity of an exile; Baines didn't complain; he had chosen his fate; and if his fate was Mrs. Baines he had only himself to blame.

But today, because the house was almost empty and Mrs. Baines was upstairs and there was nothing to do, he allowed himself a little acidity.

"I'd go back tomorrow if I had the chance."

"Did you ever shoot a nigger?"

"I never had any call to shoot," Baines said. "Of course I carried a gun. But you didn't need to treat them bad. That just made them stupid. Why," Baines said, bowing his thin grey hair with embarrassment over the ginger pop, "I loved some of those damned niggers. I couldn't help loving them. There they'd be, laughing, holding hands; they liked to touch each other; it made them feel fine to know the other fellow was round.

"It didn't mean anything we could understand; two of them would go about all day without loosing hold, grown men; but it wasn't love; it didn't mean anything we could understand."

"Eating between meals," Mrs. Baines said. "What would your mother say, Master Philip?"

She came down the steep stairs to the basement, her hands full of pots of cream and salve, tubes of grease and paste. "You oughtn't to encourage him, Baines," she said, sitting down in a wicker arm-chair and screwing up her small ill-humoured eyes at the Coty lip-stick, Pond's cream, the Leichner rouge and Cyclax powder and Elizabeth Arden astringent.

She threw them one by one into the wastepaper basket. She saved only the cold cream. "Telling the boy stories," she said. "Go along to the nursery, Master Philip, while I get lunch."

Philip climbed the stairs to the baize door. He heard Mrs. Baines's voice like the voice in a nightmare when the small Price light has guttered in the saucer and the curtains move; it was sharp and shrill and full of malice, louder than people ought to speak, exposed.

"Sick to death of your ways, Baines, spoiling the boy. Time you did some work about the house," but he couldn't hear what Baines said in reply. He pushed open the baize door, came up like a small earth animal in his grey flannel shorts into a wash of sunlight on a parquet floor, the gleam of mirrors dusted and polished and beau-tified by Mrs. Baines.

Something broke downstairs, and Philip sadly mounted the stairs to the nursery. He pitied Baines; it occurred to him how happily they could live together in the empty house if Mrs. Baines were called away. He didn't want to play with his Meccano sets; he wouldn't take out his train or his soldiers; he sat at the table with his chin on his hands: this is life; and suddenly he felt responsible for Baines, as if he were the master of the house and Baines an ageing servant who deserved to be cared for. There was not much one could do; he decided at least to be good.

He was not surprised when Mrs. Baines was agreeable at lunch; he was used to her changes. Now it was "another helping of meat, Master Philip," or "Master Philip, a little more of this nice pud-ding." It was a pudding he liked, Queen's pudding with a perfect meringue, but he wouldn't eat a second helping lest she might count that a victory. She was the kind of woman who thought that any injustice could be counterbalanced by something good to eat.

She was sour, but she liked making sweet things; one never had to complain of a lack of jam or plums; she ate well herself and added soft sugar to the meringue and the strawberry jam. The half light through the basement window set the motes moving above her pale hair like dust as she sifted the sugar, and Baines crouched over his plate saying nothing.

Again Philip felt responsibility. Baines had looked forward to this, and Baines was disappointed: everything was being spoilt. The sensation of disappointment was one which Philip could share; knowing nothing of love or jealousy or passion, he could understand better than anyone this grief, something hoped for not happening, something promised not fulfilled, something exciting turning dull. "Baines," he said, "will you take me for a walk this afternoon?"

"No," Mrs. Baines said, "no. That he won't. Not with all the silver to clean."

"There's a fortnight to do it in," Baines said.

"Work first, pleasure afterwards." Mrs. Baines helped herself to some more meringue.

Baines suddenly put down his spoon and fork and pushed his plate away. "Blast," he said.

"Temper," Mrs. Baines said softly, "temper. Don't you go breaking any more things, Baines, and I won't have you swearing in front of the boy. Master Philip, if you've finished you can get down." She skinned the rest of the meringue off the pudding.

"I want to go for a walk," Philip said.

"You'll go and have a rest."

"I will go for a walk."

"Master Philip," Mrs. Baines said. She got up from the table, leaving her meringue unfinished, and came towards him, thin, menacing, dusty in the basement room. "Master Philip, you do as you're told." She took him by the arm and squeezed it gently; she watched him with a joyless passionate glitter and above her head the feet of the typists trudged back to the Victoria offices after the lunch interval.

"Why shouldn't I go for a walk?" But he weakened; he was scared and ashamed of being scared. This was life; a strange passion he couldn't understand moving in the basement room. He saw a small pile of broken glass swept into a corner by the wastepaper basket. He looked to Baines for help and only intercepted hate; the sad hopeless hate of something behind bars.

"Why shouldn't I?" he repeated.

"Master Philip," Mrs. Baines said, "you've got to do as you're told. You mustn't think just because your father's away there's nobody here to—"

"You wouldn't dare," Philip cried, and was startled by Baines's low interjection, "There's nothing she wouldn't dare."

"I hate you," Philip said to Mrs. Baines. He pulled away from her and ran to the door, but she was there before him; she was old, but she was quick.

"Master Philip," she said, "you'll say you're sorry." She stood in front of the door quivering with excitement. "What would your father do if he heard you say that?"

She put a hand out to seize him, dry and white with constant soda, the nails cut to the quick, but he backed away and put the table between them, and suddenly to his surprise she smiled; she became again as servile as she had been arrogant. "Get along with you, Master Philip," she said with glee. "I see I'm going to have my hands full till your father and mother come back."

She left the door unguarded and when he passed her she slapped him playfully. "I've got too much to do today to trouble about you. I haven't covered half the chairs," and suddenly even the upper part of the house became unbearable to him as he thought of Mrs. Baines moving round shrouding the sofas, laying out the dust-sheets.

So he wouldn't go upstairs to get his cap but walked straight out across the shining hall into the street, and again, as he looked this way and looked that way, it was life he was in the middle of.

2

It was the pink sugar cakes in the window on a paper doily, the ham, the slab of mauve sausage, the wasps driving like small torpedoes across the pane that caught Philip's attention. His feet were tired by pavements; he had been afraid to cross the road, had simply walked first in one direction, then in the other. He was nearly home now; the square was at the end of the street; this was a shabby outpost of Pimlico, and he smudged the pane with his nose, looking for sweets, and saw between the cakes and ham a different Baines. He hardly recognized the bulbous eyes, the bald forehead. It was a happy, bold and buccaneering Baines, even though it was, when you looked closer, a desperate Baines.

Philip had never seen the girl. He remembered Baines had a niece and he thought that this might be her. She was thin and drawn, and she wore a white mackintosh; she meant nothing to Philip; she belonged to a world about which he knew nothing at all. He couldn't make up stories about her, as he could make them up about withered Sir Hubert Reed, the Permanent Secretary, about Mrs. Wince-Dudley, who came up once a year from Penstanley in Suffolk with a green umbrella and an enormous black handbag, as he could make them up about the upper servants in all the houses where he went to tea and games. She just didn't belong; he thought of mermaids and Undine; but she didn't belong there either, nor to the adventures of Emil, nor to the Bastables. She sat there looking at an iced pink cake in the detachment and mystery of the completely disinherited, looking at the half-used pots of powder which Baines had set out on the marble-topped table between them.

Baines was urging, hoping, entreating, commanding, and the girl looked at the tea and the china pots and cried. Baines passed his handkerchief across the table, but she wouldn't wipe her eyes; she screwed it in her palm and let the tears run down, wouldn't do anything, wouldn't speak, would only put up a silent despairing resistance to what she dreaded and wanted and refused to listen to at any price. The two brains battled over the tea-cups loving each other, and there came to Philip outside, beyond the ham and wasps and dusty Pimlico pane, a confused indication of the struggle.

He was inquisitive and he didn't understand and he wanted to know. He went and stood in the doorway to see better, he was less sheltered than he had ever been; other people's lives for the first time touched and pressed and moulded. He would never escape that scene. In a week he had forgotten it, but it conditioned his career, the long austerity of his life; when he was dying he said, "Who is she?"

Baines had won; he was cocky and the girl was happy. She wiped her face, she opened a pot of powder, and their fingers touched across the table. It occurred to Philip that it would be amusing to imitate Mrs. Baines's voice and call "Baines" to him from the door.

It shrivelled them; you couldn't describe it in any other way; it made them smaller, they weren't happy any more and they weren't bold. Baines was the first to recover and trace the voice, but that didn't make things as they were. The sawdust was spilled out of the afternoon; nothing you did could mend it, and Philip was scared. "I didn't mean . . ." He wanted to say that he loved Baines, that he had only wanted to laugh at Mrs. Baines. But he had discovered that you couldn't laugh at Mrs. Baines. She wasn't Sir Hubert Reed, who used steel nibs and carried a pen-wiper in his pocket; she wasn't Mrs. Wince-Dudley; she was darkness when the night-light went out in a draught; she was the frozen blocks of earth he had seen one winter in a graveyard when someone said, "They need an electric drill"; she was the flowers gone bad and smelling in the little closet room at Penstanley. There was nothing to laugh about. You had to endure her when she was there and forget about her quickly when she was away, suppress the thought of her, ram it down deep.

Baines said, "It's only Phil," beckoned him in and gave him the pink iced cake the girl hadn't eaten, but the afternoon was broken, the cake was like dry bread in the throat. The girl left them at once; she even forgot to take the powder; like a small blunt icicle in her white mackintosh she stood in the doorway with her back to them, then melted into the afternoon.

"Who is she?" Philip asked. "Is she your niece?"

"Oh, yes," Baines said, "that's who she is; she's my niece," and poured the last drops of water on to the coarse black leaves in the teapot.

"May as well have another cup," Baines said.

"The cup that cheers," he said hopelessly, watching the bitter black fluid drain out of the spout.

"Have a glass of ginger pop, Phil?"

"I'm sorry. I'm sorry, Baines."

"It's not your fault, Phil. Why, I could believe it wasn't you at all, but her. She creeps in everywhere." He fished two leaves out of his cup and laid them on the back of his hand, a thin soft flake and a hard stalk. He beat them with his hand: "Today," and the stalk detached itself, "tomorrow, Wednesday, Thursday, Friday, Saturday, Sunday," but the flake wouldn't come, stayed where it was, drying under his blows, with a resistance you wouldn't believe it to possess. "The tough one wins," Baines said.

He got up and paid the bill and out they went into the street. Baines said, "I don't ask you to say what isn't true. But you needn't mention to Mrs. Baines you met us here."

"Of course not," Philip said, and catching something of Sir

Hubert Reed's manner, "I understand, Baines." But he didn't understand a thing; he was caught up in other people's darkness.

"It was stupid," Baines said. "So near home, but I hadn't time to think, you see. I'd got to see her."

"Of course, Baines."

"I haven't time to spare," Baines said. "I'm not young. I've got to see that she's all right."

"Of course you have, Baines."

"Mrs. Baines will get it out of you if she can."

"You can trust me, Baines," Philip said in a dry important Reed voice; and then, "Look out. She's at the window watching." And there indeed she was, looking up at them, between the lace curtains, from the basement room, speculating. "Need we go in, Baines?" Philip asked, cold lying heavy on his stomach like too much pudding; he clutched Baines's arm.

"Careful," Baines said softly, "careful."

"But need we go in, Baines? It's early. Take me for a walk in the park."

"Better not."

"But I'm frightened, Baines."

"You haven't any cause," Baines said. "Nothing's going to hurt you. You just run along upstairs to the nursery. I'll go down by the area and talk to Mrs. Baines." But even he stood hesitating at the top of the stone steps, pretending not to see her where she watched between the curtains. "In at the front door, Phil, and up the stairs."

Philip didn't linger in the hall; he ran, slithering on the parquet Mrs. Baines had polished, to the stairs. Through the drawing-room doorway on the first floor he saw the draped chairs; even the china clock on the mantel was covered like a canary's cage; as he passed it, it chimed the hour, muffled and secret under the duster. On the nursery table he found his supper laid out: a glass of milk and a piece of bread and butter, a sweet biscuit and a little cold Queen's pudding without the meringue. He had no appetite; he strained his ears for Mrs. Baines's coming, for the sound of voices, but the basement held its secrets; the green baize door shut off that world. He drank the milk and ate the biscuit, but he didn't touch the rest, and presently he could hear the soft precise footfalls of Mrs. Baines

on the stairs: she was a good servant, she walked softly; she was
a determined woman, she walked precisely.

But she wasn't angry when she came in; she was ingratiating as
she opened the night nursery door—"Did you have a good walk,
Master Philip?"—pulled down the blinds, laid out his pyjamas, came
back to clear his supper. "I'm glad Baines found you. Your mother
wouldn't have liked your being out alone." She examined the tray.
"Not much appetite, have you, Master Philip? Why don't you try
a little of this nice pudding? I'll bring you up some more jam for it."

"No, no, thank you, Mrs. Baines," Philip said.

"You ought to eat more," Mrs. Baines said. She sniffed round the
room like a dog. "You didn't take any pots out of the wastepaper
basket in the kitchen, did you, Master Philip?"

"No," Philip said.

"Of course you wouldn't. I just wanted to make sure." She patted
his shoulder and her fingers flashed to his lapel; she picked off a
tiny crumb of pink sugar. "Oh, Master Philip," she said, "that's why
you haven't any appetite. You've been buying sweet cakes. That's
not what your pocket money's for."

"But I didn't," Philip said. "I didn't."

She tasted the sugar with the tip of her tongue.

"Don't tell lies to me, Master Philip. I won't stand for it any
more than your father would."

"I didn't, I didn't," Philip said. "They gave it me. I mean Baines,"
but she had pounced on the word "they." She had got what she
wanted; there was no doubt about that, even when you didn't
know what it was she wanted. Philip was angry and miserable and
disappointed because he hadn't kept Baines's secret. Baines oughtn't
to have trusted him; grown-up people should keep their own
secrets, and yet here was Mrs. Baines immediately entrusting him
with another.

"Let me tickle your palm and see if you can keep a secret." But
he put his hand behind him; he wouldn't be touched. "It's a secret
between us, Master Philip, that I know all about them. I suppose
she was having tea with him," she speculated.

"Why shouldn't she?" he said, the responsibility for Baines weighing on his spirit, the idea that he had got to keep her secret when
he hadn't kept Baines's making him miserable with the unfairness
of life. "She was nice."

"She was nice, was she?" Mrs. Baines said in a bitter voice he wasn't used to.

"And she's his niece."

"So that's what he said," Mrs. Baines struck softly back at him like the clock under the duster. She tried to be jocular. "The old scoundrel. Don't you tell him I know, Master Philip." She stood very still between the table and the door, thinking very hard, planning something. "Promise you won't tell. I'll give you that Meccano set, Master Philip. . . ."

He turned his back on her; he wouldn't promise, but he wouldn't tell. He would have nothing to do with their secrets, the responsibilities they were determined to lay on him. He was only anxious to forget. He had received already a larger dose of life than he had bargained for, and he was scared. "A 2A Meccano set, Master Philip." He never opened his Meccano set again, never built anything, never created anything, died, the old dilettante, sixty years later, with nothing to show rather than preserve the memory of Mrs. Baines's malicious voice saying good night, her soft determined footfalls on the stairs to the basement, going down, going down.

3

The sun poured in between the curtains and Baines was beating a tattoo on the water-can. "Glory, glory," Baines said. He sat down on the end of the bed and said, "I beg to announce that Mrs. Baines has been called away. Her mother's dying. She won't be back till tomorrow."

"Why did you wake me up so early?" Philip said. He watched Baines with uneasiness; he wasn't going to be drawn in; he'd learnt his lesson. It wasn't right for a man of Baines's age to be so merry. It made a grown person human in the same way that you were human. For if a grown-up could behave so childishly, you were liable too to find yourself in their world. It was enough that it came at you in dreams: the witch at the corner, the man with a knife. So "It's very early," he complained, even though he loved Baines, even though he couldn't help being glad that Baines was happy. He was divided by the fear and the attraction of life.

"I want to make this a long day," Baines said. "This is the best time." He pulled the curtains back. "It's a bit misty. The cat's been out all night. There she is, sniffing round the area. They haven't taken in any milk at 59. Emma's shaking out the mats at 63." He said, "This was what I used to think about on the Coast: somebody shaking mats and the cat coming home. I can see it today," Baines said, "just as if I was still in Africa. Most days you don't notice what you've got. It's a good life if you don't weaken." He put a penny on the washstand. "When you've dressed, Phil, run and get a *Mail* from the barrow at the corner. I'll be cooking the sausages."

"Sausages?"

"Sausages," Baines said. "We're going to celebrate today. A fair bust." He celebrated at breakfast, reckless, cracking jokes, unaccountably merry and nervous. It was going to be a long, long day, he kept on coming back to that: for years he had waited for a long day, he had sweated in the damp Coast heat, changed shirts, gone down with fever, lain between the blankets and sweated, all in the hope of this long day, that cat sniffing round the area, a bit of mist, the mats beaten at 63. He propped the *Mail* in front of the coffee-pot and read pieces aloud. He said, "Cora Down's been married for the fourth time." He was amused, but it wasn't his idea of a long day. His long day was the Park, watching the riders in the Row, seeing Sir Arthur Stillwater pass beyond the rails ("He dined with us once in Bo; up from Freetown; he was governor there"), lunch at the Corner House for Philip's sake (he'd have preferred himself a glass of stout and some oysters at the York bar), the Zoo, the long bus ride home in the last summer light: the leaves in the Green Park were beginning to turn and the motors nuzzled out of Berkeley Street with the low sun gently glowing on their wind-screens. Baines envied no one, not Cora Down, or Sir Arthur Stillwater, or Lord Sandale, who came out on to the steps of the Army and Navy and then went back again because he hadn't got anything to do and might as well look at another paper. "I said don't let me see you touch that black again." Baines had led a man's life; everyone on top of the bus pricked their ears when he told Philip all about it.

"Would you have shot him?" Philip asked, and Baines put his head back and tilted his dark respectable man-servant's hat to a better angle as the bus swerved round the artillery memorial.

"I wouldn't have thought twice about it. I'd have shot to kill," he boasted, and the bowed figure went by, the steel helmet, the heavy cloak, the down-turned rifle and the folded hands.

"Have you got the revolver?"

"Of course I've got it," Baines said. "Don't I need it with all the burglaries there've been?" This was the Baines whom Philip loved: not Baines singing and carefree, but Baines responsible, Baines behind barriers, living his man's life.

All the buses streamed out from Victoria like a convoy of aeroplanes to bring Baines home with honour. "Forty blacks under me," and there waiting near the area steps was the proper conventional reward, love at lighting-up time.

"It's your niece," Philip said, recognizing the white mackintosh, but not the happy sleepy face. She frightened him like an unlucky number; he nearly told Baines what Mrs. Baines had said; but he didn't want to bother, he wanted to leave things alone.

"Why, so it is," Baines said. "I shouldn't wonder if she was going to have a bite of supper with us." But he said they'd play a game, pretend they didn't know her, slip down the area steps, "and here," Baines said, "we are," lay the table, put out the cold sausages, a bottle of beer, a bottle of ginger pop, a flagon of harvest burgundy. "Everyone his own drink," Baines said. "Run upstairs, Phil, and see if there's been a post."

Philip didn't like the empty house at dusk before the lights went on. He hurried. He wanted to be back with Baines. The hall lay there in quiet and shadow prepared to show him something he didn't want to see. Some letters rustled down, and someone knocked. "Open in the name of the Republic." The tumbrils rolled, the head bobbed in the bloody basket. Knock, knock, and the postman's footsteps going away. Philip gathered the letters. The slit in the door was like the grating in a jeweller's window. He remembered the policeman he had seen peer through. He had said to his nurse, "What's he doing?" and when she said, "He's seeing if everything's all right," his brain immediately filled with images of all that might be wrong. He ran to the baize door and the stairs. The girl was already there and Baines was kissing her. She leant breathless against the dresser.

"This is Emmy, Phil."

"There's a letter for you, Baines."

"Emmy," Baines said, "it's from her." But he wouldn't open it. "You bet she's coming back."

"We'll have supper, anyway," Emmy said. "She can't harm that."

"You don't know her," Baines said. "Nothing's safe. Damn it," he said, "I was a man once," and he opened the letter.

"Can I start?" Philip asked, but Baines didn't hear; he presented in his stillness and attention an example of the importance grown-up people attached to the written word: you had to write your thanks, not wait and speak them, as if letters couldn't lie. But Philip knew better than that, sprawling his thanks across a page to Aunt Alice who had given him a doll he was too old for. Letters could lie all right, but they made the lie permanent: they lay as evidence against you; they made you meaner than the spoken word.

"She's not coming back till tomorrow night," Baines said. He opened the bottles, he pulled up the chairs, he kissed Emmy again against the dresser.

"You oughtn't to," Emmy said, "with the boy here."

"He's got to learn," Baines said, "like the rest of us," and he helped Philip to three sausages. He only took one himself; he said he wasn't hungry; but when Emmy said she wasn't hungry either he stood over her and made her eat. He was timid and rough with her; he made her drink the harvest burgundy because he said she needed building up; he wouldn't take no for an answer, but when he touched her his hands were light and clumsy too, as if he were afraid to damage something delicate and didn't know how to handle anything so light.

"This is better than milk and biscuits, eh?"

"Yes," Philip said, but he was scared, scared for Baines as much as for himself. He couldn't help wondering at every bite, at every draught of the ginger pop, what Mrs. Baines would say if she ever learnt of this meal; he couldn't imagine it, there was a depth of bit-terness and rage in Mrs. Baines you couldn't sound. He said, "She won't be coming back tonight?" but you could tell by the way they immediately understood him that she wasn't really away at all; she was there in the basement with them, driving them to longer drinks and louder talk, biding her time for the right cutting word. Baines wasn't really happy; he was only watching happiness from close to instead of from far away.

"No," he said, "she'll not be back till late tomorrow." He couldn't keep his eyes off happiness; he'd played around as much as other men, he kept on reverting to the Coast as if to excuse himself for his innocence; he wouldn't have been so innocent if he'd lived his life in London, so innocent when it came to tenderness. "If it was you, Emmy," he said, looking at the white dresser, the scrubbed chairs, "this'd be like a home." Already the room was not quite so harsh; there was a little dust in corners, the silver needed a final polish, the morning's paper lay untidily on a chair. "You'd better go to bed, Phil; it's been a long day."

They didn't leave him to find his own way up through the dark shrouded house; they went with him, turning on lights, touching each other's fingers on the switches; floor after floor they drove the night back; they spoke softly among the covered chairs; they watched him undress, they didn't make him wash or clean his teeth, they saw him into bed and lit his night-light and left his door ajar. He could hear their voices on the stairs, friendly, like the guests he heard at dinner-parties when they moved down to the hall, saying good night. They belonged; wherever they were they made a home. He heard a door open and a clock strike, he heard their voices for so long while, so that he felt they were not far away and he was safe. The voices didn't dwindle, they simply went out, and he could be sure that they were still somewhere not far from him, silent together in one of the many empty rooms, growing sleepy together as he grew sleepy after the long day.

He just had time to sigh faintly with satisfaction, because this too perhaps had been life, before he slept and the inevitable terrors of sleep came round him: a man with a tricolour hat beat at the door on His Majesty's service, a bleeding head lay on the kitchen table in a basket, and the Siberian wolves crept closer. He was bound hand and foot and couldn't move; they leapt round him breathing heavily; he opened his eyes and Mrs. Baines was there, her grey untidy hair in threads over his face, her black hat askew. A loose hairpin fell on the pillow and one musty thread brushed his mouth. "Where are they?" she whispered. "Where are they?"

4

Philip watched her in terror. Mrs. Baines was out of breath as if she had been searching all the empty rooms, looking under loose covers.

With her untidy grey hair and her black dress buttoned to her throat, her gloves of black cotton, she was so like the witches of his dreams that he didn't dare to speak. There was a stale smell in her breath.

"She's here," Mrs. Baines said; "you can't deny she's here." Her face was simultaneously marked with cruelty and misery; she wanted to "do things" to people, but she suffered all the time. It would have done her good to scream, but she daren't do that: it would warn them. She came ingratiatingly back to the bed where Philip lay rigid on his back and whispered, "I haven't forgotten the Meccano set. You shall have it tomorrow, Master Philip. We've got secrets together, haven't we? Just tell me where they are."

He couldn't speak. Fear held him as firmly as any nightmare. She said, "Tell Mrs. Baines, Master Philip. You love your Mrs. Baines, don't you?" That was too much; he couldn't speak, but he could move his mouth in terrified denial, wince away from her dusty image.

She whispered, coming closer to him, "Such deceit. I'll tell your father. I'll settle with you myself when I've found them. Yc smart; I'll see you smart." Then immediately she was still, liste ing. A board had creaked on the floor below, and a moment later, while she stooped listening above his bed, there came the whispers of two people who were happy and sleepy together after a long day. The night-light stood beside the mirror and Mrs. Baines could see bitterly there her own reflection, misery and cruelty wavering in the glass, age and dust and nothing to hope for. She sobbed without tears, a dry, breathless sound; but her cruelty was a kind of pride which kept her going; it was her best quality, she would have been merely pitiable without it. She went out of the door on tiptoe, feeling her way across the landing, going so softly down the stairs that no one behind a shut door could hear her. Then there was complete silence again; Philip could move; he raised his knees; he sat up in bed; he wanted to die. It wasn't fair, the walls were down again between his world and theirs; but this time it was something worse than merriment that the grown people made him share; a passion moved in the house he recognized but could not understand.

It wasn't fair, but he owed Baines everything: the Zoo, the ginger pop, the bus ride home. Even the supper called on his loyalty. But he was frightened; he was touching something he touched in dreams: the bleeding head, the wolves, the knock, knock, knock.

Life fell on him with savagery: you couldn't blame him if he never faced it again in sixty years. He got out of bed, carefully from habit put on his bedroom slippers, and tiptoed to the door: it wasn't quite dark on the landing below because the curtains had been taken down for the cleaners and the light from the street came in through the tall windows. Mrs. Baines had her hand on the glass door-knob; she was very carefully turning it; he screamed, "Baines, Baines."

Mrs. Baines turned and saw him cowering in his pyjamas by the banisters; he was helpless, more helpless even than Baines, and cruelty grew at the sight of him and drove her up the stairs. The nightmare was on him again and he couldn't move; he hadn't any more courage left for ever; he'd spent it all, had been allowed no time to let it grow, no years of gradual hardening; he couldn't even scream.

But the first cry had brought Baines out of the best spare bed-room and he moved quicker than Mrs. Baines. She hadn't reached the top of the stairs before he'd caught her round the waist. She drove her black cotton gloves at his face and he bit her hand. He hadn't time to think, he fought her savagely like a stranger, but she fought back with knowledgeable hate. She was going to teach them all and it didn't really matter whom she began with; they had all deceived her; but the old image in the glass was by her side, telling her she must be dignified, she wasn't young enough to yield her dignity; she could beat his face, but she mustn't bite; she could push, but she mustn't kick.

Age and dust and nothing to hope for were her handicaps. She went over the banisters in a flurry of black clothes and fell into the hall; she lay before the front door like a sack of coals which should have gone down the area into the basement. Philip saw; Emmy saw; she sat down suddenly in the doorway of the best spare bed-room with her eyes open as if she were too tired to stand any longer. Baines went slowly down into the hall.

It wasn't hard for Philip to escape; they'd forgotten him completely; he went down the back, the servants' stairs because Mrs. Baines was in the hall; he didn't understand what she was doing lying there; like the startling pictures in a book no one had read to him, the things he didn't understand terrified him. The whole house had been turned over to the grown-up world; he wasn't safe in the night nursery; their passions had flooded it. The only thing he could do was to get away, by the back stair, and up through the area, and never come back. You didn't think of the cold, of the need of food and sleep; for an hour it would seem quite possible to escape from people for ever.

He was wearing pyjamas and bedroom slippers when he came up into the square, but there was no one to see him. It was that hour of the evening in a residential district when everyone is at the theatre or at home. He climbed over the iron railings into the little garden: the plane-trees spread their large pale palms between him and the sky. It might have been an illimitable forest into which he had escaped. He crouched behind a trunk and the wolves retreated; it seemed to him between the little iron seat and the tree-trunk that no one would ever find him again. A kind of embittered happiness and self-pity made him cry; he was lost; there wouldn't be any more secrets to keep; he surrendered responsibility once and for all. Let grown-up people keep to their world and he would keep to his, safe in the small garden between the plane-trees. "In the lost childhood of Judas Christ was betrayed"; you could almost see the small unformed face hardening into the deep dilettante selfishness of age.

Presently the door of 48 opened and Baines looked this way and that; then he signalled with his hand and Emmy came; it was as if they were only just in time for a train, they hadn't a chance of saying good-bye; she went quickly by, like a face at a window swept past the platform, pale and unhappy and not wanting to go. Baines went in again and shut the door; the light was lit in the basement, and a policeman walked round the square, looking into the areas. You could tell how many families were at home by the lights behind the first-floor curtains.

Philip explored the garden: it didn't take long: a twenty-yard square of bushes and plane-trees, two iron seats and a gravel path, a padlocked gate at either end, a scuffle of old leaves. But he couldn't stay: something stirred in the bushes and two illuminated eyes peered out at him like a Siberian wolf, and he thought how terrible it would be if Mrs. Baines found him there. He'd have no time to climb the railings; she'd seize him from behind.

He left the square at the unfashionable end and was immediately among the fish-and-chip shops, the little stationers selling Bagatelle, among the accommodation addresses and the dingy hotels with open doors. There were few people about because the pubs were open, but a blowzy woman carrying a parcel called out to him across the street and the commissionaire outside a cinema would have stopped him if he hadn't crossed the road. He went deeper: you could go farther and lose yourself more completely here than among the plane-trees. On the fringe of the square he was in danger of being stopped and taken back: it was obvious where he belonged: but as he went deeper he lost the marks of his origin. It was a warm night: any child in those free-living parts might be expected to play truant from bed. He found a kind of camaraderie even among grown-up people; he might have been a neighbour's child as he went quickly by, but they weren't going to tell on him, they'd been young once themselves. He picked up a protective coating of dust from the pavements, of smuts from the trains which passed along the backs in a spray of fire. Once he was caught in a knot of children running away from something or somebody, laughing as they ran; he was whirled with them round a turning and abandoned, with a sticky fruit-drop in his hand.

He couldn't have been more lost; but he hadn't the stamina to keep on. At first he feared that someone would stop him; after an hour he hoped that someone would. He couldn't find his way back, and in any case he was afraid of arriving home alone; he was afraid of Mrs. Baines, more afraid than he had ever been. Baines was his friend, but something had happened which gave Mrs. Baines all the power. He began to loiter on purpose to be noticed, but no one noticed him. Families were having a last breather on the doorsteps, the refuse bins had been put out and bits of cabbage stalks soiled his slippers. The air was full of voices, but he was cut off; these people were strangers and would always now be strangers; they were marked by Mrs. Baines and he shied away from them into a deep class-consciousness. He had been afraid of policemen, but now he wanted one to take him home; even Mrs. Baines could do nothing against a policeman. He sidled past a constable who was directing traffic, but he was too busy to pay him any attention. Philip sat down against a wall and cried.

It hadn't occurred to him that that was the easiest way, that all you had to do was to surrender, to show you were beaten and accept kindness. . . . It was lavished on him at once by two women and a pawnbroker. Another policeman appeared, a young man

with a sharp incredulous face. He looked as if he noted everything
he saw in pocketbooks and drew conclusions. A woman offered to
see Philip home, but he didn't trust her: she wasn't a match for
Mrs. Baines immobile in the hall. He wouldn't give his address;
he said he was afraid to go home. He had his way; he got his
protection. "I'll take him to the station," the policeman said, and
holding him awkwardly by the hand (he wasn't married; he had
his career to make) he led him round the corner, up the stone
stairs into the little bare overheated room where Justice waited.

5

Justice waited behind a wooden counter on a high stool; it wore
a heavy moustache; it was kindly and had six children ("three of
them nippers like yourself"); it wasn't really interested in Philip,
but it pretended to be, it wrote the address down and sent a constable to fetch a glass of milk. But the young constable was interested; he had a nose for things.

"Your home's on the telephone, I suppose," Justice said. "We'll
ring them up and say you are safe. They'll fetch you very soon.
What's your name, sonny?"

"Philip."

"Your other name."

"I haven't got another name." He didn't want to be fetched; he
wanted to be taken home by someone who would impress even
Mrs. Baines. The constable watched him, watched the way he
drank the milk, watched him when he winced away from questions.

"What made you run away? Playing truant, eh?"

"I don't know."

"You oughtn't to do it, young fellow. Think how anxious your
father and mother will be."

"They are away."

"Well, your nurse."

"I haven't got one."

"Who looks after you, then?" That question went home. Philip
saw Mrs. Baines coming up the stairs at him, the heap of black
cotton in the hall. He began to cry.

"Now, now, now," the sergeant said. He didn't know what to

do; he wished his wife were with him; even a policewoman might have been useful.

"Don't you think it's funny," the constable said, "that there hasn't been an inquiry?"

"They think he's tucked up in bed."

"You are scared, aren't you?" the constable said. "What scared you?"

"I don't know."

"Somebody hurt you?"

"No."

"He's had bad dreams," the sergeant said. "Thought the house was on fire, I expect. I've brought up six of them. Rose is due back. She'll take him home."

"I want to go home with you," Philip said; he tried to smile at the constable, but the deceit was immature and unsuccessful.

"I'd better go," the constable said. "There may be something wrong."

"Nonsense," the sergeant said. "It's a woman's job. Tact is what you need. Here's Rose. Pull up your stockings, Rose. You're a disgrace to the Force. I've got a job of work for you." Rose shambled in: black cotton stockings drooping over her boots, a gawky Girl Guide manner, a hoarse hostile voice. "More tarts, I suppose."

"No, you've got to see this young man home." She looked at him owlishly.

"I won't go with her," Philip said. He began to cry again. "I don't like her."

"More of that womanly charm, Rose," the sergeant said. The telephone rang on his desk. He lifted the receiver. "What? What's that?" he said. "Number 48? You've got a doctor?" He put his hand over the telephone mouth. "No wonder this nipper wasn't reported," he said. "They've been too busy. An accident. Woman slipped on the stairs."

"Serious?" the constable asked. The sergeant mouthed at him; you didn't mention the word death before a child (didn't he know? he had six of them), you made noises in the throat, you grimaced, a complicated shorthand for a word of only five letters anyway.

"You'd better go, after all," he said, "and make a report. The doctor's there."

Rose shambled from the stove; pink apply-dapply cheeks, loose stockings. She stuck her hands behind her. Her large morgue-like mouth was full of blackened teeth. "You told me to take him and now just because something interesting . . . I don't expect justice from a man . . ."

"Who's at the house?" the constable asked.

"The butler."

"You don't think," the constable said, "he saw . . ."

"Trust me," the sergeant said. "I've brought up six. I know 'em through and through. You can't teach me anything about children."

"He seemed scared about something."

"Dreams," the sergeant said.

"What name?"

"Baines."

"This Mr. Baines," the constable said to Philip, "you like him, eh? He's good to you?" They were trying to get something out of him; he was suspicious of the whole roomful of them; he said "yes" without conviction because he was afraid at any moment of more responsibilities, more secrets.

"And Mrs. Baines?"

"Yes."

They consulted together by the desk: Rose was hoarsely aggrieved; she was like a female impersonator, she bore her womanhood with an unnatural emphasis even while she scorned it in her creased stockings and her weather-exposed face. The charcoal shifted in the stove; the room was overheated in the mild late summer evening. A notice on the wall described a body found in the Thames, or rather the body's clothes: wool vest, wool pants, wool shirt with blue stripes, size ten boots, blue serge suit worn at the elbows, fifteen and a half celluloid collar. They couldn't find anything to say about the body, except its measurements, it was just an ordinary body.

"Come along," the constable said. He was interested, he was glad to be going, but he couldn't help being embarrassed by his company, a small boy in pyjamas. His nose smelt something, he didn't know what, but he smarted at the sight of the amusement they caused: the pubs had closed and the streets were full again of men making as long a day of it as they could. He hurried through the less frequented streets, chose the darker pavements, wouldn't loiter, and Philip wanted more and more to loiter, pulling at his hand, dragging with his feet. He dreaded the sight of Mrs. Baines waiting in the hall: he knew now that she was dead. The sergeant's mouthings had conveyed that; but she wasn't buried, she wasn't out of sight; he was going to see a dead person in the hall when the door opened.

The light was on in the basement, and to his relief the constable made for the area steps. Perhaps he wouldn't have to see Mrs. Baines at all. The constable knocked on the door because it was too dark to see the bell, and Baines answered. He stood there in the doorway of the neat bright basement room and you could see the sad complacent plausible sentence he had prepared wither at the sight of Philip; he hadn't expected Philip to return like that in the policeman's company. He had to begin thinking all over again; he wasn't a deceptive man; if it hadn't been for Emmy he would have been quite ready to let the truth lead him where it would.

"Mr. Baines?" the constable asked.

He nodded; he hadn't found the right words; he was daunted by the shrewd knowing face, the sudden appearance of Philip there.

"This little boy from here?"

"Yes," Baines said. Philip could tell that there was a message he was trying to convey, but he shut his mind to it. He loved Baines, but Baines had involved him in secrets, in fears he didn't understand. The glowing morning thought, "This is life," had become under Baines's tuition the repugnant memory, "That was life": the musty hair across the mouth, the breathless cruel tortured inquiry, "Where are they," the heap of black cotton tipped into the hall. That was what happened when you loved: you got involved; and Philip extricated himself from life, from love, from Baines, with a merciless egotism.

There had been things between them, but he laid them low, as a retreating army cuts the wires, destroys the bridges. In the abandoned country you may leave much that is dear—a morning in the Park, an ice at a corner house, sausages for supper—but more is concerned in the retreat than temporary losses. There are old people who, as the tractors wheel away, implore to be taken, but you can't risk the rearguard for their sake: a whole prolonged retreat from life, from care, from human relationships is involved.

"The doctor's here," Baines said. He nodded at the door, moistened his mouth, kept his eyes on Philip, begging for something like a dog you can't understand. "There's nothing to be done. She slipped on these stone basement stairs. I was in here. I heard her fall." He wouldn't look at the notebook, at the constable's tiny spidery writing which got a terrible lot on one page.

"Did the boy see anything?"

"He can't have done. I thought he was in bed. Hadn't he better go up? It's a shocking thing. Oh," Baines said, losing control, "it's a shocking thing for a child."

"She's through there?" the constable asked.

"I haven't moved her an inch," Baines said.

"He'd better then—"

"Go up the area and through the hall," Baines said and again he begged dumbly like a dog: one more secret, keep this secret, do this for old Baines, he won't ask another.

"Come along," the constable said. "I'll see you up to bed. You're a gentleman; you must come in the proper way through the front door like the master should. Or will you go along with him, Mr. Baines, while I see the doctor?"

"Yes," Baines said, "I'll go." He came across the room to Philip, begging, begging, all the way with his soft old stupid expression: this is Baines, the old Coaster; what about a palm-oil chop, eh?; a man's life; forty niggers; never used a gun; I tell you I couldn't help loving them: it wasn't what we call love, nothing we could understand. The messages flickered out from the last posts at the border, imploring, beseeching, reminding: this is your old friend Baines; what about an eleven's; a glass of ginger pop won't do you any harm; sausages; a long day. But the wires were cut, the messages just faded out into the enormous vacancy of the neat scrubbed room in which there had never been a place where a man could hide his secrets.

"Come along, Phil, it's bedtime. We'll just go up the steps . . ." Tap, tap, tap, at the telegraph; you may get through, you can't tell, somebody may mend the right wire. "And in at the front door."

"No" Philip said, "no. I won't go. You can't make me go. I'll fight. I won't see her."

The constable turned on them quickly. "What's that? Why won't you go?"

"She's in the hall," Philip said. "I know she's in the hall. And she's dead. I won't see her."

"You moved her then?" the constable said to Baines. "All the way down here? You've been lying, eh? That means you had to tidy up. . . . Were you alone?"

"Emmy," Philip said, "Emmy." He wasn't going to keep any more secrets: he was going to finish once and for all with everything, with Baines and Mrs. Baines and the grown-up life beyond him; it wasn't his business and never, never again, he decided, would he share their confidences and companionship. "It was all Emmy's fault," he protested with a quaver which reminded Baines that after all he was only a child; it had been hopeless to expect help there; he was a child; he didn't understand what it all meant; he couldn't read this shorthand of terror; he'd had a long day and he was tired out. You could see him dropping asleep where he stood against the dresser, dropping back into the comfortable nursery peace. You couldn't blame him. When he woke in the morning, he'd hardly remember a thing.

"Out with it," the constable said, addressing Baines with professional ferocity, "who is she?" just as the old man sixty years later startled his secretary, his only watcher, asking, "Who is she? Who is she?" dropping lower and lower into death, passing on the way perhaps the image of Baines: Baines hopeless, Baines letting his head drop, Baines "coming clean."

COMMENT

Greene's story brings together elements that we have seen in various preceding stories: the subject of infidelity, and the use of the child's point of view. Here the infidelity is used quite differently—not as a means of presenting the character of husband or wife or mistress, but as an example of a complicated adult relationship which the child, when it impinges upon him, cannot cope with; and the child's point of view is used not to create the ironic discrepancy between what he understands and what the reader understands, but as the best way of defining an experience which influences his life from early childhood even into old age. Although Baines, Mrs. Baines, and Emmy figure largely in the action, we are not invited to study their characters and personalities as we are those of the protagonists in the Mansfield and Huxley stories; except for a hint or two that Baines may not be quite so "good" or Mrs. Baines so "bad" as they appear to Philip (hints which the reader should check up and make an estimate of), the trio exist almost entirely as they are seen by Philip. To lead us to speculate about them would be to deflect attention from their actual significance in the story, which is the impact they have upon Philip. Hence we never see them acting alone, without the presence of Philip, the central character.

Nor is the story concerned with the accuracy or completeness of Philip's view of the trio. Hence, with the very slight exceptions noted above, the author does not introduce any materials which would lead us strongly to speculate about Philip's rightness or wrongness. (The author's care not to go beyond Philip's view of his elders, with its ignorance, distortions, and self-interest, will remind some readers of Dickens's management of children's perceptions. This reminiscence is quite strong in the early part of Section 5.) All we see is the love or fear with which he responds to them. But as a rule a child's point of view on experience has to be measured against something else if the story is to be more than a quaint record of juvenile impressions. Now Greene is not at all interested in the juvenile as such, and he does measure Philip's experience against something else—namely, all the remaining sixty years of Philip's life. The meaning of Philip's experience is seen, not in the rightness or wrongness of his observations, but in the influence on his whole life.

The introduction of Philip's later years brings up another technical problem. The author could introduce the later years by using the elder Philip's point of view throughout, but this method would probably interfere with his securing the immediate effect of terror which is possible when the earlier scenes are presented just as the young Philip felt them. Greene solves the problem by sticking, in the main, to the boy's point of view. Thus he gets the values of both points of view—of immediacy on the one hand, and of wide perspective on the other. Notice that the omniscient author is introduced into the story very unobtrusively, without formal breaks; a single paragraph may slip gradually from one point of view to the other. Two-thirds of the way through Section 5, the paragraph beginning " 'Yes,' Baines said. Philip could tell there was a message" first represents Philip's point of view, and then quietly shifts to that of the detached commentator.

Since the author does not have time in which to present fully the adult Philip, and since the entire effect of the story depends upon our having a clear picture of him, the author has another problem—that of giving sufficient emphasis to the passages describing the old man. He tries in several ways to secure this emphasis. He uses position: the final paragraph of the story is about the old man. He uses *vigorous language*, *often implying a sharp moral judgment*, in commenting on the later Philip: "*merciless egotism*"; "*the deep dilettante selfishness of age*"; "*never built anything, never created anything*"; and introduces the Judas-Christ comparison. A careful reader will not fail to recognize the force of these and other such comments. Again, Greene uses virtually a definite pattern of language: such words as *life* and responsibility are used repeatedly, and their very recurrence is a way of emphasizing the theme. The reader will find it useful to hunt up all these passages and see how they elaborate and reinforce each other.

The reader will be repaid by a systematic study of the author's imagery. Notice particularly the metaphor about a third of the way through Section 2: "*The sawdust was spilled out of the afternoon.*" What is the full meaning implied by this figure?

How does Greene avoid sentimental effects in his treatment of the child? What does he not do which would tend to make the reader merely feel sorry for the child?

This is the first story we have seen in which the main material is primarily psychological. But does the author stop at making a psychological case history? Are any more general ideas introduced? Is there any implied comment upon the nature of adult life?

Normally our business is to see the relation between the themes of a story and its form, between the *what* and the *how* of a story. Occasionally, however, it may be profitable to compare stories in terms of theme. Do you observe any thematic relationships between Greene's story and "*Shivaree Before Breakfast*" or "*The Gioconda Smile*"?

In "*The Fallen Idol*," the moving picture based on "*The Basement Room*," the references to Philip's later life are entirely eliminated. How does this omission change the story? Is the omission a serious one? Perhaps as a substitute for this part of the story which it does not attempt to reproduce, the picture adds something new: it shows Philip trying to lie to the police and openly makes the point that lying is bad. This addition of a "moral" may at first glimpse appear to make the movie version of the story more serious than the story itself. But does the movie seem really to be a more mature and profound work?

FANTASY

H. F. Heard

Henry Fitz Gerald Heard (who usually writes under the name Gerald Heard) was born in England in 1889, was educated at Cambridge, and since 1937 has lived in the United States. He has been a very productive writer, although most of his work has not been in fiction. His first work, *Narcissus: An Anatomy of Clothes* (1924), endeavored to trace the relationship between clothes and architecture. His philosophic and religious interests appear in such works as *The Ascent of Humanity* (1929), *The Source of Civilization* (1935), and *The Creed of Christ* (1940). At the same time he has been a student of science and has written, among other works, *Science in the Making* (1935) and *Exploring the Stratosphere* (1936). His volumes of short stories, *The Great Fog* (1944) and *The Lost Cavern* (1948), show to a considerable extent the influence of his scientific training. He has written two unusual mystery stories.

The Great Fog

THE FIRST symptom was a mildew. Very few people have ever looked carefully at such "molds"; indeed, only a specialized branch of botanists knows about them. Nor is this knowledge—except rarely—of much use. Every now and then a low growth of this sort may attack a big cash crop. Then the mycologists, whose lifework is to study these spore growths, are called in by the growers. These botanists can sometimes find another mold which will eat its fellow. That closes the matter. The balance of life, which had been slightly upset, has been righted. It is not a matter of any general interest.

This particular mildew did not seem to have even that special importance. It did not, apparently, do any damage to the trees on which it grew. Indeed, most fruit growers never noticed it. The botanists found it themselves; no one called their attention to it. It was simply a form of spore growth different in its growth rate from any previously recorded. It did not seem to do any harm to any other form of life. But it did do amazingly well for itself. It was not a new plant, but a plant with quite a new power of growth.

It was this fact which puzzled the botanists, or rather that special branch of the botanists, the mycologists. That was why they finally called in the meteorologists. They asked for "another opinion," as baffled doctors say. What made the mycologists choose the meteorologists for consultation was this: Here was a mildew which spread faster than any other mold had ever been known to grow. It flourished in places where such mildews had been thought incapable of growing. But there seemed to be no botanical change either in the mold or in the plants it grew on. Therefore the cause must be climatic: only a weather change could account for the unprecedented growth.

The meteorologists saw the force of this argument. They became interested at once. The first thing to do, they said, was to study the mildew, not as a plant, but as a machine, an indicator. "You know," said Sersen the weatherman to Charles the botanist (they had been made colleagues for the duration of the study), "the astronomers have a thing called a thermocouple that will tell the heat of a summer day on the equator of Mars. Well, here is a little gadget I've made. It's almost as sensitive to damp as the thermocouple is to heat."

Sersen spent some time rigging it up and then "balancing" it, as he called it. "Find the normal humidity and then see how much the damp at a particular spot exceeds that." But he went on fiddling about far longer than Charles thought an expert who was handling his own gadget should. He was evidently puzzled. And after a while he confessed that he was.

"Queer, very queer," said Sersen. "Of course, I expected to get a good record of humidity around the mold itself. As you say, it can't grow without that: it wouldn't be here unless the extra damp was here too. But, look here," he said, pointing to a needle that quivered near a high number on a scale. "*That* is the humidity actually around the mold itself—what we might expect, if a trifle high. That's not the surprise. It's *this*." He had swung the whole instrument on its tripod until it pointed a foot or more from the mold; for the tree they were studying was a newly attacked one and, as far as Charles had been able to discover, had on it only this single specimen of the mildew.

Charles looked at the needle. It remained hovering about the high figure it had first chosen. "Well?" he queried.

"Don't you see?" urged Sersen. "This odd high humidity is present not only around the mold itself but for more than a foot beyond."

"I don't see much to that."

"I see two things," snapped Sersen; "one's odd; the other's damned odd. The odd one anyone not blind would see. The other one is perhaps too big to be seen until one can stand well back."

"Sorry to be stupid," said Charles, a gentle-spoken but close-minded little fellow; "we botanists are small-scale men."

"Sorry to be a snapper," apologized Sersen. "But, as I suppose you've guessed, I'm startled. I've got a queer feeling that we're on the track of something big, yes, and something maybe moving pretty fast. The first odd thing isn't a complete surprise: it's that you botanists have shown us what could turn out to be a meteorological instrument more delicate and more accurate than any we have been able to make. Perhaps we ought to have been on the outlook for some such find. After all, living things are always the most sensitive detectors—can always beat mechanical instruments when they want to. You know about the mitogenetic rays given out by breeding seeds. Those rays can be recorded only by yeast cells—which multiply rapidly when exposed to the rays, thus giving an indication of their range and strength."

"Umph," said Charles. Sersen's illustration had been unfortunate, for Charles belonged to that majority of conservative botanists to whom the mitogenetic radiation was mere moonshine.

Sersen, again vexed, went on: "Well, whether you accept them or not, I still maintain that here we have a superdetector. This mildew can notice an increase in humidity long before any of our instruments. There's proof that something has changed in the climate. This mold is the first to know about it—and to profit by it. I prophesy it will soon be over the whole world."

"But your second discovery, or supposition?" Charles had no use for prophecy. These weathermen, he thought; well, after all, they aren't quite scientists, so one mustn't blame them, one supposes, for liking forecasts—forecasting is quite unscientific.

Charles was a courteous man, but Sersen was sensitive. "Well," he said defensively, "that's nothing but supposition." And yet, he thought to himself as he packed up his instrument, if it *is* true it may mean such a change that botany will be blasted and meteorology completely mistified. His small private joke relieved his temper. By the time they returned to headquarters he and Charles were friendly enough. They agreed to make a joint report which would stick severely to the facts.

Meanwhile, botanists everywhere were observing and recording the spreading of the mildew. Before long, they began to get its drift. It was spreading from a center, spreading like a huge ripple from where a stone has been flung into a lake. The center, there could be no doubt, was eastern Europe. Spain, Britain, and North Africa showed the same "high incidence." France showed an even higher one. The spread of the mold could be watched just as well in North or South America. Such and such a percentage of shrubs and trees was attacked on the Atlantic coasts; a proportionately lower percentage on the Pacific coasts; but everywhere the incidence was rising. On every sector of the vast and widening circle, America, Africa, India, the mildew was advancing rapidly.

Sersen continued his own research on the mold itself, on the "field of humidity" around each plant. He next made a number of calculations correlating the rapid rate of dispersal, the average increase of infestation of all vegetation by the mold, and the degree of humidity which must result. Then, having checked and counterchecked, at last he was ready to read his paper and give his conclusions at a joint meeting of the plant men and the weathermen.

Just before Sersen went up to the platform, he turned to Charles. "I'm ready now to face the music," he said, "because I believe we are up against something which makes scientific respectability nonsense. We've got to throw caution aside and tell the world." "That's serious," said Charles cautiously. "It's damned serious," said Sersen, and went up the steps to the rostrum.

When he came down, the audience was serious too; for a moment, as serious as he. He had begun by showing the world map with its spreading, dated lines showing where the mildew in its present profusion had reached; showing also where, in a couple of months, the two sides of the ripple would meet. Soon, almost every tree and shrub throughout the world would be infested, and, of course, the number of molds per tree and bush would increase. That was interesting and queer, but of no popular concern. The molds still remained harmless to their tree hosts and to animal life—indeed, some insects seemed rather happy about the botanical change. As far, then, as the change was only a change in mildew reproduction there was no cause for much concern, still less for alarm. The mold had gone ahead, because it was the first to benefit from some otherwise undetectable change in climate. The natural expectation would, then, be that insects, the host plants, or some other species of mold would in turn advance and so readjust the disturbed balance of nature.

But that was only the first part of Sersen's lecture. At that phrase, "balance of nature," he paused. He turned from the world map with its charting of the mold's growth. For a moment he glanced at another set of statistical charts; then he seemed to change his mind and touched the buzzer. The lights went out, and the beam from the stereopticon shot down through the darkened hall. The lighted screen showed a tree; on its branches and trunk a number of red crosses had been marked. Around each cross was a large circle, so large that some of the circles intersected.

"Gentlemen," said Sersen, "this is the discovery that really matters. Until now, perhaps unwisely, I have hesitated to communicate it. That the mold spreads, you know. That it is particularly sensitive to some otherwise undetected change in the weather, you know. Now, you must know a third fact about it—it is a weather *creator*. Literally, it can brew a climate of its own.

"I have proved that in each of these circles—and I am sure they are spreading circles—the mold is going far to create its own peculiar atmosphere—a curiously high and stable humidity. The statistically arranged readings which I have prepared, and which I have here, permit, I believe, of no other conclusion. I would also add that I believe we can see why this has happened. It is now clear what permitted this unprecedented change to get under way. We have pulled the trigger that has fired this mine. No doubt the mold first began to increase because a slight change in humidity helped it. But now it is—how shall I put it—co-operating. It is *making the humidity increase.*

"There has probably been present, these past few years, one of those small increases in atmospheric humidity which occur periodically. In itself, it would have made no difference to our lives and, indeed, would have passed unperceived. But it was at this meteorological moment that European scientists began to succeed in making a new kind of quick-growing mold which could create fats. It is, perhaps, the most remarkable of all the war efforts, perhaps the most powerful of all the new defensive weapons— against a human enemy. But in regard to the extra human world in which we live it may prove as dangerous as a naked flame in a mine chamber filled with firedamp. For, need I remind you, molds are spore-reproducing growths. Fungus is by far the strongest form of life. It breeds incessantly and will grow under conditions no other form of life will endure. When you play with spore life you may at any moment let loose something the sheer power of which makes dynamite look like a damp squib. I believe what man has now done is precisely that—he has let the genie out of its bottle, and we may find ourselves utterly helpless before it."

Sersen paused. The lights came on. Dr. Charles rose and caught the chairman's eye. Dr. Charles begged to state on behalf of the botanical world that he hoped Dr. Sersen's dramatic remarks would not be taken gravely by the press or the public. Dr. Sersen had spoken of matters botanical. Dr. Charles wished to say that he and his colleagues had had the mildew under protracted observation. He could declare categorically that it was not dangerous.

Sersen had not left the platform. He strode back to the rostrum. "I am not speaking as a botanist," he exclaimed, "I am speaking as a meteorologist. I have told you of what I am sure—the balance of life has been upset. You take for granted that the only balance is life against life, animal against animal, vegetable against vege-table. You were right to call in a weatherman, but that's of no use unless you understand what he is telling you."

The audience shifted offendedly in its seats. It wasn't scientific to be as urgent as all that. Besides, hadn't Charles said there was no danger? But what was their queer guest now saying?

"I know, every meteorologist knows, that this nature-balance is far vaster and more delicately poised than you choose to suspect. All life is balanced against its environment. Cyclones are brought on, climate can change, a glacial age can begin as the result of atmospheric alterations far too small for the layman to notice. In our atmosphere, that wonderful veil and web under which we are sheltered and in which we grow, we have a condition of extraordinary delicacy. The right—or rather the precisely wrong—catalytic agent can send the whole thing suddenly into quite another arrangement, one which can well be desperately awkward for man. It has taken an amazing balance of forces to allow human beings to live. That's the balance you've upset. Look out."

He studied his audience. There they sat, complacent, assured, only a little upset that an overexcitable colleague should be behaving unscientifically—hysterically, almost. Suddenly, with a shock of despair, Sersen realized that it was no use hoping to stir these learned experts. These were the actual minds which had patiently, persistently, purblindly worked the very changes which must bring the house down on their heads. They'd never asked, never wished to ask, what might be the general and ultimate effects of their burrowing. We're just another sort of termite, thought Sersen, as he looked down on the rows of plump faces and dull-ivory-colored pates. We tunnel away trying to turn everything into "consumable goods" until suddenly the whole structure of things collapses round us.

He left the rostrum, submitted to polite thanks, and went home. A week later his botanical hosts had ceased even to talk about his strange manners. Hardly anyone else heard of his speech.

The first report of trouble—or rumor rather (for such natural-history notes were far too trivial to get into the battle-crammed papers)—came from orchard growers in deep valleys. Then fruit growers began to gossip when the Imperial Valley, hot and dry as hell, began to report much the same thing. It was seen at night at the start and cleared off in the day; so it seemed no more than an odd, inconsequent little phenomenon. But if you went out at full moon you did see a queer sight. Every tree seemed to have a sort of iridescent envelope, a small white cloud or silver shroud all its own.

Of course, soon after that, the date growers had something to howl about. The dates wouldn't stand for damp—and each silver shroud was, for the tree about which it hung, a vapor bath. But the date growers, all the other growers decided, were done for anyway; they'd have made a howl in any case when the new Colorado water made the irrigation plans complete. The increase in humidity would inevitably spoil their crop when the valley became one great oasis.

The botanists didn't want to look into the matter again. Botanically, it was uninteresting. The inquiry had been officially closed. But the phenomenon continued to be noticed farther and farther afield.

The thing seemed then to reach a sort of saturation point. A new sort of precipitation took place. The cloud around each tree and bush, which now could be seen even during the day, would, at a certain moment, put out feeler-like wisps and join up with the other spreading and swelling ground clouds stretching out from the neighboring trees. Sersen, who had thrown up his official job just to keep track of this thing, described that critical night when, with a grim prophetic pleasure, he saw his forecast fulfilled before his eyes. His last moldering papers have remained just decipherable for his great-grandchildren.

"I stood," he said, "on a rock promontory south of Salton Sea. The full moon was rising behind me and lighted the entire Valley. I could see the orchards glistening, each tree surrounded by its own cloud. It was like a gargantuan dew; each dew-globule tree-size. And then, as I watched, just like a great tide, an obliterating flood of whiteness spread over everything. The globules ran into one another until I was looking down on a solid sea of curd-white, far denser than mist or fog. It looked as firm, beautiful, and dead as the high moon which looked down on it. 'A new Deluge,' I said to myself. 'May I not ask who has been right? Did I not foretell its coming and did not I say that man had brought it on his own head?'"

Certainly Sersen had been justified. For, the morning after his vigil, when the sun rose, the Fog did not. It lay undisturbed, level, dazzling white as a sheet of snow-covered ice, throwing back into space every ray of heat that fell on it. The air immediately above it was crystal clear. The valley was submerged under an element that looked solid enough to be walked on. The change was evidently so complete because it was a double one, a sudden reciprocal process. All the damp had been gathered below the Fog's surface, a surface as distinct as the surface of water. Conversely, all the cloud, mist, and aqueous vapor in the air above the Fog was evidently drained out of it by this new dense atmosphere. It was as though the old atmosphere had been milk. The mold acted as a kind of rennet, and so, instead of milk, there remained only this hard curd and the clear whey. The sky above the Fog was not so much the deepest of blues—it was almost a livid black; the sun in it was an intense, harsh white and most of the big stars were visible throughout the day. So, outside the Fog it was desperately cold. At night it was agonizingly so. Under that cold the Fog lay packed dense like a frozen drift of snow.

Beneath the surface of the Fog, conditions were even stranger. Passing into it was like going suddenly into night. All lights had to be kept on all day. But they were not much use. As in a bad old-fashioned fog, but now to a far worse degree, the lights would not penetrate the air. For instance, the rays of a car's headlights formed a three-foot cone, the base of which looked like a circular patch of light thrown on an opaque white screen. It was possible to move about in the Fog, but only at a slow walking pace—otherwise you kept running into things. It was a matter of groping about, with objects suddenly looming up at you—the kind of world in which a severe myopic case must live if he loses his spectacles.

Soon, of course, people began to notice with dismay the Fog's effect on crops and gardens, on houses and goods. Nothing was ever again dry. Objects did not become saturated, but they were, if at all absorbent, thoroughly damp. Paper molded, wood rotted, iron rusted. But concrete, glass, pottery, all stone ware and ceramics remained unaffected. Cloth, too, served adequately, provided the wearer could stand its never being dry.

The first thought in the areas which had been first attacked was, naturally, to move out. But the Fog moved too. Every night some big valley area suddenly "went over." The tree fog around each tree would billow outward, join up with all its fellows, and so make a solid front and surface. Then came the turn for each fog-submerged valley, each fog-lake, to link with those adjacent to it. The general level of these lakes then rose. Instead of there being, as until now, large flooded areas of lowland, but still, in the main, areas of clear upland, this order was now reversed. The mountain ranges had become strings of islands which emerged from a shining ocean that covered the whole earth's surface, right up to the six-thousand-foot level.

Any further hope of air travel was extinguished. In the Fog, lack of visibility, of course, made it impossible. Above the Fog, you could see to the earth's edge: the horizons, cleared of every modulation of mist, seemed so close that you would have thought you could have touched them with your hand. As far as sight was concerned, above the Fog, near and far seemed one. But even if men could have lived in that thin air and "unscreened" light, no plane could be sustained by it.

Sea travel was hardly more open. True, the surface of the oceans lay under the Fog-blanket, as still as the water, a thousand fathoms down. But on that oily surface—that utterly featureless desert of motionless water—peering man, only a few yards from the shore, completely lost his way. Neither sun nor stars ever again appeared over the sea to give him his bearings. So man soon abandoned the sea beyond the closest inshore shallows. Even if he could have seen his way over the ocean, he could not have taken it. There was never a breath of wind to fill a sail, and the fumes from any steamship or motorboat would have hung around the vessel and would have almost suffocated the crew.

Retreat upward was cut off. For when the Fog stabilized at six thousand feet, it was no use thinking of attempting to live above it. Even if the limited areas could have given footing, let alone feeding, to the fugitive populations, no hope lay in that direction. For the cold was now so intense above the Fog that no plant would grow. And, worse, it was soon found, to the cost of those who ventured out there, that through this unscreened air—air which was so thin that it could scarcely be breathed—came also such intense ultraviolet radiations from the sun and outer space that a short exposure to them was fatal.

So the few ranges and plateaus which rose above the six-thousand-foot level stood gaunt as the ribs of a skeleton carcass under the untwinkling stars and the white glaring sun. After a very few exploratory expeditions out into that open, men realized that they must content themselves with a sub-surface life, a new kind of fish existence, nosing about on the floor of a pool which henceforth was to be their whole world. It might be a poor, confined way of living, but above that surface was death. A few explorers returned, but, though fish taken out of water may recover if put back soon enough, every above-the-Fog explorer succumbed from the effect. After a few days the lesions and sores of bad X-ray burning appeared. If, after that, the nervous system did not collapse, the wretched man literally began to fall to pieces.

Underneath the Fog-blanket men painfully, fumblingly worked out a new answer to living. Of course, it had to be done without preparation, so the cost was colossal. All who were liable to rheumatic damage and phthisis died off. Only a hardy few remained. Man had been clever enough to pull down the atmosphere-roof which had hung so loftily over his head, but he never learned again how to raise a cover as high, spacious, and pleasant as the sky's blue dome. The dividing out of the air was a final precipitation, a nonreversible change-down toward the final entropy. Man might stay on, but only at the price of being for the rest of his term on earth confined under a thick film of precipitated air. Maybe, even if he had been free and had had the power to move fast and see far, it would have been too great a task for him to have attempted to "raise the air." As he now found himself, pinned under the collapse he had caused, he had not a chance of even beginning to plan such a vast reconstruction.

His job, then, was just to work at making lurking livable. And, within the limits imposed, it was not absolutely impossible. True, all his passion for speed and travel and seeing far and quick, all that had to go. He who had just begun to feel that it was natural to fly, now was confined not even to the pace of a brisk walk but to a crawl. It was a life on the lowest gear. Of course, great numbers died just in the first confusion, when the dark came on, before the permanent change in humidity and light swept off the other many millions who could not adapt themselves. But, after a while, not only men's health but their eyes became adapted to the perpetual dusk. They began to see that the gloom was not pitch-dark. Gradually, increasing numbers learned to be able to go about without lamps. Indeed, they found that they saw better if they cultivated this "nightsight," this ancient part of the eye so long neglected by man when he thought he was master of things. They were greatly helped also by a type of faint phosphorescence, a "cold-light," which (itself probably another mold-mutation) appeared on most surfaces if they were left untouched, and so outlined objects with faint, ghostly highlights.

So, as decentralized life worked itself out, men found that they had enough. War was gone, so that huge social hemorrhage stopped

Money went out of gear, and so that odd strangle hold on goods-exchange was loosed. Men just couldn't waste what they had, so they found they had much more than they thought. For one reason, it wasn't worth hoarding anything, holding back goods, real, edible, and wearable goods, for a rise in price. They rotted. The old medieval epitaph proved itself true in this new dark age: "What I spent I had: what I saved I lost." Altogether, life became more immediate and, what people had never suspected, more real because less diffused. It was no use having a number of things which had been thought to be necessities. Cars? You could not see to travel at more than four miles an hour, and not often at that. Radios? They just struck; either insulation against the damp was never adequate or the electric conditions, the radio-resonant layers of the upper atmosphere, had been completely altered. A wailing static was the only answer to any attempt to re-establish wireless communication.

It was a low-built, small-housed, pedestrian world. Even horses were too dashing; and they were blinder in the Fog than were men. As for your house, you could seldom see more than its front door. Metal was little used. Smelting it was troublesome (the fumes could hardly get away and nearly suffocated everyone within miles of a furnace), and when you got your iron and steel it began rusting at once. Glass knives were used instead. They were very sharp. Men learned again, after tens of thousands of years of neglect, how to flake flints, crystal, and all the silica rocks to make all manner of neat, sharp tools.

Man's one primary need, which had made for nearly all his hoarding, the animal craving to accumulate food stocks, that fear which, since the dawn of civilization, has made his granaries as vast as his fortresses, this need, this enemy, was wiped out by another freak botanical by-product of the Fog. The curious sub-fog climate made an edible fungus grow. It was a sort of manna. It rotted if you stored it. But it grew copiously everywhere, of itself. Indeed, it replaced grass: wherever grass had grown the fungus grew. Eaten raw, it was palatable and highly nutritious—more tasty and more wholesome than when cooked (which was a blessing in itself, since all fires burnt ill and any smoke was offensive in the dense air). Man, like the fishes, lived in a dim but fruitful element.

The mean temperature under the Fog stayed precisely at 67

degrees Fahrenheit, owing, evidently, to some basic balance, like that which keeps the sea below a certain depth always at 36 degrees, four degrees above freezing. Men, then, were never cold.

They stayed mainly at home, around their small settlements. What was the use of going about? All you needed and could use was at your door. There was nothing to see—your view was always limited to four feet. There was no use in trying to seize someone else's territory. You all had the same: you all had enough.

Art, too, changed. The art of objects was gone. So a purer, less collectible art took its place. Books would not last; and so memory increased enormously, and men carried their libraries in their heads —a cheaper way and much more convenient. As a result, academic accuracy, the continual quoting of authorities, disappeared. A new epic age resulted. Men in the dusk composed, extemporized, jointly developed great epics, sagas, and choruses, which grew like vast trees, generation after generation, flowering, bearing fruit, putting out new limbs. And, as pristine, bardic poetry returned, it united again with its nursery foster-brother, music. Wood winds and strings were ruined by the damp. But stone instruments, like those used by the dawn cultures, returned—giving beautiful pure notes. An orchestra of jade and marble flutes, lucid gongs, crystal-clear xylophones grew up. Just as the Arabs, nomads out on the ocean of sand, had had no plastic art, but, instead, a wonderful aural art of chant and singing verse, so the creative power of the men of the Umbral Epoch swung over from eye to ear. Indeed, the thick air which baffled the eye made fresh avenues and extensions for the ear. Men could hear for miles: their ears grew as keen as a dog's. And with this keenness went subtlety. They appreciated intervals of sound which to the old men of the open air would have been imperceptible. Men lived largely for music and felt they had made a good exchange when they peered at the last moldering shreds of pictorial art.

"Yes," said Sersen's great-grandson, when the shock of the change was over and mankind had accustomed itself to its new conditions, "yes, I suspect we were not fit for the big views, the vast world into which the old men tumbled up. It was all right to give animal men the open. But, once they had got power without vision, then either they had to be shut up or they would have shot and bombed everything off the earth's surface. Why, they were already living in tunnels when the Fog came. And out in the open, men, powerful as never before, nevertheless died by millions, died the way insects used to die in a frost, but died by one another's hands. The plane drove men off the fields. That was the thing, I believe, that made Mind decide we were not fit any longer to be at large. We were going too fast and too high to see what we were actually doing. So, then, Mind let man fancy that all he had to do was to make food apart from the fields. That was the Edible Mold, and that led straight, as my great-grandfather saw, to the atmospheric upset, the meteorological revolution. It really was a catalyst, making the well-mixed air, which we had always taken for granted as the only possible atmosphere, divide out into two layers as distinct as water and air. We're safer as we are. Mind knew that, and already we are better for our Fog cure, though it had to be drastic.

"Perhaps, one day, when we have learned enough, the Fog will lift, the old high ceiling will be given back to us. Once more Mind may say: 'Try again. The Second Flood is over. Go forth and replenish the earth, and this time remember that you are all one.' Meanwhile I'm thankful that we are as we are."

COMMENT

The stories preceding "The Great Fog" all belong in varying ways to the general category of realism. Some of them do seem to have symbolic as well as literal meanings, but all of them are to be understood primarily in terms of their reference to a known world, to familiar or probable situations and characters. In this respect they differ from Heard's "The Great Fog" and the next several stories, which are examples of fantasy. In its popular usage, the word fantasy describes unreal and improbable situations, in which the known facts of experience are distorted, reversed, or ignored entirely; it is associated with mental disorder, caprice, deliberate nonsense, and so on. As a literary form—an old one, regularly and often brilliantly practiced—fantasy also deals in what by everyday standards is unreal and improbable, and, like some practical joke or elaborate entertainment, it may do so simply for the fun of it. But fantasy is also a way of saying serious things about the world and people as we know them, and as such it may be used very effectively, as it was by Swift in Gulliver's Travels. Used seriously, fantasy relies basically upon a sharp change in the usual perspective, upon a fresh seeing of well-known objects, and its success depends partly upon creating an illusion of truth, partly upon consistency of method. "The Great Fog" may be examined in the light of these criteria.

Heard uses entirely normal characters in his story, but alters the usual perspective by radically changing the physical world in which they live. The initial appeal is to the reader's wonder, which should carry him through the account of a frightening new world. The account of mankind's efforts at survival leads the reader to an awareness of modern man's major predicament: that the marvelous powers he has acquired coupled with his lack of sufficient spiritual development to use the powers may well lead to his destruction.

Heard uses extreme care in trying to create an illusion. His style is the scientist's: he uses highly technical terms when necessary but otherwise his manner is plain, objective, factual, unexcited. The use of scientists as his main characters is a device for suggesting dependable, disinterested observation of actual phenomena. The very difference of opinion among scientists assures us that there is a tangible occurrence to disagree about. The account is very concrete; Heard is ingenious in the invention of the gradual steps by which the world is transformed.

It is in the matter of consistency, in his ability or willingness to adhere to his method, that Heard falls short. Once he starts describing the adjustment to the Fog, the tempo of the story is greatly accelerated. This is most true of what should be the most important part of the story— the moral and spiritual change brought about in the world. For emphasis, this part could well be longer and more carefully worked out. The author tends toward a quick encyclopedic account instead of continuing to give a careful dramatic account of a gradual, painful change. He virtually slips outside his illusion to comment on the new developments. Perhaps this is due, ultimately, to another aspect of his method—his failure to create one or two individual characters to carry all the way through the experience. Fiction works through individuals rather than masses; the latter are the material of journalism, and indeed the latter part of the story is presented from an external, reportorial view. The quick pace here suggests that the author is really more interested in the scientific wonders which he works out so carefully at the start than in the human significations to which he comes later.

The concluding statement by Sersen's great-grandson has a generally religious cast. How is this interpretation aided by the several references to the "New Deluge," the "Second Flood," and to manna?

V. S. Pritchett

Victor Sawdon Pritchett was born in England in 1900 and educated at Alleyn's School. He has engaged in various occupations. From 1917 to 1920 he was a salesman; from 1923 to 1928 a news correspondent in Ireland, Spain, and France; since 1930 he has been a broadcaster and critic. In 1946 he became literary editor of *The New Statesman and Nation*, and he writes literary news from London for the New York *Times*. His ten published volumes include *In My Good Books*, 1942, and *The Living Novel*, 1946, books of criticism; and *You Make Your Own Life*, 1938, and *It May Never Happen*, 1946, collections of short stories. The last volume has been praised for its sharp perceptions, which often appear in unusual situations.

The Ape

THE FRUIT robbery was over. It was the greatest fruit robbery, and from our point of view, the most successful ever known in our part of the jungle. Not that we can take all the credit for that, for it was not ourselves who started the fight, but our enemies, a colony of apes who live in another tree. They were the first to attack and by the time the great slaughter was over hundreds of their dead, of both sexes, lay on the ground, and we had taken all their fruit. It was a fortunate triumph for us.

But apes are not a complacent or ungrateful race. Once we were back in our tree binding up our wounds, we thought at once of commemorating our victory and thanking our god for it. For we are aware that if we do not thank our god for his benefactions he might well think twice before he sent us another fruit robbery of this triumphant kind. We thought therefore of how we might best please him. We tried to put ourselves in his place. What would most impress him? There were many discussions about this: we

screamed and screeched in passionate argument and the din grew
so loud—far louder than the noise we make in the ordinary business
of eating or defending our places in the tree or making love and
dying—that at last our oldest and wisest ape who lived at the very
top, slyly observed: "If I were god and had been looking down at
this tree of screeching monkeys for thousands of years, the thing
that would really impress me would be silence." We were dumb-
founded. Then one or two of us shouted: "That's got it. Let silence
be the commemoration of our victory."

So at last it was arranged. On the anniversary of the day when
the great fruit robbery began, we arranged that all of us would
stop whatever we were doing and would be silent.

But nothing is perfect in the jungle. You would think that all
apes would be proud to be alike, and would have the wisdom to
abide by the traditions of their race and the edicts of their leader.
You would think all would destroy the individual doubt with the
reflection that however different an ape may fancy he is, the glory
of the ape is that as he is now so he always has been, unchangeable
and unchanged. There were, however, some and one in particular,
as you will see, who did not think so.

We heard of them from a pterodactyl, a rather ridiculous neighbour of ours.

The pterodactyl lived on a cliff just above our tree and often,
scaly and long necked, he would flop clumsily down to talk to us.
He was a sensationalist and newsmonger, a creature with more
curiosity than brains. He was always worried. What (he would ask
us) is the meaning of life? We scratched our heads. Where was it
all leading? We spat our fruit pips. Did we apes think that we
would always go on as we were? That question was easy. Of course,
we said. How fortunate we were, he said, for he had doubts about
himself. "It seems to me that I am becoming—extinct," he said.

It was all very well of us to make light of it, he said, but "if I
had not lived near you such an idea would never have entered my
head." We replied that we did not see what we had done to upset
him. "Oh, not you in particular," he said. "It is your young apes
that are worrying me. They keep talking about their tails."—"No
livelier or more flourishing subject," we said. "We apes delight in
our tails."—"As far as I can see," the pterodactyl said, "among your
younger apes, they are being worn shorter and will soon be dis-

carded altogether."—"What!" we exclaimed—he could have touched us on no more sensitive spot—"How dare you make such a suggestion!"—"The suggestion," the pterodactyl said, "does not come from me but from your young apes. There's a group of them. They caught me by the neck the other day—I am very vulnerable in the neck—and ridiculed me publicly before a large audience. 'A flying reptile,' they said. 'Study him while you can for the species won't exist much longer—any more than *we apes shall go about on four legs and have tails*. We shall, at some unknown time in the future, but a time that comes rapidly nearer, cease to be apes. We shall become man. The pterodactyl, poor creature, came to the end of his evolutionary possibilities long ago.' "

"Man!" we exclaimed. "Man! What is that?" And what on earth, we asked the pterodactyl, did he mean by "evolution." We had never heard of it. We pressed the pterodactyl to tell us more, but he would only repeat what he had already said. When he had flopped back to his cliff again we sat scratching ourselves, deep in thought. Presently our old and wisest ape, a horny and scarred old warrior who sits dribbling away quietly to himself all day and rubbing his scars on the highest branch of all, gave a snigger and said, "Cutting off their tails to spite the ape." We did not laugh. We couldn't take the matter as lightly as he took it. We, on the contrary, raged. It was blasphemy. The joy, the pride, the whole apehood of us apes is in our tails. They are the flag under which we fight, the sheet-anchor of our patriotism, the vital insignia of our race. This young, decadent post-fruit-robbery generation was proposing to mutilate the symbol which is at the base of all our being. We did not hesitate. Spies were at once sent down to the lower branches to see if what the pterodactyl had told us was true and to bring the leader into our presence.

But before I tell what happened I must describe what life in our tree is like. The tree is a vast and leafy one, dense in the ramification of its twigs and branches. In the upper branches where the air is freer and purer and the sunlight is plentiful, live those of us who are called the higher apes; in the branches below, and even to the bottom of the trunk, swarm the thousands of lower apes, clawing and scrambling over one another's backs, massing on the boughs until they nearly break, clutching at twigs and leaves, hanging on to one another's legs and tails and all bellowing and screeching in the struggle to get up a little higher and to find a place to sit, so that when we say, as we do, that the nature of life is struggle and war we are giving a faithful report from what is going on below us.

We in the upper branches eat our fruit in peace and spit out the pips and drop the rind upon the crowd below. It is they who, without of course intending to do so, bring us our food. Each of them carries fruit for himself, but the struggle is so violent that it is hard for them to hold the fruit or to find a quiet place where they can eat it. Accordingly we send down some of our cleverer apes—those who are not quite at the top of the tree yet and perhaps will never get there because they have more brain than claw—and these hang down by their tails and adroitly flick the fruit out of the hands of the climbers. Very amusing it is to watch the astonishment of the climbers when they see their fruit go, because a minute before, they were full of confidence; then astonishment changes to anger and you see them grab the fruit from their nearest neighbours who in turn grab from the next. Failing in this, they have to go down once more to the bottom to get more fruit and begin again; and as no part of the struggle is more difficult than the one which takes place at the bottom, an ape will go to any lengths, even to the risk of his life, to avoid that catastrophe. So for thousands of years have we lived and only when fruit on our own tree is short or when we can bear no longer the sight of an abundance of fruit on another tree, occupied by just such a tribe of apes as ourselves, do our masses cease their engaging civil struggle and at an order from us higher apes above, go forth upon our great fruit robberies. It is plain that if in any respect an ape ceased to be an ape, our greatness would decline, and anarchy would follow, i.e., how would we at the top get our food?—and we should lose our tree and be destroyed by some stronger tribe. Our thoughts can therefore be imagined when the spies brought before us the leader of that group of apes who were preparing to monkey with our dearest emblem. He stood before us—and that is astonishing, for we apes do not habitually stand for long. Then he was paler than our race usually is, less hairy, fearless—very un-ape-like that—and upright on his hind legs, not seeking support for his forelegs on some branch. These hung at his side or fidgeted with an aimless embarrassment behind his back. We growled at him and averted our eyes from his stupidly steadfast stare—for as a fighting race we are made subtle by fear and look restlessly, suspiciously around us, continually preparing for the sudden feint, the secret calculation, the necessary retreat, the unexpected attack. Nothing delivers an ape more readily to his enemy than a transparently straight-forward look; but this upright ape had already lost so much of his apehood that he had forgotten the evasions of a warrior race. He was not even furtive. And in another way, too, he had lost our tradition. He spoke what was in his mind. This, I need hardly say, is ridiculous in a warrior whose business is to conceal his real purpose from his enemy. I note these facts merely as a matter of curiosity and to show how this new ape, from the very beginning, gave himself helplessly into our hands. We had supposed him to be guilty of race-treachery only, a bodily perversion which is, perhaps, a sin and not a crime—but the moment he spoke he went much further. He accused himself of sedition from his own mouth. He spoke as follows:

"Since my arrest has given me an opportunity of speaking to higher apes for the first time in my life, I will speak what (perhaps unknown to you), has been in the minds of us who are lower in the tree for hundreds of years. We think that there is no greater evil than the vast fruit slaughters. Now there could be no slaughter if our teeth and claws were not sharp, and they would not be sharp if we were not perpetually engaged in struggle. We believe that a crucial time has arrived in the evolution" (we pricked up our ears at that word) "of the ape. Our tails, that used to swirl us (as they waved above our heads) into blood-thirsty states of mind, are shortening; we have not shortened them ourselves by any act of will. If we apes will work to order our lives in a new way, the struggle will cease, no more great fruit slaughters will be necessary and everyone will have all the fruit he needs and can eat in peace in his appropriate place in the tree. For we do not think that even you in the higher branches for whom unconsciously we labour, really benefit by the great slaughters. Some of you are killed as thousands of us are, many of you are maimed and carry unbeautiful scars. From what we below hear of your private lives and talk in the upper branches, your privileges do not make you either sensible or happy."

We were ready to fall upon him after this blasphemous speech, but our oldest ape, steeped in the wisdom and slyness of his great age, silenced us. "And when there is a shortage of fruit for every-

one in the tree, high and low alike?" he asked. "If our teeth and
claws are not sharpened," replied the new ape, "we shall not want to
attack other trees but, when we need fruit, we shall go to the others
and instead of tearing them apart we shall talk to them, stroke
them and persuade them. They, seeing how gentle our hands are,
will like being stroked and will smile and coo in their pleasure;
for, as all of us apes know from intimate experience, there is nothing more delightful than a gentle tickling and scratching—and then
they will share their fruit with us."—"What a hope!" we laughed.
And some cried with disgust, "That ape's a pansy!" But a shout
went up from the lower branches where a mass of his supporters
were gathered. "You'd better do as he says," the cry came, "or soon
there will be none of us left to bring you your fruit." "Yes," said the
leader, "another fruit robbery and there will be no more workers
for you to steal from."

"Now," we whispered to our oldest ape on the highest branch,
"now let us kill him."

"Remember," said the old one, "that he has followers. They are
too many for us and we are unprepared."

This was true, so, reluctantly, we let the leader go and swing
back down the branches to his own people.

After he had gone we gathered in conference in the upper
branches. When we were seated our oldest ape said, "No doubt to
you there seems to be something new, startling and dangerous in
the speech you have just heard. I expect you think it the speech
of a revolutionary. So it is—but there's nothing new in that. From
the beginning of time there have been revolutions and what difference do they make? None whatever. Everything goes on afterwards
exactly as it went on before. Do not worry therefore about revolu-
tionaries. I have seen dozens of such people and with a little art they
can be made to die very comfortably of their own enthusiasm. And,
in one way, I agree with what that strange ape said. He said that
violence is wasteful. It is—for to exterminate our own workers
would mean that we would be without food or would have to go
down out of our comfortable places in the tree and get it for ourselves. That would indeed be a calamity. No, I think if we wish
to remove the danger from this particular movement we should
support it."

"Support blasphemy and treachery!" we cried with indignation.

"Ah!" exclaimed the old ape wistfully. "There speaks the honest warrior. But I am old and political and it would seem to me a mistake to let all that enthusiasm get out of our hands. After our last great fruit robbery we are rather tired, you know, and enthusiasm is not easily come by again."

"But our tails!" we shouted.

"Your honour and your tails!" said our weary and ancient one. "I guarantee to show you such a display of tails wagging, curling, prehensile and triumphant as you have never seen before."

"Well, if your plan will safeguard our sacred tails and preserve us from evolution," we said, "there may be something in it. Tell us what it is."

"It is very simple," he said. "First of all we shall announce the end of all fruit robbery . . ."

"Impossible," we interrupted.

"It is never impossible to *announce* anything," he said. "I repeat we shall announce the end of all fruit robbery. But the lower ape is an emotional creature. It is useless to argue with him—indeed we know that the free interchange of ideas in open argument is extremely dangerous, for the lower apes are hungry and hunger sharpens the mind, just as it sharpens the claws. No, we must appeal to his emotions, for it is here that he is untrained and inexperienced. So when we announce the end of all fruit robbery we must perform an act which shall symbolize our intention. That is easy. Almost anything would do. The best, I think, would be merely to alter the date of the commemoration of our last robbery from the anniversary of its call to battle, to the day on which it ended and when peace was declared. I'll lay you a hundred to one in pomegranates that you will see the tails wag on that day."

We who listened were doubtful of the success of a trick so simple and, moreover, we were disappointed not to have the opportunity of killing the rebel ape. But when we heard the enthusiasm in the lower branches, we realized that our oldest ape had judged rightly. Those short-tailed evolutionists were so diddled that they shouted for joy. "Peace!" "The end of all fruit robberies," "To each according to his needs"—we above heard their delirious cries and winked. And when the inquisitive pterodactyl came down to see what it was all about, we slapped him on the back and pulled his wings about merrily and nearly choked him with pomegranate seeds which do not agree with him. "Cheer up, you're not extinct yet," we said. And even that cheerless reptile, though he said his nerves couldn't stand monkey tricks any more, had to smile.

And the ceremony took place. We appointed the day, and just before noon the yelling ceased and all the struggling and climbing. Just where they were, on whatever twig or branch, our apes coiled their tails and squatted in silence. The only movement was the blinking of our eyes, thousands of eyes in the hot rays of the sun. I do not know if you have ever seen a tree full of apes squatting in silence on their haunches. It is an impressive sight. There was our oldest ape on the topmost branch; a little beneath him was our circle of privileged ones, and below, thick in the descending hierarchy, were the others.

And then, before a minute had gone by, an event occurred which filled us with horror. The lengths to which blasphemy will go were revealed to us. Taking advantage of the stillness of the multitude, an ape leapt up the tree, from back to back, from branch to branch and burst through our unprepared ranks at the top. It was the leader to whom we had spoken.

"This is a fraud," he shouted. "You are pretending to commemorate peace when all the time you are planning greater robberies. You are not even silent. Listen to the grinding and sharpening of your claws and teeth."

It was, of course, our habit. We do it unconsciously.

Too startled for a moment to act, we hesitated. Then: "Lynch him. Kill him," cried the crowd with a sudden roar. We hesitated no more and at least a score of us leapt upon him. You would think we had an easy task. But there was extraordinary strength in that creature. He fought like a god, skilfully, and he had laid out half of our number with a science and ferocity such as we had never seen before our numbers overwhelmed him. Some spirit must have been in him and we still wonder, not without apprehension, if that spirit is lying asleep in his followers. However that may be, we threw him down at last upon the branch. Our oldest ape came down to look upon the panting creature and then what we saw made us gasp. He was lying on his face. There was a backside bare and hairless—he had no tail. No tail at all.

"It is man!" we cried. And our stomachs turned.

COMMENT

In Mr. Pritchett's story the fantasy appears in the characters rather than in the situation. Readers who are familiar with fables will probably have little sense of the fantastic, for they will easily recognize the tradition of giving animal form to human characters and altering the setting and the other properties accordingly. In fact, the human situation is so completely recognizable in the apes and their life in the tree that the story is virtually an allegory—a form of narrative in which all the elements (characters, situations, and so forth) have exact equivalents in another scale of meaning. In general, we may say that the allegorical narrative has greater value when it more successfully engages our imagination, that is, when the story works in its own terms and thus is not merely a transparent disguise for something else. In a very primitive allegory, for instance, the old ape might merely have been called "Mr. Ruling Class." Mr. Pritchett goes far beyond that simple form, and indeed many details serve to make the ape life come through in its own terms—the furtive look, for instance, and the grinding and sharpening of teeth and claws which goes on "unconsciously." But how about the arrangement of apes on the tree? Is it plausible, or is it merely a mechanical way of expressing a certain meaning?

The reader should decide how successful the allegory is in stimulating the imagination. As we have said, one of the criteria is the consistency with which the author works out his primary, literal terms. But this is not the sole test. Ultimately, what counts is the freshness with which he reveals the situation he is writing about. Does Pritchett compel us to see, in a new light, such matters as the competitive nature of modern life, the struggle to "get to the top," the relationship of this struggle to world wars, the strategies used to maintain the status quo? In pursuing his allegory, does one have a real sense of discovery?

One of the factors that bear upon these questions is Pritchett's choice of the apes to represent mankind. He might have chosen various other animals, which could perhaps have exhibited human relationships just as well. But the advantage of the apes is that they are not merely an allegorical figure for man, but have also a metaphorical value: because of their relation to the human race, they suggest an actual retrogression by the human race, as if we had retained certain human qualities but in many ways were basically animal. Since, considered in their relationship to man, they represent a prehistoric era, the apes make possible the introduction of the pterodactyl, which is a good symbol of extinction, *of the passage of things which at any given period may seem inevitable and permanent. Notice how important this idea is in the story. Further, the use of apes makes it logical to introduce the concept of evolution as a metaphor for revolution—a metaphor which suggests, at the same time, that a good deal of what is considered revolutionary at any given time will turn out to be only a phase of an evolutionary process. Finally, the use of evolution as a part of the narrative prepares the way for the very effective ending—the appearance of a man and the dramatically proper disgust of the apes at this manifestation.*

Note that the identification of the man by his physical form follows after his character has been explicitly developed by his actions. The stress is entirely upon his mental and moral make-up. In effect, then, the story is making a definition of manliness—of the essentially human as against the essentially animal. The theme is a very broad one, not one of limited historical or topical interest. What are the ingredients of manliness which are dramatically presented?

Another test of an allegory is its flexibility. Is the reader held to a single set of meanings which exhaust the possibilities of the text, or can the narrative accommodate a rich body of interpretation? Can each element suggest more than one thing to an imaginative reader? Again, how profound or limited are the meanings which the allegory is able to suggest? Such questions as these should be asked with respect to "The Ape."

Franz Kafka

Franz Kafka was born in Prague in 1883, took a law degree in 1906, obtained a position in the workmen's compensation division of the government, and, after repeated visits to sanitariums, died of tuberculosis in 1924. Kafka is known for three novels, none of which is complete— *The Trial, The Castle,* and *America,* for a volume of short stories, and for several volumes of sketches, aphorisms, and journals. He had directed that most of this work be destroyed, but it was saved by his friend Max Brod. Kafka is one of the most brilliant and influential writers of the twentieth century. Realistic and quiet in detail, the writings have in general a dreamlike and surrealist quality which has called forth a variety of interpretations ranging from the psychoanalytical to the theological. The basic situation in the novels is that of human isolation, guilt, and frustration in an apparently incoherent universe.

A Hunger Artist

URING these last decades the interest in professional fasting has markedly diminished. It used to pay very well to stage such great performances under one's own management, but today that is quite impossible. We live in a different world now. At one time the whole town took a lively interest in the hunger artist; from day to day of his fast the excitement mounted; everybody wanted to see him at least once a day; there were people who bought season tickets for the last few days and sat from morning till night in front of his small barred cage; even in the nighttime there were visiting hours, when the whole effect was heightened by torch flares; on fine days the cage was set out in the open air, and then it was the children's special treat to see the hunger artist; for their elders he was often just a joke that happened to be in fashion, but the children stood open-mouthed, holding each other's hands for greater security, marveling at him as he sat there pallid in black tights, with his ribs sticking out so prominently, not even on a seat but down among straw on the ground, sometimes giving a courteous nod, answering questions with a constrained smile, or perhaps stretching an arm through the bars so that one might feel how thin it was, and then again withdrawing deep into himself, paying no attention to anyone or anything, not even to the all-important striking of the clock that was the only piece of furniture in his cage, but merely staring into vacancy with half-shut eyes, now and then taking a sip from a tiny glass of water to moisten his lips.

Besides casual onlookers there were also relays of permanent watchers selected by the public, usually butchers, strangely enough, and it was their task to watch the hunger artist day and night, three of them at a time, in case he should have some secret recourse to nourishment. This was nothing but a formality, instituted to reassure the masses, for the initiates knew well enough that during his fast the artist would never in any circumstances, not even under forcible compulsion, swallow the smallest morsel of food; the honor of his profession forbade it. Not every watcher, of course, was capable of understanding this, there were often groups of night watchers who were very lax in carrying out their duties and deliberately huddled together in a retired corner to play cards with great absorption, obviously intending to give the hunger artist the chance of a little refreshment, which they supposed he could draw from some private hoard. Nothing annoyed the artist more than such watchers; they made him miserable; they made his fast seem unendurable; sometimes he mastered his feebleness sufficiently to sing during their watch for as long as he could keep going, to show them how unjust their suspicions were. But that was of little use; they only wondered at his cleverness in being able to fill his mouth even while singing. Much more to his taste were the watchers who sat close up to the bars, who were not content with the dim night lighting of the hall but focused him in the full glare of the electric pocket torch given them by the impresario. The harsh light did not trouble him at all, in any case he could never sleep properly, and he could always drowse a little, whatever the light, at any hour, even when the hall was thronged with noisy onlookers. He was quite happy at the prospect of spending a sleepless night with such watchers; he was ready to exchange jokes with them, to tell them stories out of his nomadic life, anything at all to keep them awake and demonstrate to them again that he had no eatables in his cage and that he was fasting as not one of them could fast. But his happiest moment was when the morning came and an enormous breakfast was brought them, at his expense, on which they flung themselves with the keen appetite of healthy men after a weary night of wakefulness. Of course there were people who argued that this breakfast was an unfair attempt to bribe the watchers, but that was going rather too far, and when they were invited to take on a night's vigil without a breakfast, merely for the sake of the cause, they made themselves scarce, although they stuck stubbornly to their suspicions.

Such suspicions, anyhow, were a necessary accompaniment to the profession of fasting. No one could possibly watch the hunger artist continuously, day and night, and so no one could produce first-hand evidence that the fast had really been rigorous and continuous; only the artist himself could know that, he was therefore bound to be the sole completely satisfied spectator of his own fast. Yet for other reasons he was never satisfied; it was not perhaps mere fasting that had brought him to such skeleton thinness that many people had regretfully to keep away from his exhibitions, because the sight of him was too much for them, perhaps it was dissatisfaction with himself that had worn him down. For he alone knew, what no other initiate knew, how easy it was to fast. It was the easiest thing in the world. He made no secret of this, yet people did not believe him, at the best they set him down as modest, most of them, however, thought he was out for publicity or else was some kind of cheat who found it easy to fast because he had discovered a way of making it easy, and then had the impudence to admit the fact, more or less. He had to put up with all that, and in the course of time had got used to it, but his inner dissatisfaction always rankled, and never yet, after any term of fasting—this must be granted to his credit—had he left the cage of his own free will. The longest period of fasting was fixed by his impresario at forty days, beyond that term he was not allowed to go, not even in great cities, and there was good reason for it, too. Experience had proved that for about forty days the interest of the public could be stimulated by a steadily increasing pressure of advertisement, but after that the town began to lose interest, sympathetic support began

notably to fall off; there were of course local variations as between
one town and another or one country and another, but as a general
rule forty days marked the limit. So on the fortieth day the flower-
bedecked cage was opened, enthusiastic spectators filled the hall,
a military band played, two doctors entered the cage to measure
the results of the fast, which were announced through a mega-
phone, and finally two young ladies appeared, blissful at having
been selected for the honor, to help the hunger artist down the
few steps leading to a small table on which was spread a carefully
chosen invalid repast. And at this very moment the artist always
turned stubborn. True, he would entrust his bony arms to the
outstretched helping hands of the ladies bending over him, but
stand up he would not. Why stop fasting at this particular moment,
after forty days of it? He had held out for a long time, an illimit-
ably long time; why stop now, when he was in his best fasting
form, or rather, not yet quite in his best fasting form? Why should
he be cheated of the fame he would get for fasting longer, for
being not only the record hunger artist of all time, which presumably he was already, but for beating his own record by a performance beyond human imagination, since he felt that there were no
limits to his capacity for fasting? His public pretended to admire
him so much, why should it have so little patience with him; if
he could endure fasting longer, why shouldn't the public endure it?
Besides, he was tired, he was comfortable sitting in the straw, and
now he was supposed to lift himself to his full height and go down
to a meal the very thought of which gave him a nausea that only
the presence of the ladies kept him from betraying, and even that
with an effort. And he looked up into the eyes of the ladies who
were apparently so friendly and in reality so cruel, and shook his
head, which felt too heavy on its strengthless neck. But then there
happened yet again what always happened. The impresario came
forward, without a word—for the band made speech impossible—
lifted his arms in the air above the artist, as if inviting Heaven
to look down upon its creature here in the straw, this suffering
martyr, which indeed he was, although in quite another sense;
grasped him round the emaciated waist, with exaggerated caution,
so that the frail condition he was in might be appreciated; and
committed him to the care of the blenching ladies, not without
secretly giving him a shaking so that his legs and body tottered

and swayed. The artist now submitted completely; his head lolled on his breast as if it had landed there by chance; his body was hollowed out; his legs in a spasm of self-preservation clung close to each other at the knees, yet scraped on the ground as if it were not really solid ground, as if they were only trying to find solid ground; and the whole weight of his body, a featherweight after all, relapsed onto one of the ladies, who, looking round for help and panting a little—this post of honor was not at all what she had expected it to be—first stretched her neck as far as she could to keep her face at least free from contact with the artist, then finding this impossible, and her more fortunate companion not coming to her aid but merely holding extended on her own trembling hand the little bunch of knucklebones that was the artist's, to the great delight of the spectators burst into tears and had to be replaced by an attendant who had long been stationed in readiness. Then came the food, a little of which the impresario managed to get between the artist's lips, while he sat in a kind of half-fainting trance, to the accompaniment of cheerful patter designed to distract the public's attention from the artist's condition; after that, a toast was drunk to the public, supposedly prompted by a whisper from the artist in the impresario's ear; the band confirmed it with a mighty flourish, the spectators melted away, and no one had any cause to be dissatisfied with the proceedings, no one except the hunger artist himself, he only, as always.

So he lived for many years, with small regular intervals of recuperation, in visible glory, honored by the world, yet in spite of that troubled in spirit, and all the more troubled because no one would take his trouble seriously. What comfort could he possibly need? What more could he possibly wish for? And if some good-natured person, feeling sorry for him, tried to console him by pointing out that his melancholy was probably caused by fasting, it could happen, especially when he had been fasting for some time, that he reacted with an outburst of fury and to the general alarm began to shake the bars of his cage like a wild animal. Yet the impresario had a way of punishing these outbreaks which he rather enjoyed putting into operation. He would apologize publicly for the artist's behavior, which was only to be excused, he admitted, because of the irritability caused by fasting; a condition hardly to be understood by well-fed people; then by natural transition he went on to mention the artist's equally incomprehensible boast that he could fast for much longer than he was doing; he praised the high ambition, the good will, the great self-denial undoubtedly implicit in such a statement; and then quite simply countered it by bringing out photographs, which were also on sale to the public, showing the artist on the fortieth day of a fast lying in bed almost dead from exhaustion. This perversion of the truth, familiar to the artist though it was, always unnerved him afresh and proved too much for him. What was a consequence of the premature ending of his fast was here presented as the cause of it! To fight against this lack of understanding, against a whole world of non-understanding, was impossible. Time and again in good faith he stood by the bars listening to the impresario, but as soon as the photographs appeared he always let go and sank with a groan back on to his straw, and the reassured public could once more come close and gaze at him.

A few years later when the witnesses of such scenes called them to mind, they often failed to understand themselves at all. For meanwhile the aforementioned change in public interest had set in; it seemed to happen almost overnight; there may have been profound causes for it, but who was going to bother about that; at any rate the pampered hunger artist suddenly found himself deserted one fine day by the amusement seekers, who went streaming past him to other more favored attractions. For the last time the impresario hurried him over half Europe to discover whether the old interest might still survive here and there; all in vain; everywhere, as if by secret agreement, a positive revulsion from professional fasting was in evidence. Of course it could not really have sprung up so suddenly as all that, and many premonitory symptoms which had not been sufficiently remarked or suppressed during the rush and glitter of success now came retrospectively to mind, but it was now too late to take any countermeasures. Fasting would surely come into fashion again at some future date, yet that was no comfort for those living in the present. What, then, was the hunger artist to do? He had been applauded by thousands in his time and could hardly come down to showing himself in a street booth at village fairs, and as for adopting another profession, he was not only too old for that but too fanatically devoted to fasting. So he took leave of the impresario, his partner in an unparalleled career, and hired himself to a large circus; in order to spare his own feelings he avoided reading the conditions of his contract.

A large circus with its enormous traffic in replacing and recruiting men, animals and apparatus can always find a use for people at any time, even for a hunger artist, provided of course that he does not ask too much, and in this particular case anyhow it was not only the artist who was taken on but his famous and long-known name as well, indeed considering the peculiar nature of his performance, which was not impaired by advancing age, it could not be objected that here was an artist past his prime, no longer at the height of his professional skill, seeking a refuge in some quiet corner of a circus; on the contrary, the hunger artist averred that he could fast as well as ever, which was entirely credible, he even alleged that if he were allowed to fast as he liked, and this was at once promised him without more ado, he could astound the world by establishing a record never yet achieved, a statement which certainly provoked a smile among the other professionals, since it left out of account the change in public opinion, which the hunger artist in his zeal conveniently forgot.

He had not, however, actually lost his sense of the real situation and took it as a matter of course that he and his cage should be stationed, not in the middle of the ring as a main attraction, but outside, near the animal cages, on a site that was after all easily accessible. Large and gaily painted placards made a frame for the cage and announced what was to be seen inside it. When the public came thronging out in the intervals to see the animals, they could hardly avoid passing the hunger artist's cage and stopping there for a moment, perhaps they might even have stayed longer had not those pressing behind them in the narrow gangway, who did not understand why they should be held up on their way toward the excitements of the menagerie, made it impossible for anyone to stand gazing quietly for any length of time. And that was the reason why the hunger artist, who had of course been looking forward to these visiting hours as the main achievement of his life, began instead to shrink from them. At first he could hardly wait for the intervals; it was exhilarating to watch the crowds come streaming his way, until only too soon—not even the most obstinate self-deception, clung to almost consciously, could hold out against the fact—the conviction was borne in upon him that these people, most of them, to judge from their actions, again and again, without exception, were all on their way to the menagerie. And the first sight of them from the distance remained the best. For when they reached his cage he was at once deafened by the storm of shouting and abuse that arose from the two contending factions, which renewed themselves continuously, of those who wanted to stop and stare at him—he soon began to dislike them more than the others—not out of real interest but only out of obstinate self-assertiveness, and those who wanted to go straight on to the animals. When the first great rush was past, the stragglers came along, and these, whom nothing could have prevented from stopping to look at him as long as they had breath, raced past with long strides, hardly even glancing at him, in their haste to get to the menagerie in time. And all too rarely did it happen that he had a stroke of luck, when some father of a family fetched up before him with his children, pointed a finger at the hunger artist and explained at length what the phenomenon meant, telling stories of earlier years when he himself had watched similar but much more thrilling performances, and the children, still rather uncomprehending, since neither inside nor outside school had they been sufficiently prepared for this lesson—what did they care about fasting?—yet showed by the brightness of their intent eyes that new and better times might be coming. Perhaps, said the hunger artist to himself many a time, things would be a little better if his cage were set not quite so near the menagerie. That made it too easy for people to make their choice, to say nothing of what he suffered from the stench of the menagerie, the animals' restlessness by night, the carrying past of raw lumps of flesh for the beasts of prey, the roaring at feeding times, which depressed him continually. But he did not dare to lodge a complaint with the management; after all, he had the animals to thank for the troops of people who passed his cage, among whom there might always be one here and there to take an interest in him, and who could tell where they might seclude him if he called attention to his existence and thereby to the fact that, strictly speaking, he was only an impediment on the way to the menagerie.

A small impediment, to be sure, one that grew steadily less. People grew familiar with the strange idea that they could be expected, in times like these, to take an interest in a hunger artist, and with this familiarity the verdict went out against him. He might fast as much as he could, and he did so; but nothing could save him now, people passed him by. Just try to explain to anyone the art of fasting! Anyone who has no feeling for it cannot be made to understand it. The fine placards grew dirty and illegible, they were torn down; the little notice board telling the number of fast days achieved, which at first was changed carefully every day, had long stayed at the same figure, for after the first few weeks even this small task seemed pointless to the staff; and so the artist simply fasted on and on, as he had once dreamed of doing, and it was no trouble to him, just as he had always foretold, but no one counted the days, no one, not even the artist himself, knew what records he was already breaking, and his heart grew heavy. And when once in a time some leisurely passer-by stopped, made merry over the old figure on the board and spoke of swindling, that was in its way the stupidest lie ever invented by indifference and inborn malice, since it was not the hunger artist who was cheating; he was working honestly, but the world was cheating him of his reward.

Many more days went by, however, and that too came to an end. An overseer's eye fell on the cage one day and he asked the attendants why this perfectly good cage should be left standing there unused with dirty straw inside it; nobody knew, until one man, helped out by the notice board, remembered about the hunger artist. They poked into the straw with sticks and found him in it. "Are you still fasting?" asked the overseer. "When on earth do you mean to stop?" "Forgive me, everybody," whispered the hunger artist; only the overseer, who had his ear to the bars, understood him. "Of course," said the overseer, and tapped his forehead with a finger to let the attendants know what state the man was in, "we forgive you." "I always wanted you to admire my fasting," said the hunger artist. "We do admire it," said the overseer, affably. "But you shouldn't admire it," said the hunger artist. "Well, then we don't admire it," said the overseer, "but why shouldn't we admire it?" "Because I have to fast, I can't help it," said the hunger artist. "What a fellow you are," said the overseer, "and why can't you help it?" "Because," said the hunger artist, lifting his head a little and speaking, with his lips pursed, as if for a kiss, right into the overseer's ear, so that no syllable might be lost, "because I couldn't find the food I liked. If I had found it, believe me, I should have made no fuss and stuffed myself like you or anyone else." These were his last words, but in his dimming eyes remained the firm though no longer proud persuasion that he was still continuing to fast.

"Well, clear this out now!" said the overseer, and they buried the hunger artist, straw and all. Into the cage they put a young panther. Even the most insensitive felt it refreshing to see this wild creature leaping around the cage that had so long been dreary. The panther was all right. The food he liked was brought him without hesitation by the attendants; he seemed not even to miss his freedom; his noble body, furnished almost to the bursting point with all that it needed, seemed to carry freedom around with it too; somewhere in his jaws it seemed to lurk; and the joy of life streamed with such ardent passion from his throat that for the onlookers it was not easy to stand the shock of it. But they braced themselves, crowded round the cage, and did not want ever to move away.

COMMENT

Kafka's fantasy is of a different order than that of Pritchett or Heard. It does not derive from the use of animal characters or of amazing events. The world and the characters are in the main recognizable; in days of hunger strikes and assorted kinds of endurance contests, even the main character's unusual way of life is not entirely incredible. Everything that happens is recorded in a full and solid way, with a calm, unhurried reasonableness. One of Kafka's gifts is the ability to give to all the surfaces of the life he describes, and to almost any individual moment of that life, a kind of everyday, commonplace actuality. In some stories this note of the substantial and the ordinary is maintained at the same time that monstrous characters or happenings are presented and this combination is quite characteristic of Kafka. But in "The Hunger Artist" nearly all of the story might be read as if it were realistic—a literary transcript of experience.

It is, of course, not a realistic story at bottom. Despite all the details drawn from life, the meaning cannot be pinned down by a mere putting together of those details. Something other than an everyday logic is at work. Perhaps we may say that it is like a very logical and orderly dream, which may be entirely consistent within itself, which may look very

much like life and be based on life, and yet not be meaningful in the
ordinary terms of life. (In their different ways Heard and Pritchett depart much further from a realistic version of life; yet their meanings are
comparatively easy to trace.) It is in that sense that this story is a fantasy.
If we can compare the hunger artist with a hunger striker, we find that
in everyday logic the striker has some objective outside himself, such as
a release of prisoners or a relaxation of a rule; but the hunger artist's
endurance does not have this kind of meaning. By everyday logic the
hunger artist may be viewed as a circus freak, but a circus freak would
not present the psychological problems of the artist and would not dis-
appear into the straw and be forgotten. And so on throughout the story:
the ordinary avenues of approach take us only part way to the heart
of the story.

The concreteness of the story, its substantialness on its own grounds
as story, plus the elusiveness of its meaning, show that it is hardly an
allegory. Its meaning must be sought rather in symbolism, in the power
of various parts of the story to suggest nonliteral meanings. The career
of the hunger artist, for instance, may suggest that fame depends upon
a coincidence of some personal gift—or even eccentricity—and a fashion
in public taste. In the watchers of the artist a reader may find the skepti-
cal spirit, the spirit of the checkup, even the scientific spirit, which can
never quite capture the whole truth. The artist's anger at the cynical
watcher and his preference for devoted watchers may suggest either
idealism or a desire for attention. The replacement of the hunger artist
by the young panther obviously symbolizes a sharp shift of values. The
panther loves food and is full of vitality: he suggests the vigorous and
the affirmative—in a word, life instead of death. Yet he is animal, not
human; this seems to be a bar against accepting him as an unqualified
symbol of value. On the other hand, the author goes out of his way to
emphasize the panther's apparent freedom—a highly important point if
the story is at all concerned with moral values.

The ambiguity of the final paragraph is characteristic of the story as
a whole, of which a number of widely different interpretations have been
made. According to one of these, the artist's experience represents the
fate of religion, the modern shift from spiritual to physical values.
According to another, the hunger artist is the artist in general, whose
fate has been like that of the religious hero. According to a quite different
theory, the life of the hunger artist really represents the life of a neurotic
personality, presented comically; the neurosis is finally overcome, and
at the end a happy state of health is achieved.

Many of the details present great difficulties for one or another of
these interpretations, and in a sense we may have to accept all these

meanings as latent in the story. Is this a doctrine of despair? By no means. It is all to the story's credit that it contains so much of a stimulus to the imagination; it drives us to a rewarding discovery of meanings that a straight realistic story or a mere extravaganza cannot have. It is rich rather than confused, and it compels us, like all the finest art, both to sense the ambiguity of experience and to seek the difficult synthesis of meanings. We have various clues: it is clear, for instance, that the artist is not a political or business figure. The impresario we can see, in general, as the agency which mediates between the specialized hero and the rest of the world: we could conceive of him as the artist's exhibitor, the writer's publisher, the ecclesiastical organization in which the spiritual life is channeled, the part of the human personality which keeps the neurotic part in touch with reality, and so on. A study of the different elements in the story will suggest a series of meaningful relationships.

What is the suggestive value of the forty days of the fast? Of the self-revelation which the artist makes just before his death? Does the use of the circus resemble the use of the circus in Alexander's story?

E. M. Forster

Edward Morgan Forster was born in England in 1879 and has lived there for most of his life. After completing his education at Cambridge, he wrote, during his 20's, a series of four novels, of which *Howards End* (1910) was the last. During World War I he was stationed in Egypt. It was many years before he returned to novel writing; then in 1924 appeared his best-known work, *A Passage to India,* the product of a two-year residence in India. In 1927 he published *Aspects of the Novel,* a volume of criticism generally held in high esteem. His two volumes of short stories, which he says are all that he is likely to do in that form, are strikingly original. Most of them belong to the category of fantasy, which is used as a means of commenting on human character.

Mr. Andrews

THE SOULS of the dead were ascending towards the Judgment Seat and the Gate of Heaven. The world soul pressed them on every side, just as the atmosphere presses upon rising bubbles, striving to vanquish them, to break their thin envelope of personality, to mingle their virtue with its own. But they resisted, remembering their glorious individual life on earth, and hoping for an individual life to come.

Among them ascended the soul of a Mr. Andrews who, after a beneficent and honourable life, had recently deceased at his house in town. He knew himself to be kind, upright and religious, and though he approached his trial with all humility, he could not be doubtful of its result. God was not now a jealous God. He would not deny salvation merely because it was expected. A righteous soul may reasonably be conscious of its own righteousness and Mr. Andrews was conscious of his.

"The way is long," said a voice, "but by pleasant converse the way becomes shorter. Might I travel in your company?"

MR. ANDREWS From *The Eternal Moment and Other Stories* by E. M. Forster, copyright, 1920, by Harcourt, Brace and Company, Inc., and used with their permission.

"Willingly," said Mr. Andrews. He held out his hand, and the two souls floated upwards together.

"I was slain fighting the infidel," said the other exultantly, "and I go straight to those joys of which the Prophet speaks."

"Are you not a Christian?" asked Mr. Andrews gravely.

"No, I am a Believer. But you are a Moslem, surely?"

"I am not," said Mr. Andrews. "I am a Believer."

The two souls floated upwards in silence, but did not release each other's hands. "I am broad church," he added gently. The word "broad" quavered strangely amid the interspaces.

"Relate to me your career," said the Turk at last.

"I was born of a decent middle-class family, and had my education at Winchester and Oxford. I thought of becoming a missionary, but was offered a post in the Board of Trade, which I accepted. At thirty-two I married, and had four children, two of whom have died. My wife survives me. If I had lived a little longer I should have been knighted."

"Now I will relate my career. I was never sure of my father, and my mother does not signify. I grew up in the slums of Salonika. Then I joined a band and we plundered the villages of the infidel. I prospered and had three wives, all of whom survive me. Had I lived a little longer I should have had a band of my own."

"A son of mine was killed travelling in Macedonia. Perhaps you killed him."

"It is very possible."

The two souls floated upward, hand in hand. Mr. Andrews did not speak again, for he was filled with horror at the approaching tragedy. This man, so godless, so lawless, so cruel, so lustful, believed that he would be admitted into Heaven. And into what a heaven—a place full of the crude pleasures of a ruffian's life on earth! But Mr. Andrews felt neither disgust nor moral indignation. He was only conscious of an immense pity, and his own virtues confronted him not at all. He longed to save the man whose hand he held more tightly, who, he thought, was now holding more tightly on to him. And when he reached the Gate of Heaven, instead of saying, "Can I enter?" as he had intended, he cried out, "Cannot *he* enter?"

And at the same moment the Turk uttered the same cry. For the same spirit was working in each of them.

From the gateway a voice replied, "Both can enter." They were filled with joy and pressed forward together.

Then the voice said, "In what clothes will you enter?"

"In my best clothes," shouted the Turk, "the ones I stole." And he clad himself in a splendid turban and a waistcoat embroidered with silver, and baggy trousers, and a great belt in which were stuck pipes and pistols and knives.

"And in what clothes will you enter?" said the voice to Mr. Andrews.

Mr. Andrews thought of his best clothes, but he had no wish to wear them again. At last he remembered and said, "Robes."

"Of what colour and fashion?" asked the voice.

Mr. Andrews had never thought about the matter much. He replied, in hesitating tones, "White, I suppose, of some flowing soft material," and he was immediately given a garment such as he had described. "Do I wear it rightly?" he asked.

"Wear it as it pleases you," replied the voice. "What else do you desire?"

"A harp," suggested Mr. Andrews. "A small one."

A small gold harp was placed in his hand.

"And a palm—no, I cannot have a palm, for it is the reward of martyrdom; my life has been tranquil and happy."

"You can have a palm if you desire it."

But Mr. Andrews refused the palm, and hurried in his white robes after the Turk, who had already entered Heaven. As he passed in at the open gate, a man, dressed like himself, passed out with gestures of despair.

"Why is he not happy?" he asked.

The voice did not reply.

"And who are all those figures, seated inside on thrones and mountains? Why are some of them terrible, and sad, and ugly?"

There was no answer. Mr. Andrews entered, and then he saw that those seated figures were all the gods who were then being worshipped on the earth. A group of souls stood round each, singing his praises. But the gods paid no heed, for they were listening to the prayers of living men, which alone brought them nourishment. Sometimes a faith would grow weak, and then the god of that faith also drooped and dwindled and fainted for his daily portion of incense. And sometimes, owing to a revivalist movement, or to a great commemoration, or to some other cause, a faith would grow strong, and the god of that faith grow strong also. And, more frequently still, a faith would alter, so that the features of its god altered and became contradictory, and passed from ecstasy to respectability, or from mildness and universal love to the ferocity of battle. And at times a god would divide into two gods, or three, or more, each with his own ritual and precarious supply of prayer.

Mr. Andrews saw Buddha, and Vishnu, and Allah, and Jehovah, and the Elohim. He saw little ugly determined gods who were worshipped by a few savages in the same way. He saw the vast shadowy outlines of the neo-Pagan Zeus. There were cruel gods, and coarse gods, and tortured gods, and, worse still, there were gods who were peevish, or deceitful, or vulgar. No aspiration of humanity was unfulfilled. There was even an intermediate state for those who wished it, and for the Christian Scientists a place where they could demonstrate that they had not died.

He did not play his harp for long, but hunted vainly for one of his dead friends. And though souls were continually entering Heaven, it still seemed curiously empty. Though he had all that he expected, he was conscious of no great happiness, no mystic contemplation of beauty, no mystic union with good. There was nothing to compare with that moment outside the gate, when he prayed that the Turk might enter and heard the Turk uttering the same prayer for him. And when at last he saw his companion, he hailed him with a cry of human joy.

The Turk was seated in thought, and round him, by sevens, sat the virgins who are promised in the Koran.

"Oh, my dear friend!" he called out. "Come here and we will never be parted, and such as my pleasures are, they shall be yours also. Where are my other friends? Where are the men whom I love, or whom I have killed?"

"I, too, have only found you," said Mr. Andrews. He sat down by the Turk, and the virgins, who were all exactly alike, ogled them with coal black eyes.

"Though I have all that I expected," said the Turk, "I am conscious of no great happiness. There is nothing to compare with that moment outside the gate when I prayed that you might enter, and heard you uttering the same prayer for me. These virgins are as beautiful and good as I had fashioned, yet I could wish that they were better."

As he wished, the forms of the virgins became more rounded, and their eyes grew larger and blacker than before. And Mr. Andrews, by a wish similar in kind, increased the purity and softness of his garment and the glitter of his harp. For in that place their expectations were fulfilled, but not their hopes.

"I am going," said Mr. Andrews at last. "We desire infinity and we cannot imagine it. How can we expect it to be granted? I have never imagined anything infinitely good or beautiful excepting in my dreams."

"I am going with you," said the other.

Together they sought the entrance gate, and the Turk parted with his virgins and his best clothes, and Mr. Andrews cast away his robes and his harp.

"Can we depart?" they asked.

"You can both depart if you wish," said the voice, "but remember what lies outside."

As soon as they passed the gate, they felt again the pressure of the world soul. For a moment they stood hand in hand resisting it. Then they suffered it to break in upon them, and they, and all the experience they had gained, and all the love and wisdom they had generated, passed into it, and made it better.

COMMENT

Forster offers us still another kind of fantasy. Whereas Kafka gives us a real world in which some rather puzzling events occur, Forster forms his story out of disembodied spirits, the "world soul," and Heaven. Kafka's story is the harder, since we must find the meanings of his human beings and their experiences. Forster, on the other hand, employs traditional, mythical figures and concepts of which the general meaning is quickly apparent.

But Forster does not use his traditional counters in a conventional way; rather he rearranges them sharply, so that, instead of reading platitudes, we are driven to a fresh examination of familiar positions. Irony is Forster's chief instrument; it is used more regularly here than in almost any other story. Both Mr. Andrews and the Moslem assert,

I am a Believer"—a term which automatically excludes the other. Each is sorry that the other will have to be excluded, and each is pleasantly surprised by the way things come out. Then comes the ultimate and unpleasant surprise—that Heaven is not as satisfying as they had supposed.

This constant reversal of expectations is a way of commenting upon a certain aspect of human nature—its constant belief that it can define, and its effort to define, a permanent state of happiness. It can specify certain rewards for itself, but it can never guarantee that these rewards will make it feel as it hopes to feel. The reader should examine the story to see how this idea is worked out dramatically. (Why is it effective to have two quite different aspirants to Heaven? Forster constantly stresses their differences. Are the differences as important as the likenesses? If not, why stress the differences?)

Does Forster, then, merely register the irony of failure? Or does he also present another irony—the irony of success in an unexpected quarter? What contribution to the meaning of the story is made by the wish that each soul makes for the other? This episode is very important, and the reader should not neglect it because of the almost casual way in which Forster slides over it.

One of the very important concepts in modern civilization is individualism. To what extent is the story a criticism of this concept? Consider, in this connection, the wish that each soul makes for the other, and the place of the "world soul" in the plot.

Note that Forster achieves a special effect by the casualness of his manner. The story is like an anecdote told, in not very great detail and without much emphasis, in a passing conversation. It is the method of understatement. Only the last sentence has a slightly more formal and emphatic style. What arrangement of words contributes to this effect

METHODS OF
CHARACTER STUDY

George Milburn

George Milburn was born at Coweta, Indian Territory, in 1906. He attended various colleges and finally graduated from the University of Oklahoma in 1930. By this time he had already had a career as a reporter in Oklahoma and as a free-lance writer in Chicago and New Orleans. After graduation he was again a journalist for a time; later he engaged in radio serial writing; and since 1943 he has done motion-picture writing in Hollywood. The source of many of his best-known stories is the life of the cities and towns of Oklahoma. Some of his works are *Oklahoma Town* (1931), *No More Trumpets* (1933), and *Catalogue* (1936).

The Apostate

HARRY, you been jacking me up about how I been neglecting Rotary here lately, so I'm just going to break down and tell you something. Now I don't want you to take this personal, Harry, because it's not meant personal at all. No siree! Not *a*-tall! But, just between you and I, Harry, I'm not going to be coming out to Rotary lunches any more. I mean I'm quitting Rotary! . . .

Now whoa there! Whoa! Whoa just a minute and let me get in a word edgeways. Just let me finish my little say.

Don't you never take it into your head that I haven't been wrestling with this thing plenty. I mean I've argued it all out with myself. Now I'm going to tell you the whyfor and the whereof and the howcome about this, Harry, but kindly don't let what I say go no further. Please keep it strictly on the Q.T. Because I guess the rest of the boys would suspicion that I was turning highbrow on them. But you've always been a buddy to me, Harry, you mangy old son of a hoss thief, you, so what I'm telling you is the straight dope.

THE APOSTATE Reprinted from *The New Yorker;* copyright, 1932, The F-R Publishing Corporation; and from *No More Trumpets* by permission of the author and of Harcourt, Brace and Company, Inc.

Harry, like you no doubt remember, up till a few months ago Rotary was about "the most fondest thing I is of," as the nigger says. There wasn't nothing that stood higher for me than Rotary.

Well, here, about a year ago last fall I took a trip down to the university to visit my son and go to a football game. You know Hubert Junior, my boy. Sure. Well, this is his second year down at the university. Yes sir, that boy is getting a college education. I mean, I'm all for youth having a college education.

Of course I think there is such a thing as too much education working a detriment. Take, for instance, some of these longhairs running around knocking the country right now. But what I mean is, a good, sound, substantial college education. I don't mean a string of letters a yard long for a man to write after his John Henry. I just mean that I want my boy to have his sheepskin, they call it, before he starts out in the world. Like the fellow says, I want him to get his A.B. degree, and then he can go out and get his J.O.B.

Now, Harry, I always felt like a father has got certain responsibilities to his son. That's just good Rotary. That's all that is. You know that that's just good Rotary yourself, Harry. Well, I always wanted Hubert to think about me just like I was a pal to him, or say an older brother, maybe. Hubert always knew that all he had to do was come to me, and I would act like a big buddy to him, irregardless.

Well, like I was telling you, Harry, I started Hubert in to the university two years ago, and after he had been there about two months, I thought I would run down and see how he was getting along and go to a football game. So I and Mrs. T. drove over one Friday. We didn't know the town very well, so we stopped at a filling station, and I give Hubert a ring, and he come right on down to where we was to show us the way. Just as soon as he come up, I could see right then that he had something on his mind bothering him.

He called me aside and took me into the filling-station rest-room, and says: "For the love of God, Dad, take that Rotary button out of your coat lapel," he says to me.

Harry, that come as a big surprise to me, and I don't mind telling you that it just about took the wind out of my sails. But I wasn't going to let on to him, so I rared back on my dignity, and says,

"Why, what do you mean, take that Rotary button out of my lapel, young man?" I says to him.

"Dad," Hubert says to me, serious, "any frat house has always got a few cynics in it. If you was to wear that Rotary button in your lapel out to the frat house, just as soon as you got out of sight, some of those boys at the house would razz the life out of me," he says.

"Hubert," I says, "there's not a thing that this lapel badge represents that any decent, moral person could afford to make fun of. If that's the kind of Reds you got out at your fraternity, the kind that would razz a what you might call sacred thing—yes sir, a sacred thing—like Rotary, well I and your mamma can just go somewheres else and put up. I don't guess the hotels have quit running," I says to him.

By now I was on my high horse right, see?

"Now, Dad," Hubert says, "it's not that. I mean, person'ly I'm awful proud of you. It's just that I haven't been pledged to this fraternity long, see, and when some of those older members found out you was a Rotarian they would deal me a lot of misery, and I couldn't say nothing. Person'ly I think Rotary is all right," he says to me.

"Well, you better, son," I says, "or I'm going to begin to think that you're sick in the head."

The way he explained it, though, Harry, that made it a horse of a different tail, as the saying goes, so I give in and took off my Rotary button right there. Stuck it in my pocket, see? So we went on out and visited at Hubert's fraternity house, and do you know that those boys just got around there and treated we folks like we was princes of the blood. I mean you would of thought that I was an old ex-graduate of that university. And we saw the big pigskin tussle the next day, fourteen to aught, favor us, and we had such a scrumptious time all around I forgot all about what Hubert had said.

Ever'thing would of been all right, except for what happened later. I guess some of those older boys at the frat house begin using their form of psychology on Hubert. I mean they finely got his mind set against Rotary, because when he come home for the summer vacation that was about the size of things.

I mean all last summer, I thought Hubert never would let up. He just kept it up, making sarcastic remarks about Rotary, see? Even when we was on our vacation trip. You know we drove out to California and back last summer, Harry. Come back with the same air in the tires we started out with. Well, I thought it would be kind of nice to drop in and eat with the Hollywood Rotary— you know, just to be able to say I had. Well, do you know that that boy Hubert made so much fun of the idea I just had to give it up? That was the way it was the whole trip. He got his mother around on his side, too. Just to be frank with you, I never got so sick and tired of anything in all my born days.

Well, Harry, I had my dander up there for a while, and all the bickering in the world couldn't of shook me from my stand. But finely Hubert went back to college in September, and I thought I would have a little peace. Then I just got to thinking about it, and it all come over me. "Look here, Mister Man," I says to myself, "your faith and loyalty to Rotary may be a fine thing, and all that, but it's just costing you the fellowship of your own son." Now a man can't practice Rotary in the higher sense, and yet at the same time be letting his own son's fellowship get loose from him. So there it was. Blood's thicker than water, Harry. You'll have to admit that.

Right along in there, Harry, was the first time I begin to attending meetings irregular. I'll tell you—you might not think so—but it was a pretty tough struggle for me. I remember one Monday noon, Rotary-meeting day, I happened to walk past the Hotel Beckman just at lunchtime. The windows of the Venetian Room was open, and I could hear you boys singing a Rotary song. You know that one we sing set to the tune of "Last Night on the Back Porch." It goes:

> I love the Lions in the morning,
>   The Exchange Club at night,
> I love the Y's men in the evening,
>   And Kiwanis are all right . . .

Well, I couldn't carry a tune if I had it in a sack, but anyway that's the way it goes. So I just stopped in my tracks and stood there listening to that song coming out of the Hotel Beckman dining room. And when the boys come to the last verse,

I love the Optimists in the springtime,
The Ad Club in the fall,
But each day—and in every way—
I love Rotary best of all. . . .

I tell you, Harry, that just got me. I had a lump in my throat big enough to choke a cow. The tears begin coming up in my eyes, and it might sound ridiculous to hear me tell it now, but I could of broke down and bawled right there on the street. I got a grip on myself and walked on off, but right then I says to myself, "The hell with Hubert and his highbrow college-fraternity ideas; I'm going back to Rotary next week."

Well, I did go back the next week, and what happened decided me on taking the step I decided on. Here's what decided me. You know, I never got very well acquainted with Gay Harrison, the new secretary. I mean, of course, I know him all right, but he hasn't been in Rotary only but about a year. Well, on that particular day, I just happened to let my tongue slip and called him Mister Harrison, instead of by his nickname. Well, of course, the boys slapped a dollar fine on me right then and there. I haven't got no kick to make about that, but the point is, I had a letter from Hubert in my pocket right then, telling me that he had run short of money. So I just couldn't help but be struck by the idea "I wish I was giving Hubert this dollar." So that's what decided me on devoting my time and finances to another kind of fellowship, Harry.

I get down to the university to see Hubert more frequent now. I make it a point to. And the boys come to me, and I been helping them a little on their frat building fund. There's a fine spirit of fellowship in an organization like that. Some boys from the best families of the State are members, too. You might think from what I said that they'd be uppish, but they're not. No siree. Not a bit of it. I been down there enough for them to know me, now, and they all pound me on the back and call me H.T., just like I was one of them. And I do them, too. And I notice that when they sit down to a meal, they have some songs they sing just as lively and jolly as any we had at Rotary. Of course, like Hubert said, a few of them might have some wild-haired ideas about Rotary, but they're young yet. And as far as I can see there's not a knocker nor a sourbelly among them. Absolutely democratic.

It puts me in mind of a little incidence that happened last month when the frat threw a big Dad's Day banquet for us down there. All the fathers of the boys from all over the State was there. Well, to promote the spirit of fellowship between dad and son, the fraternity boys all agreed to call their dads by their first name, just treating the dads like big buddies. So at the table Hubert happened to forget for a minute, and says to me "Dad" something. Well sir, the president of the frat flashed right out, "All right, Hubie, we heard you call H.T. 'Dad.' So that'll just cost you a dollar for the ice-cream fund." Ever'body had a good laugh at Hubert getting caught like that, but do you know, that boy of mine just forked right over without making a kick. That shows the stuff, don't it, Harry? Nothing wrong with a boy like that.

And the whole bunch is like that, ever' one of them. I'll tell you, Harry, the boys at that frat of Hubert's are the builders in the coming generation. Any man of vision can see that.

Well, that's that. Now what was you going to say?

COMMENT

To read Milburn's story after a group of fantasies is to shift very sharply back into the basic methods of realism: everything from the language to the characters and their actions is drawn directly from the immediate, everyday world. In that sense the story might be called photographic. Is the author content, however, to make a recognizable picture, or does he use his materials in such a way as to make a comment upon them?

The story consists entirely of a monologue by H. T.—a form which prevents the author from making direct comments. But we do not merely read what H. T. says; as we read, we are led to take a certain attitude toward him. We realize that he is a kindly, well-intending father; yet we hardly identify ourselves with him or admire him. Note how his style influences our conception of him—his grammar, his mispronunciations ("finely," "incidence"), his repetitions and inaccuracy (note the sixth paragraph in the story), his total dependence on clichés. It is not that he is incorrect but that he is extremely dull and undiscriminating.

Milburn, then, in his skillful reproduction of a certain kind of spoken English (even the rhythm of it is well done), has not merely produced an imitation for imitation's sake, but has prepared us to look over the head of the speaker, as it were, and to see things that he does not see. What we see, of course, is that Rotary and college fraternity life are very much alike, or, in more general terms, that social organizations tend to fall into a standard pattern. H. T. makes this clear by his recital of the activities, habits, and rules of each. Yet the story is aimed less at making this point than at exhibiting it in the midst of its attendant ironies—H. T.'s unimaginative failure to see the resemblances even while he is in effect listing them, the way in which two generations resemble each other socially despite all their other differences, the supercilious attitude of the boys toward a group so like their own.

What other comments does the story make either on characters or on organizations? What does its acceptance of H. T. tell us about the fraternity? Merely that it is "democratic"?

What this story should make clear is that a realistic story may be quite different things: it may try noncommittally to record experience ("transcript of life" or "slice of life"), or it may frankly interpret by all the means at its disposal. Milburn's story, for instance, is highly selective: the author chooses both a certain kind of character and a certain kind of language to make us respond in a certain way, to sense a situation as ironically amusing. He does not merely record all the facts and "let the facts speak for themselves." How, for instance, would the story differ in its effect if H. T. were shrewd, humorous, and tolerant?

The word apostate is usually used in a religious sense. How does Milburn's choice of it add to his meaning?

A study of H. T.'s clichés will reveal most of H. T.'s mental furnishings. What are they?

How does H. T. compare, as a father, with Henry Garnet in "The Facts of Life"?

J. F. Powers

James F. Powers was born in Jacksonville, Illinois, in 1917. He attended various schools in Illinois and received his high-school education under Franciscan friars. He has worked in bookstores in Chicago and as editor on the Historical Records Survey. His first story appeared in *Accent* and since then his work has been published in various magazines. He has received several prizes and distinctions, including a Guggenheim Fellowship in 1948. In 1949 he began teaching creative writing at Marquette University. His volume of collected stories, *Prince of Darkness and Other Stories* (1947), published both in the United States and in England, has won a great deal of praise.

The Forks

THAT summer when Father Eudex got back from saying Mass at the orphanage in the morning, he would park Monsignor's car, which was long and black and new like a politician's, and sit down in the cool of the porch to read his office. If Monsignor was not already standing in the door, he would immediately appear there, seeing that his car had safely returned, and inquire:

"Did you have any trouble with her?"

Father Eudex knew too well the question meant, Did you mistreat my car?

"No trouble, Monsignor."

"Good," Monsignor said, with imperfect faith in his curate, who was not a car owner. For a moment Monsignor stood framed in the screen door, fumbling his watch fob as for a full-length portrait, and then he was suddenly not there.

"Monsignor," Father Eudex said, rising nervously, "I've got a chance to pick up a car."

At the door Monsignor slid into his frame again. His face expressed what was for him intense interest.

"Yes? Go on."

"I don't want to have to use yours every morning."

"It's all right."

"And there are other times." Father Eudex decided not to be maudlin and mention sick calls, nor be entirely honest and admit he was tired of busses and bumming rides from parishioners. "And now I've got a chance to get one—cheap."

Monsignor, smiling, came alert at *cheap*.

"New?"

"No, I wouldn't say it's new."

Monsignor was openly suspicious now. "What kind?"

"It's a Ford."

"And not new?"

"Not new, Monsignor—but in good condition. It was owned by a retired farmer and had good care."

Monsignor sniffed. He *knew* cars. "V-Eight, Father?"

"No," Father Eudex confessed. "It's a Model A."

Monsignor chuckled as though this were indeed the damnedest thing he had ever heard.

"But in very good condition, Monsignor."

"You said that."

"Yes. And I could take it apart if anything went wrong. My uncle had one."

"No doubt." Monsignor uttered a laugh at Father Eudex's rural origins. Then he delivered the final word, long delayed out of amusement. "It wouldn't be prudent, Father. After all, this isn't a country parish. You know the class of people we get here."

Monsignor put on his Panama hat. Then, apparently mistaking the obstinacy in his curate's face for plain ignorance, he shed a little more light. "People watch a priest, Father. *Damnant quod non intelligunt.* It would never do. You'll have to watch your tendencies."

Monsignor's eyes tripped and fell hard on the morning paper lying on the swing where he had finished it.

"Another flattering piece about that crazy fellow. . . . There's a man who might have gone places if it weren't for his mouth! A bishop doesn't have to get mixed up in all that stuff!"

Monsignor, as Father Eudex knew, meant unions, strikes, race riots—all that stuff.

"A parishioner was saying to me only yesterday it's getting so you can't tell the Catholics from the Communists, with the priests as bad as any. Yes, and this fellow is the worst. He reminds me of that bishop a few years back—at least he called himself a bishop, a Protestant—that was advocating companionate marriages. It's not that bad, maybe, but if you listened to some of them you'd think that Catholicity and capitalism were incompatible!"

"The Holy Father—"

"The Holy Father's in Europe, Father. Mr. Memmers lives in this parish. I'm his priest. What can I tell him?"

"Is it Mr. Memmers of the First National, Monsignor?"

"It is, Father. And there's damned little cheer I can give a man like Memmers. Catholics, priests, and laity alike—yes, and princes of the Church, all talking atheistic communism!"

This was the substance of their conversation, always, the deadly routine in which Father Eudex played straight man. Each time it happened he seemed to participate, and though he should have known better he justified his participation by hoping that it would not happen again, or in quite the same way. But it did, it always did, the same way, and Monsignor, for all his alarums, had nothing to say really and meant one thing only, the thing he never said— that he dearly wanted to be, and was not, a bishop.

Father Eudex could imagine just what kind of bishop Monsignor would be. His reign would be a wise one, excessively so. His mind was made up on everything, excessively so. He would know how to avoid the snares set in the path of the just man, avoid them, too, in good taste and good conscience. He would not be trapped as so many good shepherds before him had been trapped, poor souls— caught in fair-seeming dilemmas of justice that were best left alone, like the first apple. It grieved him, he said, to think of those great hearts broken in silence and solitude. It was the worst kind of exile, alas! But just give him the chance and he would know what to do, what to say, and, more important, what not to do, not to say—neither yea nor nay for him. He had not gone to Rome for nothing. For him the dark forest of decisions would not exist; for him, thanks to hours spent in prayer and meditation, the forest would vanish as dry grass before fire, his fire. He knew the mask of evil already—birth control, indecent movies, salacious books— and would call these things by their right names and dare to deal with them for what they were, these new occasions for the old sins of the cities of the plains.

But in the meantime—oh, to have a particle of the faith that God had in humanity! Dear, trusting God forever trying them beyond their feeble powers, ordering terrible tests, fatal trials by nonsense (the crazy bishop). And keeping Monsignor steadily warming up on the side lines, ready to rush in, primed for the day that would perhaps never dawn.

At one time, so the talk went, there had been reason to think that Monsignor was headed for a bishopric. Now it was too late; Monsignor's intercessors were all dead; the cupboard was bare; he knew it at heart, and it galled him to see another man, this *crazy* man, given the opportunity, and making such a mess of it.

Father Eudex searched for and found a little salt for Monsignor's wound. "The word's going around he'll be the next archbishop," he said.

"I won't believe it," Monsignor countered hoarsely. He glanced at the newspaper on the swing and renewed his horror. "If that fellow's right, Father, I'm"—his voice cracked at the idea—"*wrong!*"

Father Eudex waited until Monsignor had started down the steps to the car before he said, "It could be."

"I'll be back for lunch, Father. I'm taking her for a little spin."

Monsignor stopped in admiration a few feet from the car—her. He was as helpless before her beauty as a boy with a birthday bicycle. He could not leave her alone. He had her out every morning and afternoon and evening. He was indiscriminate about picking people up for a ride in her. He kept her on a special diet—only the best of gas and oil and grease, with daily rubdowns. He would run her only on the smoothest roads and at so many miles an hour. That was to have stopped at the first five hundred, but only now, nearing the thousand mark, was he able to bring himself to increase her speed, and it seemed to hurt him more than it did her.

Now he was walking around behind her to inspect the tires. Apparently O.K. He gave the left rear fender an amorous chuck and eased into the front seat. Then they drove off, the car and he, to see the world, to explore each other further on the honeymoon.

Father Eudex watched the car slide into the traffic, and waited, on edge. The corner cop, fulfilling Father Eudex's fears, blew his whistle and waved his arms up in all four directions, bringing traffic to a standstill. Monsignor pulled expertly out of line and drove down Clover Boulevard in a one-car parade; all others stalled respectfully. The cop, as Monsignor passed, tipped his cap, showing a bald head. Monsignor, in the circumstances, could not acknowledge him, though he knew the man well—a parishioner. He was occupied with keeping his countenance kindly, grim, and exalted, that the cop's faith remain whole, for it was evidently inconceivable to him that Monsignor should ever venture abroad unless to bear the Holy Viaticum, always racing with death.

Father Eudex, eyes baleful but following the progress of the big black car, saw a hand dart out of the driver's window in a wave. Monsignor would combine a lot of business with pleasure that morning, creating what he called "good will for the Church"—all morning in the driver's seat toasting passers-by with a wave that was better than a blessing. How he loved waving to people!

Father Eudex overcame his inclination to sit and stew about things by going down the steps to meet the mailman. He got the usual handful for the Monsignor—advertisements and amazing offers, the unfailing crop of chaff from dealers in church goods, organs, collection schemes, insurance, and sacramental wines. There were two envelopes addressed to Father Eudex, one a mimeographed plea from a missionary society which he might or might not acknowledge with a contribution, depending upon what he thought of the cause—if it was really lost enough to justify a levy on his poverty—and the other a cheque for a hundred dollars.

The cheque came in an eggshell envelope with no explanation except a tiny card, "Compliments of the Rival Tractor Company," but even that was needless. All over town clergymen had known for days that the cheques were on the way again. Some, rejoicing, could hardly wait. Father Eudex, however, was one of those who could.

With the passing of hard times and the coming of the fruitful war years, the Rival Company, which was a great one for public relations, had found the best solution to the excess-profits problem to be giving. Ministers and even rabbis shared in the annual jack pot, but Rival employees were largely Catholic and it was the cheques to the priests that paid off. Again, some thought it was a wonderful idea, and others thought that Rival, plagued by strikes and justly so, had put their alms to work.

There was another eggshell envelope, Father Eudex saw, among the letters for Monsignor, and knew his cheque would be for two hundred, the premium for pastors.

Father Eudex left Monsignor's mail on the porch table by his cigars. His own he stuck in his back pocket, wanting to forget it, and went down the steps into the yard. Walking back and forth on the shady side of the rectory where the lilies of the valley grew and reading his office, he gradually drifted into the back yard, lured by a noise. He came upon Whalen, the janitor, pounding pegs into the ground.

Father Eudex closed the breviary on a finger. "What's it all about, Joe?"

Joe Whalen snatched a piece of paper from his shirt and handed it to Father Eudex. "He gave it to me this morning."

He—it was the word for Monsignor among them. A docile pronoun only, and yet when it meant the Monsignor it said, and concealed, nameless things.

The paper was a plan for a garden drawn up by the Monsignor in his fine hand. It called for a huge fleur-de-lis bounded by smaller crosses—and these Maltese—a fountain, a sundial, and a cloister walk running from the rectory to the garage. Later there would be birdhouses and a ten-foot wall of thick grey stones, acting as a moat against the eyes of the world. The whole scheme struck Father Eudex as expensive and, in this country, Presbyterian.

When Monsignor drew the plan, however, he must have been in his medieval mood. A spouting whale jostled with Neptune in the choppy waters of the fountain. North was indicated in the legend by a winged cherub huffing and puffing.

Father Eudex held the plan up against the sun to see the watermark. The stationery was new to him, heavy, simulated parchment, with the Church of the Holy Redeemer and Monsignor's name embossed, three initials, W. F. X., William Francis Xavier. With all those initials the man could pass for a radio station, a chancery wit had observed, or if his last name had not been Sweeney, Father Eudex added now, for high Anglican.

Father Eudex returned the plan to Whalen, feeling sorry for him and to an extent guilty before him—if only because he was a priest like Monsignor (now turned architect) whose dream of a monastery garden included the overworked janitor under the head of "labour."

Father Eudex asked Whalen to bring another shovel. Together, almost without words, they worked all morning spading up crosses, leaving the big fleur-de-lis to the last. Father Eudex removed his coat first, then his collar, and finally was down to his undershirt.

Toward noon Monsignor rolled into the driveway.

He stayed in the car, getting red in the face, recovering from the pleasure of seeing so much accomplished as he slowly recognized his curate in Whalen's helper. In a still, appalled voice he called across the lawn, "Father," and waited as for a beast that might or might not have sense enough to come.

Father Eudex dropped his shovel and went over to the car, shirtless.

Monsignor waited a moment before he spoke, as though annoyed by the everlasting necessity, where this person was concerned, to explain. "Father," he said quietly at last, "I wouldn't do any more of that—if I were you. Rather, in any event, I wouldn't."

"All right, Monsignor."

"To say the least, it's not prudent. If necessary"—he paused as Whalen came over to dig a cross within earshot—"I'll explain later. It's time for lunch now."

The car, black, beautiful, fierce with chromium, was quiet as Monsignor dismounted, knowing her master. Monsignor went around to the rear, felt a tire, and probed a nasty cinder in the tread.

"Look at that," he said, removing the cinder.

Father Eudex thought he saw the car lift a hoof, gaze around, and thank Monsignor with her headlights.

Monsignor proceeded at a precise pace to the back door of the rectory. There he held the screen open momentarily, as if remembering something or reluctant to enter before himself—such was his humility—but then called to Whalen with an intimacy that could never exist between them.

"Better knock off now, Joe."

Whalen turned in on himself. "*Joe*—is it!"

Father Eudex removed his clothes from the grass. His hands were all blisters, but in them he found a little absolution. He apologized to Joe for having to take the afternoon off. "I can't make it, Joe. Something turned up."

"Sure, Father."

Father Eudex could hear Joe telling his wife about it that night —yeah, the young one got in wrong with the old one again. Yeah, the old one, he don't believe in it, work, for them.

Father Eudex paused in the kitchen to remember he knew not what. It was in his head, asking to be let in, but he did not place it until he heard Monsignor in the next room complaining about the salad to the housekeeper. It was the voice of dear, dead Aunt Hazel, coming from the summer he was ten. He translated the past into the present: I can't come out and play this afternoon, Joe, on account of my monsignor won't let me.

In the dining room Father Eudex sat down at the table and said grace. He helped himself to a chop, creamed new potatoes, pickled beets, jelly, and bread. He liked jelly. Monsignor passed the butter.

"That's supposed to be a tutti-frutti salad," Monsignor said, grimacing at his. "But she used green olives."

Father Eudex said nothing.

"I said she used green olives."

"I like green olives all right."

"*I* like green olives, but *not* in tutti-frutti salad."

Father Eudex replied by eating a green olive, but he knew it could not end there.

"Father," Monsignor said in a new tone. "How would you like to go away and study for a year?"

"Don't think I'd care for it, Monsignor. I'm not the type."

"You're no canonist, you mean?"

"That's one thing."

"Yes. Well, there are other things it might not hurt you to know. To be quite frank with you, Father, I think you need broadening."

"I guess so," Father Eudex said thickly.

"And still, with your tendencies . . . and with the universities honeycombed with Communists. No, that would never do. I think I meant seasoning, not broadening."

"Oh."

"No offence?"

"No offence."

Who would have thought a little thing like an olive could lead to all this, Father Eudex mused—who but himself, that is, for his association with Monsignor had shown him that anything could lead to everything. Monsignor was a master at making points. Nothing had changed since the day Father Eudex walked into the rectory saying he was the new assistant. Monsignor had evaded Father Eudex's hand in greeting, and a few days later, after he began to get the range, he delivered a lecture on the whole subject of handshaking. It was Middle West to shake hands, or South West, or West in any case, and it was not done where he came from, and—why had he ever come from where he came from? Not to be reduced to shaking hands, you could bet! Handshaking was worse than foot washing and unlike that pious practice there was nothing to support it. And from handshaking Monsignor might go into a general discussion of Father Eudex's failings. He used the open forum method, but he was the only speaker and there was never time enough for questions from the audience. Monsignor seized his examples at random from life. He saw Father Eudex coming out of his bedroom in pyjama bottoms only and so told him about the dressing gown, its purpose, something of its history. He advised Father Eudex to barber his armpits, for it was being done all over now. He let Father Eudex see his bottle of cologne, "Steeple," special for clergymen, and said he should not be afraid of it. He suggested that Father Eudex shave his face oftener, too. He loaned him his Rogers Peet catalogue, which had sketches of clerical blades togged out in the latest, and prayed that he would stop going around looking like a rabbinical student.

He found Father Eudex reading *The Catholic Worker* one day and had not trusted him since. Father Eudex's conception of the priesthood was evangelical in the worst sense, barbaric, gross, foreign to the mind of the Church, which was one of two terms he used as sticks to beat him with. The other was taste. The air of the rectory was often heavy with The Mind of the Church and Taste.

Another thing. Father Eudex could not conduct a civil conversation. Monsignor doubted that Father Eudex could even think to himself with anything like agreement. Certainly any discussion with Father Eudex ended inevitably in argument or sighing. Sighing! Why didn't people talk up if they had anything to say? No, they'd rather sigh! Father, don't ever, ever sigh at me again!

Finally, Monsignor did not like Father Eudex's table manners. This came to a head one night when Monsignor, seeing his curate's plate empty and all the silverware at his place unused except for a single knife, fork, and spoon, exploded altogether, saying it had been on his mind for weeks, and then descending into the vernacular he declared that Father Eudex did not know the forks—now perhaps he could understand that! Meals, unless Monsignor had guests or other things to struggle with, were always occasions of instruction for Father Eudex, and sometimes of chastisement.

And now he knew the worst—if Monsignor was thinking of recommending him for a year of study, in a Sulpician seminary probably, to learn the forks. So this was what it meant to be a priest. *Come, follow me. Going forth, teach ye all nations. Heal the sick, raise the dead, cleanse the lepers, cast out devils.* Teach the class of people we get here? Teach Mr. Memmers? Teach Communists? Teach Monsignors? And where were the poor? The lepers of old? The lepers were in their colonies with nuns to nurse them. The poor were in their holes and would not come out. Mr. Memmers was in his bank, without cheer. The Communists were in their universities, awaiting a sign. And he was at table with Monsignor, and it was enough for the disciple to be as his master, but the housekeeper had used green olives.

Monsignor inquired, "Did you get your cheque today?"

Father Eudex looked up, considered. "I got *a* cheque," he said.

"From the Rival people, I mean?"

"Yes."

"Good. Well, I think you might apply it on the car you're wanting. A decent car. That's a worthy cause." Monsignor noticed that he was not taking it well. "Not that I mean to dictate what you shall do with your little windfall, Father. It's just that I don't like to see you mortifying yourself with a Model A—and disgracing the Church."

"Yes," Father Eudex said, suffering.

"Yes. I dare say you don't see the danger, just as you didn't a while ago when I found you making a spectacle of yourself with Whalen. You just don't see the danger because you just don't think. Not to dwell on it, but I seem to remember some overshoes."

The overshoes! Monsignor referred to them as to the Fall. Last winter Father Eudex had given his overshoes to a freezing picket.

It had got back to Monsignor and—good Lord, a man could have his sympathies, but he had no right clad in the cloth to endanger the prestige of the Church by siding in these wretched squabbles. Monsignor said he hated to think of all the evil done by people doing good! Had Father Eudex ever heard of the Albigensian heresy, or didn't the seminary teach that any more?

Father Eudex declined dessert. It was strawberry mousse.

"Delicious," Monsignor said. "I think I'll let her stay."

At that moment Father Eudex decided that he had nothing to lose. He placed his knife next to his fork on the plate, adjusted them this way and that until they seemed to work a combination in his mind, to spring a lock which in turn enabled him to speak out.

"Monsignor," he said. "I think I ought to tell you I don't intend to make use of that money. In fact—to show you how my mind works—I have even considered endorsing the cheque to the strikers' relief fund."

"So," Monsignor said calmly—years in the confessional had prepared him for anything.

"I'll admit I don't know whether I can in justice. And even if I could I don't know that I would. I don't know why . . . I guess hush money, no matter what you do with it, is lousy."

Monsignor regarded him with piercing baby blue eyes. "You'd find it pretty hard to prove, Father, that *any* money *in se* is . . . what you say it is. I would quarrel further with the definition 'hush money.' It seems to me nothing if not rash that you would presume to impugn the motive of the Rival Company in sending out those cheques. You would seem to challenge the whole concept of good works—not that I am ignorant of the misuses to which money can be put." Monsignor, changing tack, tucked it all into a sigh. "Perhaps I'm just a simple soul, and it's enough for me to know personally some of the people in the Rival Company and to know them good people. Many of them Catholic . . ." A throb had crept into Monsignor's voice. He shut it off.

"I don't mean anything that subtle, Monsignor," Father Eudex said. "I'm just telling you, as my pastor, what I'm going to do with the cheque. Or what I'm not going to do with it. I don't know what I'm going to do with it. Maybe send it back."

Monsignor rose from the table, slightly smiling. "Very well, Father. But there's always the poor."

Monsignor took leave of Father Eudex with a laugh. Father Eudex felt it was supposed to fool him into thinking that nothing he had said would be used against him. It showed, rather, that Monsignor was not winded, that he had broken wild curates before, plenty of them, and that he would ride again.

Father Eudex sought the shade of the porch. He tried to read his office, but was drowsy. He got up for a glass of water. The saints in Ireland used to stand up to their necks in cold water, but not for drowsiness. When he came back to the porch a woman was ringing the doorbell. She looked like a customer for rosary beads.

"Hello," he said.

"I'm Mrs. Klein, Father, and I was wondering if you could help me out."

Father Eudex straightened a porch chair for her. "Please sit down."

"It's a German name, Father. Klein was German descent," she said, and added with a silly grin, "It ain't what you think, Father."

"I beg your pardon."

"Klein. Some think it's a Jew name. But they stole it from Klein."

Father Eudex decided to come back to that later. "You were wondering if I could help you?"

"Yes, Father. It's personal."

"Is it matter for confession?"

"Oh no, Father." He had made her blush.

"Then go ahead."

Mrs. Klein peered into the honeysuckle vines on either side of the porch for alien ears.

"No one can hear you, Mrs. Klein."

"Father—I'm just a poor widow," she said, and continued as though Father Eudex had just slandered the man. "Klein was awful good to me, Father."

"I'm sure he was."

"So good . . . and he went and left me all he had." She had begun to cry a little.

Father Eudex nodded gently. She was after something, probably not money, always the best bet—either that or a drunk in the family —but this one was not Irish. Perhaps just sympathy.

"I come to get your advice, Father. Klein always said, 'If you got a problem, Freda, see the priest.'"

"Do you need money?"

"I got more than I can use from the bakery."

"You have a bakery?"

Mrs. Klein nodded down the street. "That's my bakery. It was Klein's. The Purity."

"I go by there all the time," Father Eudex said, abandoning himself to her. He must stop trying to shape the conversation and let her work it out.

"Will you give me your advice, Father?" He felt that she sensed his indifference and interpreted it as his way of rejecting her. She either had no idea how little sense she made or else supreme faith in him, as a priest, to see into her heart.

"Just what is it you're after, Mrs. Klein?"

"He left me all he had, Father, but it's just laying in the bank."

"And you want me to tell you what to do with it?"

"Yes, Father."

Father Eudex thought this might be interesting, certainly a change. He went back in his mind to the seminary and the class in which they had considered the problem of inheritances. Do we have any unfulfilled obligations? Are we sure? . . . Are there any impedimenta?

"Do you have any dependents, Mrs. Klein—any children?"

"One boy, Father. I got him running the bakery. I pay him good—too much, Father."

"Is 'too much' a living wage?"

"Yes, Father. He ain't got a family."

"A living wage is not too much," Father Eudex handed down, sailing into the encyclical style without knowing it.

Mrs. Klein was smiling over having done something good without knowing precisely what it was.

"How old is your son?"

"He's thirty-six, Father."

"Not married?"

"No, Father, but he's got him a girl." She giggled, and Father Eudex, embarrassed, retied his shoe.

"But you don't care to make a will and leave this money to your son in the usual way?"

"I guess I'll have to . . . if I die." Mrs. Klein was suddenly crushed and haunted, but whether by death or charity, Father Eudex did not know.

"You don't have to, Mrs. Klein. There are many worthy causes. And the worthiest is the cause of the poor. My advice to you, if I understand your problem, is to give what you have to someone who needs it."

Mrs. Klein just stared at him.

"You could even leave it to the archdiocese," he said, completing the sentence to himself: but I don't recommend it in your case . . . with your tendencies. You look like an Indian giver to me.

But Mrs. Klein had got enough. "Huh!" she said, rising. "Well! You *are* a funny one!"

And then Father Eudex realized that she had come to him for a broker's tip. It was in the eyes. The hat. The dress. The shoes. "If you'd like to speak to the pastor," he said, "come back in the evening."

"You're a nice young man," Mrs. Klein said, rather bitter now and bent on getting away from him. "But I got to say this—you ain't much of a priest. And Klein said if I got a problem, see the priest—huh! You ain't much of a priest! What time's your boss come in?"

"In the evening," Father Eudex said. "Come any time in the evening."

Mrs. Klein was already down the steps and making for the street.

"You might try Mr. Memmers at the First National," Father Eudex called, actually trying to help her, but she must have thought it was just some more of his nonsense and did not reply.

After Mrs. Klein had disappeared Father Eudex went to his room. In the hallway upstairs Monsignor's voice, coming from the depths of the clerical nap, halted him.

"Who was it?"

"A woman," Father Eudex said. "A woman seeking good counsel."

He waited a moment to be questioned, but Monsignor was not awake enough to see anything wrong with that, and there came only a sigh and a shifting of weight that told Father Eudex he was simply turning over in bed.

Father Eudex walked into the bathroom. He took the Rival cheque from his pocket. He tore it into little squares. He let them flutter into the toilet. He pulled the chain—hard.

He went to his room and stood looking out the window at nothing. He could hear the others already giving an account of their stewardship, but could not judge them. I bought baseball uniforms for the school. I bought the nuns a new washing machine. I purchased a Mass kit for a Chinese missionary. I bought a set of matched irons. Mine helped pay for keeping my mother in a rest home upstate. I gave mine to the poor.

And you, Father?

COMMENT

In Milburn's story character is secondary to situation: the author is less interested in picturing H. T. than in using him as a medium through which certain ironies of social conduct may be seen. But in Powers's story the focus is directly upon Father Eudex, and the various situations introduced serve primarily to show the operation of his conscience and his efforts to come to terms with himself. This problem is canvassed rather fully: we see Father Eudex in his relationship with the janitor, with a parishioner, with his superior, and with himself. This last relationship is developed throughout the story; the author uses an omniscient point of view which does not limit him to an account of what happened to Father Eudex externally but permits him to give a running account of the priest's reflections and questions. This is the real issue of the story: his struggle to find a satisfactory way of life, and to feel secure in it. Mr. Powers gives the emphatic final position in the story to an account of Father Eudex's self-questioning: our last impression is not of a pathetic defeat, nor of a glorious victory, but of the intense difficulty of being sure of the quality of one's actions.

Of the other characters, the Monsignor is developed most fully: the contrast between the two men is a way of defining Father Eudex's problem. The opposition is between an idealistic cast of mind which draws its inspiration from original Christian sources, and an expedient cast of mind which tends to identify institutional well-being with material comfort, good manners, and so on. While the sympathies of the author are clear, we should observe how the author keeps the materials under control. He does not let Father Eudex become a self-assured zealot, nor the Monsignor become an all-powerful enemy. The reader should recognize the effect secured by the Monsignor's failure to become a bishop, and by the references to the "crazy bishop" whom he despises.

Like other stories in this volume, "The Forks" does not have a plot in the conventional sense of the word. Rather there are several scenes bound together by a common theme and contributing to a common impression. Compare this kind of structure with that of the stories by Maugham, Coppard, and Huxley, which belong rather to the well-made type of story.

The language in this story is often very interesting. What is the effect, for example, of the metaphorical terms used in the two paragraphs beginning, "Monsignor stopped in admiration a few feet from the car"? Of Father Eudex's thinking, "I can't come out and play . . . on account of my monsignor won't let me"? "I guess hush money . . . is lousy"? Does his style of speaking tell us anything about him? Again, we find such colorful phrases as "straight man," "warming up on the sidelines," "cupboard was bare," "annual jackpot," "clerical blades togged out in the latest," "had broken wild curates before . . . and . . . would ride again." Do these serve merely to provide a shock by their unexpectedness in a church story? Or do they amplify the meaning? Do they serve to make a comment on the matters to which they refer? Do they suggest a relation between church problems and those of life generally?

What is the symbolic value of the title of the story?

Virginia Woolf

Virginia Woolf, one of the brilliant experimental novelists of the twentieth century, was descended from or related to many distinguished English families. She was the daughter of Sir Leslie Stephen, noted biographer and literary critic. Born in 1882, she was educated entirely at home, a home which was frequented by many literary and intellectual figures of the day. Later she became one of the leaders of a famous group—known as "the Bloomsbury Group"—of literary figures which included E. M. Forster, Lytton Strachey, John Maynard Keynes, and Leonard Woolf. She became the wife of Leonard Woolf in 1912. Together they founded the Hogarth Press, which subsequently became very successful. As novelist—*Mrs. Dalloway*, *To the Lighthouse*, *The Waves*, and so forth—Mrs. Woolf tried constantly to rely less and less upon conventional plot and to achieve a more and more subtle and precise expression of psychological reality. The stresses of the early years of the war led to her suicide in 1941.

The New Dress

MABEL had her first serious suspicion that something was wrong as she took her cloak off and Mrs. Barnet, while handing her the mirror and touching the brushes and thus drawing her attention, perhaps rather markedly, to all the appliances for tidying and improving hair, complexion, clothes, which existed on the dressing table, confirmed the suspicion—that it was not right, not quite right, which growing stronger as she went upstairs and springing at her with conviction as she greeted Clarissa Dalloway, she went straight to the far end of the room, to a shaded corner where a looking-glass hung and looked. No! It was not right. And at once the misery which she always tried to hide, the profound dissatisfaction—the sense she had had, ever since she was a child, of being inferior to other people—set upon her, relentlessly, remorselessly, with an intensity which she could not beat off, as she would when she woke at night at home, by reading Borrow or Scott; for, oh, these men, oh, these women, all were thinking—"What's Mabel wearing? What a fright she looks! What a hideous new dress!"—their eyelids flickering as they came up and then their lids shutting rather tight. It was her own appalling inadequacy; her cowardice; her mean, water-sprinkled blood that depressed her. And at once the whole of the room where, for ever so many hours, she had planned with the little dressmaker how it was to go, seemed sordid, repulsive; and her own drawing-room so shabby, and herself, going out, puffed up with vanity as she touched the letters on the hall table and said: "How dull!" to show off—all this now seemed unutterably silly, paltry, and provincial. All this had been absolutely destroyed, shown up, exploded, the moment she came into Mrs. Dalloway's drawing-room.

What she had thought that evening when, sitting over the tea-cups, Mrs. Dalloway's invitation came, was that, of course, she could not be fashionable. It was absurd to pretend to even—fashion meant cut, meant style, meant thirty guineas at least—but why not be original? Why not be herself, anyhow? And, getting up, she had taken that old fashion book of her mother's, a Paris fashion book of the time of the Empire, and had thought how much prettier, more dignified, and more womanly, they were then, and so set herself—oh, it was foolish—trying to be like them, pluming herself in fact upon being modest and old-fashioned and very charming, giving herself up, no doubt about it, to an orgy of self-love which deserved to be chastised, and so rigged herself out like this.

But she dared not look in the glass. She could not face the whole horror—the pale yellow, idiotically old-fashioned silk dress with its long skirt and its high sleeves and its waist and all the things that looked so charming in the fashion book, but not on her, not among all these ordinary people. She felt like a dressmaker's dummy standing there for young people to stick pins into.

"But, my dear, it's perfectly charming!" Rose Shaw said, looking her up and down with that little satirical pucker of the lips which she expected—Rose herself being dressed in the height of the fashion, precisely like everybody else, always.

"We are all like flies trying to crawl over the edge of the saucer," Mabel thought, and repeated the phrase as if she were crossing herself, as if she were trying to find some spell to annul this pain, to make this agony endurable. Tags of Shakespeare, lines from books she had read ages ago, suddenly came to her when she was in agony, and she repeated them over and over again. "Flies trying to crawl," she repeated. If she could say that over often enough and make herself see the flies, she would become numb, chill, frozen, dumb. Now she could see flies crawling slowly out of a saucer of milk with their wings stuck together; and she strained and strained (standing in front of the looking-glass, listening to Rose Shaw) to make herself see Rose Shaw and all the other people there as flies, trying to hoist themselves out of something, or into something, meagre, insignificant, toiling flies. But she could not see them like that, not other people. She saw herself like that—she was a fly, but the others were dragonflies, butterflies, beautiful insects, dancing, fluttering, skimming, while she alone dragged herself up out of the saucer. (Envy and spite, the most detestable of the vices, were her chief faults.)

"I feel like some dowdy, decrepit, horribly dingy old fly," she said, making Robert Haydon stop just to hear her say that, just to reassure herself by furbishing up a poor weak-kneed phrase and so showing how detached she was, how witty, that she did not feel in the least out of anything. And, of course, Robert Haydon answered something quite polite, quite insincere, which she saw through instantly, and said to herself, directly he went (again from some book), "Lies, lies, lies!" For a party makes things either much more real or much less real, she thought; she saw in a flash to the bottom of Robert Haydon's heart; she saw through everything. She saw the truth. This was true, this drawing-room, this self, and the other false. Miss Milan's little work-room was really terribly hot, stuffy, sordid. It smelt of clothes and cabbage cooking; and yet, when Miss Milan put the glass in her hand, and she looked at herself with the dress on, finished, an extraordinary bliss shot through her heart. Suffused with light, she sprang into existence. Rid of cares and wrinkles, what she had dreamed of herself was there—a beautiful woman. Just for a second (she had not dared look longer, Miss Milan wanted to know about the length of the skirt), there looked at her, framed in the scrolloping mahogany, a grey-white, mysteriously smiling, charming girl, the core of herself, the soul of herself; and it was not vanity only, not only self-love that made her think it good, tender, and true. Miss Milan said that the skirt could not well be longer; if anything the skirt, said Miss Milan, puckering her forehead, considering with all her wits about her, must be shorter; and she felt, suddenly, honestly, full of love for Miss Milan, much, much fonder of Miss Milan than of anyone in the whole world, and could have cried for pity that she should be crawling on the floor with her mouth full of pins and her face red and her eyes bulging—that one human being should be doing this for another, and she saw them all as human beings merely, and herself going off to her party, and Miss Milan pulling the cover over the canary's cage, or letting him pick a hemp-seed from between her lips, and the thought of it, of this side of human nature and its patience and its endurance and its being content with such miserable, scanty, sordid, little pleasures filled her eyes with tears.

And now the whole thing had vanished. The dress, the room, the love, the pity, the scrolloping looking-glass, and the canary's cage—all had vanished, and here she was in a corner of Mrs. Dalloway's drawing-room, suffering tortures, woken wide awake to reality.

But it was all so paltry, weak-blooded, and petty-minded to care so much at her age with two children, to be still so utterly dependent on people's opinions and not have principles or convictions, not to be able to say as other people did, "There's Shakespeare! There's death! We're all weevils in a captain's biscuit"—or whatever it was that people did say.

She faced herself straight in the glass; she pecked at her left shoulder; she issued out into the room, as if spears were thrown at her yellow dress from all sides. But instead of looking fierce or tragic, as Rose Shaw would have done—Rose would have looked like Boadicea—she looked foolish and self-conscious and simpered like a schoolgirl and slouched across the room, positively slinking, as if she were a beaten mongrel, and looked at a picture, an engraving. As if one went to a party to look at a picture! Everybody knew why she did it—it was from shame, from humiliation.

"Now the fly's in the saucer," she said to herself, "right in the middle, and can't get out, and the milk," she thought, rigidly staring at the picture, "is sticking its wings together."

"It's so old-fashioned," she said to Charles Burt, making him stop (which by itself he hated) on his way to talk to someone else.

She meant, or she tried to make herself think that she meant, that it was the picture and not her dress, that was old-fashioned. And one word of praise, one word of affection from Charles would have made all the difference to her at the moment. If he had only said, "Mabel, you're looking charming tonight!" it would have changed her life. But then she ought to have been truthful and direct. Charles said nothing of the kind, of course. He was malice itself. He always saw through one, especially if one were feeling particularly mean, paltry, or feeble-minded.

"Mabel's got a new dress!" he said, and the poor fly was absolutely shoved into the middle of the saucer. Really, he would like her to drown, she believed. He had no heart, no fundamental kindness, only a veneer of friendliness. Miss Milan was much more real, much kinder. If only one could feel that and stick to it, always. "Why," she asked herself—replying to Charles much too pertly, letting him see that she was out of temper, or "ruffled" as he called it ("Rather ruffled?" he said and went on to laugh at her with some woman over there)—"Why," she asked herself, "can't I feel one thing always, feel quite sure that Miss Milan is right, and Charles wrong and stick to it, feel sure about the canary and pity and love and not be whipped all round in a second by coming into a room full of people?" It was her odious, weak, vacillating character again, always giving at the critical moment and not being seriously interested in conchology, etymology, botany, archeology, cutting up potatoes and watching them fructify like Mary Dennis, like Violet Searle.

Then Mrs. Holman, seeing her standing there, bore down upon her. Of course a thing like a dress was beneath Mrs. Holman's notice, with her family always tumbling downstairs or having the scarlet fever. Could Mabel tell her if Elmthorpe was ever let for August and September? Oh, it was a conversation that bored her unutterably!—it made her furious to be treated like a house agent or a messenger boy, to be made use of. Not to have value, that was it, she thought, trying to grasp something hard, something real, while she tried to answer sensibly about the bathroom and the south aspect and the hot water to the top of the house; and all the time she could see little bits of her yellow dress in the round looking-glass which made them all the size of boot-buttons or tad-poles; and it was amazing to think how much humiliation and agony and self-loathing and effort and passionate ups and downs of feeling were contained in a thing the size of a threepenny bit. And what was still odder, this thing, this Mabel Waring, was sepa-rate, quite disconnected; and though Mrs. Holman (the black button) was leaning forward and telling her how her eldest boy had strained his heart running, she could see her, too, quite de-tached in the looking-glass, and it was impossible that the black dot, leaning forward, gesticulating, should make the yellow dot, sitting solitary, self-centred, feel what the black dot was feeling, yet they pretended.

"So impossible to keep boys quiet"—that was the kind of thing one said.

And Mrs. Holman, who could never get enough sympathy and snatched what little there was greedily, as if it were her right (but she deserved much more for there was her little girl who had come down this morning with a swollen knee-joint), took this miser-able offering and looked at it suspiciously, grudgingly, as if it were a halfpenny when it ought to have been a pound and put it away in her purse, must put up with it, mean and miserly though it was, times being hard, so very hard; and on she went, creaking, injured Mrs. Holman, about the girl with the swollen joints. Ah, it was tragic, this greed, this clamour of human beings, like a row of cor-morants, barking and flapping their wings for sympathy—it was tragic, could one have felt it and not merely pretended to feel it!

But in her yellow dress tonight she could not wring out one drop more; she wanted it all, all for herself. She knew (she kept on looking into the glass, dipping into that dreadfully showing-up blue pool) that she was condemned, despised, left like this in a backwater, because of her being like this—a feeble, vacillating crea-ture; and it seemed to her that the yellow dress was a penance which she had deserved, and if she had been dressed like Rose Shaw, in lovely, clinging green with a ruffle of swansdown, she would have deserved that; and she thought that there was no escape for her—none whatever. But it was not her fault altogether, after all. It was being one of a family of ten; never having money enough, always skimping and paring; and her mother carrying great cans, and the linoleum worn on the stair edges, and one sordid little domestic tragedy after another—nothing catastrophic, the sheep farm failing, but not utterly; her eldest brother marrying beneath him but not very much—there was no romance, nothing extreme about them all. They petered out respectably in seaside resorts; every watering-place had one of her aunts even now asleep in some lodging with the front windows not quite facing the sea. That was so like them—they had to squint at things always. And she had done the same—she was just like her aunts. For all her dreams of living in India, married to some hero like Sir Henry Lawrence, some empire builder (still the sight of a native in a turban filled her with romance), she had failed utterly. She had married Hubert, with his safe, permanent underling's job in the Law Courts, and they managed tolerably in a smallish house, without proper maids, and hash when she was alone or just bread and butter, but now and then—Mrs. Holman was off, thinking her the most dried-up, unsympathetic twig she had ever met, absurdly dressed, too, and would tell everyone about Mabel's fantastic appearance—now and then, thought Mabel Waring, left alone on the blue sofa, punching the cushion in order to look occupied, for she would not join Charles Burt and Rose Shaw, chattering like magpies and perhaps laughing at her by the fireplace—now and then, there did come to her delicious moments, reading the other night in bed, for instance, or down by the sea on the sand in the sun, at Easter—let her recall it—a great tuft of pale sand-grass, standing all twisted like a shock of spears against the sky, which was blue like a smooth china egg, so firm, so hard, and then the melody of the waves—"Hush, hush," they said, and the children's shouts paddling—yes, it was a divine moment, and there she lay, she felt, in the hand of the Goddess who was the world; rather a hard-hearted, but very beautiful Goddess, a little lamb laid on the altar (one did think these silly things, and it didn't matter so long as one never said them). And also with Hubert sometimes she had quite unexpectedly—carving the mutton for Sunday lunch, for no reason, opening a letter, coming into a room—divine moments, when she said to herself (for she would never say this to anybody else), "This is it. This has happened. This is it!" And the other way about it was equally surprising—that is, when everything was arranged—music, weather, holidays, every reason for happiness was there—then nothing happened at all. One wasn't happy. It was flat, just flat, that was all.

Her wretched self again, no doubt! She had always been a fretful, weak, unsatisfactory mother, a wobbly wife, lolling about in a kind of twilight existence with nothing very clear or very bold, or more one thing than another, like all her brothers and sisters, except perhaps Herbert—they were all the same poor water-veined creatures who did nothing. Then in the midst of this creeping, crawling life suddenly she was on the crest of a wave. That wretched fly—where had she read the story that kept coming into her mind about the fly and the saucer?—struggled out. Yes, she had those moments. But now that she was forty, they might come more and more seldom. By degrees she would cease to struggle any more. But that was deplorable! That was not to be endured! That made her feel ashamed of herself!

She would go to the London Library tomorrow. She would find some wonderful, helpful, astonishing book, quite by chance, a book by a clergyman, by an American no one had ever heard of; or she would walk down the strand and drop, accidentally, into a hall where a miner was telling about the life in the pit, and suddenly she would become a new person. She would be absolutely transformed. She would wear a uniform; she would be called Sister Somebody; she would never give a thought to clothes again. And forever after she would be perfectly clear about Charles Burt and Miss Milan and this room and that room; and it would be always, day after day, as if she were lying in the sun or carving the mutton. It would be it!

So she got up from the blue sofa, and the yellow button in the looking-glass got up too, and she waved her hand to Charles and Rose to show them she did not depend on them one scrap, and the yellow button moved out of the looking-glass, and all the spears were gathered into her breast as she walked towards Mrs. Dalloway and said, "Good night."

"But it's too early to go," said Mrs. Dalloway, who was always so charming.

"I'm afraid I must," said Mabel Waring. "But," she added in her weak, wobbly voice which only sounded ridiculous when she tried to strengthen it, "I have enjoyed myself enormously."

"I have enjoyed myself," she said to Mr. Dalloway, whom she met on the stairs.

"Lies, lies, lies!" she said to herself, going downstairs, and "Right in the saucer!" she said to herself as she thanked Mrs. Barnet for helping her and wrapped herself, round and round and round, in the Chinese cloak she had worn these twenty years.

COMMENT

Virginia Woolf's "The New Dress" is another study of character, but it differs from previous studies in this volume by the severity with which the point of view is maintained. All that the author permits to come into the story is Mabel's view of herself; she relies entirely on inner action. It is true that we see Mabel going through various motions at the party, speaking to a number of people, and observing the activity of others, but these matters are permitted to exist only dimly in the background. The foreground is taken up entirely by the scurrying reflections, recollections, and feelings which are called forth in Mabel by a series of relatively slight external stimuli.

This careful staying within the mind and feelings of Mabel, this exclusion of all materials that would permit us to see Mabel in any light other than her own, indicates that the story is not primarily concerned with establishing the rightness or wrongness of Mabel's view of herself. The author does not play, as she might, with the ironic disparity between several views of the same character. The method does not, of course, commit the reader to a literal acceptance of everything that Mabel says about herself. The very vehemence of her self-excoriation leads one to make corrections against Mabel's emotional drift, and her very capacity for self-criticism modifies for us her self-condemnatory view.

But the problem of Mabel's character is not the main business of the story. The meticulous tracing of Mabel's various moods and emotions suggests that primarily the story is trying to give reality to the feelings a certain situation evokes in a given personality. Mabel is a kind of embodiment of all self-consciousness, diffidence, self-distrust, sensitiveness to slight; if others do not go more than halfway with her, she falls into an agony of self-abasement. She is imaginative enough to try an unusual expedient (the dress) but she lacks staying power, and ultimately her imagination recoils upon her with an immense burden of disparagement, made openly by herself and assumed to be made by others.

Is this portrait of Mabel only the portrait of a specialized, neurotic character? Or has Mrs. Woolf really made her a representative of a habit of mind which is rather general? Note the seventh and eighth paragraphs from the end of the story, in which Mabel describes certain experiences which are very familiar to everybody. Is the author not really, by excluding other elements in a personality, endeavoring to give the utmost reality to those qualities which may make an experience painfully frustrating? In another sense, is she not exhibiting the private reality as against the public façade, the inner life which is withheld in any situation dominated by the conventions? In any case, the conspicuous thing in the story is the author's wonderful care in tracing the subtle ingredients of psychological experience.

To what extent may this be considered a story of atmosphere?

Note that the story "plunges into the middle of things": the action has started, so to speak, before the reader comes in on it. This is a conventional way of getting into a story quickly. But the author who uses it has to manage the exposition without falling into awkward delays while he feeds the necessary information directly to the reader. Mrs. Woolf successfully uses Mabel's thoughts to tell the reader everything that is necessary.

Compared with the style of Hemingway, whose story appears later in this book, Mrs. Woolf's involves a rather complicated sentence structure. Is this appropriate for the psychological theme? Why?

D. H. Lawrence

The son of a coal miner, David Herbert Lawrence was born in England in 1885. He was trained as an elementary-school teacher, but this career was brought to an end both by recurrent lung trouble and by his interest in writing. In search of a healthful climate, he lived in many parts of the world, including Taos, New Mexico, where he believed he would help create an ideal intellectual community. He left America for the last time in 1925 and died of tuberculosis in 1930. In his last years his closest friend was Aldous Huxley, who in *Point Counter Point* based the character Rampion on Lawrence. Lawrence's personality called forth considerable controversy, which was raised to a hysterical pitch by a whole series of books that appeared after his death. His writings were equally controversial, primarily because of their outspokenness. He himself considered his best books to be *Sons and Lovers*, *Women in Love*, and *Lady Chatterley's Lover*.

The Lovely Lady

AT SEVENTY-TWO, Pauline Attenborough could still sometimes be mistaken, in the half-light, for thirty. She really was a wonderfully preserved woman, of perfect *chic*. Of course, it helps a great deal to have the right frame. She would be an exquisite skeleton, and her skull would be an exquisite skull, like that of some Etruscan woman, with feminine charm still in the swerve of the bone and the pretty naïve teeth.

Mrs. Attenborough's face was of the perfect oval and slightly flat type that wears best. There is no flesh to sag. Her nose rode serenely, in its finely bridged curve. Only her big grey eyes were a tiny bit prominent on the surface of her face, and they gave her away most. The bluish lids were heavy, as if they ached sometimes with the strain of keeping the eyes beneath them arch and bright; and at the corners of the eyes were fine little wrinkles which

would slacken with haggardness, then be pulled up tense again,
to that bright, gay look, like a Leonardo woman who really could
laugh outright.

Her niece Cecilia was perhaps the only person in the world who
was aware of the invisible little wire which connected Pauline's
eye-wrinkles with Pauline's will power. Only Cecilia *consciously*
watched the eyes go haggard and old and tired, and remain so, for
hours; until Robert came home. Then, ping!—the mysterious little
wire that worked between Pauline's will and her face went taut;
the weary, haggard, prominent eyes suddenly began to gleam; the
eyelids arched; the queer curved eyebrows, which floated in such
frail arches on Pauline's forehead, began to gather a mocking significance, and you had the *real* lovely lady, in all her charm.

She really had the secret of everlasting youth; that is to say, she
could don her youth again like an eagle. But she was sparing of
it. She was wise enough not to try being young for too many
people. Her son Robert, in the evenings, and Sir Wilfred Knipe
sometimes in the afternoon to tea; then occasional visitors on Sunday, when Robert was home; for these she was her lovely and
changeless self, that age could not wither, nor custom stale; so
bright and kindly and yet subtly mocking, like Mona Lisa who
knew a thing or two. But Pauline knew more, so she needn't be
smug at all, she could laugh that lovely mocking Bacchante laugh
of hers, which was at the same time never malicious, always good-
naturedly tolerant, both of virtues and vices. The former, of course,
taking much more tolerating. So she suggested, roguishly.

Only with her niece Cecilia she did not trouble to keep up the
glamour. Ciss was not very observant, anyhow; and more than that,
she was plain; more still, she was in love with Robert; and most
of all, she was thirty, and dependent on her Aunt Pauline. Oh,
Cecilia! Why make music for her!

Cecilia, called by her aunt and by her cousin Robert just Ciss,
like a cat spitting, was a big dark-complexioned pug-faced young
woman who very rarely spoke, and, when she did, couldn't get it
out. She was the daughter of a poor Congregational minister who
had been, while he lived, brother to Ronald, Aunt Pauline's husband. Ronald and the Congregational minister were both well dead,
and Aunt Pauline had had charge of Ciss for the last five years.

They lived all together in a quite exquisite though rather small Queen Anne house some twenty-five miles out of town, secluded in a little dale, and surrounded by small but very quaint and pleasant grounds. It was an ideal place and an ideal life for Aunt Pauline, at the age of seventy-two. When the kingfishers flashed up the little stream in the garden, going under the alders, something still flashed in her heart. She was that kind of woman.

Robert, who was two years older than Ciss, went every day to town, to his chambers in one of the Inns. He was a barrister, and, to his secret but very deep mortification, he earned about a hundred pounds a year. He simply *couldn't* get above that figure, though it was rather easy to get below it. Of course, it didn't matter. Pauline had money. But then what was Pauline's was Pauline's, and, though she could give almost lavishly, still, one was always aware of having a *lovely* and *undeserved* present made to one: presents are so much nicer when they are undeserved, Aunt Pauline would say.

Robert too was plain, and almost speechless. He was medium-sized, rather broad and stout, though not fat. Only his creamy, clean-shaven face was rather fat, and sometimes suggestive of an Italian priest, in its silence and its secrecy. But he had grey eyes like his mother but very shy and uneasy, not bold like hers. Perhaps Ciss was the only person who fathomed his awful shyness and *malaise,* his habitual feeling that he was in the wrong place: almost like a soul that has got into the wrong body. But he never did anything about it. He went up to his chambers, and read law. It was, however, all the weird old processes that interested him. He had, unknown to everybody but his mother, a quite extraordinary collection of old Mexican legal documents, reports of processes and trials, pleas, accusations, the weird and awful mixture of ecclesiastical law and common law in seventeenth-century Mexico. He had started a study in this direction through coming across a report of a trial of two English sailors, for murder, in Mexico in 1620, and he had gone on, when the next document was an accusation against a Don Miguel Estrada for seducing one of the nuns of the Sacred Heart Convent in Oaxaca in 1680.

Pauline and her son Robert had wonderful evenings with these old papers. The lovely lady knew a little Spanish. She even looked a trifle Spanish herself, with a high comb and a marvellous dark brown shawl embroidered in thick silvery silk embroidery. So she would sit at the perfect old table, soft as velvet in its deep brown surface, a high comb in her hair, ear-rings with dropping pendants in her ears, her arms bare and still beautiful, a few strings of pearls round her throat, a puce velvet dress on, and this or another beautiful shawl, and by candlelight she looked, yes, a Spanish high-bred beauty of thirty-two or three. She set the candles to give her face just the chiaroscuro she knew suited her; her high chair that rose behind her face was done in old green brocade, against which her face emerged like a Christmas rose.

They were always three at table; and they always drank a bottle of champagne: Pauline two glasses, Ciss two glasses, Robert the rest. The lovely lady sparkled and was radiant. Ciss, her black hair bobbed, her broad shoulders in a very nice and becoming dress that Aunt Pauline had helped her to make, stared from her aunt to her cousin and back again, with rather confused, mute, hazel eyes, and played the part of an audience suitably impressed. She *was* impressed, somewhere, all the time. And even rendered speechless by Pauline's brilliancy, even after five years. But at the bottom of her consciousness were the data of as weird a document as Robert ever studied: all the things she knew about her aunt and cousin.

Robert was always a gentleman, with an old-fashioned punctilious courtesy that covered his shyness quite completely. He was, and Ciss knew it, more confused than shy. He was worse than she was. Cecilia's own confusion dated from only five years back— Robert's must have started before he was born. In the lovely lady's womb he must have felt *very* confused.

He paid all his attention to his mother, drawn to her as a humble flower to the sun. And yet, priest-like, he was all the time aware, with the tail of his consciousness, that Ciss was there, and that she was a bit shut out of it, and that something wasn't right. He was aware of the third consciousness in the room. Whereas, to Pauline, her niece Cecilia was an appropriate part of her own setting, rather than a distinct consciousness.

Robert took coffee with his mother and Ciss in the warm drawing-room, where all the furniture was so lovely, all collectors' pieces— Mrs. Attenborough had made her own money, dealing privately in pictures and furniture and rare things from barbaric countries— and the three talked desultorily till about eight or half-past. It was very pleasant, very cosy, very homely even: Pauline made a real home cosiness out of so much elegant material. The chat was simple, and nearly always bright. Pauline was her *real* self, emanating a friendly mockery and an odd, ironic gaiety. Till there came a little pause.

At which Ciss always rose and said good night and carried out the coffee tray, to prevent Burnett from intruding any more.

And then! Oh, then, the lovely glowing intimacy of the evening, between mother and son, when they deciphered manuscripts and discussed points, Pauline with that eagerness of a girl, for which she was famous. And it was quite genuine. In some mysterious way she had *saved up* her power for being thrilled, in connexion with a man. Robert, solid, rather quiet and subdued, seemed like the elder of the two: almost like a priest with a young girl pupil. And that was rather how he felt.

Ciss had a flat for herself just across the courtyard, over the old coachhouse and stables. There were no horses. Robert kept his car in the coachhouse. Ciss had three very nice rooms up there, stretching along in a row one after another, and she had got used to the ticking of the stable clock.

But sometimes she did not go up to her rooms. In the summer she would sit on the lawn, and from the open window of the drawing-room upstairs she would hear Pauline's wonderful heart-searching laugh. And in the winter the young woman would put on a thick coat and walk slowly to the little balustrated bridge over the stream, and then look back at the three lighted windows of that drawing-room where mother and son were so happy together.

Ciss loved Robert, and she believed that Pauline intended the two of them to marry: when she was dead. But poor Robert, he was so convulsed with shyness already, with man or woman. What would he be when his mother was dead?—in a dozen more years. He would be just a shell, the shell of a man who had never lived.

The strange unspoken sympathy of the young with one another, when they are overshadowed by the old, was one of the bonds between Robert and Ciss. But another bond, which Ciss did not know how to draw tight, was the bond of passion. Poor Robert was by nature a passionate man. His silence and his agonized, though hidden, shyness were both the result of a secret physical passionateness. And how Pauline could play on this! Ah, Ciss was not blind to the eyes which he fixed on his mother, eyes fascinated yet humiliated, full of shame. He was ashamed that he was not a man. And he did not love his mother. He was fascinated by her. Completely fascinated. And for the rest, paralyzed in a life-long confusion.

Ciss stayed in the garden till the lights leapt up in Pauline's bed-room—about ten o'clock. The lovely lady had retired. Robert would now stay another hour or so, alone. Then he too would retire. Ciss, in the dark outside, sometimes wished she could creep up to him and say: "Oh, Robert! It's all wrong!" But Aunt Pauline would hear. And anyhow, Ciss couldn't do it. She went off to her own rooms, once more, and so for ever.

In the morning, coffee was brought up on a tray to each of the three relatives. Ciss had to be at Sir Wilfred Knipe's at nine o'clock, to give two hours' lessons to his little granddaughter. It was her sole serious occupation, except that she played the piano for the love of it. Robert set off to town about nine. And, as a rule, Aunt Pauline appeared to lunch, though sometimes not until tea-time. When she appeared, she looked fresh and young. But she was in-clined to fade rather quickly, like a flower without water, in the daytime. Her hour was the candle hour.

So she always rested in the afternoon. When the sun shone, if possible she took a sun bath. This was one of her secrets. Her lunch was very light, she could take her sun-and-air bath before noon or after, as it pleased her. Often it was in the afternoon, when the sun shone very warmly into a queer little yew-walled square just behind the stables. Here Ciss stretched out the lying-chair and rugs, and put the light parasol handy in the silent little enclosure of thick dark yew hedges beyond the red walls of the unused stables. And hither came the lovely lady with her book. Ciss then had to be on guard in one of her own rooms, should her aunt, who was very keen-eared, hear a footstep.

One afternoon it occurred to Cecilia that she herself might while away this rather long afternoon by taking a sun bath. She was grow-ing restive. The thought of the flat roof of the stable buildings, to which she could climb from a loft at the end, started her on a new adventure. She often went on to the roof: she had to, to wind up the stable clock, which was a job she had assumed to herself. Now she took a rug, climbed out under the heavens, looked at the sky and the great elm-tops, looked at the sun, then took off her things and lay down perfectly serenely, in a corner of the roof under the parapet, full in the sun.

It was rather lovely, to bask all one's length like this in warm sun and air. Yes, it was very lovely! It even seemed to melt some of the hard bitterness of her heart, some of that core of unspoken resentment which never dissolved. Luxuriously, she spread herself, so that the sun should touch her limbs fully, fully. If she had no other lover, she should have the sun! She rolled voluptuously. And suddenly, her heart stood still in her body, and her hair almost rose on end as a voice said very softly, musingly in her ear:

"No, Henry dear! It was not my fault you died instead of marrying that Claudia. No, darling. I was quite, quite willing for you to marry her, unsuitable though she was."

Cecilia sank down on her rug powerless and perspiring with dread. That awful voice, so soft, so musing, yet so unnatural. Not a human voice at all. Yet there must, there must be someone on the roof! Oh! how unspeakably awful!

She lifted her weak head and peeped across the sloping leads. Nobody! The chimneys were far too narrow to shelter anybody. There was nobody on the roof. Then it must be someone in the trees, in the elms. Either that, or terror unspeakable, a bodiless voice! She reared her head a little higher.

And as she did so, came the voice again:

"No, darling! I told you you would tire of her in six months. And you see, it was true, dear. It was true, true, true! I wanted to spare you that. So it wasn't I who made you feel weak and disabled, wanting that very silly Claudia; poor thing, she looked so woebegone afterwards! Wanting her and not wanting her, you got *yourself* into that perplexity, my dear. I only warned you. What else could I do? And you lost your spirit and died without ever knowing me again. It was bitter, bitter—"

The voice faded away. Cecilia subsided weakly on to her rug, after the anguished tension of listening. Oh, it was awful. The sun shone, the sky was blue, all seemed so lovely and afternoony and summery. And yet, oh, horror!—she was going to be forced to believe in the supernatural! And she loathed the supernatural, ghosts and voices and rappings and all the rest.

But that awful creepy bodiless voice, with its rusty sort of whisper of an overtone! It had something so fearfully familiar in it too!

and yet was so utterly uncanny. Poor Cecilia could only lie there unclothed, and so all the more agonizingly helpless, inert, collapsed in sheer dread.

And then she heard the thing sigh! A deep sigh that seemed weirdly familiar, yet was not human. "Ah, well; ah, well, the heart must bleed! Better it should bleed than break. It is grief, grief! But it wasn't my fault, dear. And Robert could marry our poor dull Ciss tomorrow, if he wanted her. But he doesn't care about it, so why force him into anything!" The sounds were very uneven, sometimes only a husky sort of whisper. Listen! Listen!

Cecilia was about to give vent to loud and piercing screams of hysteria, when the last two sentences arrested her. All her caution and her cunning sprang alert. It was Aunt Pauline! It must be Aunt Pauline, practising ventriloquism or something like that! What a devil she was!

Where was she? She must be lying down there, right below where Cecilia herself was lying. And it was either some fiend's trick of ventriloquism, or else thought transference that conveyed itself like sound. The sounds were very uneven. Sometimes quite inaudible, sometimes only a brushing sort of noise. Ciss listened intently. No, it could not be ventriloquism. It was worse, some form of thought transference. Some horror of that sort. Cecilia still lay weak and inert, terrified to move, but she was growing calmer, with suspicion. It was some diabolic trick of that unnatural woman.

But *what a devil* of a woman! She even knew that she, Cecilia, had mentally accused her of killing her son Henry. Poor Henry was Robert's elder brother, twelve years older than Robert. He had died suddenly when he was twenty-two, after an awful struggle with himself, because he was passionately in love with a young and very good-looking actress, and his mother had humorously despised him for the attachment. So he had caught some sudden ordinary disease, but the poison had gone to his brain and killed him, before he ever regained consciousness. Ciss knew the few facts from her own father. And lately, she had been thinking that Pauline was going to kill Robert as she had killed Henry. It was clear murder: a mother murdering her sensitive sons, who were fascinated by her: the Circe!

"I suppose I may as well get up," murmured the dim unbreaking voice. "Too much sun is as bad as too little. Enough sun, enough love thrill, enough proper food, and not too much of any of them, and a woman might live for ever. I verily believe for ever. If she absorbs as much vitality as she expends! Or perhaps a trifle more!"

It was certainly Aunt Pauline! How, how horrible! She, Ciss, was hearing Aunt Pauline's thoughts. Oh, how ghastly! Aunt Pauline was sending out her thoughts in a sort of radio, and she, Ciss, had to *hear* what her aunt was thinking. How ghastly! How insufferable! One of them would surely have to die.

She twisted and she lay inert and crumpled, staring vacantly in front of her. Vacantly! Vacantly! And her eyes were staring almost into a hole. She was staring into it unseeing, a hole going down in the corner from the lead gutter. It meant nothing to her. Only it frightened her a little more.

When suddenly out of the hole came a sigh and a last whisper. "Ah, well! Pauline! Get up, it's enough for today!"—Good God! Out of the hole of the rain-pipe! The rain-pipe was acting as a speaking-tube! Impossible! No, quite possible. She had read of it even in some book. And Aunt Pauline, like the old and guilty woman she was, talked aloud to herself. That was it!

A sullen exultance sprang into Ciss's breast. *That* was why she would never have anybody, not even Robert, in her bedroom. That was why she never dozed in a chair, never sat absent-minded anywhere, but went to her room, and kept to her room, except when she roused herself to be alert. When she slackened off, she talked to herself! She talked in a soft little crazy voice, to herself. But she was not crazy. It was only her thoughts murmuring themselves aloud.

So she had qualms about poor Henry! Well she might have! Ciss believed that Aunt Pauline had loved her big, handsome, brilliant first-born much more than she loved Robert, and that his death had been a terrible blow and a chagrin to her. Poor Robert had been only ten years old when Henry died. Since then he had been the substitute.

Ah, how awful!

But Aunt Pauline was a strange woman. She had left her husband when Henry was a small child, some years even before Robert was born. There was no quarrel. Sometimes she saw her husband again, quite amicably, but a little mockingly. And she even gave him money.

For Pauline earned all her own. Her father had been a Consul in the East and in Naples, and a devoted collector of beautiful and exotic things. When he died, soon after his grandson Henry was born, he left his collection of treasures to his daughter. And Pauline, who had really a passion and a genius for loveliness, whether in texture or form or colour, had laid the basis of her fortune on her father's collection. She had gone on collecting, buying where she could, and selling to collectors and to museums. She was one of the first to sell old, weird African wooden figures to the museums, and ivory carvings from New Guinea. She bought Renoir as soon as she saw his pictures. But not Rousseau. And all by herself, she made a fortune.

After her husband died, she had not married again. She was not even *known* to have had lovers. If she did have lovers, it was not among the men who admired her most and paid her devout and open attendance. To these she was a "friend."

Cecilia slipped on her clothes and caught up her rug, hastening carefully down the ladder to the loft. As she descended she heard the ringing musical call: "All right, Ciss!" which meant that the lovely lady was finished, and returning to the house. Even her voice was marvellously young and sonorous, beautifully balanced and self-possessed. So different from the little voice in which she talked to herself. *That* was much more the voice of an old woman.

Ciss hastened round to the yew enclosure, where lay the comfortable chaise-longue with the various delicate rugs. Everything Pauline had was choice, to the fine straw mat on the floor. The great yew walls were beginning to cast long shadows. Only in the corner, where the rugs tumbled their delicate colours, was there hot, still sunshine.

The rugs folded up, the chair lifted away, Cecilia stooped to look at the mouth of the rain-pipe. There it was, in the corner, under a little hood of masonry and just projecting from the thick leaves of the creeper on the wall. If Pauline, lying there, turned her face towards the wall, she would speak into the very mouth of the hole. Cecilia was reassured. She had heard her aunt's thoughts indeed, but by no uncanny agency.

That evening, as if aware of something, Pauline was a little quicker than usual, though she looked her own serene, rather mysterious self. And after coffee she said to Robert and Ciss: "I'm so sleepy. The sun has made me so sleepy. I feel full of sunshine like a bee. I shall go to bed, if you don't mind. You two sit and have a talk."

Cecilia looked quickly at her cousin.

"Perhaps you would rather be alone," she said to him.

"No, no," he replied. "Do keep me company for a while, if it doesn't bore you."

The windows were open, the scent of the honeysuckle wafted in, with the sound of an owl. Robert smoked in silence. There was a sort of despair in the motionless, rather squat body. He looked like a caryatid bearing a weight.

"Do you remember Cousin Henry?" Cecilia asked him suddenly.

He looked up in surprise.

"Yes, very well," he said.

"What did he look like?" she said, glancing into her cousin's big secret-troubled eyes, in which there was so much frustration.

"Oh, he was handsome; tall and fresh-coloured, with mother's soft brown hair." As a matter of fact, Pauline's hair was grey. "The ladies admired him very much; he was at all the dances."

"And what kind of character had he?"

"Oh, very good-natured and jolly. He liked to be amused. He was rather quick and clever, like mother, and very good company."

"And did he love your mother?"

"Very much. She loved him too—better than she does me, as a matter of fact. He was so much more nearly her idea of a man."

"Why was he more her idea of a man?"

"Tall—handsome—attractive, and very good company—and would, I believe, have been very successful at law. I'm afraid I am merely negative in all those respects."

Ciss looked at him attentively, with her slow-thinking hazel eyes. Under his impassive mask, she knew he suffered.

"Do you think you are so much more negative than he?" she said.

He did not lift his face. But after a few moments he replied:

"My life, certainly, is a negative affair."

She hesitated before she dared ask him:

"And do you mind?"

He did not answer her at all. Her heart sank.

"You see, I am afraid my life is as negative as yours is," she said. "And I'm beginning to mind bitterly. I'm thirty."

She saw his creamy, well-bred hand tremble.

"I suppose," he said, without looking at her, "one will rebel when it is too late."

That was queer, from him.

"Robert," she said, "do you like me at all?"

She saw his dusky creamy face, so changeless in its folds, go pale.

"I am very fond of you," he murmured.

"Won't you kiss me? Nobody ever kisses me," she said pathetically.

He looked at her, his eyes strange with fear and a certain haughtiness. Then he rose and came softly over to her, and kissed her gently on the cheek.

"It's an awful shame, Ciss!" he said softly.

She caught his hand and pressed it to her breast.

"And sit with me sometime in the garden," she said, murmuring with difficulty. "Won't you?"

He looked at her anxiously and searchingly.

"What about mother?" he said.

Ciss smiled a funny little smile, and looked into his eyes. He suddenly flushed crimson, turning aside his face. It was a painful sight.

"I know," he said, "I am no lover of women."

He spoke with sarcastic stoicism against himself, but even she did not know the shame it was to him.

"You never try to be!" she said.

Again his eyes changed uncannily.

"Does one have to try?" he said.

"Why, yes! One never does anything if one doesn't try."

He went pale again.

"Perhaps you are right," he said.

In a few minutes she left him, and went to her rooms. At least, she had tried to take off the everlasting lid from things.

The weather continued sunny, Pauline continued her sun baths, and Ciss lay on the roof eavesdropping in the literal sense of the word. But Pauline was not to be heard. No sound came up the pipe. She must be lying with her face away into the open. Ciss listened with all her might. She could just detect the faintest, faintest murmur away below, but no audible syllable.

And at night, under the stars, Cecilia sat and waited in silence, on the seat which kept in view the drawing-room windows and the side door into the garden. She saw the light go up in her aunt's room. She saw the lights at last go out in the drawing-room. And she waited. But he did not come. She stayed on in the darkness half the night, while the owl hooted. But she stayed alone.

Two days she heard nothing, her aunt's thoughts were not revealed, and at evening nothing happened. Then the second night, as she sat with heavy, helpless persistence in the garden, suddenly she started. He had come out. She rose and went softly over the grass to him.

"Don't speak," he murmured.

And in silence, in the dark, they walked down the garden and over the little bridge to the paddock, where the hay, cut very late, was in cock. There they stood disconsolate under the stars.

"You see," he said, "how can I ask for love, if I don't feel any love in myself. You know I have a real regard for you—"

"How can you feel any love, when you never feel anything?" she said.

"That is true," he replied.

And she waited for what next.

"And how can I marry?" he said. "I am a failure even at making money. I can't ask my mother for money."

She sighed deeply.

"Then don't bother yet about marrying," she said. "Only love me a little. Won't you?"

He gave a short laugh.

"It sounds so atrocious, to say it is hard to begin," he said.

She sighed again. He was so stiff to move.

"Shall we sit down a minute?" she said. And then as they sat on the hay, she added: "May I touch you? Do you mind?"

"Yes, I mind! But do as you wish," he replied, with that mixture of shyness and queer candour which made him a little ridiculous, as he knew quite well. But in his heart there was almost murder.

She touched his black, always tidy hair with her fingers.

"I suppose I shall rebel one day," he said again, suddenly.

They sat some time, till it grew chilly. And he held her hand fast, but he never put his arms round her. At last she rose and went indoors, saying good night.

The next day, as Cecilia lay stunned and angry on the roof, taking her sun bath, and becoming hot and fierce with sunshine, suddenly she started. A terror seized her in spite of herself. It was the voice.

"Caro, caro, tu non l'hai visto!" it was murmuring away, in a language Cecilia did not understand. She lay and writhed her limbs in the sun, listening intently to words she could not follow. Softly, whisperingly, with infinite caressiveness and yet with that subtle, insidious arrogance under its velvet, came the voice, murmuring in Italian: "Bravo, si, molto bravo, poverino, ma uomo come te non lo sara mai, mai, mai!" Oh, especially in Italian Cecilia heard the poisonous charm of the voice, so caressive, so soft and flexible, yet so utterly egoistic. She hated it with intensity as it sighed and whispered out of nowhere. Why, why should it be so delicate, so subtle and flexible and beautifully controlled, while she herself was so clumsy! Oh, poor Cecilia, she writhed in the afternoon sun, knowing her own clownish clumsiness and lack of suavity, in comparison.

"No, Robert dear, you will never be the man your father was, though you have some of his looks. He was a marvellous lover, soft as a flower yet piercing as a humming-bird. No, Robert dear, you will never know how to serve a woman as Monsignor Mauro did. Cara, cara mia bellisima, ti ho aspettato come l'agonizzante aspetta la morte, morte deliziosa, quasi quasi troppo deliziosa per un' anima humana—Soft as a flower, yet probing like a humming-bird. He gave himself to a woman as he gave himself to God. Mauro! Mauro! How you loved me!"

The voice ceased in reverie, and Cecilia knew what she had guessed before, that Robert was not the son of her Uncle Ronald, but of some Italian.

"I am disappointed in you, Robert. There is no poignancy in you. Your father was a Jesuit, but he was the most perfect and poignant lover in the world. You are a Jesuit like a fish in a tank. And that Ciss of yours is the cat fishing for you. It is less edifying even than poor Henry."

Cecilia suddenly bent her mouth down to the tube, and said in a deep voice:

"Leave Robert alone! Don't kill him as well."

There was a dead silence, in the hot July afternoon that was lowering for thunder. Cecilia lay prostrate, her heart beating in great thumps. She was listening as if her whole soul were an ear. At last she caught the whisper:

"Did someone speak?"

She leaned again to the mouth of the tube.

"Don't kill Robert as you killed me," she said with slow enunciation, and a deep but small voice.

"Ah!" came the sharp little cry. "Who is that speaking?"

"Henry!" said the deep voice.

There was dead silence. Poor Cecilia lay with all the use gone out of her. And there was dead silence. Till at last came the whisper:

"I didn't kill Henry. No, NO! Henry, surely you can't blame me! I loved you, dearest. I only wanted to help you."

"You killed me!" came the deep, artificial, accusing voice. "Now, let Robert live. Let him go! Let him marry!"

There was a pause.

"How very, very awful!" mused the whispering voice. "Is it possible, Henry, you are a spirit, and you condemn me?"

"Yes! I condemn you!"

Cecilia felt all her pent-up rage going down that rain-pipe. At the same time, she almost laughed. It was awful.

She lay and listened and listened. No sound! As if time had ceased, she lay inert in the weakening sun. The sky was yellowing. Quickly she dressed herself, went down, and out to the corner of the stables.

"Aunt Pauline!" she called discreetly. "Did you hear thunder?"

"Yes! I am going in. Don't wait," came a feeble voice.

Cecilia retired, and from the loft watched, spying, as the figure of the lovely lady, wrapped in a lovely wrap of old blue silk, went rather totteringly to the house.

The sky gradually darkened, Cecilia hastened in with the rugs. Then the storm broke. Aunt Pauline did not appear to tea. She found the thunder trying. Robert also did not arrive till after tea, in the pouring rain. Cecilia went down the covered passage to her own house, and dressed carefully for dinner, putting some white columbines at her breast.

The drawing-room was lit with a softly shaded lamp. Robert, dressed, was waiting, listening to the rain. He too seemed strangely crackling and on edge. Cecilia came in, with the white flowers nodding at her breast. Robert was watching her curiously, a new look on his face. Cecilia went to the bookshelves near the door, and was peering for something, listening acutely. She heard a rustle, then the door softly opening. And as it opened, Ciss suddenly switched on the strong electric light by the door.

Her aunt, in a dress of black lace over ivory colour, stood in the doorway. Her face was made up, but haggard with a look of unspeakable irritability, as if years of suppressed exasperation and dislike of her fellow-men had suddenly crumpled her into an old witch.

"Oh, aunt!" cried Cecilia.

"Why, mother, you're a little old lady!" came the astounded voice of Robert; like an astonished boy; as if it were a joke.

"Have you only just found it out?" snapped the old woman venomously.

"Yes! Why, I thought—" his voice trailed out in misgiving.

The haggard, old Pauline, in a frenzy of exasperation, said:

"Aren't we going down?"

She had never even noticed the excess of light, a thing she shunned. And she went downstairs almost tottering.

At table she sat with her face like a crumpled mask of unspeakable irritability. She looked old, very old, and like a witch. Robert and Cecilia fetched furtive glances at her. And Ciss, watching Robert, saw that he was so astonished and repelled by his mother's looks, that he was another man.

"What kind of a drive home did you have?" snapped Pauline, with an almost gibbering irritability.

"It rained, of course," he said.

"How clever of you to have found that out!" said his mother, with the grisly grin of malice that had succeeded her arch smirk.

"I don't understand," he said with quiet suavity.

"It's apparent," said his mother, rapidly and sloppily eating her food.

She rushed through the meal like a crazy dog, to the utter consternation of the servant. And the moment it was over, she darted in a queer, crab-like way upstairs. Robert and Cecilia followed her, thunderstruck, like two conspirators.

"You pour the coffee. I loathe it! I'm going! Good night!" said the old woman, in a succession of sharp shots. And she scrambled out of the room.

There was a dead silence. At last he said:

"I'm afraid mother isn't well. I must persuade her to see a doctor."

"Yes!" said Cecilia.

The evening passed in silence. Robert and Ciss stayed on in the drawing-room, having lit a fire. Outside was cold rain. Each pretended to read. They did not want to separate. The evening passed with ominous mysteriousness, yet quickly.

At about ten o'clock, the door suddenly opened, and Pauline appeared, in a blue wrap. She shut the door behind her, and came to the fire. Then she looked at the two young people in hate, real hate.

"You two had better get married quickly," she said in an ugly voice. "It would look more decent; such a passionate pair of lovers!"

Robert looked up at her quietly.

"I thought you believed that cousins should not marry, mother," he said.

"I do! But you're not cousins. Your father was an Italian priest." Pauline held her daintily slippered foot to the fire, in an old coquettish gesture. Her body tried to repeat all the old graceful gestures. But the nerve had snapped, so it was a rather dreadful caricature.

"Is that really true, mother?" he asked.

"True! What do you think? He was a distinguished man, or he wouldn't have been my lover. He was far too distinguished a man to have had you for a son. But that joy fell to me."

"How unfortunate all round," he said slowly.

"Unfortunate for you? *You* were lucky. It was *my* misfortune," she said acidly to him.

She was really a dreadful sight, like a piece of lovely Venetian glass that has been dropped, and gathered up again in horrible, sharp-edged fragments.

Suddenly she left the room again.

For a week it went on. She did not recover. It was as if every nerve in her body had suddenly started screaming in an insanity of discordance. The doctor came, and gave her sedatives, for she never slept. Without drugs, she never slept at all, only paced back and forth in her room, looking hideous and evil, reeking with malevolence. She could not bear to see either her son or her niece. Only when either of them came, she asked in pure malice:

"Well! When's the wedding? Have you celebrated the nuptials yet?"

At first Cecilia was stunned by what she had done. She realized vaguely that her aunt, once a definite thrust of condemnation had penetrated her beautiful armour, had just collapsed squirming inside her shell. It was too terrible. Ciss was almost terrified into repentance. Then she thought: This is what she always was. Now let her live the rest of her days in her true colours.

But Pauline would not live long. She was literally shrivelling away. She kept her room, and saw no one. She had her mirrors taken away.

Robert and Cecilia sat a good deal together. The jeering of the mad Pauline had not driven them apart, as she had hoped. But Cecilia dared not confess to him what she had done.

"Do you think your mother ever loved anybody?" Ciss asked him tentatively, rather wistfully, one evening.

He looked at her fixedly.

"Herself!" he said at last.

"She didn't even *love* herself," said Ciss. "It was something else —what was it?" She lifted a troubled, utterly puzzled face to him.

"Power!" he said curtly.

"But what power?" she asked. "I don't understand."

"Power to feed on other lives," he said bitterly. "She was beautiful, and she fed on life. She has fed on me as she fed on Henry. She put a sucker into one's soul, and sucked up one's essential life."

"And don't you forgive her?"

"No."

"Poor Aunt Pauline!"

But even Ciss did not mean it. She was only aghast.

"I *know* I've got a heart," he said, passionately striking his breast. "But it's almost sucked dry. I *know* people who want power over others."

Ciss was silent; what was there to say?

And two days later, Pauline was found dead in her bed, having taken too much veronal, for her heart was weakened. From the grave even she hit back at her son and her niece. She left Robert the noble sum of one thousand pounds; and Ciss one hundred. All the rest, with the nucleus of her valuable antiques, went to form the "Pauline Attenborough Museum."

COMMENT

As a characterization of a woman, Lawrence's story is developed by means directly opposite those used by Virginia Woolf. The reader saw Mrs. Woolf's protagonist entirely from the inside and saw other characters only as they made an impression on her; but Pauline Attenborough is seen entirely from the outside and in terms of the effect she has upon other characters. Notice that the difference in method is related to the type of character to be presented: as a hypersensitive, withdrawing individual, Mabel is best shown by her inner response to various external influences; as a lover of power, Pauline must be shown in her exercise of power over others. Her power becomes the more real as its effect is shown on people who are themselves made real for us; hence Robert and Cecilia are fully characterized, and we are even given some glimpse of a dead husband and son in relation to the forceful Pauline. Perhaps the most skillful part of the story is the presentation of Robert and Cecilia, not so much as the victims of immediate tyrannical acts, but rather in terms of the cumulative effect of Pauline's influence upon their character—their negativeness and virtual inability to revolt. How, of course, is Robert distinguished from Cecilia?

The means by which Cecilia does finally revolt is a rather artificial device which depends upon several coincidences and imposes a considerable strain upon the reader's credulity. For the moment Lawrence has fallen out of the character story and into a kind of popular narrative which rests its appeal upon delightfully ingenious and strange occurrences (this part of the story is rather suggestive of Maugham's methods in "The Facts of Life"). There is even a little of the mystery story—with some originality of handling in that the mysterious event occurs in broad daylight instead of in conventional nocturnal surroundings. But Lawrence does return quickly to the problem of character, and here he clearly stays away from the popular effect which he could easily have secured by having Pauline shocked into some more admirable kind of conduct. The shock does make an apparent change in Pauline, and in some ways even a startling change, but her basic motives continue the same. Lawrence refuses to sentimentalize her. In what ways, also, does Lawrence keep his portraits of Robert and Cecilia consistent?

What is the purpose of giving the final position in the story to Pauline instead of to Robert and Cecilia?

SYMBOLISM

William Carlos Williams

William Carlos Williams has engaged in two professions throughout his adult life—medicine and literature. He has practiced medicine in Rutherford, New Jersey, for forty years, and the first of his many volumes of poetry appeared in 1909. He was born in Rutherford in 1883, had an athletic boyhood, took his M.D. at the University of Pennsylvania, and did a year's graduate work in pediatrics at Leipzig. His poems are characterized by freshness of language and by a departure from conventional forms, and they have won him a number of prizes. In recent years he has been working on a long poem entitled *Paterson*. He has also been interested in fiction and has published a novel as well as a volume of sketches and short stories, *Life Along the Passaic River*.

The Use of Force

THEY were new patients to me, all I had was the name, Olson. Please come down as soon as you can, my daughter is very sick.

When I arrived I was met by the mother, a big startled looking woman, very clean and apologetic who merely said, Is this the doctor? and let me in. In the back, she added. You must excuse us, doctor, we have her in the kitchen where it is warm. It is very damp here sometimes.

The child was fully dressed and sitting on her father's lap near the kitchen table. He tried to get up, but I motioned for him not to bother, took off my overcoat and started to look things over. I could see that they were all very nervous, eyeing me up and down distrustfully. As often, in such cases, they weren't telling me more than they had to, it was up to me to tell them; that's why they were spending three dollars on me.

The child was fairly eating me up with her cold, steady eyes, and no expression to her face whatever. She did not move and seemed, inwardly, quiet; an unusually attractive little thing, and as strong as a heifer in appearance. But her face was flushed, she was breathing rapidly, and I realized that she had a high fever. She had magnificent blonde hair, in profusion. One of those picture children often reproduced in advertising leaflets and the photogravure sections of the Sunday papers.

She's had a fever for three days, began the father and we don't know what it comes from. My wife has given her things, you know, like people do, but it don't do no good. And there's been a lot of sickness around. So we tho't you'd better look her over and tell us what is the matter.

As doctors often do I took a trial shot at it as a point of departure. Has she had a sore throat?

Both parents answered me together, No . . . No, she says her throat don't hurt her.

Does your throat hurt you? added the mother to the child. But the little girl's expression didn't change nor did she move her eyes from my face.

Have you looked?

I tried to, said the mother, but I couldn't see.

As it happens we had been having a number of cases of diphtheria in the school to which this child went during that month and we were all, quite apparently, thinking of that, though no one had as yet spoken of the thing.

Well, I said, suppose we take a look at the throat first. I smiled in my best professional manner and asking for the child's first name I said, come on, Mathilda, open your mouth and let's take a look at your throat.

Nothing doing.

Aw, come on, I coaxed, just open your mouth wide and let me take a look. Look, I said opening both hands wide, I haven't anything in my hands. Just open up and let me see.

Such a nice man, put in the mother. Look how kind he is to you. Come on, do what he tells you to. He won't hurt you.

At that I ground my teeth in disgust. If only they wouldn't use the word "hurt" I might be able to get somewhere. But I did not allow myself to be hurried or disturbed but speaking quietly and slowly I approached the child again.

As I moved my chair a little nearer suddenly with one catlike movement both her hands clawed instinctively for my eyes and she almost reached them too. In fact she knocked my glasses flying and they fell, though unbroken, several feet away from me on the kitchen floor.

Both the mother and father almost turned themselves inside out in embarrassment and apology. You bad girl, said the mother, taking her and shaking her by one arm. Look what you've done. The nice man . . .

For heaven's sake, I broke in. Don't call me a nice man to her. I'm here to look at her throat on the chance that she might have diphtheria and possibly die of it. But that's nothing to her. Look here, I said to the child, we're going to look at your throat. You're old enough to understand what I'm saying. Will you open it now by yourself or shall we have to open it for you?

Not a move. Even her expression hadn't changed. Her breaths however were coming faster and faster. Then the battle began. I had to do it. I had to have a throat culture for her own protection. But first I told the parents that it was entirely up to them. I explained the danger but said that I would not insist on a throat examination so long as they would take the responsibility.

If you don't do what the doctor says you'll have to go to the hospital, the mother admonished her severely.

Oh yeah? I had to smile to myself. After all, I had already fallen in love with the savage brat, the parents were contemptible to me. In the ensuing struggle they grew more and more abject, crushed, exhausted while she surely rose to magnificent heights of insane fury of effort bred of her terror of me.

The father tried his best, and he was a big man but the fact that she was his daughter, his shame at her behavior and his dread of hurting her made him release her just at the critical times when I had almost achieved success, till I wanted to kill him. But his dread also that she might have diphtheria made him tell me to go on, go on though he himself was almost fainting, while the mother moved back and forth behind us raising and lowering her hands in an agony of apprehension.

Put her in front of you on your lap, I ordered, and hold both her wrists.

But as soon as he did the child let out a scream. Don't, you're hurting me. Let go of my hands. Let them go I tell you. Then she shrieked terrifyingly, hysterically. Stop it! Stop it! You're killing me!

Do you think she can stand it, doctor! said the mother.

You get out, said the husband to his wife. Do you want her to die of diphtheria?

Come on now, hold her, I said.

Then I grasped the child's head with my left hand and tried to get the wooden tongue depressor between her teeth. She fought, with clenched teeth, desperately! But now I also had grown furious —at a child. I tried to hold myself down but I couldn't. I know how to expose a throat for inspection. And I did my best. When finally I got the wooden spatula behind the last teeth and just the point of it into the mouth cavity, she opened up for an instant but before I could see anything she came down again and gripping the wooden blade between her molars she reduced it to splinters before I could get it out again.

Aren't you ashamed, the mother yelled at her. Aren't you ashamed to act like that in front of the doctor?

Get me a smooth-handled spoon of some sort, I told the mother. We're going through with this. The child's mouth was already bleeding. Her tongue was cut and she was screaming in wild hysterical shrieks. Perhaps I should have desisted and come back in an hour or more. No doubt it would have been better. But I have seen at least two children lying dead in bed of neglect in such cases, and feeling that I must get a diagnosis now or never I went at it again. But the worst of it was that I too had got beyond reason. I could have torn the child apart in my own fury and enjoyed it. It was a pleasure to attack her. My face was burning with it.

The damned little brat must be protected against her own idiocy, one says to one's self at such times. Others must be protected against her. It is a social necessity. And all these things are true. But a blind fury, a feeling of adult shame, bred of a longing for muscular release are the operatives. One goes on to the end.

In a final unreasoning assault I overpowered the child's neck and jaws. I forced the heavy silver spoon back of her teeth and down her throat till she gagged. And there it was—both tonsils covered with membrane. She had fought valiantly to keep me from knowing her secret. She had been hiding that sore throat for three days at least and lying to her parents in order to escape just such an outcome as this.

Now truly she was furious. She had been on the defensive before but now she attacked. Tried to get off her father's lap and fly at me while tears of defeat blinded her eyes.

COMMENT

"The Use of Force" interests us immediately because it is written from a point of view relatively rare in fiction—that of the doctor. But the use of a novel point of view cannot in itself make a good story, and we have to ask further questions. For instance, what makes this a story at all rather than a mere sketch of a physician's call and his difficulties with a patient? For one thing, of course, there is a conflict, which becomes more intense as it works toward a climax; the conflict is not merely described but is presented in images of sound and feeling so that the reader is led to participate in it. The writer selects his materials: there is almost no description of scene; our attention is focused on the human participants, who are gradually distinguished from each other. The parents are prominent at the start but gradually fade away until at the end they have virtually disappeared—as when a camera is moved closer and closer to a central object, eliminating all else from the field of vision. The chief combatants are characterized; they are more than merely neutral antagonists whose blows are seen but whose motivations are unknown. Most important of all, the characterization is not at all obvious, but is complicated. The child is not only scared; she has an obscure sense of shame, of defending herself against a violation; and she becomes actively hostile. This irony points to a more general level of meaning: a kind of self-defense, heroic in its way, may serve to conceal a danger to both oneself and others. Or again, the very state of affairs which needs disclosure may itself lead to an intense concealment.

But it is in the narrator's characterization of himself that the most interesting contradictions are laid bare and the meaning is carried farthest beyond the limits of the immediate scene. The narrator has a sharp awareness of his own motives. He has a sense of duty and responsibility, and this we can see operating. But he also recognizes the instinctive, animal-like impulse to physical victory that operates powerfully, and this he presents fully. He goes further and shows how the recognition of this element brings the combatant to the need of justification. It is just after he has said, "I could have torn the child apart in my fury," that he talks of the need of protecting others against her, and her against herself. How does he show that he does not fool himself with the platitude, even though the platitude is, as he says, a truth?

At this point the reader needs hardly to glance at the title, "The Use of Force," to feel the symbolic value of the story as a commentary on force generally—on the kind of hostility, love of conquest, and madness that the use of force brings into play, whatever the apparent necessity of or justification for vigorous action. It would be a mistake, however, to read the story as a treatise against the use of force. The narrator does say, "Perhaps I should have desisted and come back in an hour or more," but he also presents a fairly compelling reason for acting when he did. The very fact that he has balanced the arguments keeps his story from becoming a statement of either a negative or affirmative position. Instead it remains a fine portrayal by means of a specific dramatic situation of the basic ways in which human nature works.

Although the story is short, and the parents have a secondary role, the author develops a certain amount of conflict even in them. What is it?

How is the theme of this story related to the theme of "Sailor off the Bremen"? Does Shaw's story have the symbolic implications that Williams's does?

Shirley Jackson

Shirley Jackson's life has been passed in widely separated parts of
the United States. She was born in California, was educated in New
York, and now lives in Vermont. She graduated from Syracuse University
in 1940 and married a fellow student, Stanley Hyman, who is a well-
known critic. Her short stories have appeared in *The New Yorker* and
elsewhere. When the volume of stories, *The Lottery*, appeared in 1949,
it attracted a great deal of attention. The title story, which is reprinted
here, has been much discussed. The author says of it: "I would explain
it as an attempt to define a present-day state of mind by a ritual of
blood sacrifice still dormant in our minds."

The Lottery

THE MORNING of June 27th was clear and sunny, with the
fresh warmth of a full-summer day; the flowers were blos-
soming profusely and the grass was richly green. The people
of the village began to gather in the square, between the post
office and the bank, around ten o'clock; in some towns there were
so many people that the lottery took two days and had to be
started on June 26th, but in this village, where there were only
about three hundred people, the whole lottery took less than two
hours, so it could begin at ten o'clock in the morning and still be
through in time to allow the villagers to get home for noon dinner.

The children assembled first, of course. School was recently over
for the summer, and the feeling of liberty sat uneasily on most of
them; they tended to gather together quietly for a while before
they broke into boisterous play, and their talk was still of the classroom and the teacher, of books and reprimands. Bobby Martin
had already stuffed his pockets full of stones, and the other boys

THE LOTTERY Reprinted from *The New Yorker* by permission of the author. Copyright 1948 The New Yorker Magazine, Inc. Also copyright 1949
by Shirley Jackson and published in the volume of the same name by Farrar
Straus and Company.

soon followed his example, selecting the smoothest and roundest stones; Bobby and Harry Jones and Dickie Delacroix—the villagers pronounced this name "Dellacroy"—eventually made a great pile of stones in one corner of the square and guarded it against the raids of the other boys. The girls stood aside, talking among themselves, looking over their shoulders at the boys, and the very small children rolled in the dust or clung to the hands of their older brothers or sisters.

Soon the men began to gather, surveying their own children, speaking of planting and rain, tractors and taxes. They stood together, away from the pile of stones in the corner, and their jokes were quiet and they smiled rather than laughed. The women, wearing faded house dresses and sweaters, came shortly after their menfolk. They greeted one another and exchanged bits of gossip as they went to join their husbands. Soon the women, standing by their husbands, began to call to their children, and the children came reluctantly, having to be called four or five times. Bobby Martin ducked under his mother's grasping hand and ran, laughing, back to the pile of stones. His father spoke up sharply, and Bobby came quickly and took his place between his father and his oldest brother.

The lottery was conducted—as were the square dances, the teen-age club, the Halloween program—by Mr. Summers, who had time and energy to devote to civic activities. He was a round-faced, jovial man and he ran the coal business, and people were sorry for him, because he had no children and his wife was a scold. When he arrived in the square, carrying the black wooden box, there was a murmur of conversation among the villagers, and he waved and called, "Little late today, folks." The postmaster, Mr. Graves, followed him, carrying a three-legged stool, and the stool was put in the center of the square and Mr. Summers set the black box down on it. The villagers kept their distance, leaving a space between themselves and the stool, and when Mr. Summers said, "Some of you fellows want to give me a hand?" there was a hesitation before two men, Mr. Martin and his oldest son, Baxter, came forward to hold the box steady on the stool while Mr. Summers stirred up the papers inside it.

The original paraphernalia for the lottery had been lost long ago, and the black box now resting on the stool had been put into use

even before Old Man Warner, the oldest man in town, was born.
Mr. Summers spoke frequently to the villagers about making a
new box, but no one liked to upset even as much tradition as was
represented by the black box. There was a story that the present
box had been made with some pieces of the box that had preceded
it, the one that had been constructed when the first people settled
down to make a village here. Every year, after the lottery, Mr.
Summers began talking again about a new box, but every year the
subject was allowed to fade off without anything's being done. The
black box grew shabbier each year; by now it was no longer completely black but splintered badly along one side to show the
original wood color, and in some places faded or stained.

Mr. Martin and his oldest son, Baxter, held the black box securely
on the stool until Mr. Summers had stirred the papers thoroughly
with his hand. Because so much of the ritual had been forgotten
or discarded, Mr. Summers had been successful in having slips of
paper substituted for the chips of wood that had been used for
generations. Chips of wood, Mr. Summers had argued, had been
all very well when the village was tiny, but now that the population was more than three hundred and likely to keep on growing,
it was necessary to use something that would fit more easily into
the black box. The night before the lottery, Mr. Summers and Mr.
Graves made up the slips of paper and put them in the box, and it
was then taken to the safe of Mr. Summers' coal company and
locked up until Mr. Summers was ready to take it to the square
next morning. The rest of the year, the box was put away, sometimes one place, sometimes another; it had spent one year in Mr.
Graves's barn and another year underfoot in the post office, and
sometimes it was set on a shelf in the Martin grocery and left there.

There was a great deal of fussing to be done before Mr. Summers declared the lottery open. There were the lists to make up—
of heads of families, heads of households in each family, members
of each household in each family. There was the proper swearing-in
of Mr. Summers by the postmaster, as the official of the lottery; at
one time, some people remembered, there had been a recital of
some sort, performed by the official of the lottery, a perfunctory,
tuneless chant that had been rattled off duly each year; some people
believed that the official of the lottery used to stand just so when
he said or sang it, others believed that he was supposed to walk

among the people, but years and years ago this part of the ritual had been allowed to lapse. There had been, also, a ritual salute, which the official of the lottery had had to use in addressing each person who came up to draw from the box, but this also had changed with time, until now it was felt necessary only for the official to speak to each person approaching. Mr. Summers was very good at all this; in his clean white shirt and blue jeans, with one hand resting carelessly on the black box, he seemed very proper and important as he talked interminably to Mr. Graves and the Martins.

Just as Mr. Summers finally left off talking and turned to the assembled villagers, Mrs. Hutchinson came hurriedly along the path to the square, her sweater thrown over her shoulders, and slid into place in the back of the crowd. "Clean forgot what day it was," she said to Mrs. Delacroix, who stood next to her, and they both laughed softly. "Thought my old man was out back stacking wood," Mrs. Hutchinson went on, "and then I looked out the window and the kids was gone, and then I remembered it was the twenty-seventh and came a-running." She dried her hands on her apron, and Mrs. Delacroix said, "You're in time, though. They're still talking away up there."

Mrs. Hutchinson craned her neck to see through the crowd and found her husband and children standing near the front. She tapped Mrs. Delacroix on the arm as a farewell and began to make her way through the crowd. The people separated good-humoredly to let her through; two or three people said, in voices just loud enough to be heard across the crowd, "Here comes your Missus, Hutchinson," and "Bill, she made it after all." Mrs. Hutchinson reached her husband, and Mr. Summers, who had been waiting, said cheerfully, "Thought we were going to have to get on without you, Tessie." Mrs. Hutchinson said, grinning, "Wouldn't have me leave m'dishes in the sink, now, would you, Joe?," and soft laughter ran through the crowd as the people stirred back into position after Mrs. Hutchinson's arrival.

"Well, now," Mr. Summers said soberly, "guess we better get started, get this over with, so's we can go back to work. Anybody ain't here?"

"Dunbar," several people said. "Dunbar, Dunbar."

Mr. Summers consulted his list. "Clyde Dunbar," he said. "That's right. He's broke his leg, hasn't he? Who's drawing for him?"

"Me, I guess," a woman said, and Mr. Summers turned to look at her. "Wife draws for her husband," Mr. Summers said. "Don't you have a grown boy to do it for you, Janey?" Although Mr. Summers and everyone else in the village knew the answer perfectly well, it was the business of the official of the lottery to ask such questions formally. Mr. Summers waited with an expression of polite interest while Mrs. Dunbar answered.

"Horace's not but sixteen yet," Mrs. Dunbar said regretfully. "Guess I gotta fill in for the old man this year."

"Right," Mr. Summers said. He made a note on the list he was holding. Then he asked, "Watson boy drawing this year?"

A tall boy in the crowd raised his hand. "Here," he said. "I'm drawing for m'mother and me." He blinked his eyes nervously and ducked his head as several voices in the crowd said things like "Good fellow, Jack," and "Glad to see your mother's got a man to do it."

"Well," Mr. Summers said, "guess that's everyone. Old Man Warner make it?"

"Here," a voice said, and Mr. Summers nodded.

A sudden hush fell on the crowd as Mr. Summers cleared his throat and looked at the list. "All ready?" he called. "Now, I'll read the names—heads of families first—and the men come up and take a paper out of the box. Keep the paper folded in your hand without looking at it until everyone has had a turn. Everything clear?"

The people had done it so many times that they only half listened to the directions; most of them were quiet, wetting their lips, not looking around. Then Mr. Summers raised one hand high and said, "Adams." A man disengaged himself from the crowd and came forward. "Hi, Steve," Mr. Summers said, and Mr. Adams said, "Hi, Joe." They grinned at one another humorlessly and nervously. Then Mr. Adams reached into the black box and took out a folded paper. He held it firmly by one corner as he turned and went hastily back to his place in the crowd, where he stood a little apart from his family, not looking down at his hand.

"Allen," Mr. Summers said. "Anderson. . . . Bentham."

"Seems like there's no time at all between lotteries any more," Mrs. Delacroix said to Mrs. Graves in the back row. "Seems like we got through with the last one only last week."

"Time sure goes fast," Mrs. Graves said.

"Clark. . . . Delacroix."

"There goes my old man," Mrs. Delacroix said. She held her breath while her husband went forward.

"Dunbar," Mr. Summers said, and Mrs. Dunbar went steadily to the box while one of the women said, "Go on, Janey," and another said, "There she goes."

"We're next," Mrs. Graves said. She watched while Mr. Graves came around from the side of the box, greeted Mr. Summers gravely, and selected a slip of paper from the box. By now, all through the crowd there were men holding the small folded papers in their large hands, turning them over and over nervously. Mrs. Dunbar and her two sons stood together, Mrs. Dunbar holding the slip of paper.

"Harburt. . . . Hutchinson."

"Get up there, Bill," Mrs. Hutchinson said, and the people near her laughed.

"Jones."

"They do say," Mr. Adams said to Old Man Warner, who stood next to him, "that over in the north village they're talking of giving up the lottery."

Old Man Warner snorted. "Pack of crazy fools," he said. "Listening to the young folks, nothing's good enough for *them*. Next thing you know, they'll be wanting to go back to living in caves, nobody work any more, live *that* way for a while. Used to be a saying about 'Lottery in June, corn be heavy soon.' First thing you know, we'd all be eating stewed chickweed and acorns. There's *always* been a lottery," he added petulantly. "Bad enough to see young Joe Summers up there joking with everybody."

"Some places have already quit lotteries," Mrs. Adams said.

"Nothing but trouble in *that*," Old Man Warner said stoutly. "Pack of young fools."

"Martin." And Bobby Martin watched his father go forward. "Overdyke. . . . Percy."

"I wish they'd hurry," Mrs. Dunbar said to her older son. "I wish they'd hurry."

"They're almost through," her son said.

"You get ready to run tell Dad," Mrs. Dunbar said.

Mr. Summers called his own name and then stepped forward precisely and selected a slip from the box. Then he called, "Warner."

"Seventy-seventh year I been in the lottery," Old Man Warner said as he went through the crowd. "Seventy-seventh time."

"Watson." The tall boy came awkwardly through the crowd. Someone said, "Don't be nervous, Jack," and Mr. Summers said, "Take your time, son."

"Zanini."

After that, there was a long pause, a breathless pause, until Mr. Summers, holding his slip of paper in the air, said, "All right, fellows." For a minute, no one moved, and then all the slips of paper were opened. Suddenly, all the women began to speak at once, saying, "Who is it?," "Who's got it?," "Is it the Dunbars?," "Is it the Watsons?" Then the voices began to say, "It's Hutchinson. It's Bill," "Bill Hutchinson's got it."

"Go tell your father," Mrs. Dunbar said to her older son.

People began to look around to see the Hutchinsons. Bill Hutchinson was standing quiet, staring down at the paper in his hand. Suddenly, Tessie Hutchinson shouted to Mr. Summers, "You didn't give him time enough to take any paper he wanted. I saw you. It wasn't fair."

"Be a good sport, Tessie," Mrs. Delacroix called, and Mrs. Graves said, "All of us took the same chance."

"Shut up, Tessie," Bill Hutchinson said.

"Well, everyone," Mr. Summers said, "that was done pretty fast, and now we've got to be hurrying a little more to get done in time." He consulted his next list. "Bill," he said, "you draw for the Hutchinson family. You got any other households in the Hutchinsons?"

"There's Don and Eva," Mrs. Hutchinson yelled. "Make them take their chance!"

"Daughters draw with their husbands' families, Tessie," Mr. Summers said gently. "You know that as well as anyone else."

"It wasn't fair," Tessie said.

"I guess not, Joe," Bill Hutchinson said regretfully. "My daughter draws with her husband's family, that's only fair. And I've got no other family except the kids."

"Then, as far as drawing for families is concerned, it's you," Mr. Summers said in explanation, "and as far as drawing for households is concerned, that's you, too. Right?"

"Right," Bill Hutchinson said.

"How many kids, Bill?" Mr. Summers asked formally.

"Three," Bill Hutchinson said. "There's Bill, Jr., and Nancy, and little Dave. And Tessie and me."

"All right, then," Mr. Summers said. "Harry, you got their tickets back?"

Mr. Graves nodded and held up the slips of paper. "Put them in the box, then," Mr. Summers directed. "Take Bill's and put it in."

"I think we ought to start over," Mrs. Hutchinson said, as quietly as she could. "I tell you it wasn't *fair*. You didn't give him time enough to choose. *Every*body saw that."

Mr. Graves had selected the five slips and put them in the box, and he dropped all the papers but those onto the ground, where the breeze caught them and lifted them off.

"Listen, everybody," Mrs. Hutchinson was saying to the people around her.

"Ready, Bill?" Mr. Summers asked, and Bill Hutchinson, with one quick glance around at his wife and children, nodded.

"Remember," Mr. Summers said, "take the slips and keep them folded until each person has taken one. Harry, you help little Dave." Mr. Graves took the hand of the little boy, who came willingly with him up to the box. "Take a paper out of the box, Davy," Mr. Summers said. Davy put his hand into the box and laughed. "Take just *one* paper," Mr. Summers said. "Harry, you hold it for him." Mr. Graves took the child's hand and removed the folded paper from the tight fist and held it while little Dave stood next to him and looked up at him wonderingly.

"Nancy next," Mr. Summers said. Nancy was twelve, and her school friends breathed heavily as she went forward, switching her skirt, and took a slip daintily from the box. "Bill, Jr.," Mr. Summers said, and Billy, his face red and his feet over-large, nearly knocked the box over as he got a paper out. "Tessie," Mr. Summers said. She hesitated for a minute, looking around defiantly, and then set her lips and went up to the box. She snatched a paper out and held it behind her.

"Bill," Mr. Summers said, and Bill Hutchinson reached into the box and felt around, bringing his hand out at last with the slip of paper in it.

The crowd was quiet. A girl whispered, "I hope it's not Nancy," and the sound of the whisper reached the edges of the crowd.

"It's not the way it used to be," Old Man Warner said clearly. "People ain't the way they used to be."

"All right," Mr. Summers said. "Open the papers. Harry, you open little Dave's."

Mr. Graves opened the slip of paper and there was a general sigh through the crowd as he held it up and everyone could see that it was blank. Nancy and Bill, Jr., opened theirs at the same time, and both beamed and laughed, turning around to the crowd and holding their slips of paper above their heads.

"Tessie," Mr. Summers said. There was a pause, and then Mr. Summers looked at Bill Hutchinson, and Bill unfolded his paper and showed it. It was blank.

"It's Tessie," Mr. Summers said, and his voice was hushed. "Show us her paper, Bill."

Bill Hutchinson went over to his wife and forced the slip of paper out of her hand. It had a black spot on it, the black spot Mr. Summers had made the night before with the heavy pencil in the coal-company office. Bill Hutchinson held it up, and there was a stir in the crowd.

"All right, folks," Mr. Summers said. "Let's finish quickly."

Although the villagers had forgotten the ritual and lost the original black box, they still remembered to use stones. The pile of stones the boys had made earlier was ready; there were stones on the ground with the blowing scraps of paper that had come out of the box. Mrs. Delacroix selected a stone so large she had to pick it up with both hands and turned to Mrs. Dunbar. "Come on," she said. "Hurry up."

Mrs. Dunbar had small stones in both hands, and she said, gasping for breath, "I can't run at all. You'll have to go ahead and I'll catch up with you."

The children had stones already, and someone gave little Davy Hutchinson a few pebbles.

Tessie Hutchinson was in the center of a cleared space by now, and she held her hands out desperately as the villagers moved in on her. "It isn't fair," she said. A stone hit her on the side of the head.

Old Man Warner was saying, "Come on, come on, everyone." Steve Adams was in the front of the crowd of villagers, with Mrs. Graves beside him.

"It isn't fair, it isn't right," Mrs. Hutchinson screamed, and then they were upon her.

COMMENT

Miss Jackson's story is remarkable for the tremendous shock produced by the ending. Let us ignore the problem of meaning for the moment and see how the shock is created. In general, the method is quite easily recognized. Up to the last six paragraphs the story is written in the manner of a realistic transcript of small-town experience: the day is a special one, true, but the occasion is familiar, and for the most part the people are presented as going through a well-known routine. We see them as decent, friendly, neighborly people; in fact, most of the details could be used just as they are in a conventional picture of idyllic small-town life. Things are easily, simply told, as if in a factual chronicle (note the use of date and hour). Suddenly, in the midst of this ordinary, matter-of-fact environment, there occurs a terrifyingly cruel action, official, accepted, yet for the reader mysterious and unexplained. It is entirely out of line with all the terms of actual experience in which the story has otherwise dealt. It is as if ordinary life had suddenly ceased and were replaced, without warning, without break, and without change of scene, by some horrifying nightmare. Hence the shock, which the author has very carefully worked up to. Note how the shock is enhanced by the deadpan narrative style, which in no way suggests that anything unusual is going on.

In one sense the author has prepared for the ending. A few slight notes of nervousness, the talk about giving up the tradition, and the emotional outburst by Mrs. Hutchinson all suggest some not entirely happy outcome. Still more important in building up an unusually strong sense of expectation is the entire absence of explanation of the public ceremony. (At the end, the reader recalls the gathering of stones earlier in the story. This unobtrusive introduction of stage properties for later use exemplifies the well-made kind of construction.) But all these preparations still look forward to an outcome which will fall within the realistic framework that the author has chosen to use. Yet the ending is not realistic: it is symbolic. We may summarize the method of the story by saying that it suddenly, without notice, shifts from a realistic to a symbolic technique. This is another way of describing the shock.

Here we come to the problem of meaning. The experienced reader will recognize immediately what Miss Jackson has done: she has taken the ancient ritual of the scapegoat—the sacrificing of an individual on whom the evils of the community are ceremonially laid (by looking up "scapegoat" in Frazer's Golden Bough the student can find accounts of many such practices)—and plunged it into an otherwise realistic account of contemporary American life. What the story appears to be saying, then, is that though ancient rituals die out, the habits of mind which brought them into being persist; that we still find scapegoats and "innocent victims."

The critical question is: Does the effect of shock really serve the symbolic intention of the story? Ideally, shock should have the effect of shaking up the accustomed habits of mind and, therefore, of compelling a more incisive observation of familiar ways of life. But shock may disturb as well as stimulate the mind and may leave the reader only feeling shaken up. The question here is whether the shock "seizes stage," so to speak, and so crowds out the revelation to which it should be secondary. It is difficult to shift from genial chatter—even with some overtones of fear—to ritual murder without leaving a sense of an unclosed gap. The risk would have been greatly lessened if atmosphere, instead of being used intentionally to emphasize the sense of the ordinary, had been used earlier in the story to introduce an element of the sinister. It would clearly have been most difficult to suggest the coexistence of the sinister and the innocuous from the start. But this would have been an ideal method, since that coexistence is really the human fact with which the story is concerned. But the story gives us the sinister after the innocuous, instead of the two simultaneously. To put it in other terms, the symbolic intention of the story could have been made clear earlier so that throughout the story we would have been seeking the symbolic level instead of being driven to look for it only retrospectively, after it has suddenly become apparent that a realistic reading will not work. (In "The Hunger Artist," for instance, we have the symbolic figure —the hunger artist—as the center of attention from the start; we know immediately that the story goes beyond realism, and so we always read with an eye on the underlying meaning.) To set us immediately on the track of the symbolism would probably reduce the shock, but it might result in a more durable story.

Paragraphs five and six of the story tell of some of the changes that have taken place in connection with the lottery. Why does the author include such matters? Is there a secondary level of meaning here?

In the second section of the story there is some talk about the other towns giving up the lottery. Such a possibility calls forth the expression of two points of view. What larger issues are really being referred to here?

Point out the ways in which, from the beginning of the lottery to Mrs. Hutchinson's final choice of a paper, the tension is gradually heightened.

Ernest Hemingway

The writings of Ernest Hemingway, who was born in 1898, reflect many of the aspects of his varied life. The short stories of *In Our Time* recount childhood experiences with his father, an Illinois doctor who took him on professional calls and taught him hunting and fishing. The background of the novel *A Farewell to Arms* is the author's experience in World War I, in which, as a volunteer in the Italian infantry, he was severely wounded. After the war Hemingway returned to his earlier career of reporter and spent most of a decade in Paris; out of the life of expatriates came the novel *The Sun Also Rises*. From a subsequent residence in Florida came the materials of *To Have and Have Not*, and from the Spanish War, in which Hemingway was again a correspondent, came the play *The Fifth Column* and the novel *For Whom the Bell Tolls*. Hemingway has been interested in, and has written about, bull-fighting, hunting in Africa, deep-sea fishing, war, and the whole gamut of activities primarily masculine.

A Clean, Well-Lighted Place

IT WAS late and every one had left the café except an old man who sat in the shadow the leaves of the tree made against the electric light. In the day time the street was dusty, but at night the dew settled the dust and the old man liked to sit late because he was deaf and now at night it was quiet and he felt the difference. The two waiters inside the café knew that the old man was a little drunk, and while he was a good client they knew that if he became too drunk he would leave without paying, so they kept watch on him.

"Last week he tried to commit suicide," one waiter said.

"Why?"

"He was in despair."

"What about?"

"Nothing."

"How do you know it was nothing?"

"He has plenty of money."

They sat together at a table that was close against the wall near the door of the café and looked at the terrace where the tables were all empty except where the old man sat in the shadow of the leaves of the tree that moved slightly in the wind. A girl and a soldier went by in the street. The street light shone on the brass number on his collar. The girl wore no head covering and hurried beside him.

"The guard will pick him up," one waiter said.

"What does it matter if he gets what he's after?"

"He had better get off the street now. The guard will get him. They went by five minutes ago."

The old man sitting in the shadow rapped on his saucer with his glass. The younger waiter went over to him.

"What do you want?"

The old man looked at him. "Another brandy," he said.

"You'll be drunk," the waiter said. The old man looked at him. The waiter went away.

"He'll stay all night," he said to his colleague. "I'm sleepy now. I never get into bed before three o'clock. He should have killed himself last week."

The waiter took the brandy bottle and another saucer from the counter inside the café and marched out to the old man's table. He put down the saucer and poured the glass full of brandy.

"You should have killed yourself last week," he said to the deaf man. The old man motioned with his finger. "A little more," he said. The waiter poured on into the glass so that the brandy slopped over and ran down the stem into the top saucer of the pile. "Thank you," the old man said. The waiter took the bottle back inside the café. He sat down at the table with his colleague again.

"He's drunk now," he said.

"He's drunk every night."

"What did he want to kill himself for?"

"How should I know."

"How did he do it?"

"He hung himself with a rope."

"Who cut him down?"

"His niece."

"Why did they do it?"

"Fear for his soul."

"How much money has he got?"

"He's got plenty."

"He must be eighty years old."

"Anyway I should say he was eighty."

"I wish he would go home. I never get to bed before three o'clock. What kind of hour is that to go to bed?"

"He stays up because he likes it."

"He's lonely. I'm not lonely. I have a wife waiting in bed for me."

"He had a wife once too."

"A wife would be no good to him now."

"You can't tell. He might be better with a wife."

"His niece looks after him."

"I know. You said she cut him down."

"I wouldn't want to be that old. An old man is a nasty thing."

"Not always. This old man is clean. He drinks without spilling. Even now, drunk. Look at him."

"I don't want to look at him. I wish he would go home. He has no regard for those who must work."

The old man looked from his glass across the square, then over at the waiters.

"Another brandy," he said, pointing to his glass. The waiter who was in a hurry came over.

"Finished," he said, speaking with that omission of syntax stupid people employ when talking to drunken people or foreigners. "No more tonight. Close now."

"Another," said the old man.

"No. Finished." The waiter wiped the edge of the table with a towel and shook his head.

The old man stood up, slowly counted the saucers, took a leather coin purse from his pocket and paid for the drinks, leaving half a peseta tip.

The waiter watched him go down the street, a very old man walking unsteadily but with dignity.

"Why didn't you let him stay and drink?" the unhurried waiter asked. They were putting up the shutters. "It is not half-past two."

"I want to go home to bed."

"What is an hour?"

"More to me than to him."

"An hour is the same."

"You talk like an old man yourself. He can buy a bottle and drink at home."

"It's not the same."

"No, it is not," agreed the waiter with a wife. He did not wish to be unjust. He was only in a hurry.

"And you? You have no fear of going home before your usual hour?"

"Are you trying to insult me?"

"No, hombre, only to make a joke."

"No," the waiter who was in a hurry said, rising from pulling down the metal shutters. "I have confidence. I am all confidence."

"You have youth, confidence, and a job," the older waiter said. "You have everything."

"And what do you lack?"

"Everything but work."

"You have everything I have."

"No. I have never had confidence and I am not young."

"Come on. Stop talking nonsense and lock up."

"I am of those who like to stay late at the café," the older waiter said. "With all those who do not want to go to bed. With all those who need a light for the night."

"I want to go home and into bed."

"We are of two different kinds," the older waiter said. He was now dressed to go home. "It is not only a question of youth and confidence although those things are very beautiful. Each night I am reluctant to close up because there may be some one who needs the café."

"Hombre, there are bodegas open all night long."

"You do not understand. This is a clean and pleasant café. It is well lighted. The light is very good and also, now, there are shadows of the leaves."

"Good night," said the younger waiter.

"Good night," the other said. Turning off the electric light he continued the conversation with himself. It is the light of course but it is necessary that the place be clean and pleasant. You do not want music. Certainly you do not want music. Nor can you stand before a bar with dignity although that is all that is provided for these hours. What did he fear? It was not fear or dread. It was a nothing that he knew too well. It was all a nothing and a man was nothing too. It was only that and light was all it needed and a certain cleanness and order. Some lived in it and never felt it but he knew it all was nada y pues nada y nada y pues nada. Our nada who art in nada, nada be thy name thy kingdom nada thy will be nada in nada as it is in nada. Give us this nada our daily nada and nada us our nada as we nada our nadas and nada us not into nada but deliver us from nada; pues nada. Hail nothing full of nothing, nothing is with thee. He smiled and stood before a bar with a shining steam pressure coffee machine.

"What's yours?" asked the barman.

"Nada."

"Otro loco mas," said the barman and turned away.

"A little cup," said the waiter.

The barman poured it for him.

"The light is very bright and pleasant but the bar is unpolished," the waiter said.

The barman looked at him but did not answer. It was too late at night for conversation.

"You want another copita?" the barman asked.

"No, thank you," said the waiter and went out. He disliked bars and bodegas. A clean, well-lighted café was a very different thing. Now, without thinking further, he would go home to his room. He would lie in the bed and finally, with daylight, he would go to sleep. After all, he said to himself, it is probably only insomnia. Many must have it.

COMMENT

Like others we have read, this story does not have a plot in the narrower sense of the word. At first glance it may seem to be little more than a sketch: an old man leaves a café, the two waiters talk while closing up, one waiter stops for a cup of coffee on the way home and does not sleep until morning. But on examination we find that all parts of the story bear a heavy burden of meaning; it is one of the most compact stories in this volume.

Initially there is a problem of structure: first our attention is focused on the old man, and then the old man disappears; after that, our attention is split between the two waiters, and finally one of these has the stage alone. But these different characters are not a set of disconnected individuals; we come to realize that the older waiter and the old man are in truth the same character. They are allied by the waiter's sympathy for the old man, by the fact that neither is young, and most of all by the fact that the waiter's stopping at a coffee bar is really a duplication of the old man's drinking at the café. The story is unified because the same feeling, the same need, animates the two characters and makes them behave almost identically. The recurrent pattern of action emphasizes the fact that the motivation is typical rather than special and peculiar.

The story is like Powers's "The Forks" in that contrast is the basic means of development. There is a fleeting contrast between the old man in the café and the soldier and his girl who walk past—between his solitary drinking and their active companionship. The major contrast is that developed between the two waiters, who at first seem only two participants in a casual dialogue but become mouthpieces of two antithetical attitudes toward life. The younger wants to finish work on schedule and go home; his satisfying home life is evidence of his assured, unquestioning, matter-of-fact existence. To him only poverty is an excuse for suicide, and he can see no difference between drinking at home and drinking in public. Before he is identified as "the younger waiter," ten lines of dialogue have been spoken by him and his colleague. Are these speeches differentiated enough to permit their being assigned to one speaker or the other?

The contrast between the old man and the younger waiter, and then between the younger waiter and the old waiter, might seem at first to be based on the familiar opposition between youth and age. But the older waiter makes clear that this is not the main point when he says, "It is not only a question of youth and confidence. . . ." Hemingway wants, too, to keep before us the possibility that the old man and the waiter are not unique cases. The old waiter wants to keep the café open for others who may "need" it, and the last line in the story is his comment on his wakefulness, "Many must have it." What is it that the old man, the waiter, and others have in common? The old man's attempted suicide gives the first clue; it suggests that he suffers from some essential despair—not a private despair, but one felt also by others. The real definition of this despair, of course, is given by the older waiter in his reflections before he enters the coffee bar (the longest single paragraph in the story). The world is all nothing; there is no meaning to which he can hold, no reality in which he can believe. The story is, then, a philosophic story. And the philosophic problem is given a specifically religious turn when the waiter recites a parody of the Lord's Prayer, using nada (nothing) as the main word throughout. He cannot hold to the religious assurance which would make life orderly and intelligible. Everything is nothing.

Why, then, drink? Note that the emphasis is less upon the drinking than upon the scene of the drinking, "a clean, well-lighted place." It is significant that the adjectives are clean and well-lighted rather than exciting, glamorous, exotic, cute or other adjectives that might conventionally be applied to a place of entertainment. They suggest the orderly and the clear—the opposite of the dirty and dark, the messy and meaningless universe from which some men are in flight. It is as if the old waiter were in his own way calling, "Let there be light," in a chaotic world. Too, it is not drinking alone that is the thing, but drinking in an appointed place; and although both the old man and the waiter drink alone in the place at which they stop, still they are having a kind of association with other human beings. May this not be read as a kind of secular communion? How far such an interpretation may be carried is debatable, but by now it should at least be clear that the story is functioning on the symbolic level.

Are we invited to take the side of the younger waiter against the older? Does his having "confidence" mean that he is more admirable? That he has a firm set of beliefs upon which to found an existence?

Although the story deals with very large issues, the style is very plain and simple. What is the effect of using such a style?

Robert Penn Warren, the novelist and critic, regards this story as an expression of a central belief that appears throughout Hemingway's writing. Readers who are interested in pursuing this idea further should consult Mr. Warren's introduction to Hemingway's A Farewell to Arms (1949).

Thomas Mann

A major figure in the modern literary world, Thomas Mann was born in Lübeck, Germany, in 1875. After working for a short time in an insurance office, Mann entered upon a permanent career of writing. His first major work, the novel *Buddenbrooks* (1901), was an examination of the well-to-do mercantile class to which his parents belonged. *The Magic Mountain* (1924) is a study of European civilization treated symbolically in a story of patients in a tuberculosis sanitarium. In addition Mann has written many novelettes, short stories, and essays, as well as other novels, in some of which the political views expressed led to the banning of his books in Nazi Germany. He has lived in the United States since 1938. During the 1930's and 1940's he issued various novels in a series dealing symbolically with the Biblical character Joseph. His short stories and novelettes have been collected in *Stories of Three Decades*.

Mario and the Magician

THE ATMOSPHERE of Torre di Venere remains unpleasant in the memory. From the first moment the air of the place made us uneasy, we felt irritable, on edge; then at the end came the shocking business of Cipolla, that dreadful being who seemed to incorporate, in so fateful and so humanly impressive a way, all the peculiar evilness of the situation as a whole. Looking back, we had the feeling that the horrible end of the affair had been preordained and lay in the nature of things; that the children had to be present at it was an added impropriety, due to the false colours in which the weird creature presented himself. Luckily for them, they did not know where the comedy left off and the tragedy began; and we let them remain in their happy belief that the whole thing had been a play up till the end.

Torre di Venere lies some fifteen kilometres from Portoclemente, one of the most popular summer resorts on the Tyrrhenian Sea.

Portoclemente is urban and elegant and full to overflowing for months on end. Its gay and busy main street of shops and hotels runs down to a wide sandy beach covered with tents and pennanted sand-castles and sunburnt humanity, where at all times a lively social bustle reigns, and much noise. But this same spacious and inviting fine-sanded beach, this same border of pine grove and near, presiding mountains, continues all the way along the coast. No wonder then that some competition of a quiet kind should have sprung up further on. Torre di Venere—the tower that gave the town its name is gone long since, one looks for it in vain—is an off-shoot of the larger resort, and for some years remained an idyll for the few, a refuge for more unworldly spirits. But the usual history of such places repeated itself: peace has had to retire further along the coast, to Marina Petriera and dear knows where else. We all know how the world at once seeks peace and puts her to flight—rushing upon her in the fond idea that they two will wed, and where she is, there it can be at home. It will even set up its Vanity Fair in a spot and be capable of thinking that peace is still by its side. Thus Torre—though its atmosphere so far is more modest and contemplative than that of Portoclemente—has been quite taken up, by both Italians and foreigners. It is no longer the thing to go to Portoclemente—though still so much the thing that it is as noisy and crowded as ever. One goes next door, so to speak; to Torre. So much more refined, even, and cheaper to boot. And the attractiveness of these qualities persists, though the qualities themselves long ago ceased to be evident. Torre has got a Grand Hotel. Numerous pensions have sprung up, some modest, some pretentious. The people who own or rent the villas and pinetas overlooking the sea no longer have it all their own way on the beach. In July and August it looks just like the beach at Portoclemente: it swarms with a screaming, squabbling, merrymaking crowd, and the sun, blazing down like mad, peels the skin off their necks. Garish little flat-bottomed boats rock on the glittering blue, manned by children, whose mothers hover afar and fill the air with anxious cries of Nino! and Sandro! and Bice! and Maria! Pedlars step across the legs of recumbent sun-bathers, selling flowers and corals, oysters, lemonade, and *cornetti al burro,* and crying their wares in the breathy, full-throated southern voice.

Such was the scene that greeted our arrival in Torre: pleasant enough, but after all, we thought, we had come too soon. It was the middle of August, the Italian season was still at its height, scarcely the moment for strangers to learn to love the special charms of the place. What an afternoon crowd in the cafés on the front! For instance, in the Esquisito, where we sometimes sat and were served by Mario, that very Mario of whom I shall have presently to tell. It is well-nigh impossible to find a table; and the various orchestras contend together in the midst of one's conversation with bewildering effect. Of course, it is in the afternoon that people come over from Portoclemente. The excursion is a favourite one for the restless denizens of that pleasure resort, and a Fiat motor-bus plies to and fro, coating inch-thick with dust the oleander and laurel hedges along the highroad—a notable if repulsive sight.

Yes, decidedly one should go to Torre in September, when the great public has left. Or else in May, before the water is warm enough to tempt the Southerner to bathe. Even in the before and after seasons Torre is not empty, but life is less national and more subdued. English, French, and German prevail under the tent-awnings and in the pension dining-rooms; whereas in August—in the Grand Hotel, at least, where, in default of private addresses, we had engaged rooms—the stranger finds the field so occupied by Florentine and Roman society that he feels quite isolated and even temporarily *déclassé*.

We had, rather to our annoyance, this experience on the evening we arrived, when we went in to dinner and were shown to our table by the waiter in charge. As a table, it had nothing against it, save that we had already fixed our eyes upon those on the veranda beyond, built out over the water, where little red-shaded lamps glowed—and there were still some tables empty, though it was as full as the dining-room within. The children went into raptures at the festive sight, and without more ado we announced our intention to take our meals by preference in the veranda. Our words, it appeared, were prompted by ignorance; for we were informed, with somewhat embarrassed politeness, that the cosy nook outside was reserved for the clients of the hotel: *ai nostri clienti*. Their clients? But we were their clients. We were not tourists or trippers, but boarders for a stay of some three or four weeks. However, we forbore to press for an explanation of the difference between the likes of us and that clientèle to whom it was vouchsafed to eat out there in the glow of the red lamps, and took our dinner by the prosaic common light of the dining-room chandelier—a thoroughly ordinary and monotonous hotel bill of fare, be it said. In Pensione Eleonora, a few steps landward, the table, as we were to discover, was much better.

And thither it was that we moved, three or four days later, before we had had time to settle in properly at the Grand Hotel. Not on account of the veranda and the lamps. The children, straightway on the best of terms with waiters and pages, absorbed in the joys of life on the beach, promptly forgot those colourful seductions. But now there arose, between ourselves and the veranda clientèle—or perhaps more correctly with the compliant management—one of those little unpleasantnesses which can quite spoil the pleasure of a holiday. Among the guests were some high Roman aristocracy, a Principe X and his family. These grand folk occupied rooms close to our own, and the Principessa, a great and a passionately maternal lady, was thrown into a panic by the vestiges of a whooping-cough which our little ones had lately got over, but which now and then still faintly troubled the unshatterable slumbers of our youngest-born. The nature of this illness is not clear, leaving some play for the imagination. So we took no offence at our elegant neighbour for clinging to the widely held view that whooping-cough is acoustically contagious and quite simply fearing lest her children yield to the bad example set by ours. In the fullness of her feminine self-confidence she protested to the management, which then, in the person of the proverbial frock-coated manager, hastened to represent to us, with many expressions of regret, that under the circumstances they were obliged to transfer us to the annexe. We did our best to assure him that the disease was in its very last stages, that it was actually over, and presented no danger of infection to anybody. All that we gained was permission to bring the case before the hotel physician—not one chosen by us—by whose verdict we must then abide. We agreed, convinced that thus we should at once pacify the Princess and escape the trouble of moving. The doctor appeared, and behaved like a faithful and honest servant of science. He examined the child and gave his opinion: the disease was quite over, no danger of contagion was present. We drew a long breath and considered the incident closed—until the manager announced that despite the doctor's verdict it would still be necessary for us to give up our rooms and retire to the *dépendance*. Byzantinism like this outraged us. It is not likely that the Principessa was responsible for the wilful breach of faith. Very likely the fawning management had not even dared to tell her what the physician said. Anyhow, we made it clear to his understanding that we preferred to leave the hotel altogether and at once—and packed our trunks. We could do so with a light heart, having already set up casual friendly relations with Casa Eleonora. We had noticed its pleasant exterior and formed the acquaintance of its proprietor, Signora Angiolieri, and her husband: she slender and black-haired, Tuscan in type, probably at the beginning of the thirties, with the dead ivory complexion of the southern woman, he quiet and bald and carefully dressed. They owned a larger establishment in Florence and presided only in summer and early autumn over the branch in Torre di Venere. But earlier, before her marriage, our new landlady had been companion, fellow-traveller, wardrobe mistress, yes, friend, of Eleonora Duse and manifestly regarded that period as the crown of her career. Even at our first visit she spoke of it with animation. Numerous photographs of the great actress, with affectionate inscriptions, were displayed about the drawing-room, and other souvenirs of their life together adorned the little tables and étagères. This cult of a so interesting past was calculated, of course, to heighten the advantages of the signora's present business. Nevertheless our pleasure and interest were quite genuine as we were conducted through the house by its owner and listened to her sonorous and staccato Tuscan voice relating anecdotes of that immortal mistress, depicting her suffering saintliness, her genius, her profound delicacy of feeling.

Thither, then, we moved our effects, to the dismay of the staff of the Grand Hotel, who, like all Italians, were very good to children. Our new quarters were retired and pleasant, we were within easy reach of the sea through the avenue of young plane trees that ran down to the esplanade. In the clean, cool dining-room Signora Angiolieri daily served the soup with her own hands, the service was attentive and good, the table capital. We even discovered some Viennese acquaintances, and enjoyed chatting with them after luncheon, in front of the house. They, in their turn, were the means of our finding others—in short, all seemed for the best, and we were heartily glad of the change we had made. Nothing was now wanting to a holiday of the most gratifying kind.

And yet no proper gratification ensued. Perhaps the stupid occasion of our change of quarters pursued us to the new ones we had found. Personally, I admit that I do not easily forget these collisions with ordinary humanity, the naïve misuse of power, the injustice, the sycophantic corruption. I dwelt upon the incident too much, it irritated me in retrospect—quite futilely, of course, since such phenomena are only all too natural and all too much the rule. And we had not broken off relations with the Grand Hotel. The children were as friendly as ever there, the porter mended their toys, and we sometimes took tea in the garden. We even saw the Principessa. She would come out, with her firm and delicate tread, her lips emphatically corallined, to look after her children, playing under the supervision of their English governess. She did not dream that we were anywhere near, for so soon as she appeared in the offing we sternly forbade our little one even to clear his throat.

The heat—if I may bring it in evidence—was extreme. It was African. The power of the sun, directly one left the border of the indigo-blue wave, was so frightful, so relentless, that the mere thought of the few steps between the beach and luncheon was a burden, clad though one might be only in pyjamas. Do you care for that sort of thing? Weeks on end? Yes, of course, it is proper to the south, it is classic weather, the sun of Homer, the climate wherein human culture came to flower—and all the rest of it. But after a while it is too much for me, I reach a point where I begin to find it dull. The burning void of the sky, day after day, weighs one down; the high coloration, the enormous naïveté of the unrefracted light—they do, I dare say, induce light-heartedness, a carefree mood born of immunity from downpours and other meteorological caprices. But slowly, slowly, there makes itself felt a lack: the deeper, more complex needs of the northern soul remain unsatisfied. You are left barren—even, it may be, in time, a little contemptuous. True, without that stupid business of the whooping-cough I might not have been feeling these things. I was annoyed, very likely I wanted to feel them and so half-unconsciously seized upon an idea lying ready to hand to induce, or if not to induce, at least to justify and strengthen, my attitude. Up to this point, then, if you like, let us grant some ill will on our part. But the sea; and the mornings spent extended upon the fine sand in face of its eternal splendours—no, the sea could not conceivably induce such feelings. Yet it was none the less true that, despite all previous experience, we were not at home on the beach, we were not happy.

It was too soon, too soon. The beach, as I have said, was still in the hands of the middle-class native. It is a pleasing breed to look at, and among the young we saw much shapeliness and charm. Still, we were necessarily surrounded by a great deal of very average humanity—a middle-class mob, which, you will admit, is not more charming under this sun than under one's own native sky. The voices these women have! It was sometimes hard to believe that we were in the land which is the western cradle of the art of song. "*Fuggièro!*" I can still hear that cry, as for twenty mornings long I heard it close behind me, breathy, full-throated, hideously stressed, with a harsh open *e*, uttered in accents of mechanical despair. "*Fuggièro! Rispondi almeno!*" Answer when I call you! The *sp* in *rispondi* was pronounced like *shp*, as Germans pronounce it; and this, on top of what I felt already, vexed my sensitive soul. The cry was addressed to a repulsive youngster whose sunburn had made disgusting raw sores on his shoulders. He outdid anything I have ever seen for ill-breeding, refractoriness, and temper and was a great coward to boot, putting the whole beach in an uproar, one day, because of his outrageous sensitiveness to the slightest pain. A sand-crab had pinched his toe in the water, and the minute injury made him set up a cry of heroic proportions—the shout of an antique hero in his agony—that pierced one to the marrow and called up visions of some frightful tragedy. Evidently he considered himself not only wounded, but poisoned as well; he crawled out on the sand and lay in apparently intolerable anguish, groaning "*Ohi!*" and "*Ohimè!*" and threshing about with arms and legs to ward off his mother's tragic appeals and the questions of the bystanders. An audience gathered round. A doctor was fetched—the same who had pronounced objective judgment on our whooping-cough—and here again acquitted himself like a man of science. Good-naturedly he reassured the boy, telling him that he was not hurt at all, he should simply go into the water again to relieve the smart. Instead of which, Fuggièro was borne off the beach, followed by a concourse of people. But he did not fail to appear next morning, nor did he leave off spoiling our children's sand-castles. Of course, always by accident. In short, a perfect terror.

And this twelve-year-old lad was prominent among the influences that, imperceptibly at first, combined to spoil our holiday and render it unwholesome. Somehow or other, there was a stiffness, a lack of innocent enjoyment. These people stood on their dignity—just why, and in what spirit, it was not easy at first to tell. They displayed much self-respectingness; towards each other and towards the foreigner their bearing was that of a person newly conscious of a sense of honour. And wherefore? Gradually we realized the political implications and understood that we were in the presence of a national ideal. The beach, in fact, was alive with patriotic children—a phenomenon as unnatural as it was depressing. Children are a human species and a society apart, a nation of their own, so to speak. On the basis of their common form of life, they find each other out with the greatest ease, no matter how different their small vocabularies. Ours soon played with natives and foreigners alike. Yet they were plainly both puzzled and disappointed at times. There were wounded sensibilities, displays of assertiveness—or rather hardly assertiveness, for it was too self-conscious and too didactic to deserve the name. There were quarrels over flags, disputes about authority and precedence. Grown-ups joined in, not so much to pacify as to render judgment and enunciate principles. Phrases were dropped about the greatness and dignity of Italy, solemn phrases that spoilt the fun. We saw our two little ones retreat, puzzled and hurt, and were put to it to explain the situation. These people, we told them, were just passing through a certain stage, something rather like an illness, perhaps; not very pleasant, but probably unavoidable.

We had only our own carelessness to thank that we came to blows in the end with this "stage"—which, after all, we had seen and sized up long before now. Yes, it came to another "cross-purposes," so evidently the earlier ones had not been sheer accident. In a word, we became an offence to the public morals. Our small daughter—eight years old, but in physical development a good year younger and thin as a chicken—had had a good long bathe and gone playing in the warm sun in her wet costume. We told her that she might take off her bathing-suit, which was stiff with sand, rinse it in the sea, and put it on again, after which she must take care to keep it cleaner. Off goes the costume and she runs down naked to the sea, rinses her little jersey, and comes back. Ought we to have foreseen the outburst of anger and resentment which her conduct, and thus our conduct, called forth? Without delivering a homily on the subject, I may say that in the last decade our attitude towards the nude body and our feelings regarding it have undergone, all over the world, a fundamental change. There are things we "never think about" any more, and among them is the freedom we had permitted to this by no means provocative little childish body. But in these parts it was taken as a challenge. The patriotic children hooted. Fuggièro whistled on his fingers. The sudden buzz of conversation among the grown people in our neighbourhood boded no good. A gentleman in city togs, with a not very apropos bowler hat on the back of his head, was assuring his outraged womenfolk that he proposed to take punitive measures; he stepped up to us, and a philippic descended on our unworthy heads, in which all the emotionalism of the sense-loving south spoke in the service of morality and discipline. The offence against decency of which we had been guilty was, he said, the more to be condemned because it was also a gross ingratitude and an insulting breach of his country's hospitality. We had criminally injured not only the letter and spirit of the public bathing regulations, but also the honour of Italy; he, the gentleman in the city togs, knew how to defend that honour and proposed to see to it that our offence against the national dignity should not go unpunished.

We did our best, bowing respectfully, to give ear to this eloquence. To contradict the man, overheated as he was, would probably be to fall from one error into another. On the tips of our tongues we had various answers: as, that the word "hospitality," in its strictest sense, was not quite the right one, taking all the circumstances into consideration. We were not literally the guests of Italy, but of Signora Angiolieri, who had assumed the rôle of dispenser of hospitality some years ago on laying down that of familiar friend to Eleonora Duse. We longed to say that surely this beautiful country had not sunk so low as to be reduced to a state of hypersensitive prudishness. But we confined ourselves to assuring the gentleman that any lack of respect, any provocation on our parts, had been the furthest from our thoughts. And as a mitigating circumstance we pointed out the tender age and physical slightness of the little culprit. In vain. Our protests were waved away, he did not believe in them; our defence would not hold water. We must be made an example of. The authorities were notified, by telephone, I believe, and their representative appeared on the beach. He said the case was *"molto grave."* We had to go with him to the Municipio up in the Piazza, where a higher official confirmed the previous verdict of *"molto grave,"* launched into a stream of the usual didactic phrases—the selfsame tune and words as the man in the bowler hat—and levied a fine and ransom of fifty lire. We felt that the adventure must willy-nilly be worth to us this much of a contribution to the economy of the Italian government; paid, and left. Ought we not at this point to have left Torre as well?

If we only had! We should thus have escaped that fatal Cipolla. But circumstances combined to prevent us from making up our minds to a change. A certain poet says that it is indolence that makes us endure uncomfortable situations. The *aperçu* may serve as an explanation for our inaction. Anyhow, one dislikes voiding the field immediately upon such an event. Especially if sympathy from other quarters encourages one to defy it. And in the Villa Eleonora they pronounced as with one voice upon the injustice of our punishment. Some Italian after-dinner acquaintances found that the episode put their country in a very bad light, and proposed taking the man in the bowler hat to task, as one fellow-citizen to another. But the next day he and his party had vanished from the beach. Not on our account, of course. Though it might be that the consciousness of his impending departure had added energy to his rebuke; in any case his going was a relief. And, furthermore, we stayed because our stay had by now become remarkable in our own eyes, which is worth something in itself, quite apart from the comfort or discomfort involved. Shall we strike sail, avoid a certain experience so soon as it seems not expressly calculated to increase our enjoyment or our self-esteem? Shall we go away whenever life looks like turning in the slightest uncanny, or not quite normal, or even rather painful and mortifying? No, surely not. Rather stay and look matters in the face, brave them out; perhaps precisely in so doing lies a lesson for us to learn. We stayed on and reaped as the awful reward of our constancy the unholy and staggering experience with Cipolla.

I have not mentioned that the after season had begun, almost on the very day we were disciplined by the city authorities. The worshipful gentleman in the bowler hat, our denouncer, was not the only person to leave the resort. There was a regular exodus, on every hand you saw luggage-carts on their way to the station. The beach denationalized itself. Life in Torre, in the cafés and the pinetas, became more homelike and more European. Very likely we might even have eaten at a table in the glass veranda, but we refrained, being content at Signora Angiolieri's—as content, that is, as our evil star would let us be. But at the same time with this turn for the better came a change in the weather: almost to an hour it showed itself in harmony with the holiday calendar of the general public. The sky was overcast; not that it grew any cooler, but the unclouded heat of the entire eighteen days since our arrival, and probably long before that, gave place to a stifling sirocco air, while from time to time a little ineffectual rain sprinkled the velvety surface of the beach. Add to which, that two-thirds of our intended stay at Torre had passed. The colourless, lazy sea, with sluggish jellyfish floating in its shallows, was at least a change. And it would have been silly to feel retrospective longings after a sun that had caused us so many sighs when it burned down in all its arrogant power.

At this juncture, then, it was that Cipolla announced himself. Cavaliere Cipolla he was called on the posters that appeared one day stuck up everywhere, even in the dining-room of Pensione Eleonora. A travelling virtuoso, an entertainer, *"forzatore, illusionista, prestidigatore,"* as he called himself, who proposed to wait upon the highly respectable population of Torre di Venere with a display of extraordinary phenomena of a mysterious and staggering kind. A conjuror! The bare announcement was enough to turn our children's heads. They had never seen anything of the sort, and now our present holiday was to afford them this new excitement. From that moment on they besieged us with prayers to take tickets for the performance. We had doubts, from the first, on the score of the lateness of the hour, nine o'clock; but gave way, in the idea that we might see a little of what Cipolla had to offer, probably no great matter, and then go home. Besides, of course, the children could sleep late next day. We bought four tickets of Signora Angiolieri herself, she having taken a number of the stalls on commission to sell them to her guests. She could not vouch for the man's performance, and we had no great expectations. But we were conscious of a need for diversion, and the children's violent curiosity proved catching.

The Cavaliere's performance was to take place in a hall where during the season there had been a cinema with a weekly programme. We had never been there. You reached it by following the main street under the wall of the "*palazzo,*" a ruin with a "For sale" sign, that suggested a castle and had obviously been built in lordlier days. In the same street were the chemist, the hairdresser, and all the better shops; it led, so to speak, from the feudal past the bourgeois into the proletarian, for it ended off between two rows of poor fishing-huts, where old women sat mending nets before the doors. And here, among the proletariat, was the hall, not much more, actually, than a wooden shed, though a large one, with a turreted entrance, plastered on either side with layers of gay placards. Some while after dinner, then, on the appointed evening, we wended our way thither in the dark, the children dressed in their best and blissful with the sense of so much irregularity. It was sultry, as it had been for days; there was heat lightning now and then, and a little rain; we proceeded under umbrellas. It took us a quarter of an hour.

Our tickets were collected at the entrance, our places we had to find ourselves. They were in the third row left, and as we sat down we saw that, late though the hour was for the performance, it was to be interpreted with even more laxity. Only very slowly did an audience—who seemed to be relied upon to come late—begin to fill the stalls. These comprised the whole auditorium; there were no boxes. This tardiness gave us some concern. The children's cheeks were already flushed as much with fatigue as with excitement. But even when we entered, the standing-room at the back and in the side aisles was already well occupied. There stood the manhood of Torre di Venere, all and sundry, fisherfolk, rough-and-ready youths with bare forearms crossed over their striped jerseys. We were well pleased with the presence of this native assemblage, which always adds colour and animation to occasions like the present; and the children were frankly delighted. For they had friends among these people—acquaintances picked up on afternoon strolls to the further ends of the beach. We would be turning homeward, at the hour when the sun dropped into the sea, spent with the huge effort it had made and gilding with reddish gold the oncoming surf; and we would come upon bare-legged fisherfolk standing in rows, bracing and hauling with long-drawn cries as they drew in the nets and harvested in dripping baskets their catch, often so scanty, of *frutta di mare.* The children looked on, helped to pull, brought out their little stock of Italian words, made friends. So now they exchanged nods with the "standing-room" clientèle; there was Guiscardo, there Antonio, they knew them by name and waved and called across in half-whispers, getting answering nods and smiles that displayed rows of healthy white teeth. Look, there is even Mario, Mario from the Esquisito, who brings us the chocolate. He wants to see the conjuror, too, and he must have come early, for he is almost in front; but he does not see us, he is not paying attention; that is a way he has, even though he is a waiter. So we wave instead to the man who lets out the little boats on the beach; he is there too, standing at the back.

It had got to a quarter past nine, it got to almost half past. It was natural that we should be nervous. When would the children get to bed? It had been a mistake to bring them, for now it would be very hard to suggest breaking off their enjoyment before it had got well under way. The stalls had filled in time; all Torre, apparently, was there: the guests of the Grand Hotel, the guests of Villa Eleonora, familiar faces from the beach. We heard English and German and the sort of French that Rumanians speak with Italians. Madame Angiolieri herself sat two rows behind us, with her quiet, bald-headed spouse, who kept stroking his moustache with the two middle fingers of his right hand. Everybody had come late, but nobody too late. Cipolla made us wait for him.

He made us wait. That is probably the way to put it. He heightened the suspense by his delay in appearing. And we could see the point of this, too—only not when it was carried to extremes. Towards half past nine the audience began to clap—an amiable way of expressing justifiable impatience, evincing as it does an eagerness to applaud. For the little ones, this was a joy in itself—all children love to clap. From the popular sphere came loud cries of *"Pronti!" "Cominciamo!"* And lo, it seemed now as easy to begin as before it had been hard. A gong sounded, greeted by the standing rows with a many-voiced "Ah-h!" and the curtains parted. They revealed a platform furnished more like a schoolroom than like the theatre of a conjuring performance—largely because of the blackboard in the left foreground. There was a common yellow hat-stand, a few ordinary straw-bottomed chairs, and further back a little round table holding a water carafe and glass, also a tray with a liqueur glass and a flask of pale yellow liquid. We had still a few seconds of time to let these things sink in. Then, with no darkening of the house, Cavaliere Cipolla made his entry.

He came forward with a rapid step that expressed his eagerness to appear before his public and gave rise to the illusion that he had already come a long way to put himself at their service—whereas, of course, he had only been standing in the wings. His costume supported the fiction. A man of an age hard to determine, but by no means young; with a sharp, ravaged face, piercing eyes, compressed lips, small black waxed moustache, and a so-called imperial in the curve between mouth and chin. He was dressed for the street with a sort of complicated evening elegance, in a wide black pelerine with velvet collar and satin lining; which, in the hampered state of his arms, he held together in front with his white-gloved hands. He had a white scarf round his neck; a top hat with a curving brim sat far back on his head. Perhaps more than anywhere else the eighteenth century is still alive in Italy, and with it the charlatan and mountebank type so characteristic of the period. Only there, at any rate, does one still encounter really well-preserved specimens. Cipolla had in his whole appearance much of the historic type; his very clothes helped to conjure up the traditional figure with its blatantly, fantastically foppish air. His pretentious costume sat upon him, or rather hung upon him, most curiously, being in one place drawn too tight, in another a mass of awkward folds. There was something not quite in order about his figure, both front and back—that was plain later on. But I must emphasize the fact that there was not a trace of personal jocularity or clownishness in his pose, manner, or behaviour. On the contrary, there was complete seriousness, an absence of any humorous appeal; occasionally even a cross-grained pride, along with that curious, self-satisfied air so characteristic of the deformed. None of all this, however, prevented his appearance from being greeted with laughter from more than one quarter of the hall.

All the eagerness had left his manner. The swift entry had been merely an expression of energy, not of zeal. Standing at the footlights he negligently drew off his gloves, to display long yellow hands, one of them adorned with a seal ring with a lapis-lazuli in a high setting. As he stood there, his small hard eyes, with flabby pouches beneath them, roved appraisingly about the hall, not quickly, rather in a considered examination, pausing here and there upon a face with his lips clipped together, not speaking a word. Then with a display of skill as surprising as it was casual, he rolled his gloves into a ball and tossed them across a considerable distance into the glass on the table. Next from an inner pocket he drew forth a packet of cigarettes; you could see by the wrapper that they were the cheapest sort the government sells. With his fingertips he pulled out a cigarette and lighted it, without looking, from a quick-firing benzine lighter. He drew the smoke deep into his lungs and let it out again, tapping his foot, with both lips drawn in an arrogant grimace and the grey smoke streaming out between broken and saw-edged teeth.

With a keenness equal to his own his audience eyed him. The youths at the rear scowled as they peered at this cocksure creature to search out his secret weaknesses. He betrayed none. In fetching out and putting back the cigarettes his clothes got in his way. He had to turn back his pelerine, and in so doing revealed a riding-whip with a silver claw-handle that hung by a leather thong from his left forearm and looked decidedly out of place. You could see that he had on not evening clothes but a frock-coat, and under this, as he lifted it to get at his pocket, could be seen a striped sash worn about the body. Somebody behind me whispered that this sash went with his title of Cavaliere. I give the information for what it may be worth—personally, I never heard that the title carried such insignia with it. Perhaps the sash was sheer pose, like the way he stood there, without a word, casually and arrogantly puffing smoke into his audience's face.

People laughed, as I said. The merriment had become almost general when somebody in the "standing seats," in a loud, dry voice, remarked: "*Buona sera.*"

Cipolla cocked his head. "Who was that?" asked he, as though he had been dared. "Who was that just spoke? Well? First so bold and now so modest? *Paura*, eh?" He spoke with a rather high, asthmatic voice, which yet had a metallic quality. He waited.

"That was me," a youth at the rear broke into the stillness, seeing himself thus challenged. He was not far from us, a handsome fellow in a woollen shirt, with his coat hanging over one shoulder. He wore his curly, wiry hair in a high, dishevelled mop, the style affected by the youth of the awakened Fatherland; it gave him an African appearance that rather spoiled his looks. *"Bè!* That was me. It was your business to say it first, but I was trying to be friendly."

More laughter. The chap had a tongue in his head. *"Ha sciolto la scilinguágnolo,"* I heard near me. After all, the retort was deserved.

"Ah, bravo!" answered Cipolla. "I like you, *giovanotto.* Trust me, I've had my eye on you for some time. People like you are just in my line. I can use them. And you are the pick of the lot, that's plain to see. You do what you like. Or is it possible you have ever not done what you liked—or even, maybe, what you didn't like? What somebody else liked, in short? Hark ye, my friend, that might be a pleasant change for you, to divide up the willing and the doing and stop tackling both jobs at once. Division of labour, *sistema americano, sa'!* For instance, suppose you were to show your tongue to this select and honourable audience here—your whole tongue, right down to the roots?"

"No, I won't," said the youth, hostilely. "Sticking out your tongue shows a bad bringing-up."

"Nothing of the sort," retorted Cipolla. "You would only be *doing* it. With all due respect to your bringing-up, I suggest that before I count ten, you will perform a right turn and stick out your tongue at the company here further than you knew yourself that you could stick it out."

He gazed at the youth, and his piercing eyes seemed to sink deeper into their sockets. *"Uno!"* said he. He had let his riding-whip slide down his arm and made it whistle once through the air. The boy faced about and put out his tongue, so long, so extendedly, that you could see it was the very uttermost in tongue which he had to offer. Then turned back, stony-faced, to his former position.

"That was me," mocked Cipolla, with a jerk of his head towards the youth. *"Bè!* That was me." Leaving the audience to enjoy its sensations, he turned towards the little round table, lifted the bottle, poured out a small glass of what was obviously cognac, and tipped it up with a practised hand.

The children laughed with all their hearts. They had understood practically nothing of what had been said, but it pleased them hugely that something so funny should happen, straightaway, between that queer man up there and somebody out of the audience. They had no preconception of what an "evening" would be like and were quite ready to find this a priceless beginning. As for us, we exchanged a glance and I remember that involuntarily I made with my lips the sound that Cipolla's whip had made when it cut the air. For the rest, it was plain that people did not know what to make of a preposterous beginning like this to a sleight-of-hand performance. They could not see why the *giovanotto*, who after all in a way had been their spokesman, should suddenly have turned on them to vent his incivility. They felt that he had behaved like a silly ass and withdrew their countenances from him in favour of the artist, who now came back from his refreshment table and addressed them as follows:

"Ladies and gentlemen," said he, in his wheezing, metallic voice, "you saw just now that I was rather sensitive on the score of the rebuke this hopeful young linguist saw fit to give me"—"*questo linguista di belle speranze*" was what he said, and we all laughed at the pun. "I am a man who sets some store by himself, you may take it from me. And I see no point in being wished a good-evening unless it is done courteously and in all seriousness. For anything else there is no occasion. When a man wishes me a good-evening he wishes himself one, for the audience will have one only if I do. So this lady-killer of Torre di Venere" (another thrust) "did well to testify that I have one tonight and that I can dispense with any wishes of his in the matter. I can boast of having good evenings almost without exception. One not so good does come my way now and again, but very seldom. My calling is hard and my health not of the best. I have a little physical defect which prevented me from doing my bit in the war for the greater glory of the Fatherland. It is perforce with my mental and spiritual parts that I conquer life—which after all only means conquering oneself. And I flatter myself that my achievements have aroused interest and respect among the educated public. The leading newspapers have lauded me, the *Corriere della Sera* did me the courtesy of calling me a phenomenon, and in Rome the brother of the *Duce* honoured me by his presence at one of my evenings. I should not have thought that in a relatively less important place" (laughter here, at the

expense of poor little Torre) "I should have to give up the small
personal habits which brilliant and elevated audiences had been
ready to overlook. Nor did I think I had to stand being heckled
by a person who seems to have been rather spoilt by the favours
of the fair sex." All this of course at the expense of the youth whom
Cipolla never tired of presenting in the guise of *donnaiuolo* and
rustic Don Juan. His persistent thin-skinnedness and animosity were
in striking contrast to the self-confidence and the worldly success
he boasted of. One might have assumed that the *giovanotto* was
merely the chosen butt of Cipolla's customary professional sallies,
had not the very pointed witticisms betrayed a genuine antagonism.
No one looking at the physical parts of the two men need have
been at a loss for the explanation, even if the deformed man had
not constantly played on the other's supposed success with the fair
sex. "Well," Cipolla went on, "before beginning our entertainment
this evening, perhaps you will permit me to make myself comfortable."

And he went towards the hat-stand to take off his things.

"*Parla benissimo,*" asserted somebody in our neighbourhood. So
far, the man had done nothing; but what he had said was accepted
as an achievement, by means of that he had made an impression.
Among southern peoples speech is a constituent part of the pleasure
of living, it enjoys far livelier social esteem than in the north. That
national cement, the mother tongue, is paid symbolic honours down
here, and there is something blithely symbolical in the pleasure
people take in their respect for its forms and phonetics. They enjoy
speaking, they enjoy listening; and they listen with discrimination.
For the way a man speaks serves as a measure of his personal rank;
carelessness and clumsiness are greeted with scorn, elegance and
mastery are rewarded with social éclat. Wherefore the small man
too, where it is a question of getting his effect, chooses his phrase
nicely and turns it with care. On this count, then, at least, Cipolla
had won his audience; though he by no means belonged to the
class of men which the Italian, in a singular mixture of moral and
æsthetic judgments, labels "*simpatico.*"

After removing his hat, scarf, and mantle he came to the front
of the stage, settling his coat, pulling down his cuffs with their
large cuff-buttons, adjusting his absurd sash. He had very ugly
hair; the top of his head, that is, was almost bald, while a narrow,

black-varnished frizz of curls ran from front to back as though stuck
on; the side hair, likewise blackened, was brushed forward to the
corners of the eyes—it was, in short, the hairdressing of an old-
fashioned circus-director, fantastic, but entirely suited to his out-
moded personal type and worn with so much assurance as to take
the edge off the public's sense of humour. The little physical defect
of which he had warned us was now all too visible, though the
nature of it was even now not very clear: the chest was too high,
as is usual in such cases; but the corresponding malformation of
the back did not sit between the shoulders, it took the form of a
sort of hips or buttocks hump, which did not indeed hinder his
movements but gave him a grotesque and dipping stride at every
step he took. However, by mentioning his deformity beforehand
he had broken the shock of it, and a delicate propriety of feeling
appeared to reign throughout the hall.

"At your service," said Cipolla. "With your kind permission, we
will begin the evening with some arithmetical tests."

Arithmetic? That did not sound much like sleight-of-hand. We
began to have our suspicions that the man was sailing under a
false flag, only we did not yet know which was the right one. I felt
sorry on the children's account; but for the moment they were
content simply to be there.

The numerical test which Cipolla now introduced was as simple
as it was baffling. He began by fastening a piece of paper to the
upper right-hand corner of the blackboard; then lifting it up, he
wrote something underneath. He talked all the while, relieving the
dryness of his offering by a constant flow of words, and showed
himself a practised speaker, never at a loss for conversational turns
of phrase. It was in keeping with the nature of his performance,
and at the same time vastly entertained the children, that he went
on to eliminate the gap between stage and audience, which had
already been bridged over by the curious skirmish with the fisher
lad: he had representatives from the audience mount the stage, and
himself descended the wooden steps to seek personal contact with
his public. And again, with individuals, he fell into his former
taunting tone. I do not know how far that was a deliberate feature
of his system; he preserved a serious, even a peevish air, but his
audience, at least the more popular section, seemed convinced that
that was all part of the game. So then, after he had written some-

thing and covered the writing by the paper, he desired that two persons should come up on the platform and help to perform the calculations. They would not be difficult, even for people not clever at figures. As usual, nobody volunteered, and Cipolla took care not to molest the more select portion of his audience. He kept to the populace. Turning to two sturdy young louts standing behind us, he beckoned them to the front, encouraging and scolding by turns. They should not stand there gaping, he said, unwilling to oblige the company. Actually, he got them in motion; with clumsy tread they came down the middle aisle, climbed the steps, and stood in front of the blackboard, grinning sheepishly at their comrades' shouts and applause. Cipolla joked with them for a few minutes, praised their heroic firmness of limb and the size of their hands, so well calculated to do this service for the public. Then he handed one of them the chalk and told him to write down the numbers as they were called out. But now the creature declared that he would not write! *"Non so scrivere,"* said he in his gruff voice, and his companion added that neither did he.

God knows whether they told the truth or whether they wanted to make game of Cipolla. Anyhow, the latter was far from sharing the general merriment which their confession aroused. He was insulted and disgusted. He sat there on a straw-bottomed chair in the centre of the stage with his legs crossed, smoking a fresh cigarette out of his cheap packet; obviously it tasted the better for the cognac he had indulged in while the yokels were stumping up the steps. Again he inhaled the smoke and let it stream out between curling lips. Swinging his leg, with his gaze sternly averted from the two shamelessly chuckling creatures and from the audience as well, he stared into space as one who withdraws himself and his dignity from the contemplation of an utterly despicable phenomenon.

"Scandalous," said he, in a sort of icy snarl. "Go back to your places! In Italy everybody can write—in all her greatness there is no room for ignorance and unenlightenment. To accuse her of them, in the hearing of this international company, is a cheap joke, in which you yourselves cut a very poor figure and humiliate the government and the whole country as well. If it is true that Torre di Venere is indeed the last refuge of such ignorance, then I must blush to have visited the place—being, as I already was, aware of its inferiority to Rome in more than one respect—"

Here Cipolla was interrupted by the youth with the Nubian coiffure and his jacket across his shoulder. His fighting spirit, as we now saw, had only abdicated temporarily, and he now flung himself into the breach in defence of his native heath. "That will do," said he loudly. "That's enough jokes about Torre. We all come from the place and we won't stand strangers making fun of it. These two chaps are our friends. Maybe they are no scholars, but even so they may be straighter than some folks in the room who are so free with their boasts about Rome, though they did not build it either."

That was capital. The young man had certainly cut his eye-teeth. And this sort of spectacle was good fun, even though it still further delayed the regular performance. It is always fascinating to listen to an altercation. Some people it simply amuses, they take a sort of kill-joy pleasure in not being principals. Others feel upset and uneasy, and my sympathies are with these latter, although on the present occasion I was under the impression that all this was part of the show—the analphabetic yokels no less than the *giovanotto* with the jacket. The children listened well pleased. They understood not at all, but the sound of the voices made them hold their breath. So this was a "magic evening"—at least it was the kind they have in Italy. They expressly found it "lovely."

Cipolla had stood up and with two of his scooping strides was at the footlights.

"Well, well, see who's here!" said he with grim cordiality. "An old acquaintance! A young man with his heart at the end of his tongue" (he used the word *linguaccia*, which means a coated tongue, and gave rise to much hilarity). "That will do, my friends," he turned to the yokels. "I do not need you now, I have business with this deserving young man here, *con questo torregiano di Venere,* this tower of Venus, who no doubt expects the gratitude of the fair as a reward for his prowess—"

"*Ah, non scherziamo!* We're talking earnest," cried out the youth. His eyes flashed, and he actually made as though to pull off his jacket and proceed to direct methods of settlement.

Cipolla did not take him too seriously. We had exchanged apprehensive glances; but he was dealing with a fellow-countryman and had his native soil beneath his feet. He kept quite cool and showed complete mastery of the situation. He looked at his audience, smiled, and made a sideways motion of the head towards the young cockerel as though calling the public to witness how the man's bumptiousness only served to betray the simplicity of his mind. And then, for the second time, something strange happened, which set Cipolla's calm superiority in an uncanny light, and in some mysterious and irritating way turned all the explosiveness latent in the air into matter for laughter.

Cipolla drew still nearer to the fellow, looking him in the eye with a peculiar gaze. He even came half-way down the steps that led into the auditorium on our left, so that he stood directly in front of the trouble-maker, on slightly higher ground. The riding-whip hung from his arm.

"My son, you do not feel much like joking," he said. "It is only too natural, for anyone can see that you are not feeling too well. Even your tongue, which leaves something to be desired on the score of cleanliness, indicates acute disorder of the gastric system. An evening entertainment is no place for people in your state; you yourself, I can tell, were of several minds whether you would not do better to put on a flannel bandage and go to bed. It was not good judgment to drink so much of that very sour white wine this afternoon. Now you have such a colic you would like to double up with the pain. Go ahead, don't be embarrassed. There is a distinct relief that comes from bending over, in cases of intestinal cramp."

He spoke thus, word for word, with quiet impressiveness and a kind of stern sympathy, and his eyes, plunged the while deep in the young man's, seemed to grow very tired and at the same time burning above their enlarged tear-ducts—they were the strangest eyes, you could tell that not manly pride alone was preventing the young adversary from withdrawing his gaze. And presently, indeed, all trace of its former arrogance was gone from the bronzed young face. He looked open-mouthed at the Cavaliere and the open mouth was drawn in a rueful smile.

"Double over," repeated Cipolla. "What else can you do? With a colic like that you *must* bend. Surely you will not struggle against the performance of a perfectly natural action just because somebody suggests it to you?"

Slowly the youth lifted his forearms, folded and squeezed them across his body; it turned a little sideways, then bent, lower and lower, the feet shifted, the knees turned inward, until he had become a picture of writhing pain, until he all but grovelled upon the ground. Cipolla let him stand for some seconds thus, then made a short cut through the air with his whip and went with his scooping stride back to the little table, where he poured himself out a cognac.

"*Il boit beaucoup*," asserted a lady behind us. Was that the only thing that struck her? We could not tell how far the audience grasped the situation. The fellow was standing upright again, with a sheepish grin—he looked as though he scarcely knew how it had all happened. The scene had been followed with tense interest and applauded at the end; there were shouts of "*Bravo, Cipolla!*" and "*Bravo, giovanotto!*" Apparently the issue of the duel was not looked upon as a personal defeat for the young man. Rather the audience encouraged him as one does an actor who succeeds in an unsympathetic rôle. Certainly his way of screwing himself up with cramp had been highly picturesque, its appeal was directly calculated to impress the gallery—in short, a fine dramatic performance. But I am not sure how far the audience were moved by that natural tactfulness in which the south excels, or how far it penetrated into the nature of what was going on.

The Cavaliere, refreshed, had lighted another cigarette. The numerical tests might now proceed. A young man was easily found in the back row who was willing to write down on the blackboard the numbers as they were dictated to him. Him too we knew; the whole entertainment had taken on an intimate character through our acquaintance with so many of the actors. This was the man who worked at the greengrocer's in the main street; he had served us several times, with neatness and dispatch. He wielded the chalk with clerkly confidence, while Cipolla descended to our level and walked with his deformed gait through the audience, collecting numbers as they were given, in two, three, and four places, and calling them out to the grocer's assistant, who wrote them down in a column. In all this, everything on both sides was calculated to amuse, with its jokes and its oratorical asides. The artist could not fail to hit on foreigners, who were not ready with their figures, and with them he was elaborately patient and chivalrous, to the great amusement of the natives, whom he reduced to confusion in their turn, by making them translate numbers that were given in English or French. Some people gave dates concerned with great events in Italian history. Cipolla took them up at once and made patriotic comments. Somebody shouted "Number one!" The Cavaliere, incensed at this as at every attempt to make game of him, retorted over his shoulder that he could not take less than two-place figures. Whereupon another joker cried out "Number two!" and was greeted with the applause and laughter which every reference to natural functions is sure to win among southerners.

When fifteen numbers stood in a long straggling row on the board, Cipolla called for a general adding-match. Ready reckoners might add in their heads, but pencil and paper were not forbidden. Cipolla, while the work went on, sat on his chair near the blackboard, smoked and grimaced, with the complacent, pompous air cripples so often have. The five-place addition was soon done. Somebody announced the answer, somebody else confirmed it, a third had arrived at a slightly different result, but the fourth agreed with the first and second. Cipolla got up, tapped some ash from his coat, and lifted the paper at the upper right-hand corner of the board to display the writing. The correct answer, a sum close on a million, stood there; he had written it down beforehand.

Astonishment, and loud applause. The children were overwhelmed. How had he done that, they wanted to know. We told them it was a trick, not easily explainable offhand. In short, the man was a conjuror. This was what a sleight-of-hand evening was like, so now they knew. First the fisherman had cramp, and then the right answer was written down beforehand—it was all simply glorious, and we saw with dismay that despite the hot eyes and the hand of the clock at almost half past ten, it would be very hard to get them away. There would be tears. And yet it was plain that this magician did not "magick"—at least not in the accepted sense, of manual dexterity—and that the entertainment was not at all suitable for children. Again, I do not know, either, what the audience really thought. Obviously there was grave doubt whether its answers had been given of "free choice"; here and there an individual might have answered of his own motion, but on the whole Cipolla certainly selected his people and thus kept the whole procedure in his own hands and directed it towards the given result. Even so, one had to admire the quickness of his calculations, however much one felt disinclined to admire anything else about the performance. Then his patriotism, his irritable sense of dignity—the Cavaliere's own countrymen might feel in their element with all that and continue in a laughing mood; but the combination certainly gave us outsiders food for thought.

Cipolla himself saw to it—though without giving them a name—that the nature of his powers should be clear beyond a doubt to even the least-instructed person. He alluded to them, of course, in his talk—and he talked without stopping—but only in vague, boastful, self-advertising phrases. He went on awhile with experiments on the same lines as the first, merely making them more complicated by introducing operations in multiplying, subtracting, and dividing; then he simplified them to the last degree in order to bring out the method. He simply had numbers "guessed" which were previously written under the paper; and the guess was nearly always right. One guesser admitted that he had had in mind to give a certain number, when Cipolla's whip went whistling through the air, and a quite different one slipped out, which proved to be the "right" one. Cipolla's shoulders' shook. He pretended admiration for the powers of the people he questioned. But in all his compliments there was something fleering and derogatory; the victims could scarcely have relished them much, although they smiled, and although they might easily have set down some part of the applause to their own credit. Moreover, I had not the impression that the artist was popular with his public. A certain ill will and reluctance were in the air, but courtesy kept such feelings in check, as did Cipolla's competency and his stern self-confidence. Even the riding-whip, I think, did much to keep rebellion from becoming overt.

From tricks with numbers he passed to tricks with cards. There were two packs, which he drew out of his pockets, and so much I still remember, that the basis of the tricks he played with them was as follows: from the first pack he drew three cards and thrust them without looking at them inside his coat. Another person then drew three out of the second pack, and these turned out to be the same as the first three—not invariably all the three, for it did happen that only two were the same. But in the majority of cases Cipolla triumphed, showing his three cards with a little bow in acknowledgment of the applause with which his audience conceded his possession of strange powers—strange whether for good or evil. A young man in the front row, to our right, an Italian, with proud, finely chiselled features, rose up and said that he intended to assert his own will in his choice and consciously to resist any influence, of whatever sort. Under these circumstances, what did Cipolla think would be the result? "You will," answered the Cavaliere, "make my task somewhat more difficult thereby. As for the result, your resistance will not alter it in the least. Freedom exists, and also the will exists; but freedom of the will does not exist, for a will that aims at its own freedom aims at the unknown. You are free to draw or not to draw. But if you draw, you will draw the right cards—the more certainly, the more wilfully obstinate your behaviour."

One must admit that he could not have chosen his words better, to trouble the waters and confuse the mind. The refractory youth hesitated before drawing. Then he pulled out a card and at once demanded to see if it was among the chosen three. "But why?" queried Cipolla. "Why do things by halves?" Then, as the other defiantly insisted, *"E servito,"* said the juggler, with a gesture of exaggerated servility; and held out the three cards fanwise, without looking at them himself. The left-hand card was the one drawn.

Amid general applause, the apostle of freedom sat down. How far Cipolla employed small tricks and manual dexterity to help out his natural talents, the deuce only knew. But even without them the result would have been the same: the curiosity of the entire audience was unbounded and universal, everybody both enjoyed the amazing character of the entertainment and unanimously conceded the professional skill of the performer. *"Lavora bene,"* we heard, here and there in our neighbourhood; it signified the triumph of objective judgment over antipathy and repressed resentment.

After his last, incomplete, yet so much the more telling success, Cipolla had at once fortified himself with another cognac. Truly he did "drink a lot," and the fact made a bad impression. But obviously he needed the liquor and the cigarettes for the replenishment of his energy, upon which, as he himself said, heavy demands were made in all directions. Certainly in the intervals he looked very ill, exhausted and hollow-eyed. Then the little glassful would redress the balance, and the flow of lively, self-confident chatter run on, while the smoke he inhaled gushed out grey from his lungs. I clearly recall that he passed from the card-tricks to parlour games—the kind based on certain powers which in human nature are higher or else lower than human reason: on intuition and "magnetic" transmission; in short, upon a low type of manifestation. What I do not remember is the precise order things came in. And I will not bore you with a description of these experiments; everybody knows them, everybody has at one time or another taken part in this finding of hidden articles, this blind carrying out of a series of acts, directed by a force that proceeds from organism to organism by unexplored paths. Everybody has had his little glimpse into the equivocal, impure, inexplicable nature of the occult, has been conscious of both curiosity and contempt, has shaken his head over the human tendency of those who deal in it to help themselves out with humbuggery, though, after all, the humbuggery is no disproof whatever of the genuineness of the other elements in the dubious amalgam. I can only say here that each single circumstance gains in weight and the whole greatly in impressiveness when it is a man like Cipolla who is the chief actor and guiding spirit in the sinister business. He sat smoking at the rear of the stage, his back to the audience while they conferred. The object passed from hand to hand which it was his task to find, with which he was to perform some action agreed upon beforehand. Then he would start to move zigzag through the hall, with his head thrown back and one hand outstretched, the other clasped in that of a guide who was in the secret but enjoined to keep himself perfectly passive, with his thoughts directed upon the agreed goal. Cipolla moved with the bearing typical in these experiments: now groping upon a false start, now with a quick forward thrust, now pausing as though to listen and by sudden inspiration correcting his course. The rôles seemed reversed, the stream of influence was moving in the contrary direction, as the artist himself pointed out, in his ceaseless flow of discourse. The suffering, receptive, performing part was now his, the will he had before imposed on others was shut out, he acted in obedience to a voiceless common will which was in the air. But he made it perfectly clear that it all came to the same thing. The capacity for self-surrender, he said, for becoming a tool, for the most unconditional and utter self-abnegation, was but the reverse side of that other power to will and to command. Commanding and obeying formed together one single principle, one indissoluble unity; he who knew how to obey knew also how to command, and conversely; the one idea was comprehended in the other, as people and leader were comprehended in one another. But that which was *done*, the highly exacting and exhausting performance, was in every case his, the leader's and mover's, in whom the will became obedience, the obedience will, whose person was the cradle and womb of both, and who thus suffered enormous hardship. Repeatedly he emphasized the fact that his lot was a hard one—presumably to account for his need of stimulant and his frequent recourse to the little glass.

Thus he groped his way forward, like a blind seer, led and sustained by the mysterious common will. He drew a pin set with a stone out of its hiding-place in an Englishwoman's shoe, carried it, halting and pressing on by turns, to another lady—Signora Angiolieri—and handed it to her on bended knee, with the words it had been agreed he was to utter. "I present you with this in token of my respect," was the sentence. Their sense was obvious, but the words themselves not easy to hit upon, for the reason that they had been agreed on in French; the language complication seemed to us a little malicious, implying as it did a conflict between the audience's natural interest in the success of the miracle, and their desire to witness the humiliation of this presumptuous man. It was a strange sight: Cipolla on his knees before the signora, wrestling, amid efforts at speech, after knowledge of the preordained words. "I must say something," he said, "and I feel clearly what it is I must say. But I also feel that if it passed my lips it would be wrong. Be careful not to help me unintentionally!" he cried out, though very likely that was precisely what he was hoping for. "*Pensez très fort*," he cried all at once, in bad French, and then burst out with the required words—in Italian, indeed, but with the final substantive pronounced in the sister tongue, in which he was probably far from fluent: he said *vénération* instead of *venerazione*, with an impossible nasal. And this partial success, after the complete success before it, the finding of the pin, the presentation of it on his knees to the right person—was almost more impressive than if he had got the sentence exactly right, and evoked bursts of admiring applause.

Cipolla got up from his knees and wiped the perspiration from his brow. You understand that this experiment with the pin was a single case, which I describe because it sticks in my memory. But he changed his method several times and improvised a number of variations suggested by his contact with his audience; a good deal of time thus went by. He seemed to get particular inspiration from the person of our landlady; she drew him on to the most extraordinary displays of clairvoyance. "It does not escape me, madame," he said to her, "that there is something unusual about you, some special and honourable distinction. He who has eyes to see descries about your lovely brow an aureola—if I mistake not, it once was stronger than now—a slowly paling radiance . . . hush, not a word! Don't help me. Beside you sits your husband—yes?" He turned towards the silent Signor Angiolieri. "You are the husband of this lady, and your happiness is complete. But in the midst of this happiness memories rise . . . the past, signora, so it seems to me, plays an important part in your present. You knew a king . . . has not a king crossed your path in bygone days?"

"No," breathed the dispenser of our midday soup, her golden-brown eyes gleaming in the noble pallor of her face.

"No? No, not a king; I meant that generally, I did not mean literally a king. Not a king, not a prince, and a prince after all, a king of a loftier realm; it was a great artist, at whose side you once—you would contradict me, and yet I am not wholly wrong. Well, then! It was a woman, a great, a world-renowned woman artist, whose friendship you enjoyed in your tender years, whose sacred memory overshadows and transfigures your whole existence. Her name? Need I utter it, whose fame has long been bound up with the Fatherland's, immortal as its own? Eleonora Duse," he finished, softly and with much solemnity.

The little woman bowed her head, overcome. The applause was like a patriotic demonstration. Nearly everyone there knew about Signora Angiolieri's wonderful past; they were all able to confirm the Cavaliere's intuition—not least the present guests of Casa Eleonora. But we wondered how much of the truth he had learned as the result of professional inquiries made on his arrival. Yet I see no reason at all to cast doubt, on rational grounds, upon powers which, before our very eyes, became fatal to their possessor.

At this point there was an intermission. Our lord and master withdrew. Now I confess that almost ever since the beginning of my tale I have looked forward with dread to this moment in it. The thoughts of men are mostly not hard to read; in this case they are very easy. You are sure to ask why we did not choose this moment to go away—and I must continue to owe you an answer. I do not know why. I cannot defend myself. By this time it was certainly eleven, probably later. The children were asleep. The last series of tests had been too long, nature had had her way. They were sleeping in our laps, the little one on mine, the boy on his mother's. That was, in a way, a consolation; but at the same time it was also ground for compassion and a clear leading to take them home to bed. And I give you my word that we wanted to obey this touching admonition, we seriously wanted to. We roused the poor things and told them it was now high time to go. But they were no sooner conscious than they began to resist and im-plore—you know how horrified children are at the thought of leaving before the end of a thing. No cajoling has any effect, you have to use force. It was so lovely, they wailed. How did we know what was coming next? Surely we could not leave until after the intermission; they liked a little nap now and again—only not go home, only not go to bed, while the beautiful evening was still going on!

We yielded, but only for the moment, of course—so far as we knew—only for a little while, just a few minutes longer. I cannot excuse our staying, scarcely can I even understand it. Did we think, having once said A, we had to say B—having once brought the children hither we had to let them stay? No, it is not good enough. Were we ourselves so highly entertained? Yes, and no. Our feelings for Cavaliere Cipolla were of a very mixed kind, but so were the feelings of the whole audience, if I mistake not, and nobody left. Were we under the sway of a fascination which ema-nated from this man who took so strange a way to earn his bread; a fascination which he gave out independently of the programme and even between the tricks and which paralysed our resolve? Again, sheer curiosity may account for something. One was curious to know how such an evening turned out; Cipolla in his remarks having all along hinted that he had tricks in his bag stranger than any he had yet produced.

But all that is not it—or at least it is not all of it. More correct it would be to answer the first question with another. Why had we not left Torre di Venere itself before now? To me the two questions are one and the same, and in order to get out of the impasse I might simply say that I had answered it already. For, as things had been in Torre in general: queer, uncomfortable, troublesome, tense, oppressive, so precisely they were here in this hall tonight. Yes, more than precisely. For it seemed to be the fountainhead of all the uncanniness and all the strained feelings which had oppressed the atmosphere of our holiday. This man whose return to the stage we were awaiting was the personification of all that; and, as we had not gone away in general, so to speak, it would have been inconsistent to do it in the particular case. You may call this an explanation, you may call it inertia, as you see fit. Any argument more to the purpose I simply do not know how to adduce.

Well, there was an interval of ten minutes, which grew into nearly twenty. The children remained awake. They were enchanted by our compliance, and filled the break to their own satisfaction by renewing relations with the popular sphere, with Antonio, Guiscardo, and the canoe man. They put their hands to their mouths and called messages across, appealing to us for the Italian words. "Hope you have a good catch tomorrow, a whole netful!" They called to Mario, Esquisito Mario: "*Mario, una cioccolata e biscotti!*" And this time he heeded and answered with a smile: "*Subito, signorini!*" Later we had reason to recall this kindly, if rather absent and pensive smile.

Thus the interval passed, the gong sounded. The audience, which had scattered in conversation, took their places again, the children sat up straight in their chairs with their hands in their laps. The curtain had not been dropped. Cipolla came forward again, with his dipping stride, and began to introduce the second half of the programme with a lecture.

Let me state once for all that this self-confident cripple was the most powerful hypnotist I have ever seen in my life. It was pretty plain now that he threw dust in the public eye and advertised himself as a prestidigitator on account of police regulations which would have prevented him from making his living by the exercise of his powers. Perhaps this eye-wash is the usual thing in Italy;

it may be permitted or even connived at by the authorities. Certainly the man had from the beginning made little concealment of the actual nature of his operations; and this second half of the programme was quite frankly and exclusively devoted to one sort of experiment. While he still practised some rhetorical circumlocutions, the tests themselves were one long series of attacks upon the will-power, the loss or compulsion of volition. Comic, exciting, amazing by turns, by midnight they were still in full swing; we ran the gamut of all the phenomena this natural-unnatural field has to show, from the unimpressive at one end of the scale to the monstrous at the other. The audience laughed and applauded as they followed the grotesque details; shook their heads, clapped their knees, fell very frankly under the spell of this stern, self-assured personality. At the same time I saw signs that they were not quite complacent, not quite unconscious of the peculiar ignominy which lay, for the individual and for the general, in Cipolla's triumphs.

Two main features were constant in all the experiments: the liquor glass and the claw-handled riding-whip. The first was always invoked to add fuel to his demoniac fires; without it, apparently, they might have burned out. On this score we might even have felt pity for the man; but the whistle of his scourge, the insulting symbol of his domination, before which we all cowered, drowned out every sensation save a dazed and outbraved submission to his power. Did he then lay claim to our sympathy to boot? I was struck by a remark he made—it suggested no less. At the climax of his experiments, by stroking and breathing upon a certain young man who had offered himself as a subject and already proved himself a particularly susceptible one, he had not only put him into the condition known as deep trance and extended his insensible body by neck and feet across the backs of two chairs, but had actually sat down on the rigid form as on a bench, without making it yield. The sight of this unholy figure in a frock-coat squatted on the stiff body was horrible and incredible; the audience, convinced that the victim of this scientific diversion must be suffering, expressed its sympathy: "*Ah, poveretto!*" Poor soul, poor soul! "*Poor soul!*" Cipolla mocked them, with some bitterness. "Ladies and gentlemen, you are barking up the wrong tree. *Sono io il poveretto.* I am the person who is suffering, I am the one to be pitied."

We pocketed the information. Very good. Maybe the experiment was at his expense, maybe it was he who had suffered the cramp when the *giovanotto* over there had made the faces. But appearances were all against it; and one does not feel like saying *poveretto* to a man who is suffering to bring about the humiliation of others.

I have got ahead of my story and lost sight of the sequence of events. To this day my mind is full of the Cavaliere's feats of endurance; only I do not recall them in their order—which does not matter. So much I do know: that the longer and more circumstantial tests, which got the most applause, impressed me less than some of the small ones which passed quickly over. I remember the young man whose body Cipolla converted into a board, only because of the accompanying remarks which I have quoted. An elderly lady in a cane-seated chair was lulled by Cipolla in the delusion that she was on a voyage to India and gave a voluble account of her adventures by land and sea. But I found this phenomenon less impressive than one which followed immediately after the intermission. A tall, well-built, soldierly man was unable to lift his arm, after the hunchback had told him that he could not and given a cut through the air with his whip. I can still see the face of that stately, mustachioed colonel smiling and clenching his teeth as he struggled to regain his lost freedom of action. A staggering performance! He seemed to be exerting his will, and in vain; the trouble, however, was probably simply that he could not will. There was involved here that recoil of the will upon itself which paralyses choice—as our tyrant had previously explained to the Roman gentleman.

Still less can I forget the touching scene, at once comic and horrible, with Signora Angiolieri. The Cavaliere, probably in his first bold survey of the room, had spied out her ethereal lack of resistance to his power. For actually he bewitched her, literally drew her out of her seat, out of her row, and away with him whither he willed. And in order to enhance his effect, he bade Signor Angiolieri call upon his wife by her name, to throw, as it were, all the weight of his existence and his rights in her into the scale, to rouse by the voice of her husband everything in his spouse's soul which could shield her virtue against the evil assaults of magic. And how vain it all was! Cipolla was standing at some distance from the couple, when he made a single cut with his whip through the air. It caused our landlady to shudder violently and turn her face towards him. "Sofronia!" cried Signor Angiolieri— we had not known that Signora Angiolieri's name was Sofronia. And he did well to call, everybody saw that there was no time to lose. His wife kept her face turned in the direction of the diabolical Cavaliere, who with his ten long yellow fingers was making passes at his victim, moving backwards as he did so, step by step. Then Signora Angiolieri, her pale face gleaming, rose up from her seat, turned right round, and began to glide after him. Fatal and forbidding sight! Her face as though moonstruck, stiff-armed, her lovely hands lifted a little at the wrists, the feet as it were together, she seemed to float slowly out of her row and after the tempter. "Call her, sir, keep on calling," prompted the redoubtable man. And Signor Angiolieri, in a weak voice, called: "Sofronia!" Ah, again and again he called; as his wife went further off he even curved one hand round his lips and beckoned with the other as he called. But the poor voice of love and duty echoed unheard, in vain, behind the lost one's back; the signora swayed along, moonstruck, deaf, enslaved; she glided into the middle aisle and down it towards the fingering hunchback, towards the door. We were convinced, we were driven to the conviction, that she would have followed her master, had he so willed it, to the ends of the earth.

"*Accidente!*" cried out Signor Angiolieri, in genuine affright, springing up as the exit was reached. But at the same moment the Cavaliere put aside, as it were, the triumphal crown and broke off. "Enough, signora, I thank you," he said, and offered his arm to lead her back to her husband. "Signor," he greeted the latter, "here is your wife. Unharmed, with my compliments, I give her into your hands. Cherish with all the strength of your manhood a treasure which is so wholly yours, and let your zeal be quickened by knowing that there are powers stronger than reason or virtue, and not always so magnanimously ready to relinquish their prey!"

Poor Signor Angiolieri, so quiet, so bald! He did not look as though he would know how to defend his happiness, even against powers much less demoniac than these which were now adding mockery to frightfulness. Solemnly and pompously the Cavaliere retired to the stage, amid applause to which his eloquence gave double strength. It was this particular episode, I feel sure, that set the seal upon his ascendancy. For now he made them dance, yes, literally; and the dancing lent a dissolute, abandoned, topsy-turvy air to the scene, a drunken abdication of the critical spirit which had so long resisted the spell of this man. Yes, he had had to fight to get the upper hand—for instance against the animosity of the young Roman gentleman, whose rebellious spirit threatened to serve others as a rallying-point. But it was precisely upon the importance of example that the Cavaliere was so strong. He had the wit to make his attack at the weakest point and to choose as his first victim that feeble, ecstatic youth whom he had previously made into a board. The master had but to look at him, when this young man would fling himself back as though struck by lightning, place his hands rigidly at his sides, and fall into a state of military somnambulism, in which it was plain to any eye that he was open to the most absurd suggestion that might be made to him. He seemed quite content in his abject state, quite pleased to be relieved of the burden of voluntary choice. Again and again he offered himself as a subject and gloried in the model facility he had in losing consciousness. So now he mounted the platform, and a single cut of the whip was enough to make him dance to the Cavaliere's orders, in a kind of complacent ecstasy, eyes closed, head nodding, lank limbs flying in all directions.

It looked unmistakably like enjoyment, and other recruits were not long in coming forward: two other young men, one humbly and one well dressed, were soon jigging alongside the first. But now the gentleman from Rome bobbed up again, asking defiantly if the Cavaliere would engage to make him dance too, even against his will.

"Even against your will," answered Cipolla, in unforgettable accents. That frightful *"anche se non vuole"* still rings in my ears. The struggle began. After Cipolla had taken another little glass and lighted a fresh cigarette he stationed the Roman at a point in the middle aisle and himself took up a position some distance behind him, making his whip whistle through the air as he gave the order: *"Balla!"* His opponent did not stir. *"Balla!"* repeated the Cavaliere incisively, and snapped his whip. You saw the young man move his neck round in his collar; at the same time one hand lifted slightly at the wrist, one ankle turned outward. But that was all, for the time at least; merely a tendency to twitch, now sternly repressed, now seeming about to get the upper hand. It escaped nobody that here a heroic obstinacy, a fixed resolve to resist, must needs be conquered; we were beholding a gallant effort to strike out and save the honour of the human race. He twitched but danced not; and the struggle was so prolonged that the Cavaliere had to divide his attention between it and the stage, turning now and then to make his riding-whip whistle in the direction of the dancers, as it were to keep them in leash. At the same time he advised the audience that no fatigue was involved in such activities, however long they went on, since it was not the automatons up there who danced, but himself. Then once more his eye would bore itself into the back of the Roman's neck and lay siege to the strength of purpose which defied him.

One saw it waver, that strength of purpose, beneath the repeated summons and whip-crackings. Saw with an objective interest which yet was not quite free from traces of sympathetic emotion—from pity, even from a cruel kind of pleasure. If I understand what was going on, it was the negative character of the young man's fighting position which was his undoing. It is likely that *not* willing is not a practicable state of mind; *not* to want to do something may be in the long run a mental content impossible to subsist on. Between not willing a certain thing and not willing at all—in other words, yielding to another person's will—there may lie too small a space for the idea of freedom to squeeze into. Again, there were the Cavaliere's persuasive words, woven in among the whip-crackings and commands, as he mingled effects that were his own secret with others of a bewilderingly psychological kind. "*Balla!*" said he. "Who wants to torture himself like that? Is forcing yourself your idea of freedom? *Una ballatina!* Why, your arms and legs are aching for it. What a relief to give way to them—there, you are dancing already! That is no struggle any more, it is a pleasure!" And so it was. The jerking and twitching of the refractory youth's limbs had at last got the upper hand; he lifted his arms, then his knees, his joints quite suddenly relaxed, he flung his legs and danced, and amid bursts of applause the Cavaliere led him to join the row of puppets on the stage. Up there we could see his face as he "enjoyed" himself; it was clothed in a broad grin and the eyes were half-shut. In a way, it was consoling to see that he was having a better time than he had had in the hour of his pride.

His "fall" was, I may say, an epoch. The ice was completely broken, Cipolla's triumph had reached its height. The Circe's wand, that whistling leather whip with the claw handle, held absolute sway. At one time—it must have been well after midnight—not only were there eight or ten persons dancing on the little stage, but in the hall below a varied animation reigned, and a long-toothed Anglo-Saxoness in a pince-nez left her seat of her own motion to perform a tarantella in the centre aisle. Cipolla was lounging in a cane-seated chair at the left of the stage, gulping down the smoke of a cigarette and breathing it impudently out through his bad teeth. He tapped his foot and shrugged his shoulders, looking down upon the abandoned scene in the hall; now and then he snapped his whip backwards at a laggard upon the stage. The children were awake at the moment. With shame I speak of them. For it was not good to be here, least of all for them; that we had not taken them away can only be explained by saying that we had caught the general devil-may-careness of the hour. By that time it was all one. Anyhow, thank goodness, they lacked understanding for the disreputable side of the entertainment, and in their innocence were perpetually charmed by the unheard-of indulgence which permitted them to be present at such a thing as a magician's "evening." Whole quarter-hours at a time they drowsed on our laps, waking refreshed and rosy-cheeked, with sleep-drunken eyes, to laugh to bursting at the leaps and jumps the magician made those people up there make. They had not thought it would be so jolly; they joined with their clumsy little hands in every round of applause. And jumped for joy upon their chairs, as was their wont, when Cipolla beckoned to their friend Mario from the Esquisito, beckoned to him just like a picture in a book, holding his hand in front of his nose and bending and straightening the forefinger by turns.

Mario obeyed. I can see him now going up the stairs to Cipolla, who continued to beckon him, in that droll, picture-book sort of way. He hesitated for a moment at first; that, too, I recall quite clearly. During the whole evening he had lounged against a wooden pillar at the side entrance, with his arms folded, or else with his hands thrust into his jacket pockets. He was on our left, near the youth with the militant hair, and had followed the performance attentively, so far as we had seen, if with no particular animation and God knows how much comprehension. He could not much relish being summoned thus, at the end of the evening. But it was only too easy to see why he obeyed. After all, obedience was his calling in life; and then, how should a simple lad like him find it within his human capacity to refuse compliance to a man so throned and crowned as Cipolla at that hour? Willy-nilly he left his column and with a word of thanks to those making way for him he mounted the steps with a doubtful smile on his full lips.

Picture a thickset youth of twenty years, with clipt hair, a low forehead, and heavy-lidded eyes of an indefinite grey, shot with green and yellow. These things I knew from having spoken with him, as we often had. There was a saddle of freckles on the flat nose, the whole upper half of the face retreated behind the lower, and that again was dominated by thick lips that parted to show the salivated teeth. These thick lips and the veiled look of the eyes lent the whole face a primitive melancholy—it was that which had drawn us to him from the first. In it was not the faintest trace of brutality—indeed, his hands would have given the lie to such an idea, being unusually slender and delicate even for a southerner. They were hands by which one liked being served.

We knew him humanly without knowing him personally, if I may make that distinction. We saw him nearly every day, and felt a certain kindness for his dreamy ways, which might at times be actual inattentiveness, suddenly transformed into a redeeming zeal to serve. His mien was serious, only the children could bring a smile to his face. It was not sulky, but uningratiating, without intentional effort to please—or, rather, it seemed to give up being pleasant in the conviction that it could not succeed. We should have remembered Mario in any case, as one of those homely recollections of travel which often stick in the mind better than more important ones. But of his circumstances we knew no more than that his father was a petty clerk in the Municipio and his mother took in washing.

His white waiter's-coat became him better than the faded striped suit he wore, with a gay coloured scarf instead of a collar, the ends tucked into his jacket. He neared Cipolla, who however did not leave off that motion of his finger before his nose, so that Mario had to come still closer, right up to the chair-seat and the master's legs. Whereupon the latter spread out his elbows and seized the lad, turning him so that we had a view of his face. Then gazed him briskly up and down, with a careless, commanding eye. "Well, *ragazzo mio,* how comes it we make acquaintance so late in the day? But believe me, I made yours long ago. Yes, yes, I've had you in my eye this long while and known what good stuff you were made of. How could I go and forget you again? Well, I've had a good deal to think about. . . . Now tell me, what is your name? The first name, that's all I want."

"My name is Mario," the young man answered, in a low voice.

"Ah, Mario. Very good. Yes, yes, there is such a name, quite a common name, a classic name too, one of those which preserve the heroic traditions of the Fatherland. *Bravo! Salve!*" And he flung up his arm slantingly above his crooked shoulder, palm outward, in the Roman salute. He may have been slightly tipsy by now, and no wonder; but he spoke as before, clearly, fluently, and with emphasis. Though about this time there had crept into his voice a gross, autocratic note, and a kind of arrogance was in his sprawl.

"Well, now, Mario *mio,*" he went on, "it's a good thing you came this evening, and that's a pretty scarf you've got on; it is becoming to your style of beauty. It must stand you in good stead with the girls, the pretty pretty girls of Torre—"

From the row of youths, close by the place where Mario had been standing, sounded a laugh. It came from the youth with the militant hair. He stood there, his jacket over his shoulder, and laughed outright, rudely and scornfully.

Mario gave a start. I think it was a shrug, but he may have started and then hastened to cover the movement by shrugging his shoulders, as much as to say that the neckerchief and the fair sex were matters of equal indifference to him.

The Cavaliere gave a downward glance.

"We needn't trouble about him," he said. "He is jealous, because your scarf is so popular with the girls, maybe partly because you and I are so friendly up here. Perhaps he'd like me to put him in mind of his colic—I could do it free of charge. Tell me, Mario. You've come here this evening for a bit of fun—and in the day-time you work in an ironmonger's shop?"

"In a café," corrected the youth.

"Oh, in a café. That's where Cipolla nearly came a cropper! What you are is a cup-bearer, a Ganymede—I like that, it is another classical allusion—*Salvietta!*" Again the Cavaliere saluted, to the huge gratification of his audience.

Mario smiled too. "But before that," he interpolated, in the interest of accuracy, "I worked for a while in a shop in Portoclemente." He seemed visited by a natural desire to assist the prophecy by dredging out its essential features.

"There, didn't I say so? In an ironmonger's shop?"

"They kept combs and brushes," Mario got round it.

"Didn't I say that you were not always a Ganymede? Not always at the sign of the serviette? Even when Cipolla makes a mistake, it is a kind that makes you believe in him. Now tell me: Do you believe in me?"

An indefinite gesture.

"A half-way answer," commented the Cavaliere. "Probably it is not easy to win your confidence. Even for me, I can see, it is not so easy. I see in your features a reserve, a sadness, *un tratto di malinconia* . . . tell me" (he seized Mario's hand persuasively) "have you troubles?"

"*Nossignore*," answered Mario, promptly and decidedly.

"You *have* troubles," insisted the Cavaliere, bearing down the denial by the weight of his authority. "Can't I see? Trying to pull the wool over Cipolla's eyes, are you? Of course, about the girls—it is a girl, isn't it? You have love troubles?"

Mario gave a vigorous head-shake. And again the *giovanotto's* brutal laugh rang out. The Cavaliere gave heed. His eyes were roving about somewhere in the air; but he cocked an ear to the sound, then swung his whip backwards, as he had once or twice before in his conversation with Mario, that none of his puppets might flag in their zeal. The gesture had nearly cost him his new prey: Mario gave a sudden start in the direction of the steps. But Cipolla had him in his clutch.

"Not so fast," said he. "That would be fine, wouldn't it? So you want to skip, do you, Ganymede, right in the middle of the fun, or, rather, when it is just beginning? Stay with me, I'll show you something nice. I'll convince you. You have no reason to worry, I promise you. This girl—you know her and others know her too—what's her name? Wait! I read the name in your eyes, it is on the tip of my tongue and yours too—"

"Silvestra!" shouted the *giovanotto* from below.

The Cavaliere's face did not change.

"Aren't there the forward people?" he asked, not looking down, more as in undisturbed converse with Mario. "Aren't there the young fighting-cocks that crow in season and out? Takes the word out of your mouth, the conceited fool, and seems to think he has some special right to it. Let him be. But Silvestra, your Silvestra—ah, what a girl that is! What a prize! Brings your heart into your mouth to see her walk or laugh or breathe, she is so lovely. And her round arms when she washes, and tosses her head back to get the hair out of her eyes! An angel from paradise!"

Mario stared at him, his head thrust forward. He seemed to have forgotten the audience, forgotten where he was. The red rings round his eyes had got larger, they looked as though they were painted on. His thick lips parted.

"And she makes you suffer, this angel," went on Cipolla, "or, rather, you make yourself suffer for her—there is a difference, my lad, a most important difference, let me tell you. There are misunderstandings in love, maybe nowhere else in the world are there so many. I know what you are thinking: what does this Cipolla, with his little physical defect, know about love? Wrong, all wrong, he knows a lot. He has a wide and powerful understanding of its workings, and it pays to listen to his advice. But let's leave Cipolla out, cut him out altogether and think only of Silvestra, your peerless Silvestra! What! Is she to give any young gamecock the preference, so that he can laugh while you cry? To prefer him to a chap like you, so full of feeling and so sympathetic? Not very likely, is it? It is impossible—we know better, Cipolla and she. If I were to put myself in her place and choose between the two of you, a tarry lout like that—a codfish, a sea-urchin—and a Mario, a knight of the serviette, who moves among gentlefolk and hands round refreshments with an air—my word, but my heart would speak in no uncertain tones—it knows to whom I gave it long ago. It is time that he should see and understand, my chosen one! It is time that you see me and recognize me, Mario, my beloved! Tell me, who am I?"

It was grisly, the way the betrayer made himself irresistible, wreathed and coquetted with his crooked shoulder, languished with the puffy eyes, and showed his splintered teeth in a sickly smile. And alas, at his beguiling words, what was come of our

Mario? It is hard for me to tell, hard as it was for me to see; for here was nothing less than an utter abandonment of the inmost soul, a public exposure of timid and deluded passion and rapture. He put his hands across his mouth, his shoulders rose and fell with his pantings. He could not, it was plain, trust his eyes and ears for joy, and the one thing he forgot was precisely that he could not trust them. "Silvestra!" he breathed, from the very depths of his vanquished heart.

"Kiss me!" said the hunchback. "Trust me, I love thee. Kiss me here." And with the tip of his index finger, hand, arm, and little finger outspread, he pointed to his cheek, near the mouth. And Mario bent and kissed him.

It had grown very still in the room. That was a monstrous moment, grotesque and thrilling, the moment of Mario's bliss. In that evil span of time, crowded with a sense of the illusiveness of all joy, one sound became audible, and that not quite at once, but on the instant of the melancholy and ribald meeting between Mario's lips and the repulsive flesh which thrust itself forward for his caress. It was the sound of a laugh, from the *giovanotto* on our left. It broke into the dramatic suspense of the moment, coarse, mocking, and yet—or I must have been grossly mistaken—with an undertone of compassion for the poor bewildered, victimized creature. It had a faint ring of that *"Poveretto"* which Cipolla had declared was wasted on the wrong person, when he claimed the pity for his own.

The laugh still rang in the air when the recipient of the caress gave his whip a little swish, low down, close to his chair-leg, and Mario started up and flung himself back. He stood in that posture staring, his hands one over the other on those desecrated lips. Then he beat his temples with his clenched fists, over and over; turned and staggered down the steps, while the audience applauded, and Cipolla sat there with his hands in his lap, his shoulders shaking. Once below, and even while in full retreat, Mario hurled himself round with legs flung wide apart; one arm flew up, and two flat shattering detonations crashed through applause and laughter.

There was instant silence. Even the dancers came to a full stop and stared about, struck dumb. Cipolla bounded from his seat. He stood with his arms spread out, slanting as though to ward everybody off, as though next moment he would cry out: "Stop! Keep back! Silence! What was that?" Then, in that instant, he sank back in his seat, his head rolling on his chest; in the next he had fallen sideways to the floor, where he lay motionless, a huddled heap of clothing, with limbs awry.

The commotion was indescribable. Ladies hid their faces, shuddering, on the breasts of their escorts. There were shouts for a doctor, for the police. People flung themselves on Mario in a mob, to disarm him, to take away the weapon that hung from his fingers —that small, dull-metal, scarcely pistol-shaped tool with hardly any barrel—in how strange and unexpected a direction had fate levelled it!

And now—now finally, at last—we took the children and led them towards the exit, past the pair of *carabinieri* just entering. Was that the end, they wanted to know, that they might go in peace? Yes, we assured them, that was the end. An end of horror, a fatal end. And yet a liberation—for I could not, and I cannot, but find it so!

COMMENT

"Mario and the Magician" is the richest and most complex of the stories in this volume. In a somewhat superficial way this is intimated by the number of shorter stories which seem to be included in Mann's: here we have the contrast of children's and adults' point of view used by several other authors; the use of a public entertainment with symbolic values, as in Alexander's story (and even a similarity of phrase— "part of the game") and in Kafka's; a treatment of nationalism as in March's story, and a contrast of nationalism and internationalism as in Miss Boyle's (both use beach scenes); café and hotel scenes with symbolic overtones as in the Boyle and Hemingway stories; the use of shock, as in Miss Jackson's story, by the account of a monstrous event in the midst of otherwise ordinary community life.

These resemblances are very interesting, but they do not in themselves establish the quality of a story. They do, however, give us a clue to the reason why the story is so extraordinarily impressive—namely, its having at least three different levels of meaning. At the most obvious level it is a story of a public entertainment, and even at this level the interest is of two kinds. For one thing, there are the mere goings on in the hall, the astonishing events which are entirely accessible to the chil-

dren. The use of the children in the story tells us, in effect, that it is possible to read the magician's performance simply as delightful entertainment. But this entertainment is carried on by psychological means, so that at the level of narrative the story is full of psychological interest (compare it with Mrs. Woolf's story, where the action is all psychological, and where everything else is subordinated to what goes on in the thoughts and imagination of the protagonist). The reader's attention is directed to the psychological action as such, to the techniques of the conqueror, and to the responses which he evokes in the audience.

But the alert reader is also aware that this is not all: he sees that psychological demonstrations are in effect a symbolic presentation of social and political meanings. Notice that it is at this level that the introductory episodes, which form about one-fourth of the story, are related to the main action. The narrator is careful to establish a connection between the family's remaining in the town earlier and their remaining in the hall now; perhaps their motives are not quite clear, but it is clear that what goes on in the town and what goes on in the hall are different aspects of the same thing. At the hotel the visitors observe "naive misuse of power, injustice, and sycophantic corruption"; on the beach they are the victims of a hysterical nationalism; and at the theater Cipolla introduces nationalistic ideas and boasts of being honored by the brother of the Duce. In a sense the story is about Fascism. Yet somehow it is broader even than that: Cipolla really stands for the demagogue type who, whatever the specific political framework, hypnotically dominates a public—partly by trickery, partly by real talent (the narrator takes pains to assert Cipolla's real ability), and partly by playing upon a susceptibility which is a real element in his victims. In a sense the people at the beach and the employees of the hotel are also hypotized, dominated by the wills of others (note that twice a medical man gives an opinion which is not heeded: in this irrational atmosphere, science can have no influence).

The mention of "the wills of others" introduces the third level of meaning, which we may call the philosophical. For here Mann deals with the whole question of human liberty, of the ways in which it is endangered and may be lost. The issue is raised directly by Cipolla when he urges his audience "to divide up the willing and the doing," according to the "American system," and again when, during the card tricks, he discusses freedom and says that freedom of the will does not exist, and at other times; and by the narrator when he describes the tricks as "one long series of attacks upon the will-power" and the weakness of those who do resist as lying in their purely negative attitude— "a mental content impossible to subsist on." Here the approach to the

problem goes far beyond the political level: Mann is really writing a story about human destiny generally. The narrator puts matters in the most inclusive terms when he speaks of the dancers as exhibiting "a drunken abdication of the critical spirit" and of the Roman's resistance as "a gallant effort to strike out and save the honour of the human race."
These quotations are only a small part of the passages in which the narrator reflects on what he sees, and the passages of reflection are only a small part of the story. They do not stand in the place of action, and they do not act as simple didactic signposts. They are really a kind of action in themselves, an extension of the actions of Cipolla and his victims into the realm of speculation. They amplify and extend but do not conclude. Mann raises all kinds of questions but ultimately lets his story speak for itself. It clearly presents Cipolla as evil, but it also presents his victims as in some way contributing to the evil. It does not denounce Cipolla or set forth a program of action against him; it merely shows how action against him comes about. The reader should analyze carefully this concluding episode to discover the sources of Mario's violence. What does this ending say in general terms?
The narrator calls the death of Cipolla a "liberation"—a word which connects it closely with the subject of free will. Do the other members of the crowd share the narrator's view? Does their seizure of Mario suggest that they regard this as an ordinary act of violence, without special significance? If this is their attitude, what is its significance for the reader?
Note that this is the first story since Maugham's in which there is a narrator, a character who tells about actions performed principally by other characters. However, the narrator always influences the tone of a story. Just as the lack of seriousness of Henry Garnet contributes to the triviality of Maugham's story, so the philosophic tone of Mann's story has its genesis in the maturity, the sober reflectiveness, and the moral awareness of the "I." The author uses great restraint in his management of the "I": he does not permit the narrator to draw the pat conclusions (political panaceas, philosophic answers) that would be so easy. Mann uses a very interesting technical device in that the "I," who is always very close to, conscious of, and thoughtful about the materials of the story, constantly maintains that the story is something outside himself, even outside his control and understanding. Is this attitude helpful in the avoidance of the didactic? How does it influence the effect of the story otherwise?
Note the complex treatment of Cipolla. At one level he is simply a psychological phenomenon, exciting wonder and curiosity. But strong as this effect is, it is, in the long run, kept subordinate to Cipolla as a

moral problem. Again, notice the double value of his deformity. How is it used psychologically? What does it symbolize?

With what do we associate Cipolla's use of his whip? What, then, does it symbolize?

Mann presents a variety of people as falling under Cipolla's sway. In what way is this important to the meaning of the story? What human type, or human characteristic, is suggested by the youth who "falls into a state of military somnambulism" and seems "content in his abject state, quite pleased to be relieved of the burden of voluntary choice"?

Note the order in which Cipolla's tricks are arranged. Do they become more significant morally as the end of the story is approached? Does the dancing have any especial symbolic value?

Reread the passage which describes the location of the hall in which Cipolla performs. Is there any symbolic meaning here?

The final group of four stories in the volume, although they are by no means the only stories in the book that have symbolic value, are all especially interesting because of their symbolic aspects. The Williams and Hemingway stories are both pared down to a bare skeleton of action, and the symbolic is hardly more than hinted. In Mann's story, on the contrary, a long and complicated action is developed with great fullness, and the symbolic meanings, though never stated explicitly, are always unmistakably present. In Miss Jackson's story we have a special situation: the sudden introduction of the symbolic in an otherwise literal and realistic milieu. As a final contrast we might notice that in Mann's story there is the same effect of shock as in Miss Jackson's—in fact, a stronger effect of shock. This is because of the tremendous significance with which Cipolla's performance has gradually been endowed, and not because of a clever management of the unexpected.